Cassandra Parkin grew up in Hull, and now lives in East Yorkshire. Her short story collection, *New World Fairy Tales* (Salt Publishing, 2011), won the 2011 Scott Prize for Short Stories. Her work has been published in numerous magazines and anthologies. *Lily's House* is her third novel.

Visit Cassandra at
cassandraparkin.wordpress.com
or on Twitter
@cassandrajaneuk

Lily's
House

Cassandra
Parkin

Legend Press Ltd, 107-111 Fleet Street, London EC4A 2AB
info@legend-paperbooks.co.uk | www.legendpress.co.uk

Print ISBN 978-1-7850793-4-4
Ebook ISBN 978-1-7850793-5-1
Set in Times. Printed in the United Kingdom by TJ International
Cover design by Simon Levy www.simonlevyassociates.co.uk

For Audrey, Dorothy, Millie and Anne
You stand tall in my dreams

Chapter One – Tuesday

By the time we get off at the station, I'm so tired and disoriented that nothing feels real. The judder of my suitcase wheels as we cross the broken asphalt of the car park shivers up the handle, into my hand and through my body. We've been in continuous motion for almost eleven hours.

"Is it much further, Mum?" Marianne asks. She's remembering her promise and trying not to complain, but I see her exhaustion in the shadows round her eyes. I take her hand and give it a squeeze, but I can't speak. In fact, I can hardly breathe. I'm drowning in memories.

Here are the trees in tall rows, a stately avenue to a long-vanished gateway. Here are the sharp points of gravel that I picked my way over with bare, tender feet ('You know, you could put your shoes on, Jen.' 'I'm all right, Lily, I promise!'). Here's where I'd step into the road to walk on the smooth cool yellow of the lines ('Please, Lily, I promise I won't get run over.' And the way her shoulders moved when she laughed, the brightness in her eyes; 'No, I know you won't. You've got more sense than most adults.'). Here is the place where, one hot bright summer noon, she showed me a wild buddleia swarming with a million tortoiseshell butterflies, so sudden and so lovely I thought she must have conjured them. ('Do you know, Jen, each butterfly means one happy moment in the next year? Let's see how happy you're going to be. Can you count them?' And me, swelling with nine-year-old pride;

'I can estimate them.' 'Estimate! My goodness, that sounds advanced.' 'Did you learn about estimating when you were at school, Lily? Or was it not invented when you were little?') Here against the skin of my face and neck is the soft salty dampness that comes from being three minutes' walk from the North Atlantic. The buddleia has been supplanted by a gigantic stand of bamboo. I want to take off my shoes.

"Mum? Are you all right?"

Marianne is a study in the surprising beauty that sometimes comes with poverty, lovely even though everything she wears needs replacing. Her fraying ballet pumps are covered in scuffmarks. Her thick black tights have a hole that began as small and inconspicuous, but has now stretched to reveal a large oval of her right calf. Two months ago and at my stern insistence, she reluctantly conceded that the polka-dot skirt she's had since she was nine has reached the end of an honourable three-year service and is due for retirement; and yet here it is again, short and faded, trailing nylon thread where the hem's ravelled, but (thanks to her persistent habit of growing upwards but not outwards) still just about wearable. Her lips have a smear of bright red lipstick and her wild brown corkscrew curls hang in careless clumps around her face.

It doesn't matter. Soon we'll have enough money so she won't have to dress in old clothes and laddered tights any more. My heart squeezes with love.

"Are you all right?" she repeats as we climb the hill. When I don't reply, she stops in front of me to make sure I'm listening.

At the start of the journey I talked to her, trying not to mind our fellow passengers' fascination. I told her how far we were going, how long it would take, then took a paper napkin and drew her a family tree. *That's your great-grandmother Lily. That's your great-granddad, his name was Richard and he was killed in the war. That's Lily's sister Margaret, and after they were both widowed they moved to*

8

Cornwall and opened a hotel. Margaret was married but she never had children, and she had a weak heart and she died quite young, less than a year after her husband. His name? He was called Stanley. And on the next layer, that's Lily's son, another Richard. Richard was my dad, and he married Amanda – that's my mum, your grandma. They had one child too, so another level. And that's me. I married your dad. And that's you. A sparse family tree, riddled with early deaths and notably lacking in menfolk, pruned ruthlessly down to the single green shoot that is my daughter.

As the landscape from the window changed, I laid my hands in my lap and grew silent. Now we're here, seduced by the beautiful familiarity of everything I see, I'm afraid to speak for fear of what I might say. I feel so lost and weightless without Daniel. I have to look over my shoulder to make myself understand that he's really not with me.

"Nearly there," I tell her, and start walking again.

"I'm so afraid," Daniel said to me this morning as we lay half dozing in each other's arms. We'd discussed this after sex the night before, a frantic urgent coupling driven by his distress, but he woke me before the alarm so we could talk more.

"What's wrong?" I meant to be kind and not snippy, but it was an effort to concentrate on him. For me, journeys begin in my heart and mind. My body was in the bed with him but the rest of me was already far away, reluctant to be called back.

"What if she does something to turn you against me?"

"She's dead. What can she do?"

"I don't know, but she hated me. No, don't try and tell me she liked me, we both know that's not true. And she was a witch. That's where you get it from. That's how you knew she was going to die."

Daniel's always liked to believe I have second sight, inherited from my grandmother. I've told him that what

9

he sees in me is coincidence, not magic, but his belief is unshakeable. I'm not entirely sure he's wrong about Lily.

"I should come with you."

I took a deep breath, forced myself to be patient.

"We talked about this, remember? You can't. You've got rehearsals."

"They could manage without me for a few days."

"Yes, but they don't have to, do they? Look, we won't be long there, you know we won't, I promise. And when the flat's sold we'll be rich. We'll stop renting and build our dream house."

"I hate it when you go away."

"I know, but there's no way round it. You have to stay and I have to go."

He stroked my cheek.

"I'll count the minutes until you come back."

"Mum?" Marianne pats my arm to get my attention. I force myself to stop worrying about Daniel so I can concentrate on what she's saying. "Is it like you remember it?"

I swallow hard, and nod.

"You're sure we're not lost? Because I've got my mobile, I can Google-map directions."

I roll my eyes and keep walking, the pavement tapping and tapping against my shoes. Marianne looks worried and unhappy. The faint sulkiness that comes over her when she's really tired weighs down her shoulders. Her refusal to credit me with knowing anything she doesn't is one of the most annoying signs of her growing up.

For more than thirteen years, I've visited this place only in the subtly altered perspectives of my dreams. I was afraid I'd find it unfamiliar. Now I'm here, I realise I could never, ever forget. When I'm an old woman, my body will still remember every inch of this winding road, and the ghostly histories of every vanished summer. I'd like to tell Marianne this is the landscape of my innermost heart, and I could find my way to

Lily's house even if I was dying. But it's too difficult and I'm too tired, so I rehearse stories in my head instead, considering how it might feel to share them.

That house belonged to two doctors who were married and had the same surname. The husband was called by his surname, Doctor – something, I can't remember – and his wife was called by her first name. Doctor Della. And whenever Lily's friends talked about her – which they did a lot because they were always on about their health – they'd always call her a lady doctor. They'd say, 'Doctor Della, the lady doctor, she's very good, you know.' To show they didn't feel short-changed. Then when they went home, Lily would laugh and say you'd think we were still fighting for the vote.

Tell me some more, the imaginary Marianne begs me.

The man who owned that pink bungalow there had a beautiful fat fuchsia. I used to pop the buds when I went past, and one day he saw me, and he came out and shouted at me until I cried. When Lily found out she got this look on her face, and said he should be more careful. She stole a cutting from the fuchsia and put it in a black envelope and wrote his name on it. And the very next day while we were having breakfast, he walked in front of the post-van. He was in hospital for the rest of the summer. I remember Lily hearing the ambulance and going to look. And when she found out who it was she smiled to herself, and I was never sure if she'd made it happen.

"That bungalow," I say out loud. "It was pink then too."

Marianne stares at it as if she's trying to see through the walls.

And you see that house there? I continue. *They had a huge fluffy cat that was completely insane. Its owners both worked and it got lonely, so it used to sit out on the path and meow, and if you paid it any attention at all, it followed you home and flopped around on the carpet.* I'm brittle with the need to avoid giving too much away, but surely this detail will be

11

safe. I will tell her about the cat later, and her face will turn soft and yearning at the thought of a cat so loving, it would follow a stranger home. *So, of course, I'd be out here every morning at half past eight to make it come home with me.*

Didn't Lily mind?

She just used to say, 'As long as it's not getting fed.' Every morning for weeks and weeks – as long as it's not getting fed. I think she thought it wasn't stealing unless we started feeding it.

What was the cat called? She'll want to know that, of course.

I don't know. I'll have to confess. *Lily never spoke to the people who lived in that house, so we never found out. I used to call it Molly, but I didn't even know if it was a boy or a girl.*

We're approaching the top of the hill. I can see the tall cream curve of the great house now, and the wide bow window where the red lamp bloomed behind velvet curtains. Once, before the tumbling price of tin forced the break-up of all the great estates, this pathway would have led through the newly stocked gardens. Another few paces, and I see the slate roof that the herring gulls slid down on splayed feet, glaring at you from mad yellow eyes as if everything wrong in the world was your fault and soon they'd take their revenge. I used to ache to stroke their pristine feathers. I had fantasies of taming a gull to eat from my hand. But even when I threw long rubbery strands of bacon rind in desperate supplication, holding my breath as they caught them in their fierce beaks, they'd still give me that contemptuous round-eyed glare: *We'll eat your stupid bacon rind if you're offering, but we still hate you.*

If I think about any of this too long I'll come apart.

"Nearly there now," I manage, swallowing hard. "That one."

"That one?" Marianne catches her breath in amazement.

"Not all of it. It's converted into flats."

"Which bit? Downstairs?"

Since Marianne was a very little girl, she's expressed her secret wishes in a very particular way. When she's hoping for a certain answer, she'll ask about a less desirable one instead, and then (if that happens to be what's true) she'll pretend that was what she wanted all along.

"Upstairs," I tell her, and feel the incredulous pleasure on her face lick treacherously at my heart.

"What can you see from the window? Does it look over the town?"

"Look out there," Lily tells me, beckoning me into the bay window. I'm in my green nightdress embroidered with the little cross-stitch girl in the poke bonnet. My feet enjoy the thick pile of the grass-coloured carpet. The carpet is magical to me, because you can draw patterns on by stroking the pile in the wrong direction.

"See the lights on the ocean?" Lily continues. "That's a huge ship full of rich passengers on a cruise. They're dressed up in their best clothes for dinner, and soon they'll go back to their tiny little cabins to sleep." She laughs. "Some people are such fools, Jen. All that money to sleep in a room the size of a prison cell."

On her desk is a mortar and pestle with a coarse green powder in the bottom. I peer into it with interest.

"What's this? Can I touch it?"

Lily takes it gently away. "Better not. It's for Mrs Scobell. Something to make her husband less of a lazy misery guts."

"Is it magic?"

"It's lemon balm. Good for the spirit. She can make him a tea with it. It'll make him nicer to live with."

"So it is magic."

"That's what Mrs Scobell thinks."

"So it's a real proper spell? It'll work? Really work?"

"She thinks it will, so it will. Now come on, off to bed with you. Even the seagulls are asleep by now." Her hands on my shoulders, steering and directing me in the way that would have driven me wild from anyone else, but that I always loved from her.

"That big bow window?" I point. "If you stand in it, you can see the sea."

I can't help the quiver of pride when I see Marianne's face.

The gateposts were built to accommodate the sweep of a carriage. I wonder how many years it's been since horses felt the gravel crunch and shift beneath their hooves, and if it felt rough or welcoming. I can picture them blowing through their noses, tired and patient as the steps were folded down. While the guests were led into the tall bright hallway, steam would rise from the horses' coats in the stable's comforting twilight. Perhaps the groom's hands rested briefly on their velvet muzzles as they burrowed greedily in the manger for oats. The front door is right around the sweep, looking out over the remaining fragment of gardens. It's hard work pulling our suitcases over the gravel. At the top of the stone steps, the front door waits.

"Don't sit in the middle of the steps," Lily tells me, too gentle to count as a scolding. "You're right in the way of everyone coming in and out."

"But they can go on either side of me."

"Not all of them. Mrs Shawcross from downstairs, she needs the whole width to herself. Have you watched her climbing the stairs? Huffing and puffing and rolling from side to side. She looks like a walrus, poor woman. She'd be better off going to live in the sea."

Her expression is so sweet and conspiratorial that I almost miss the spite. I'm always surprised by Lily's sharp edges. She enjoys being cruel about the neighbours who clearly find her charming, and look forward to seeing her.

This is the Lily I need to remember. Not the woman who let me bring other people's cats home and gave me bacon rind for the seagulls, but the Lily who dropped sharp bright truth from her lips, cutting everyone else to pieces. As I rummage in my handbag for the keys, Marianne turns her face towards the sunset and sighs deeply, as if she's waking from a refreshing sleep.

I know how she feels. It's how I used to feel too.

Inside the door now, and as we cross the grey stone floor made shiny by a million footsteps, my feet remember padding delicately barefoot across the glossy surface. Cold and unwelcoming as I left the yielding comfort of Lily's carpets and ran downstairs. A smooth cool relief from the gravel on the way back in. My first discovery that the pain or pleasure of all sensory experiences is provisional only, shaped by what surrounds it. Our suitcases bump and struggle as we heave them up the stone staircase and I'm conscious that we must be making noise.

Here is the subtle change in scent that comes at the top of the stairs, a slight difference in the air as the sea takes over from the garden. Here is the sage-green strip of carpet that runs down the centre of the boards to her front door. Here is the key with the loop of plaited string that surely, surely cannot be the one I made for her, decades ago. Here we are, myself and Marianne, going in through Lily's front door. My dreams have never taken me this far, and Marianne is no longer a solemn scrap who trots sturdily beside me like a little curly lamb. My girlhood's over. My daughter's tall. I'm really here. This is now.

The pink-and-gold flocked wallpaper in the hallway is shabby now, the colours fading, the edges beginning to peel above the radiator. Anxious to get my first look over, I plunge into the sitting room with its antique furniture and beautiful photographs and magnificent view of the sea, and onwards to the kitchen. I fling open the door to the walk-in pantry and see that even to the end of her life, Lily lined her shelves with paper and arranged her tins with the labels facing tidily outward. The top shelf was for the things I was forbidden to touch; the next shelf down for tins and baking ingredients and home-made jam. The lower shelves, empty now, held the things just for me: tinned rice pudding, peaches in syrup, butter-yellow sponge cake under a glass dome, the biscuit tin. From my brief glance inside, I see that Lily still kept an array of cake decorations in store and liked to hoard tinned fruit.

"Which bowl would you like for your peaches?" Lily, her chin on her hands in that gesture that makes her look like a contented cat, watches as I sit snug and peaceful in the dining alcove, smushing my boiled egg shell into the crusts of my soldiers so I won't have to eat them.

"The one with the bird on the bottom. I always have the one with the bird on the bottom." A moment of panic. "Have you still got it?"

"Of course I've still got it. I'm not like your mother, you know, I don't break my crockery. I only wanted to make sure you still liked that one." And then the eggshell and the crusts are whisked away and replaced by a bowl of peaches swimming in a luxurious bath of syrup, which I carefully conserve so that when the bird on his branch of dogwood are revealed, I can lift the bowl to my mouth and slurp it down in a long rich series of swallows. This was how Lily was always, indulging you with syrupy birds on sprays of wild roses, so you never realised until afterwards how sharp the thorns were. And besides, it was true; my mother did break a lot of china.

Back into the sitting room, where the curtains need washing and the furniture wears grey coats of dust. Lily was ninety-five; it's not surprising her standards slipped. Was she too poor, towards the end, to pay for help, or just too stubborn? Thank God the gas and the electricity are still on. I flick the switch on the immersion heater so we can have a bath later, and then rummage between the kitchen and the pantry to see what I can add to our supplies to create a meal.

"Have you texted Dad?" asks Marianne as I stare blankly at the tins in the pantry, and I flinch with guilt because I've totally forgotten to let Daniel know we've arrived. "It's all right, you're busy, I just know he worries. I'll ring him. And then I'll come and help you."

So many girls her age would rather shave their heads than traipse hundreds of miles by an assortment of trains in the company of their mother, to clear out the house of a deceased elderly relative who they never met and were barely aware even existed. Marianne begged to come with me. "You can't go by yourself," she told me. "I can help. Let me come too." And then, as the Midlands raced past in a grey smear, her sudden sweet confession: "Mum, is it all right that I wanted to come because I'm interested? But I'll help too, of course I will." If honesty can be a fault, then Marianne's compulsion to get things absolutely, scrupulously clear – even if the truth might make her look bad – falls into this category. She's curled on the William-Morris-looking sofa with the elegant wooden legs, her phone to her ear, chattering away to her dad, her discarded shoes neatly side by side on the floor. Of course I'll text Daniel anyway, he'll want to talk to me too, but perhaps I can wait a few more minutes.

I wonder if I dare brave the bedrooms.

The feel of the round black wooden door handle. The way it turns the opposite way to all the others. The keyhole beneath. I remember it all. About to push the door open and cross the threshold, my body is possessed by the ritual, and – feeling ridiculous but unable to stop myself – I kneel down on the mossy carpet.

"Why do you always do that?" Lily, shaking her head in bafflement, laughing at me as I bounce to my feet and give her a beaming smile.

"I'm checking to see if the key's still in the lock."

"But why do you do it from the outside? Why not check when you get inside?"

Instead of answering, I pull her head down so I can kiss her. I love her, but I don't want even Lily to know that I'm checking to make sure that, as long as the key remains on the inside of the lock, no one can see through the keyhole into my room while I sleep.

"And you promise you won't ever lock the door?" Lily says, as she always says, the words as much a part of the ritual as the kneeling and the peering.

"I promise," I say with a theatrical sigh, and then I'm in my room, mine even though I only live in it for a few weeks a year, and there is my bed made up with heavy white sheets, a thick brown blanket and a dusty-pink eiderdown, my fat pink lamp on the bedside table, and the book I left behind on my last visit waiting like an old friend; and when I turn around to close the door, there are shells strung over the door frame wait to catch any nightmares before they can reach me, and the porcelain cats with their round eyes and strange coiled tails and the pelican with the fat yellow beak stare back at me from the shelves above the chest of drawers.

By some strange necromantic act of housekeeping, my room is exactly as I remember.

SO SO SORRY I couldn't text as soon as we arrived. There was no signal until we got here. We made it. Although you probably know that because Marianne's just got off the phone to you. Xxxxx

So glad you're all right. I was a bit worried :(No signal at a train station??? I thought you were in Cornwall not Borneo xxxx

I know it sounds daft but it's right down between two hills. And the train was a bit late. Didn't Marianne get hold of you? I thought I saw her talking to someone.

She did but it's not the same as hearing from you. I miss you, you know.

I know, I know. I should have thought. Sorry again.

Have you found the voodoo doll yet?

???

The voodoo doll of me. You know, the one she made to try and stop me marrying you

Oh come on, she thought you were all right

She hated me on sight and you know it

Well she's dead now anyway and we're still married, so you win.

That's true. So what's it like?

Like home. Like a nightmare. Like being lost. Like being found. Like every treacherously lovely dream of my childhood coming true.

Dusty and shabby and old. You'd hate it.

Not if I was there with you I wouldn't. I'd get a giant skip and help you throw out junk all day, then fuck your brains out all night and write a million songs about how much I love you. You should be here with me. I need you xxxxx

I can't believe Lily's chosen to die now, in the month when Daniel's music career is finally about to become a paying proposition. At the station this morning, we held hands through the train window like newly parting lovers. It's been seventeen years but he still looked every bit as pretty as when we first met, his hair as fair, his mouth as endearingly expressive, his eyes as large and green. I tried not to be embarrassed by the smiles of the other passengers. At every change and every stop I texted him to assure him of our progress.

> *I can't throw anything out till it's valued. And if it's worth anything we're selling it, not binning it*

> *See, this is why you're the one who goes out to work at a proper grown-up accountancy job and I'm the musician. I'd chuck the lot and run for the hills.*

> *So when are you coming home?*

> *About a week. We did talk about this, you said you'd be all right for a week.*

> *When are you seeing the registrar? And the funeral director? Have you got appointments for everything?*

> *Yes, day after tomorrow, back to back, it's on the list, we really did talk about this remember? Look, let's not go over it again, it's boring. Tell me about your day. How was rehearsal?*

> *God, great I think. They like the new songs. Well, they all do apart from Mac but he hates new stuff on principle.*

This seems reasonable. The only time I've seen Mac smile was when Marianne brought him a cold beer after the jam session that ended with them all agreeing (with varying degrees of enthusiasm) to form Storm Interference.

And you uploaded the footage from the Rockwood gig?

I look like a dickhead in it, do I have to?

People need to see you're not just five blokes in a garage. That's the only gig you've got footage of so it needs to go up. Show the world you can make a crowd scream. Besides, you look gorgeous. :)

Okay, you're probably right. About not being five blokes in a garage, I mean. I'm standing by the dickhead thing.

But such a good-looking dickhead.

God I miss you. Why are you there and not here again?

Run away to claim our fortune, remember? It'll be worth it when we bank the cheque.

The sitting room has the mustiness of abandonment. I force the sash window upwards, savouring the salty, polleny air. Back on the sofa, my phone blinks with light.

So you're still happy about it? About the new band and everything, I mean? You really think it's going to happen?

Of course I am, you know I am. It's so cool. This is your year, I can feel it.

I know it's real if you say it. If you believe in me then I know it's true. I love being married to you. You always know what's going to happen

I should tell him again this is nonsense, but I don't have

21

the heart. A seagull perches speculatively on the window-ledge and peers beneath the sash, watching me with quick little jerks of its head. I flap my hand at it. It blinks and turns its head, checking if I look different when viewed from a different angle, but doesn't move.

It's going to cost a bit to get us started though

That's okay. Once Lily's estate's settled we will have money

Still can't quite believe it. Say it again please

My pleasure. Once Lily's estate's settled WE WILL HAVE MONEY

:-D :-D :-D :-D :-D

How much will it come to? I don't know yet exactly, but it's going to be more than we've ever had in our lives. Enough that Marianne can have shoes that don't fall apart after a month. Enough to pay Daniel's share of the band's set-up expenses. Enough to finally get us out of the succession of rented houses and into the cool white rooms and sculptured spaces Daniel's always dreamed of building. Maybe even enough so Marianne will stop sleepwalking, no longer haunted by the nightmares that force her bolt upright, screaming and flailing in terror.

And you'll quit work and we'll take Marianne out of school and you'll teach her at home and you'll both come with me everywhere and travel the world and I'll look after you for ever xoxoxoxoxox

Will any of this happen? Or have twelve years of fitting in stray gigs around his parenting duties blotted out his chances?

Music is a young man's game. Thirty-five this year; has he missed his moment? And what will happen if he has? What will become of him then?

No, I won't do this again. I've already been round this loop, assembled the evidence, reached my conclusion and committed my support. Storm Interference, formed for less than six weeks, is already attracting attention. They all like each other (apart from Mac, who doesn't like anyone). They're creating new work together. This is it, the break, the moment.

And now, miraculously, we have money to pay for equipment and recording fees and whatever else Daniel needs. Perhaps Lily's died at the perfect moment after all.

Right, I've got to go. Microwave's pinging

What are you having?

Freezer Roulette. I think it's chicken curry but I'm not sure

Yep it'll be chicken curry, there's a couple in there. There's some goulash as well, and some chicken in pesto, all the things you like

God, you're good. I'd starve without you. I love you xxxxx

I love you too xxxxx

For myself and my daughter, there's tomato soup in the pantry and a loaf of bread that I've lugged halfway down the country. Marianne is so tired she can hardly finish her soup. Against her protests, I run her a bath. She has that sallow transparent look I associate with a long night of nightmares ahead. Maybe I shouldn't have let her come. It was selfish to

23

give in to her begging, but the truth is I desperately wanted to bring her, as a companion, and as a shield against my memories. Behind the door of the little mirrored cabinet, Lily's toothbrush sits bereft beside her toothpaste and her tube of Steradent tablets.

Of course no one would have come to collect Lily's toothbrush, or fill an overnight bag with a clean nightdress and her green silk dressing gown. Marianne and I are her last living relatives, and I didn't even know she was ill until Daniel took the phone call. What was she wearing when the ambulance crew collected her? Was she dressed, or in her nightclothes? They would have spoken in that slow way she hated, big gestures and exaggerated smiles, and they would have wrapped her in a red fleecy blanket of the kind she resolutely despised. Perhaps one of them held her hand. Would she at least have had her teeth in? She hated being seen without her teeth. Marianne is hovering behind me.

"Sorry," I say, so she knows I know she's there. "Just stuck on the load-screen."

She perches against the bath and picks up the verdigris duck that stands on the black-and-white-tiled floor, running the chewed and raggedy ends of her fingers over the rough texture of its back and feeling the shape of its smiling beak. She's a compulsive fiddler. "Is it like it was when you were little?"

Beneath the grime, indifferent to the musty air, the duck still stands tall and lean like an Indian Runner duck, its beak open so it looks as if it's laughing. The store of Pears soap still sits on the top shelf of the cabinet. The wooden bath tray still holds the white soap dish with the rose in the bottom, and the pink Bakelite nail brush in the shape of a pig, which I thought for years was a grown-up bath toy. ('You mean, your mother doesn't have a nail brush in the house?' Lily, slightly overdoing her incredulity.) All the signs and signifiers of my childhood, grown old and sad with neglect. My heart hurts. I don't want to be here.

Marianne scrabbles in the bath tray and finds the flannel – dried stiff but neatly folded – then drops it again. The duck lies in her lap. I know what she's going to ask, because it's the logical thing to want to know.

Why didn't we ever visit her? What happened?

The question perches on her fingertips and I wait, wait, wait for it to take flight. Maybe she can see how much I'm dreading it. After a minute, she puts the duck back in its spot beside the bath and stands up.

"Where should I put my dirty clothes?" she asks instead.

With Marianne tidied safely away into the room that used to be mine, the monitor installed so I'll know if she cries out or sleepwalks, I'm ready to face Lily's bedroom. The huge windows (in need of painting now, perhaps even replacement) look out over the sweep of the lawn, the formal flowerbeds, the towering shrubs, and the sunny plot by the boundary wall where Lily once grew herbs. It's a beautiful view, but it was never the point of this room for me. All I wanted was to try on Lily's things.

First the jewellery, which – jackdaw that I am – still calls to me with a siren song. Lily kept her rings on the slender curved neck of a solid glass swan that I coveted almost more than the rings themselves. As a child, I crammed them on in stacks, admiring the weight they gave to my gestures, the flash as they caught the light. Decades later, I caress the swan's back and then touch the blood-dark ruby, the square inky sapphire, the huge art-deco aquamarine, the twists and twines of gold and silver and platinum, topped by the heavy hoop of rose-cut diamonds that my heart yearned for most of all.

Next I would delve into the wardrobe, which was always faintly disappointing. Lily's house was so much like a dream that I wanted to believe she spent her days draped in silks and velvets, old-fashioned dresses like the illustrations from my Ladybird fairy tales. Lily's cardigans and tea dresses, her cream leather shoes with the sensible heel, her hats for going to church in, were never what I was hoping for, but I tried them on anyway, just in case. An adult now, I open the wardrobe and disturb the cool soft folds, scented with violet and lavender.

Are you here, Lily? Are you watching me? Do you know I've come back to you at last? And what are you thinking?

I climb into her bed, wearing one of her dainty nightgowns because I seem to have forgotten my pyjamas, too tired to think about changing the sheets. I tumble into sleep wondering if this deeply personal invasion will anger Lily's spirit. But instead Lily stands by my bed, puts my book on the nightstand and tucks me in. The gold-white silk of her hair, let loose from its neat bun and falling around her shoulders, caresses my cheek as she presses her lips to my face and I feel the vibration of her voice against my cheek. *I'll always love you best,* she tells me, in words I feel, but will never hear. The gentlest of kindly hauntings.

Chapter Two – Lily

I'm six years old, and my father's been taken away by the train. I won't see him again for five weeks, a stretch of time so huge it feels like for ever. I'm aware I'm supposed to be sad about this, but I look up at the tall bony woman beside me, her white hair gleaming in the sun, and sigh. Lily's expression tells me she knows exactly how I'm feeling, and she feels it too.

On the way back up the hill, a long-haired cat waits on the wall, its squashed fluffy face impatient and eager, its gaze fixed on me. When I hold out my hand, its mouth opens pink and wide. It wipes its nose against my finger and presses the length of its back against my hand. Then it jumps off the wall and sprawls across the warm tarmac, exposing the pale soft fur of its belly.

I sit down to devote my full attention to it, knowing I'm allowed now, because I'm with Lily. No one will tell me I'll get my dress dirty. No one will mention germs. No one will tell me all the ways in which dirty dresses or germs make more work for them. I can sit on the path and talk to the cat as long as I want, and when I've finished there'll be roast chicken for lunch. Lily leans against the wall, and takes a pinch of leaves from the bush that grows from the stones.

"What's that?"

She holds out the crushed green needles between her fingers. I inhale the scent.

"Rosemary," she says. "Good for cooking with. And for sweet dreams and happy memories."

For some time now, I've thought Lily may be a witch. She seems the right age, and she knows a lot about herbs and plants. She has recipes that she keeps secret no matter how often she's asked, and she has a store of poisonous bottles that live on the top shelf of her pantry, which I'm forbidden to ever touch. *Photographic supplies*, she tells me when I ask, *there's not much room in the cellar darkroom*, but she might simply be saying that to put me off the scent. On the other hand, she doesn't have a cat, and she goes to church every Sunday.

"Why do I call you Lily?" I ask suddenly.

She laughs. "Because that's my name."

"Yes, but why don't I call you Granny, or something?"

"I don't know. You've just always called me Lily. I can't imagine you calling me anything else now. Unless you want to change."

"No. I like Lily. I just wondered."

The cat clutches imploringly at my arm with velvety paws splintered with needles. I return to stroking its side.

"Why don't you have a cat?"

"Cats are a nuisance." Nonetheless she bends down and runs her hand over it, even as she shakes her head in disdain. "Look at it. As if it's been hit in the face with a frying pan." The cat writhes blissfully as Lily caresses its cheek. "It's time I started getting lunch ready. Are you coming too? Or do you want to stay and talk to the cat?"

I blink. I can see the entrance to the gravel drive, I'm less than two minutes from the safety of Lily's front door, but no one in my family has trusted me to be by myself, inside the house or out of it, since the world turned silent.

"Am I allowed?"

"Of course, if you want to. Do you want to?"

"Did Mum say I could?"

"She didn't say you couldn't."

"But, will I be safe?"

"You'll be fine. You've got your head screwed on right. I'll leave the door on the latch."

"But what if something happens to me?" I ask, not because I think something will actually happen to me but because I want to know her answer.

"Nothing will happen to you. But if it does, I'll know, and I'll come straight back and fetch you. You come home when you're ready."

I continue petting the cat and watch her stride up the road, tall and brisk and confident. It would be a disaster if she turned around, checking I'm not jumping into the road or eating poisonous berries or climbing into a van with a stranger, or any of the other patently silly things an adult might think I'm going to do. But she turns into the driveway without looking back, and I sigh in satisfaction. Only a witch could possibly know if I'm all right without watching me. And only a witch's granddaughter could be left alone, outside, to continue seducing the cat that may, with time, become her own familiar.

I count to a hundred in my head, going as slowly as I can to give Lily time to go inside, climb the stairs, go through her own front door and begin bustling about the kitchen. Then I walk stealthily up the road. When I reach the driveway, I press into the wall so I can't be seen from Lily's windows, and keep to the shadows. I'm going to find out how Lily watches over me even when I'm not there. The downstairs front door is propped open to let the hallway breathe the flowery morning air. Before I climb the stairs, I take off my socks and shoes.

Lily's door is on the latch, exactly as she promised. Opening the door by myself is a new skill and I'm pleased when I manage it. I wedge it carefully open with my shoe so it won't make noise when it closes, and pad down the corridor into the kitchen.

A chicken sits pink and chilly in a Pyrex dish, waiting

for its coat of butter and greaseproof paper. On the table, a mound of potatoes will soon be peeled and boiled, ready for roasting. But Lily herself stands motionless, gazing at the shivering surface of a bowl of clean water, her expression stern, her attention turned inwards. I laugh in delight.

"Hello, my darling." Lily holds her hands out to me. "I thought you were on your way back. Oh, for goodness sakes, look who came with you."

I want to ask if the bowl is like a magic mirror, but I follow her pointing finger and find the cat's followed me home. When I stroke it, it closes its eyes and quivers its tail in bliss.

"Well, as long as you don't feed it," says Lily, and picks up a potato.

Chapter Three – Wednesday

I wake to sunshine and freshness and a bone-deep sensation of well-being that's instantly cancelled by the sight of Marianne, pale and frantic, standing by my bed in her pyjamas.

"Mum," she says. "Mum."

"What?" Has she been sleepwalking? Did she wake lost in a strange house, flailing and screaming, trapped in the horror of some private nightmare? Is she hurt? How did I sleep through the monitor?

She's so upset she can hardly speak. "Something awful."

"What? What?" I scrabble out from beneath the heavy sheets. "Tell me! Are you hurt? What happened? Where did you wake up?"

"I was dreaming," says Marianne. "I was in bed and I dreamed I could hear a little cat crying somewhere. It was so loud it woke me up."

"But I didn't see the monitor flash. Why didn't the monitor flash?"

"I didn't want to wake you so I unplugged it." She flaps impatiently at my objections. "No, please, you've got to listen. I was hungry and I thought it would be all right to look in the pantry. And I found… oh, Mum, I found…"

She stands straight and tall. Her bones seem intact. There are no visible cuts or bruises. My heart slows down. Perhaps this is something else entirely. I stroke her arm gently. "Calm down. Take a minute. Deep breaths. Now look at me. Go slowly. Tell me what you found." My phone sits reproachfully on the nightstand, reminding me of my other responsibilities. I reach for it, tap out a hasty message: *Morning husband, just checking in so you know we made it through the night, love you xxxxx* then turn back to Marianne.

She shakes her head miserably and leads me into the kitchen. I'm frantic to know what's drained the colour from Marianne's face and turned her hands into clutching claws, but still the scent of the pantry tempts me back into memories of the well-beloved past. Cool and very slightly damp. Hints of vanilla and biscuits, jam and trifle, clotted cream whipped with the rich skimmings from Jersey milk, and long-ago Victoria sponge cakes. Stolen chocolate and hastily devoured glacé cherries; the confounding mystery of the guilty pleasure. I force myself to stay in the present, and follow Marianne's imperious finger.

The space beneath the bottom shelf is home to such dull necessities as the carrier-bag holder, the washing powder and the old-lady breakfast cereals Lily favoured. I always wanted to believe that, when alone, she ate in the same fantastical and luxurious way that she liked to feed me: tender miniature roasts with thick gravy brewed on the back of the stove, afternoon cakes on dainty plate stands, cream with a thick gold crust concealing rich silk beneath, and a propensity to grow mould if eaten too slowly. It takes me several seconds to realise what Marianne's pointing at.

"Oh, shit," I say before I can stop myself, and see Marianne's anxiety release itself in a spasm of laughter. "Sorry. Sorry. Forget I said that." I pick up the box of cat biscuits. "Oh God."

Marianne is picking up on my distress like a radio antenna. The laughter vanishes. Her face is shrivelled misery.

"Her poor cat," she says, swiping fiercely at her tears. "Her poor, poor cat."

"Now stop it. We don't know for sure she even had a cat. She might have had a visiting cat and got biscuits in for it."

32

Except she wouldn't have bought biscuits for a visiting cat. *As long as you don't feed it.*

"She's got cat litter too." Marianne drags the bag out to show me. "You don't buy that for a visiting cat, you only buy cat litter if it's your cat. She had a cat and it's been all on its own and it must have died or got lost and thought she didn't love it any more, it must have been so sad and confused—"

"Stop that. We don't know that. We don't. Maybe she got someone to take it to a cattery."

"Then why didn't the solicitor say anything? He would have known, there'd be a bill to pay. That's not what happened, Mum. You don't have to try and make me feel better, I'm old enough to be treated like a grown-up. It's been shut in all alone and it's died, hasn't it?"

When she really gets hold of a subject, Marianne is a bit like a solicitor herself.

"Of course it hasn't been shut in and died," I say, realising as I say the words that they must be true. "There's no way there's a dead cat in here with us. We'd know."

"So where is it, then? Was it outside and it couldn't get back in, and now it's a poor lost stray cat? It must be so frightened." She stops suddenly and turns her head. "What's that?"

"What's what?"

Her eyes are black with terror. She lives so much on her nerves. No wonder she's so thin. "I heard the front door. Someone's coming in."

"There can't be. We've got the keys."

"Mum! I swear! There's someone coming in! What are we going to do?"

I take a step towards the kitchen. Marianne tries to go first, but I shake my head and push her firmly behind me. Whatever bogeyman my daughter's conjured up, there's no way I'm going to make her face up to them, and most especially not in her pyjamas, which she's cobbled together by pairing my old black camisole with some Superman boxer shorts Daniel got for Christmas in a pub Secret Santa, and that are far too small for him. Let her imaginary monsters face the full wrath of an angry half-wakened mama bear, in her grandmother's nightgown and with her hair around her face in a wild tangle. On impulse, I pick up a marble rolling pin and stalk through the sitting room. It's so heavy and unbalanced I have to support it with my spare hand. It's surely the most useless weapon imaginable. Any minute now the handle will snap.

To my enormous surprise, there is a man in Lily's hallway.

He's old and tall, and has that way of holding himself that people describe as 'military'. His hair's thick and white, clipped short against his scalp. He wears a crisp white shirt and formal navy trousers. The shirt is buttoned right to the top and I suspect he wears a tie most of the time, although not today. Clearly, housebreaking isn't an activity that demands his very best sartorial efforts. He smells of Imperial Leather soap. His eyes are blue, still bright. In his day he must have been quite a looker. It doesn't matter on any rational level, but I'd still prefer, on balance, to be greeting him with a sight other than my frowsty, unwashed face, my unbrushed hair, and my grandmother's nightgown. I find time for all of these thoughts in the moments when we stand and stare at each other. He looks far more shocked than me. His eyes widen and his mouth works, and he holds his hands up as if to defend himself.

"Who are you?" I demand, brandishing my rolling pin. I'm not seriously planning to use it, in fact I can barely even hold the thing, but perhaps this isn't as obvious as I think because the man looks terrified. His eyes are huge and his hands are trembling. Encouraged, I shake the rolling pin in his direction. "What the hell do you think you're doing?"

He swallows hard and takes a few steps back. Is he old enough that I need to worry about his heart? His gaze moves to a spot over my shoulder, staring as if he can't quite believe what he's seeing. Marianne must have followed me.

"Get out, get out, get out," I say, feeling as if I'm shooing a cat. "I mean it. I'll hit you with this, I swear. Go on. Out. Out!"

He swallows hard and squares his shoulders. Intriguingly, his expression is now one of outrage. Instead of slinking away in embarrassment, he's yelling right back at me. His face turns red, but I can't follow a word.

"Stop talking." I hold up my hand. "I didn't get any of that. Slow down and speak clearly." Marianne touches my arm. "Marianne, go and wait in the kitchen."

"I said," he repeats, "I suppose you're Lily's ungrateful little granddaughter?"

Charming.

"That's me. Which means I'm entitled to be here, and you're not. How dare you come in here?"

"How dare *you* come in here? All those years you never visited. Broke her heart, you know that?"

Who is this man who thinks he can come in here and judge me? Suddenly it's difficult to breathe. I'm filled with the kind of wild fury that gives women the strength to lift tow trucks with their bare hands and tear the heads off bears.

"And now," he continues, "now you waltz in like you own the place—"

"I do own the place," I say, although I'm not sure of this. Is it like the monarchy? Did Lily's home become mine the second she died? Or are her assets currently in unowned limbo? "Why do you care? Did you want her to leave it to you?" I'm only saying this to annoy him, but maybe he had a reason to think she might. Who is he? Who? Am I supposed to know him?

"Not been gone a week. And now here you are. Like a rat creeping in. It was her only bloody consolation, you know. Knowing you'd come back down here eventually, even if she had to die to make it happen."

Well, that certainly sounds like Lily.

35

"She was a wonderful woman," he continues. "Worth twenty of you."

"She was a—" I suddenly remember that Marianne is behind me. "I was her granddaughter. You don't need to tell me what she was like. What? *What?*"

He's staring at my hand. During the night, I must have got out of bed and slipped Lily's square-cut sapphire ring – its inky central stone bordered with tiny brilliant diamonds, its shank stretched thin and wide to slide over her poor arthritic knuckles – onto my right index finger. The sight pierces me. I fight a childish urge to put my hand behind my back.

"Couldn't wait to get your hands on her things," he says, with grim satisfaction. "Makes me feel ill."

I swallow my memories and raise my chin. "It looks better on me than it would on you. Whoever you are."

"Mum." Marianne tugs at my sleeve to get my attention and I turn away from my opponent so I can look at her. Her hands are trembling. "Mum. I'm going to call the police. Okay?"

"No, you're not," I say out loud.

"No, she's not what?" The man glares. "Bloody rude to talk so other people can't understand you."

"Really? Because people do it to me all the time. And, d'you know, some of them don't even introduce themselves?"

"James Moon," he barks at me, and in spite of himself, I see his right arm twitch as if he wants to shake hands. "I live downstairs. Been keeping an eye since – since she was taken badly. And if you're wondering why I've got a key, I'll tell you. Lily gave me it. Looked out for each other, we did, since you turned your back on her. I used to tell her, Lily, don't you leave a penny to that brat grandchild of yours, she doesn't deserve it. You give it to—"

"You?"

"—bloody charity, if you like, but don't let her see a penny."

"She didn't listen, though, did she?" I say cheerfully. "She was a horrible stubborn old witch, you see, and there was a good reason why I never came to visit, not that I have to explain that to you. What with you being a random intruder in *my* legal property."

James suddenly looks old and exhausted, and I feel the thrill of victory in my veins.

"Bet you haven't even thought about a funeral," he says, apparently with difficulty. "Helped yourself to her jewellery, all her private things, but not one second's thought to a decent send-off. Even wearing her bloody nightgown."

I drop the rolling pin on the floor, tug the nightgown over my head and crumple it into a ball. His eyes widen in shock for a second, then close tight. A flush of crimson crawls up his neck.

"Here." I hold it out towards him. "Would you like it?"

My enemy's silenced. The capricious power of the female form. I'd like to think it's my ineffable loveliness when naked, but it's more likely to be simple terror.

"Maybe you'd like me to wash it first?"

"You're not right in the head," he says, backing away towards the door, his eyes still tightly shut.

"Leave the key on the console table," I tell him.

"Like hell I will." His hand finds the door handle and scrabbles for freedom.

"I'll send you a copy of her will, if you like!" I shout after him as he finally gets the door open and makes his escape. "So you can see how much she left me!"

The door quivers in its frame, and I wince, worrying about the paintwork. On the plus side, he's gone and I've won.

I open the door again and find, as I'd hoped, that James Moon has left his key in the lock. It's slightly stiff to turn, new-looking and raw. Lily was always careful about keys. In all the years she lived here, this spare can hardly have been used.

The air is cool against my skin and I remember I'm naked. I shut the door hastily and put Lily's nightgown back on. When I emerge from the top of the crisp frail cotton, I see Marianne looking at me.

"What?"

"I can't believe you did that."

"Which bit?" I wonder if James Moon has got home yet. Perhaps he can hear us moving about above him.

"All of it! You were amazing!" Her hands are shaking and I can hardly make out what she's saying. "When he started shouting at you and calling you names, and you just shouted right back at him. I was so scared. Weren't you scared?"

"Of course I wasn't scared. Why would I be?"

"He might have hurt us! Or killed us. Or tied us up so he could steal things."

Surprisingly enough, none of this even occurred to me. For someone who turned up uninvited in someone else's home and shouted abuse at a stranger, James Moon was an oddly non-threatening person. Perhaps it helped that Lily must have known him intimately, and trusted him deeply. How else would he have the spare key to her home?

"That was horrible," Marianne adds, sniffling a little.

"He was pretty awful," I agree.

"He looked like he might be nice, but he wasn't at all. And we still haven't found the cat."

You'd think facing down an intruder would distract her, but when it comes to cats, Marianne is relentless.

"Okay, so here are the options. Either it's being looked after by someone, in which case they'll let us know so we can take it to a shelter, so we don't need to worry. Or, it's run away and found itself a new home somewhere, so we still don't need to worry."

"But what if they don't know we're here and they don't bring it back?"

"Then it'll have a lovely new home. And we still don't need to worry."

"But couldn't we—"

"The important thing is, it's definitely not here."

"But—"

"No, no more. That's it. Let's find breakfast."

There's plenty of cereal, as long as you like your cereal brown and austere and loaded with bran, but the milk in the fridge has set into a pale quivering blancmange, the bacon's turned green around the rinds and the single carton of orange juice has swollen up like a toad. The eggs are two weeks out of date. Gingerly, I take the top off the bread bin. A cloud of blue spores float out, so I cram the lid back on and back away. We'll have to make do with what we brought with us, and then we need to get dressed and go foraging. I should have thought of this when I packed, but there was no time.

While Marianne is in the bathroom, hosing herself diligently off with the pale green tap attachment that Lily – in the teeth of the evidence – insisted was a perfectly good substitute for a shower, I go to Lily's bedroom to return the sapphire ring. The swan's neck is bare, the rings scattered loosely on the dressing table. The sight causes a sinking feeling in my stomach.

"Who do you think he is?"

In Lily's little red dining alcove, Marianne and I sit opposite each other across the round mahogany table, its surface wiped hastily free of dust with a cloth I found beneath the sink. This small act of cleaning has had the unintended effect of making everything else look much dirtier. I sit in Lily's place, determined not to repeat the past. The table has a handle that unwinds it to an unfeasible length, which is something I imagine Marianne would enjoy seeing. Perhaps I'll show her later, but not today. Today we have things to do.

"He told us," I say. "He lives downstairs."

"Yes, but why did he have her key?"

I bite into my toast. It tastes of cheap margarine, faintly separated. Marianne has skimmed hers with a layer of bramble jelly from the pantry, but I prefer the taste of lightly curdled vegetable oil. "Because she gave it to him, like he said."

"Mum." Marianne gives me the patient look she uses

39

when people she loves act like idiots. "What I meant was, why would she give her key to some random man just because he lives downstairs?"

I know what Marianne's getting at, but I stubbornly refuse to pick up on her hints. "Well, maybe they used to meet on the way to collect their post or something. Eat your toast."

"Are we going to invite him to the funeral?"

"The undertakers will place a notice in the paper. If he sees it he's welcome to show up."

Marianne looks at me, then back at her plate.

"He looked so sad," she says, almost to herself. I take another bite, enjoying the sensation in my skull as the toast crunches, refusing to feel guilty. He looked angry to me, not sad; and besides, James Moon's emotional well-being is not my problem. "Mum, can I ask you something?"

"It's all right, he won't be coming back. I've got the key now. He can't get in."

"Yes, I know, I wasn't worried about that. I just wanted to ask if you'd told Dad."

The words are like an electric shock. How have I not told Daniel?

"It's all right," Marianne adds, seeing my face. "I don't think it's a good idea either. He'll only worry."

"No, you're right, I need to tell him."

"Mum, that's not what I said. I said I think you're right, we *shouldn't* tell him."

I can already imagine his reaction. Not telling him would be so easy. "No, we can't keep secrets from your dad."

"It's not a secret, it's just something he doesn't need to know about. Like if I cut my knee or something, but then you put a plaster on it and it was fine, he wouldn't need to know, would he?"

"This is different though. I'll tell him the next time I speak to him." Marianne looks disbelieving. "Look, we'll talk about it later. We need to get dressed. We're meeting the registrar in two hours."

"Well, I won't tell him, anyway," Marianne says, and returns to her toast.

Can I possibly get away with not telling Daniel? It would certainly make life easier. If he finds out he'll be devastated, but perhaps he won't ever find out. I take my plate to the kitchen and scrape crumbs into the bin, which – thank God – Lily must have emptied the day she was taken into hospital. The air is losing its chilly, unoccupied scent and now smells comfortingly of tea and toast. I like it, but I've been eating it, so I would. I need to keep Lily's flat as clean and impersonal as possible, so it will sell quickly and for a good price. I open the window to let it air out. Back in the sitting room, I'm caught by the photographs that stare out at me from the table by the fireplace.

Lily had a rare and compelling talent for photography, easily the best amateur I've ever known. Perhaps in a different life she might have made it into a profession, instead of running a hotel. Sometimes she'd let me watch, breathless, in the cellar darkroom, as my slightly younger selves swam up from their chemical bath. I pick up the picture of the little girl with the fat brown pigtails hanging over her shoulders, staring at a hermit crab picking delicately across a slab of rock. I'm someone else entirely now, but Lily has preserved my childhood self for ever, trapped until time and light steal the colour from the paper. Years before, another camera caught my dad in almost the same spot, his face round and laughing as he brandished a handful of seaweed.

"Who's this?" Marianne reaches for a photo of a small pretty young woman in a tiny, immaculate garden, reaching high into a tree to pick an apple. The wind is undoing her carefully set curls and blows the bottom of her skirt into the shape of an opening flower. "Is this Lily?"

"No, that's Margaret, her younger sister. She—"

"—had a weak heart and died." Marianne nods. "That's sad. She looks nice." She replaces Margaret in her spot and reaches for another. "And who's this?"

"My dad."

She peers at him critically. "He looks like you."

"Does he? Yes, I suppose he does."

"How old was he when he died?" she asks, all in a rush as if she's afraid of being told off for asking.

"Fifty-six."

"Is it all right to ask? I wanted to write it on the family tree."

"Of course it's all right."

"Only you never really talk about him. Oh! What's this? Have I broken it? I didn't mean to."

She holds out her hand guiltily to show a tiny wizened handful of russet-coloured berries. In spite of myself, my heart thumps.

"It's all right, you haven't broken anything. They were stuck to the back of the frame, that's all. Throw them away and get dressed, we need to get on."

"What are they?"

"Nothing, just some berries."

"But why are they there?"

"Time to get ready. Scoot. Off you go." I take the photo back from Marianne and replace it in the clean spot among the dust.

Hawthorn is good for the heart. The look on Lily's face as she cut the berries from the tree with her pocketknife, intent on her task even as she laughed at her own superstition. She knew, somehow, what was coming, what lay in her son's future; she knew what no one else ever suspected and what no doctor ever diagnosed. I will not cry. I will not cry. I reach angrily for another photo.

This one shows Lily herself. She is looking back at the camera from beneath a buddleia bush, holding a long purple frond against her cheek and laughing. A tortoiseshell butterfly sips greedily at the flowers, refusing to be dislodged. The photo lacks the crisp definition of the shots Lily herself took, and the framing is slightly too far to the left. She's also older

42

than I ever saw her; the skin over her cheekbones is more pleated, the fingers that hold the buddleia more knotted, the veins on her hand more prominent. Nonetheless, she is beautiful in this photo. I think the person who took it must have loved her.

Helping yourself to all her private things. James Moon and his burning outrage, furious with me even though he was the intruder. And here I am, doing exactly what he said I'd do. Maybe later I'll do more, rummage into all the corners to see what terrible secrets I can find. Perhaps I'll even find that voodoo doll Daniel was only half joking about. If Mr Moon had any idea what Lily was really like, he'd understand why I never visited. When I was small I was convinced she was a witch.

I wonder if James Moon can smell the food we've been eating.

I wonder if Lily ever cooked for him.

I'm surprised to find I'm a little jealous.

Chapter Four – Lily

"I can't sleep," I confess to Lily, standing on one leg in the doorway of her bedroom.

She looks at me over the top of her copy of *The Great Gatsby*, hastily removing her glasses (thick-rimmed and, she claims, ugly – she refuses to be seen wearing them). To my eight-year-old eyes she's so old that she's long past any question of ugliness or beauty, but her hair remains defiantly lovely, clean and lavender-scented, its colour a rich golden white, like sun shining on snow.

She puts her finger in her book to mark her place. "What's the matter?"

"I just can't sleep," I repeat, feeling mulish. It's the hottest week in decades, and too much time in glaring sunshine has left me with a sick headache. My room, normally a blessed peaceful sanctuary, is strange and hot and filled with unexpected shadows. I've tried putting the main light on, re-reading my favourite *Rupert Bear* annual, putting the light off again, and visiting the toilet; but my room stubbornly refuses to feel safe. It has, I feel, betrayed me. Sometimes my friends are allowed into their parents' beds when they have nightmares, although mine have never let me. I wonder if Lily will invite me to sleep with her. I'm not sure how I feel about this. Lily looks at me thoughtfully.

"Wait a minute."

She reaches across to her bedside table and tucks her

bookmark into her book. She folds back the covers of her bed, smoothing the sheet so it looks neat. Lily never likes to be hurried into leaving a mess. Her nightdress is white and crisp and voluminous. It makes me think of medieval castles.

"Back to your room," she orders.

I scurry in and start to scrabble beneath the covers, but Lily shakes her head and folds the sheets and blankets back to the foot of the bed, then snaps on my bedside light and briefly adjusts the curtains.

"Sit there," she tells me, pointing to the end of the bed.

Part of Lily's magic is that she can give orders without upsetting me. I sit obediently on the neat folds and wait. She's only gone a moment.

"I've never told you this before," she says, holding out her hand to reveal a clutch of bright treasure, nested in the pleats of her palm. "But I think you're old enough now. My rings are magical. Choose one to wear, and in five minutes you'll be cool and sleepy, and you'll stay that way all night."

My heart jumps gladly in my chest.

"Which is the most magical?" I stir them greedily with my finger. I want to choose the best one.

"I don't need to tell you that. You're my clever granddaughter. Take your time and you'll know which is the right one for you."

It takes me a long time to choose, but Lily doesn't seem impatient. She doesn't try to guide my choice, or tell me to get on with it because it's late and we both need to go to sleep. She simply sits and watches me, her face grave and still and attentive like a cat's face, as I try each ring in turn on every one of my fingers. They're far too big even on my thumb, but the jewels flash and leap in the light – sapphires and diamonds, tiny drops of ruby, a huge rectangular stone the colour of the heart of a wave.

"Where did they all come from?" I ask.

"All over the world," Lily says. "India and Burma and Africa, Australia maybe, China, Sri Lanka."

This wasn't what I meant, but it distracts me for a moment. I try a ring like a flower from an old tapestry, its tiny yellow heart surrounded with pearl petals, admiring how it looks against my smooth brown finger. Burma. China. Sri Lanka. Beautiful words to conjure with.

"But who gave them to you?" I persist, sliding the flower ring off again and returning to the magnificent sapphire surrounded with diamonds.

"That one, the one you're wearing now, that was my engagement ring from my husband, Richard."

"And he was killed in the war?"

"That's right. And that little flower ring you tried, that was my sister's engagement ring. Margaret means *Daisy*, you see, and her husband called her Daisy as a pet name."

If I had the choice, I'd much rather be called Daisy than Margaret. I slide off the sapphire and try on a ruby with its ornately crafted surround set with sprinkles of diamond.

"That's another one of Margaret's. He gave her that just before he died. She never wore it much."

"He must have really loved her."

"His family had money, so he could afford it. That one once belonged to his mother."

"And how about this diamond one?"

"That was from when your father was born. An unbroken ring of stones like that is called an eternity ring. You give one when your first child's born." I pick up a ring shaped like a Roman shield. "And that's another one of Margaret's, a birthday present I think."

"Would Margaret mind me wearing them?"

"She'd be delighted. She would have loved you. She always wanted – here, try this one." Lily hands me a slim platinum band with a huge emerald-cut aquamarine. "I bought this for myself when we moved here. I found it in an antique shop and it reminded me of the sea."

"And were the rings all magic when you got them? Or did you put a spell on them?"

"That's my secret," Lily says, and I accept this, because I want to concentrate on trying on jewellery.

I finally settle on the circle of diamonds, sliding it onto my index finger and holding it breathlessly in place so I can see the tiny fires leap and dance in the stones' cold bright hearts. Lily gives a nod of satisfaction, pats my cheek and stands up so she can tuck me in securely. So powerful is the magic of Lily's promise that the sheets now feel deliciously cold and crisp against my skin. Or maybe it's simply that she's opened the window a fraction so the garden can steal the damp heat from my bed and breathe fragrance over my cheek.

"Don't worry," she says, perhaps seeing the regret for the other rings I haven't chosen flicker across my face. "You can choose a different one tomorrow."

"Are you sure you don't mind?"

"Of course I don't mind. They'll be yours one day anyway."

"How can they be mine? They're yours."

"Well, one day you'll be grown up," Lily improvises.

I wonder what she means, then realise she's talking about her own death, which is something I don't want to think about. I can't imagine my life without Lily in it, without the glorious freedom to escape to another life every summer.

"But what if someone else wants them?" I ask, to distract myself.

"Who else would I give them to?"

"Maybe my mum," I say, knowing even as I say the words how silly I'm being. Lily would never leave anything precious or breakable to my mother.

"No, they're for you. I'll always love you best. You know that."

I wonder how my mother will feel about this, but it's so far in the future I decide not to worry about it. Instead I slide the diamonds up and down my finger, casting rainbows on the curtains.

"But what if I lose it in the night?"

"You won't lose it," Lily says, with such finality that I can't even think about arguing. "You're my granddaughter. I can trust you with anything."

And she's right. In all the years I go to bed wearing Lily's rings, I never once lose one.

Chapter Five – Thursday

Morning gorgeous husband xxxxx

Morning gorgeous favourite wife. I dreamed about you last night xxxxxx

That's funny. I dreamed about you too

Really? What was I doing?

In my dream, Daniel was in the music room, having sex with a beautiful dark-haired woman in a red satin dress. The woman was a prostitute, whose time Daniel had agreed to pay thousands of pounds for. When I looked at her, I felt anxiety rather than betrayal.

You were in the music room, talking to a woman with a red frock on. And you were drinking a beer

What?

Am I dream-stalking you again? :)

I swear to God Jen, that is so spooky how you do that. Are you sure you don't have hidden cameras or something?

Don't go all woo on me. It's a coincidence and you know it.

So what were you doing? You weren't really with a woman in a red dress were you?

Um…

Come on. Tell me

Well, I borrowed this lush red guitar from Connor. He's selling it

You're not buying it though are you?

LOL no. Just borrowing it before it disappears for ever. It's lovely mind you. I wouldn't mind buying it

But you haven't? Right?

No! It's worth thousands. You know I'll check before buying anything big. I always do, don't I? Although I was talking to my accountant the other day and apparently we are rich now.

Well in theory we are but we won't get any actual money until the probate's granted so please don't buy anything without checking okay?

Anyway, what did you dream?

Is Marianne still asleep?

Yep

Then shut the door and get back into bed and I'll tell

you all about it

Desire nibbles at my belly. Do I dare? The monitor remains black and still, but what if she's turned it off again?

Damn it, the monitor's lit up like a Christmas tree. I think our girl's awake. Sorry.

FFS :(

I'll take a rain check. You can tell me all about it later, okay?

If you're making me wait then I'll want photographs later

It's a deal

Glad to hear it

So what are you up to today?

Probate stuff. Picking estate agents to do the valuation. Find someone to look at the furniture. And I need to talk to a jeweller. Get all the rings valued.

God I remember those rings. I don't know how she moved her hands with those things on, they were like knuckle-dusters.

Bet they're worth a fortune though.

You are going to sell them, right? Oh come on, you can't be thinking of keeping them! We could get a great holiday out of it. Sell the lot and we'll take Marianne to Burning Man.

Maybe. But we can't sell anything until all the paperwork's gone through anyway, so don't book anything, okay?

Good thing I've got you to keep me honest, I'd have blown the lot on frivolities already

I know. That's why you're the musician and I'm the accountant. Right, got to get on with stuff. Talk to you later. xxxx

"Come here, sweetie." I hold my arms out to Marianne as she comes into the sitting room, sweet and unfocused with newly shed sleep. Two nights without nightmares or sleepwalking, which given we're in a strange place is nothing short of miraculous. "Did you sleep all right?"

"Mum." Marianne comes into my arms obediently. "Can I ask you something?"

"Why do you always ask if it's okay to ask? Come on, let's have it."

"Which war was Lily's husband killed in?"

"The Second World War."

"But didn't that end in nineteen forty-five?"

"You know it did. I thought you spent all last term learning about it."

"And your dad was fifty-six when he died? Is it all right to ask? I don't want to upset you."

"Of course it's all right. And yes, he was fifty-six."

Marianne's holding a notebook. She begins to write out a little sum on the edge of my page.

"So he was fifty-six," she says. "And that was the year I was born. So if you take fifty-six away…"

A little cold insect picks delicately down my spine. How have I never seen this before?

"That means he must have been born in nineteen forty-eight. I've done that right, haven't I? I checked it three times."

52

There's a mistake somewhere in the workings. There's a mistake, and I just haven't seen it yet. But what if there isn't? I'm an accountant. How have I never done this simplest of calculations before? And what does it mean? Marianne is doodling a little picture of a boat on the corner of the page.

"Maybe I got it wrong and my grandfather died *because of* the war rather than in it," I improvise. "From an old injury or something. That happened a lot."

"Did it?" Marianne's face is very innocent.

"Yes. All the time."

"And is that what happened to her sister's husband as well?"

"I… actually, I think it was his heart or something. People did die younger back then, there were a lot more things you could die of. Look, it's a lovely day. Why don't you get dressed and take your breakfast outside?"

"In the garden? Is that allowed?"

"Of course it's allowed, you daft article."

"I thought maybe it might belong to Mr Moon downstairs."

"No, it's for all of us. Go and get some fresh air."

"But what if someone asks who I am?"

"Tell them you're Lily Pascoe's great-granddaughter."

"But what if they don't believe me?"

"Then send them up to me."

"But what if—"

"No more what ifs."

"But—"

"No more buts. Go on. Get dressed, make toast, fresh air."

"And am I allowed to talk to people?"

"What?"

"If they're nice, I mean."

"No. Yes. I don't know, just… use your judgement." What harm can she come to? Three other homes beside this one. A general tendency towards richness and oldness. James Moon, rude and angry and judgemental, but probably not an actual kidnapper. Surely she wouldn't talk to him anyway, not after yesterday morning. "Don't go off with anyone."

"Of course I won't go off with anyone!"

"Then off you go." I flap towards the doorway and turn back to the paperwork that seems to be breeding every time I turn my back. Mr and Mrs Form, who got together at a paperwork dance one night. A moment of passion in the comforting dark of the box file, and now there's a whole litter of little forms, lining up for me to fill them with meaning and purpose, before I shut them away in envelopes and send them off into the world.

I've left the curtains half-drawn in an attempt to disguise the neglect, but I'm conscious of how badly Lily's house needs a good scrub. *Deep cleaning* is what it's called these days, but I prefer Lily's old phrase, the Easter Clean. Someone needs to open every nook and cranny to the fresh salty air, wipe down each wooden surface with a damp cloth scented with lemon oil, take down the curtains and wash away the dust and damp spots, empty the cupboards and clean into the corners then reline them with fresh brown paper, rinse the windows with vinegar and newspaper, vacuum the carpet back to something reminiscent of its former splendour. I know how to do all these things from watching Lily. My mother is too disorganised to keep a clean house, and my father never had time. The urge to clean is primal. Denying it makes me cross and itchy and irritable, the way I was the week before Marianne's birth.

As a compromise, I open the window. Today the sky goes on for miles, that high clear blue that comes nowhere else and promises an ocean of perfect summer days. I can't see Marianne. She must be in the shrubs somewhere.

We are sorry to hear of the death of Mrs Lily Pascoe. Before we can release details of the deceased person's assets, we need you to provide us with the following information…

My father, who died at fifty-six. The child of Lily's husband, killed during the war. His age, or his paternity;

which is the lie? And who knew about it? Is Marianne truly the first person to work out the discrepancy? If I turn my head just a little I'll see the photograph of my father as a baby, replete and splendid on a white knitted blanket, but I don't want to look. I have better things to do.

National Insurance Number. If you do not have this to hand you can write to HMRC and request...

Richard Pascoe the elder was definitely killed in the war. I remember being given the telegram to show at school. There must have been another man in Lily's life. But how did she get away with it? And since both Lily and her son are gone, does it even matter any more? I'm here to get rid of the past, not to stir up old memories.

Please enclose a copy of the deceased person's death certificate. Please note this must be an original certified copy. Photocopies cannot be accepted.

Perhaps there's a simple explanation. Perhaps my father simply lost track of how old he was. Perhaps, as an adult, he chose to lie, pretending to be a few years younger for some harmless reason of his own. I remember his fortieth birthday, the jocular parade of cards and gifts, and among them, Lily's card: *My darling Richard, you cannot possibly be forty, since this means I myself must be forty years older than when you were born*. It stuck in my mind because my mother said that, as usual, Lily was making everything about her, and then refused to be talked out of this position, referring to it every time she passed the mantelpiece but not allowing my father to throw the card away. Perhaps Lily was letting him know that she was a sly colluder in his deception? That must be it. So many of us like to pretend we're younger than we are.

Except that my father is dead, and the rituals of death strip away all pretence. I remember the warm room, the discreetly placed box of tissues, the registrar's gentle relentless questioning, while I struggled to hold my mother together well enough to complete the documentation of time, place, cause, the litany of milestones on my father's too-short journey. If there had been any irregularity in the dates, the scrupulous kind-faced official would have found it. There can't possibly have been a mistake.

I don't want to think about this, and I'm sick of the company of Mr and Mrs Form. I throw my pen down and thump across the floor to find my shoes. I can see the vibration of my feet in the quivering of the candlesticks on the dining room table. I hope I'm disturbing Mr Moon downstairs. I want to annoy him as much as he annoyed me. Who does he think he is, judging my relationship with Lily? I stamp down the stairs and hope my shoes are clattering against the stone.

The front door is ajar and the garden smells sweet and herby in the sunshine, but I don't walk out to greet it. I'm distracted by a faint draught that blows through the hallway, coiling around my legs, inviting me to pay attention to the space behind me.

I don't know what makes me take the next step on from looking, and pad down the hall towards James Moon's open door. Maybe it's the nostalgic scent of Imperial Leather soap, or else the memory of his intrusion of yesterday. Maybe it's the mutter of maternal instinct, prowling like a bear in a cavern. Maybe it's just sheer unpleasant nosiness. Why is his door open? Perhaps he has visitors? I peer inside, but can't see anything. No extra shoes in the hallway. No North Face parka or teenage anorak hanging on the peg beside the heavy camel-coloured wool overcoat.

I should give this up now, before I get into trouble. I should go back upstairs and continue my dogfight with the paperwork, and I should spend the rest of the day hunting down the local estate agents. I should do a lot of things. I take three cautious steps forward over the threshold. Let's see how James Moon likes it when an unexpected stranger invades his space.

The light has a different quality here. Filtered through greenery, it becomes softer and more diffuse, less about the ocean and more about the garden. The hallway is slightly narrower and the ceiling is lower, just enough to denote a shift in social position. At the time when this house was built, the highest-status rooms were on the first floor. Despite this, James Moon's apartment seems nice enough. It has the relentless tidiness of a neat person who lives alone in ample space, and it smells very clean. Lily would have approved. I should feel guilty and nervous, but instead I feel pleasantly at home. Perhaps this is because I associate the homes of old people with feelings of well-being and relaxation. Perhaps it's because the décor of the well-kept sitting room is oddly similar to Lily's, with a good-quality floral sofa, matching easy chair and heavy velvet curtains looped back from the windows with twisted silk ropes. Or perhaps it's because Marianne is perched on a little wooden step by the open French windows, dreamy and thoughtful, gazing into the garden with her chin in her hands. She looks so perfectly at home that it takes me a moment to realise she isn't supposed to be there.

My shock must come out in some sort of alarming noise, because James Moon appears in the kitchen doorway at almost the same moment that Marianne turns around to look at me. Marianne looks surprised and a bit worried, as though I might have come to her with some bad news. James Moon looks angry, as if I'm somehow in the wrong. I decide to deal with him first.

"Hello," I say, putting on a hard bright smile. "I see you've branched out from breaking and entering and gone into kidnapping." He starts to reply, but I turn my back on him so I don't have to pay attention and hold out my hand to Marianne. "Come on, Marianne. Time to go."

To my bewilderment, Marianne refuses to take my hand.

"It's all right," she says. "He wasn't kidnapping me. I was going past his window and I saw him, so I stopped and said hello." When she looks at him I see a faint smile in the corners of his eyes and mouth. "I said you were working upstairs and

57

we talked a bit, then I said I was thirsty. And he said I could come in and have a glass of lemonade."

James holds up the tall clear glass of bubbles like a talisman.

Both James and Marianne are talking to me now, which means I can't understand a word from either of them. I hold up a hand to James and turn to Marianne.

"We were talking about family," she says. "He was telling me about this photo of Lily."

By the stool in the window is an occasional table, an ornate piece of nonsense apparently made from gold-painted plaster. From a cluster of family photographs including a plump mop-headed baby, a moody teenage boy and a suntanned young man smiling and leaning on a surfboard, Lily's strong features send a jolt up my spine. It's a copy of the photograph she has upstairs.

Did James Moon take this? I imagine there's something of a lover's intimacy in the picture, but perhaps this is all my own projection. I wonder where it was taken, and what they did before and afterwards. I'm still looking at it when James Moon's strong brown liver-spotted hand turns all the photographs face down, *slam slam slam slam slam*, like the game I used to play with Marianne when she was smaller, where you asked questions and eliminated faces from a board showing all your opponent's possible choices. Marianne was terrible at it, because she always wanted to know about the people themselves. *Does your person like cheese sandwiches?* she would ask. *Is your person shy? Do they like going to the park?* James Moon's eyes are hot and furious. He looks as if he's caught me going through his underwear drawer.

"That photo's none of your business," he says, ridiculously.

"Why not? Didn't Lily know you had it?"

His face reddens and he starts a long and complicated rant that I can't begin to follow. Marianne's eyes are glued to my face. Probably she's wondering how severely she's going to be told off when we leave.

"Didn't get a word of it," I say to James cheerfully, when

he seems to have run out of steam. "Nice seeing you. If you try luring my daughter in here again I'll have you put on the sex offender's register."

"I said," he says, very slowly and enunciating with exaggerated care, "I only asked her in here because someone should keep an eye. Since you're clearly too busy. Should be glad she was safe. Could have been anywhere for all you knew. Career women. You're all the same. Selfish."

I pick up the tall glass of lemonade and pour it out onto the carpet. Marianne stares at me in horror.

"I realise you're very old and very stupid and probably don't get out much," I say, even more slowly and clearly, "but I don't need your advice about how to raise my child, and I don't care what you think about my career, and I don't need you to talk like this for me to understand you. Don't ever do this again. Goodbye."

This time, Marianne lets me take her hand and push her ahead of me out of the door. James Moon's eyes bore into the spot between my shoulder blades.

We scurry back up the wide stone staircase, Marianne tense and unhappy, me struggling to know what to say. How can I explain what she's done in a way that she'll understand? Doesn't she know better than this by now? Outside the front door that I utterly refuse to think of as *ours*, she stops and turns to me.

"Mum, I'm sorry," she says. "I know you're cross and I'm really sorry, I didn't mean to upset you."

"It's not about me being upset. It's about you being safe. You were supposed to be in the garden, not hanging around a strange man's house."

"I was right by the window," Marianne points out hesitantly. "And the window was open. I could have got away if I needed to."

"That's not the point. You can't tell if someone's nice or nasty by looking."

"It's just I looked in and saw him and I felt really sorry for him."

"Why?"

"Because he was crying," says Marianne.

My breath catches in my throat.

"He wasn't putting it on or anything," Marianne continues. "He didn't even know I was there to start with. And when he saw me looking he got really angry and told me it was rude to stare."

"But you talked to him anyway?"

"He was only upset because I'd seen him crying," says Marianne. "I don't mind people being grumpy when they're sad. I'm really sorry, Mum. I didn't mean to make you angry."

I harden my heart. "It's too late to be sorry now. You shouldn't have done it in the first place."

"Are you going to take me home to Dad?"

"I haven't got the time or the money to be ferrying you up and down the bloody country."

"I'm really sorry."

I don't reply.

"I could go by myself? And save up to pay for the ticket?"

"If I can't trust you on your own in the garden then I certainly can't trust you on the train," I tell Marianne with deliberate cruelty. "So it looks like I'm stuck with you until I'm done."

I expect her to cry, but instead she straightens her shoulders and nods her head, as if this is only what she deserves. How can she be so adult and also so childish? I wish Marianne came with a manual so I could know where to draw the line between giving her freedom and keeping her safe.

The next job on the list is *speak to three estate agents and arrange valuations*, but being at odds with my daughter leaves me too upset to face it. Instead, I embark on a furious frenzy of cleaning.

First the sitting room, which I attack with Lily's weary old vacuum cleaner, and a savagery that makes the ornaments shake on the mantelpiece. Marianne, hovering like a scolded dog, looks uneasy – presumably because of the noise – but doesn't dare say anything. After a few minutes watching her torture herself with anxiety, I give her a damp cloth and set her to wiping dust from frames and photographs and the turned legs and arms of the furniture. She seems happier once she's got something to do. While she scurries backwards and forwards to rinse out the dust, I finish my assault on the carpet and move onto the hall and bedrooms.

The mildly cleaner carpets and shinier wood make a difference, but I'm not satisfied. Burrowing below the sink, I pounce on the meagre cleaning supplies and begin on the kitchen. The kitchen floor disappears as I fling out the contents of each cupboard, crawling into the corners to scrub every inch clean. The hot water supply gives out, so I boil and reboil the kettle. Within minutes the windows fog up. I open them wide to let out the steam. Marianne joins me on the floor, watching what I do and copying my movements. We work side by side, avoiding speech for fear of waking the rage that lingers between us. When the kitchen is scrubbed I move onto the bathroom.

By lunchtime we've run out of cloths, cleaners and food, so I take a begrudging forty-minute break and we march into town on a supply run. On the way back I glance into a shop window and see a vacuum cleaner the size of a Dalek that promises deep shampooing action and untold suction power. Dragging it up the hill and then up the stairs nearly kills us, but we manage it somehow. As we stand sweating and panting in the hallway, I catch Marianne's eye for a second and give her a tiny smile. The rage shrinks a little.

The afternoon's work is calmer, more companionable. While Marianne fills a bucket and sponges the skirting boards, I mix white vinegar and water and wipe the mirrors, the windows and the picture frames. The smell is sharp and sour and comforting. I strip and remake the beds, then reverently set to work with the Dalek, beginning with the loops of dust on the curtains. Next, I fill its detergent compartment and begin again on the carpets, entranced and disgusted by the filth of the water I pour away down the sink. Finally I mop the kitchen floor for the third time that day, shut the Dalek away in the pantry and send Marianne to phone Daniel so I can make dinner. My muscles ache and my hands are dry and sore from their day-long soaking in water and chemicals. When Marianne returns, we sit in exhausted silence at the shining mahogany table, newly scented with lemon, and eat sausages with baked beans and jacket potatoes.

It's not until the dishes are scrubbed clean, the stove-top re-purified, the dining table purged of non-existent crumbs and the windows flung wide to let out the chemical scents of our day's work that I finally allow myself to stop. While Marianne gets ready for bed I sit at Lily's desk, in theory making a list of estate agents, but in fact staring out at the garden and the ocean beyond. Seven hours of ferocious effort have had a startling impact on Lily's house. It now looks loved rather than neglected, like a home rather than a shrine.

I've lent Marianne my dongle so she can get onto YouTube. The flickering colours of her tablet reflect off her face. Lily has a television, but Marianne has never been very interested. Her generation could well witness the slow disappearance of the box in the corner of the room. Maybe by the time I'm old, I'll reminisce fondly about the days when everyone sat around in couch-potato silence and stared with their mouths open at *the same programme*.

Lily and I rarely watched TV either. However, she sometimes took me to the moth-eaten cinema at the end of an old-fashioned shopping arcade, where the seats were worn red velvet and the floor had that ancient stickiness that's almost seductive. Often she would fall asleep, her head propped up by the sinewy slenderness of her hand and forearm, her rings gleaming in the light of the screen. I can remember all the films she took me to. *Mary Poppins*, *Bedknobs and Broomsticks*, *The Slipper and the Rose*. A double bill of *Star Wars* movies. They didn't always make sense to me because there were no subtitles, but I loved going anyway, for the darkness during daytime, the faded luxury of our surroundings.

Feeling my gaze on her, Marianne stirs a little and rearranges a cushion. From a distance, our silence probably looks companionable. It would take someone who knows us very well indeed to spot that Marianne and I are both on edge, waiting for something to happen to resolve this morning's disagreement. What sort of punishment is appropriate for what she did?

"Marianne." She's instantly alert, putting her tablet away without being asked.

"Yes?"

"Nothing. Never mind. Forget it."

She defied years of careful instruction, went alone into the house of a threatening near-stranger and accepted a drink. Or, she saw an old man, weeping for his lost love, and went to comfort him.

Yet another version: she spoke to someone who I've decided is my enemy.

A final possibility: she was kind to a man who hurt me, by telling me I betrayed and neglected Lily. I've only made him my enemy because, in spite of everything I know, in spite of what she did, I'm afraid he was right. I don't like this version.

"What did you talk about?" I ask, to distract myself. Marianne looks at me blankly. "This morning, I mean. With… him."

"He said Lily and I have the same eyebrows," says Marianne. "Is that true?"

"Yes," I say in surprise, because he's right. The fleeting resemblance that's haunted me for years can be traced to that soft triangular shape, faintly reminiscent of an owl, perfectly replicated from Lily. James Moon has effortlessly solved a question I should have answered the day she was born. Another reason to be annoyed with him. "Were you talking about Lily, then?"

"Yes. He said—" Marianne hesitates. "He says he remembers you when you were little. But you never saw him because his wife was still alive so he and Lily weren't friends then. He just remembers you playing in the garden sometimes."

This startles me. I had assumed a zero overlap between his time and mine. I don't know if I like the idea or not.

"It was interesting," Marianne says, slow and tentative. "I like hearing about you when you were little. And about Lily. She sounds nice. I wish—"

She stops abruptly. Puts her hand up to her mouth to nibble at her nails, drops her hand again. Goes to pick at a scab on her arm. Stops herself. Watches my face for clues.

She did no harm and came to no harm. I did a lot of things in the time I spent here, things that would have got me grounded for weeks if my parents found out. Except that they never did, and now, what I mainly remember is the unthinking bliss of freedom. *She did no harm and came to no harm.* I can picture Lily as clearly as if she's standing in front of me, as if my frenetic cleaning has woken her ghost. *Sometimes the best thing is not to say anything.*

"I need to text your dad," I say.

> *Hey, lovely husband. Got a joke for you. How many estate agents does it take to change a light bulb?*

Am I allowed to google it?

> *No you're not. Do you give up?*

All right, I give up. How many estate agents does it take to change a light bulb?

Ask for seven, but be prepared to go down to six for the right person.

That's TERRIBLE

Just like my day.

You found some good ones then?

I did not. There are no good ones. We're only having one house our whole lives. Just so you know. I don't ever want to have to talk to another estate agent.

Technically I haven't talked to any today either, but I've looked in Lily's Yellow Pages and made a list, so surely that counts. Daniel won't want to hear that I've spent the day cleaning. I would have had to clean before inviting anyone in to value the place. I've only done the tasks slightly out of order. I'm not used to lying to Daniel; normally we're far too entwined in each other's lives for me to get away with it. I can't decide if I like the feeling.

So what have you been doing?

Nothing special really. Worked on the new stuff. Got bored. Went shopping. Missed you.

I remember my dream about the woman in the red dress. I hope the guitar really is only borrowed. Maybe he's lying to me too.

So how's our Marianne?

Actually, that's what I wanted to talk to you about. This morning she

"No," Lily says reproachfully. "Don't do that, Jen."

> *went into someone else's house without telling me where she was going and*

"No, Jen. He doesn't need to know. Be kind."

Marianne is watching me, waiting for the sentence to be passed, the blow to fall.

I hold my thumb over the delete button.

> *You can ask her yourself if you like, she's got her phone superglued to her hand like always*

> *I called her earlier. She says she's fine and she's not bored and there's nothing much happening and she's trying to help you as much as she can but you won't let her do a lot.*

> *That sounds like Marianne all right*

> *And she said the guy who gave you the death certificate at the hospital yesterday was quite good looking. You didn't tell me that :)*

I flinch guiltily. Thank God he's not here to see me blush.

> *Well, the guy who gave me the death certificate was about twelve. Also, he was the guy who was giving me the death certificate.*

> *So he wasn't good-looking?*

> *No he wasn't. Okay? Marianne might have thought so but there's no point listening to her, she likes those terrible boys off YouTube*

I just worry. You're beautiful and amazing and I love you so much. I wish you'd let me come with you so I could look after you. Keep the vultures away

Daniel please, it's fine, he was no one, he was totally professional. And anyway, I'm only interested in you, okay? Only you. You know that.

I miss you :(

I know, I miss you too

Right, got to go. Talk to you later, okay xxxxx

xxxxxxx

"Are you all right, Mum?" Marianne is still watching me.

"Of course I am. Why?"

"You look stressed."

"It's nothing."

"Are you and Dad arguing?"

"I said it's nothing. Now let's have a talk about this morning, shall we?"

In spite of herself, she flinches. Then she takes a deep breath, squares her shoulders, lays her hands in her lap and waits, meek and accepting, for Madame Guillotine.

"I'm still not impressed about you going into Mr Moon's house by yourself," I begin.

"I know I shouldn't have done it, I know it was really stupid and you can't trust me now and—"

"Shush. Now here's what we're going to do. I don't like him, but you're allowed to like different people to me. So if you don't want to talk to him, you don't have to. But if you do want to, you can."

Marianne looks at me as if I've grown a second head.

"Really?"

"I wouldn't say it if I didn't."

"And you're not mad with me any more?"

"No," I say, not realising until my hands shape the words that this is the truth.

"But, did Dad say that was all right?"

I can't think of anything to say to this, so I look at her and hope she'll move on.

"So you don't mind if I visit him? Just while you're busy? And I'll always check with you first so you know where I am?"

Why does it mean so much to her to visit a grumpy old man who she didn't even know existed three days ago? Or is she simply relieved our cold war's at an end? The heat of her bath radiates off her skin as I stroke the damp tangle of her hair. "You need to brush this or it'll be one huge knot tomorrow. Do you want me to do it?"

"Aren't you busy?" She looks at me, then smiles. "Oh… Do you want to do it?"

"Yes."

Marianne fetches a brush, then sits at my feet. I smooth out the long thick spirally curls, marvelling at the way they hold their shape even under the weight of the water dragging them down. No matter what you do to Marianne's hair, it will always be the way it wants to be. As the tangles grow smoother, she relaxes into the brush's caress, leaning damply against my knees. Marianne's normally shy of strangers, having to be coaxed and bullied into the simplest social exchanges – buying something at a shop, asking for a book at the library. How odd that James Moon, of all people, has put her at her ease.

He was possibly the last person on this earth to love Lily. And this afternoon I shouted at him for giving Marianne a glass of lemonade and showing her a photograph of her great-grandmother. Letting him see my daughter if she wants to is the very least I can do. Perhaps I should do more, but the bare minimum is all I feel like doing. After all, I am in mourning too.

Chapter Six - Lily

I sit at the table and stare down at the food on my plate. The lamb is tender and melting, the potatoes crisp and golden with soft fluffy insides. I can't eat a bite. I'm ten years old and it's one of the rare occasions when Lily is cross with me.

It was entirely my own fault; I can see that now. "I'm going rock-pooling," I told Lily as I raced past her with my bucket, and when Lily looked up from her little pile of shells and sea glass and shook her head and replied, "No, Jen, not now, the tide's coming in," I cunningly pretended not to see.

I was going to find a snakelocks anemone. We've been studying the ancient Greek myths and I wanted Lily to photograph one for me, so I could show off my knowledge back at school. In my head, this devotion to my studies outweighed the risk to my safety. I imagined myself a heroine, bravely risking her personal safety in the quest for knowledge, applauded by all who knew me. (Although obviously, I told myself as I hopped over a little gully that was filling with seawater by the minute, I wasn't *actually* in any danger. I'd known these pools and this particular stretch of ocean all my life. Getting cut off by the tide was for tourists and idiots. Since I was neither, it was clearly going to be fine. Clearly.)

The reality of my expedition (ignominiously snatched up by a stern-faced stranger, half carried back across the rapidly vanishing rocks, wedged beneath an arm like a hoop of iron, the fascinated stares of his children, Lily's face white and frantic) is something that I will not quickly forget, however much I want to.

Lily isn't eating with me. She said something about not being very hungry yet, and is sitting at her desk in the window. She must be wondering how to tell my parents. I've already been told off in front of the entire beach by Lily, the man she sent to retrieve me and a passing mother with two very small children, who had nothing to do with it but felt compelled to join in anyway; but my parents will be the worst, because they have power. What will they say? Perhaps they'll say I can't come here again. Have I ruined every summer, and not just this one? I slip down from my chair.

For as long as I've been alive, Lily and I have hoarded up treasures from the beach: one basket for her gleanings, one for mine. Now, her collection of shells and sea glass lies scattered across a square of linen. From a length of soft grey string, held up to the light for a critical inspection, a half of mussel shell hangs resplendent like a droplet of amethyst, the centrepiece of a long necklace of sea jewels.

"What's that? It's beautiful." My hand reaches for it before I can stop myself. I want to wear it round my neck, or perhaps in my hair. I want to crown myself the daughter of the ocean.

"It's nothing." Lily tries to force a smile, but her eyes are still sad and troubled. "Have you finished eating, my darling? Let's find you some pudding."

"But it's so beautiful. Who's it for? Will you wear it to church?" In spite of herself, Lily laughs. "Then what's it for? Is it for the house? You could hang it over your mirror."

"It's nothing," Lily repeats, and starts to fold the necklace away.

"Is it because you're still mad with me? Is that why you're not telling me?" Lily stops and looks at me uncertainly. "I'm sorry. Please don't be cross any more."

70

Lily is still looking at me, not speaking, simply watching my face as if she's waiting to see something, or perhaps as if she's testing me. I stare back at her, not sure what's going on here or what kind of contest we're having, but determined not to lose.

"I'm not angry," Lily says at last. "I was never angry. I was frightened." She unfolds the linen again and lifts up the necklace. "This is for the sea. It's a gift. To make up for stealing you back."

I stare at her.

"I saw you going over the rocks," she says, and I try not to see the remembered terror in her eyes because it makes me ashamed. "I started to go after you but you were so quick, and by the time I got onto the rocks you were already so far away. I could see I wouldn't be fast enough. I thought... I thought... the sea is so greedy, Jen. I could see it wanted you. I didn't know what to do, you wouldn't look round and I didn't know how to tell you that you were in danger. If that man hadn't come along—"

I picture the hungry waves creeping closer, long arms of water reaching to drag me under. For the first time, I begin to understand. My feet feel heavy and my head very light.

"Jen. Jen. Look at me." Lily touches my arm to make sure I'm listening. "Jen, it's all right. Don't be frightened. He did come along. It's all right. You're safe. You're safe. I promise."

Like all children, I've stoically endured a lifetime of tellings-off from the adults around me. I've always assumed the lectures and the forced apologies and the time alone in rooms are simply revenge inflicted on me for requiring attention after breaking the rules – rules that seem so pointless and arbitrary that I long ago lost sight of the idea that they have any purpose. This is the first time I've understood how dangerous the world is. This is the first time I've understood that I am vulnerable.

"It's all right," Lily repeats. "You're safe. Do you

71

understand me? You're safe. It was a close call, but you did no harm and came to no harm."

"But—" the question is shaming, but I have to ask it. "But, are you going to tell Mum and Dad?"

"Why would I? You're safe. Nothing else matters."

The relief is unspeakable.

"And later on tonight," Lily continues, "we can walk down to the beach again and give my gift to the sea, and then everyone will be satisfied."

"No! You can't throw your shell necklace in the sea."

"My darling, I have to."

"But it's so beautiful," I falter.

"If it wasn't beautiful then it wouldn't be enough."

I look again at the strange perfection of the pale sand-washed glass, the pink and white and sandy gold of the limpets, the mussel shell like a teardrop jewel. The thought of all this work, all those hours of beachcombing and then the careful delicate task of assembly, being tossed away into the water, just because I was an idiot and nearly got myself drowned, hurts my heart.

"Let's make another one," I say. "I'll make it. And we'll give that one to the sea and keep this one." Lily shakes her head, but I keep speaking. "No, I want to, that's how it ought to be anyway. It was me that was stupid, so it should be my shells that get used." Lily looks doubtful. "I'll do it properly, not all limpets. I'll use all my best ones. Even my white scallop shell."

"No, you don't have to do that. The sea will be happy with this one. I don't mind."

"But I mind. It's not right. Let me do it."

"You have to work with an empty stomach." Lily's hands shape the words reluctantly.

"That's all right. I didn't eat my dinner. Please, Lily."

While Lily busies herself in the kitchen, I sit at her desk and spread out my beachcombing collection, the careful work of years. I choose ruthlessly, selecting only the bluest and rarest glass fragments, the most elegant of the bleached driftwood twigs, the cleanest of the limpet shells. For the centrepiece I choose my single pure white scallop, the most beautiful shell I own. I take fierce pleasure in the pain it causes me to add it to the necklace for the ocean.

When the necklace is finished, I go into the kitchen and touch Lily on the shoulder to tell her I've finished. The silence is a rule I made up while I was working; I don't know how to explain it to Lily, but she seems to understand anyway, and goes to put on her coat. Hand in hand, hungry and exhausted, we walk to the beach. The sand beneath my feet feels damp and chilly, and the tide has turned.

I stroke the scallop shell one last time with my fingers, then whirl the necklace around my head and fling it far out across the water, hoping it will clear the place where the waves break. I can't bear to think that my gift will be returned unwanted. But it dives into the water like a bird, then disappears. I picture it tumbling and twirling down to the ocean floor.

"There," I say, and beside me Lily stirs and smiles.

"There," she repeats. "Well done, my darling. It was a beautiful necklace."

The walk home is harder than I've ever known it. I'm so hungry that I wonder if I might die before we get home. Even the thought of my abandoned dinner, congealing and cold on the pretty willow-pattern china, turns me weak with longing. I wonder if Lily will let me eat it, even though it probably looks disgusting by now. I hope she hasn't thrown it away. I'm hungry enough to go through the rubbish and retrieve it. When we finally fling open Lily's front door with trembling hands, the scent of the tender lamb curry Lily has made from my leftovers and left simmering quietly on the stove almost makes me swoon.

Always correct in her standards, Lily insists I wash my

hands and sit nicely at the table. I devour the rich meat and spicy sauce in busy ravenous silence, mopping up every smear with thick crusty bread piled in a generous golden mound. Lady-like despite her hunger, Lily eats slowly and daintily, but watches me with indulgent pride and presses me to second and third helpings.

When I go to bed, I find Lily's necklace hung around my door frame like a dreamcatcher.

"To keep away nightmares," she tells me. "Good night, my darling."

Chapter Seven – Friday

Morning favourite wife xxxx

Just got an email. You won't believe what it says

Jen? Are you there?

Jen? It's past time. Everything all right down there?

Okay, getting worried now. Are you both okay?

Jen, please text me, I need to know you're all right

> *Sorry, we're both fine. We slept in a bit, that's all*
>
> *I know this is late, I'm so sorry*
>
> *Daniel, please, what do you want me to say? I'm sorry, I really am. I won't do it again*

You're both all right, yay :)

> *Oh come on. I said I'm sorry. Don't sulk*

I'm not sulking. I was really worried

Look I know I was late texting you but is it such a big deal?

YES IT IS A BIG DEAL. You're both in a strange place and Marianne sleepwalks. I only went there once but I remember that bloody stone staircase. If she got out and fell she could break her neck. You can't blame me for worrying when you don't text.

And did it not occur to you we might still be asleep?

You promised you'd keep your phone with you

Well I was asleep and I didn't see it flash, okay?

Are you serious? Because if you can sleep through your phone you might sleep through the monitor

Oh, shut up and leave me alone.

Jesus. What was that for?

For going on at me.

??? I'm not going on at you. I'm expressing a worry about our daughter and trying to get you to take it seriously, so we can agree how you're going to keep her safe without me there to help.

Yes you are going on. I've said sorry and you're not accepting it. You're nagging me about nothing and it's annoying.

Jen, what's the matter with you? I love you. Why are you trying to start a row?

76

I'm not trying to start a fucking row, I just want you to not pick at me for one little thing. Look I'm going to get some breakfast, I'll talk you to later.

"Dad's gone mad," Marianne announces around a slice of toast. "I had seven missed calls from him when I woke up."

"Oh God, really? Don't worry, he's fine, I promise he's fine, I've texted him."

"I know, I rang him too."

"How was he?" I try to make the question casual.

"He wanted to know if I was all right, then he asked about every single detail of what we're doing today and said he misses us about a million times."

Thank God he didn't mention that we're arguing. Marianne hates it when we argue. So do I, actually; so does he. What was wrong with me this morning? I shouldn't have spoken to him that way.

"And he wanted me to be careful on the stairs," she adds. "Why is he so worried about the stairs? I think he's getting a bit strange being all by himself."

Should I be glad or worried that she doesn't understand? Most of the time she doesn't remember what she does in her sleep. She never complains, but she must know by now that it's not normal to have a baby monitor at twelve years old, that there's a reason why we obsess over her bedtime routine and never let her go to sleepovers. I look at her carefully to see if she's thinking about any of this but she seems quite happy, crunching her way through her toast and blackberry jelly with a sticky unconscious relish and scooping up a fat red-black glob from her pyjama top with her finger.

"It's quite nice that he misses us that much," Marianne continues after a minute.

"I suppose it is really."

"I had a dream about him. We were on a train and he wanted to get on too, but you said he had the wrong ticket and then you shut the door and wouldn't speak to him and he was really sad."

My heart stutters. I breathe deeply and slowly to steady it. "But you know it was only a dream, don't you? I'd never do that to your dad."

"Mum." Marianne pats my hand tolerantly. "I'm twelve. Of course I know."

There's a knot in my stomach. We've been together for seventeen years but Daniel's never lost that honeymoon wildness. *I love you so much*, he tells me twenty times a day. *I miss you. I can't get on without you.* And I told him to fuck off and leave me alone.

"Mum." Marianne waves to get my attention. "Mum, about the funeral. What's it going to be like?"

"What? Oh. Nothing special. Just like any other funeral."

"Yes, but I've never been to one. Will everyone stand around the grave and cry and hold umbrellas?"

I wonder if Marianne has somehow managed to watch *The Sopranos*.

"No, pet. This is a cremation, not a burial."

Marianne blinks. "Are they going to cremate her in the *church*?"

"The service happens in the church, then they take the body to the crematorium afterwards."

"And do we go with her? Do we have to watch her getting burned?"

(Not unless we want to. And I don't want to. I only want it to be over.)

"Okay, so what happens is, we all go to the church, and the minister stands at the front and talks about… and talks for a bit, and there are some hymns and some things we all have to say. That's the service. Then the coffin goes by itself to the crematorium. That's the bit we won't be there for. And we stay behind and talk to everyone and eat. That's the wake." A room full of strangers, all of them silently hating me for not looking after Lily. Or, perhaps worse, just Marianne and I, and a room full only of ghosts and memories.

"So there's still a coffin, then? Even though it's going to be burned?" I imagine a funeral without a coffin and shudder. Marianne is still talking. "That's quite cool, actually. Like the Vikings. Building a longship and then setting fire to it. That's the sort of funeral I'd like. A massive boat all for me, and then you and Dad could stand around and fire arrows into it and I'd sail away into the sunset."

"By the time you die. me and your dad will be long gone, and you'll be a clucky old lady with a million great-grandchildren."

"Oh yes. Well, maybe that's what I'll do for your funeral, then. If you'd like that, I mean. It would be quite hard to organise probably. But I'd find a way."

Actually, a Viking funeral sounds rather splendid. Much better than the anaemic, by-the-numbers service I've arranged with minimum thought and effort. How wonderful it would have looked, the boat blazing on the smooth glassy water, Lily's last remains burned away into scraps and sparks and ash. I wish I'd thought of it. If things had been different, Marianne could have asked Lily herself. They could have planned her exit together, the sort of morbidly subversive conversation Lily would have enjoyed. I can picture them huddled conspiratorially on the sofa, plotting her grand finale.

Or perhaps rather than a blaze of light on a flat ocean, she would prefer the wildness of being tossed adrift in a storm. We could have built a birch-bark canoe and tucked her into it, waded through the breakers and pushed her out into churning waves. We would have stood hand in hand, Marianne and I, the salt of our tears mingling with the spray. I can see it so clearly, it's as if Lily has conjured the vision. Except that for any of this to have happened, we would all have had to be entirely different people.

"But we're not going home straight after, are we? We've still got things to get done?"

"I'm afraid so. Sorry."

"Oh, I don't mind," says Marianne. "It's just Dad was asking."

"Well, he shouldn't be. He knows how long we'll be here, I've told him enough times."

"I think he was hoping the answer might be different," says Marianne with a shrug, and takes her plate to the kitchen.

Her sweetness makes me ashamed. What was I thinking, getting so angry with Daniel? I can't leave things like this, not another minute. I take out my phone.

> *I'm so sorry I was horrible. I don't know what got into me. Do you forgive me? X*

> *Please forgive me. I was awful. I know I was. You're so lovely and I was so vile. I love you.*

I was really worried

> *I know you were. And I bit your head off. I'm really really sorry. Please say you forgive me*

Of course I do. I can't stay mad with you, you know that xx

> *You know just for the record, Marianne's actually slept really well the last few nights. I thought she'd wander for sure by now, but not a thing*

Or maybe she woke up and you didn't realise

Maybe it's the lingering remnants of the magic Lily used to work for me, the sea air and swimming combining with the rings she lent me and the shells she hung around my doorway. Or maybe Marianne has unplugged the monitor. Should I mention that she's started doing this? And if I don't mention it, who am I being most unfair to?

I've never slept through it yet have I? But I really am sorry

Let's not talk about it any more. I miss you so much. I can't work properly without you in the house. You have to come home soon or I'll be a shambling mess by the time we get into the studio for the demo

I have to smile. How many times has Daniel wandered out of the tiny space we refer to as 'the music room' to put his arms around my waist and his face in my neck, his hands fumbling over my body like a small child seeking comfort, telling me he can't work because I'm distracting him?

So now we're speaking again, isn't there something you want to ask me? :)

I scroll hastily back through our conversation.

God yes of COURSE, I can't wait to hear! What did the email say?

You know that guy who did those amazing t-shirts we saw at TribFest?

Um. Might need a little bit more

The ones with the human-object hybrids. The vacuum cleaner people and the lampshade child. You remember them.

The ones that were £68 each?

That's the ones. Well I found his website and got in touch with him AND HE'S AGREED TO DO AN ARTWORK FOR STORM INTERFERENCE

Blimey

I know!!! He likes the idea of merging us all with our instruments. Apparently I'm going to be a mic stand. Only thing is he won't work for free

Well that's fair enough I suppose. How much does he want?

He's getting really well known so it's not cheap

No I get that. How much?

It's for the rights to the artwork in all media for ever

Yes but how much?

T-shirts, album artwork, social media, everything

Come on. Let's have it

It's my idea so I said I'd put in the cash. I mean they've all bought instruments and stuff and Sol's cousin's giving us the demo recording for free so it's fair enough

And the final answer is…

Two grand

My heart judders. Daniel can spend money like water, like a man raised in lush rainy countryside who finds himself transplanted to an arid plain, with no true understanding of the horrors of drought. *Jen looks after all of that,* he tells people with pride, *she's brilliant with money, I don't dare spend anything without checking.* What frightens me most is I think he truly believes this, that the money he pours carelessly away was spent with my permission and even approval.

I swallow my panic. It's all right. It's all right. When Lily's estate is settled, we'll have all the money we need.

That's all right, I make myself type. *We can afford it.*

OH YES YES YES THANK YOU

AND THANK YOU TO YOUR DEAD GRANDMOTHER AS WELL

Sol said it was a lot of money but I knew you'd be okay with it

You're so amazing, do you know that? You're a financial wizard. Or a witch. A financial witch. I love you so much.

So do I stick it on the credit card or what?

I add up figures in my head. Groceries, which Daniel will still buy while I'm away despite the meals I left in the freezer. The train tickets, booked at short notice and therefore expensive. Funeral expenses will come out of the estate, but I haven't got around to seeing the bank yet, and in the meantime I've had to pay a deposit to the undertaker. Another two thousand on top of that. Will that take us to our credit limit? Where are we in the month? I'll have to check our account later.

If he takes credit cards then that's fine. If he doesn't then DON'T JUST CLEAR OUT OUR BANK ACCOUNT or everything will bounce. Ask him what payment methods he takes and then ask me for advice

And don't pay the whole lot upfront, hold back half for when he delivers okay?

God , you're so clever. You think of everything. It's a good job I've got you to look after me

Thank you again. As always.

What are you doing now?

> *We're finishing breakfast. Then I've got paperwork to do*

I thought you were seeing the undertaker today?

> *Yes, in about half an hour. So right now, I'm getting on with the list of twenty-seven million people I have to inform that Lily's dead. Then when it's time to meet the undertaker, I'll stop and go and do that instead. Okay?*

In the pause that follows, I reread my message and feel instantly ashamed.

> *Sorry, I didn't mean to be snippy.*

I was only asking

> *Please don't be mad. I'm really sorry. Again. I'm just stressed. But I shouldn't take it out on you, it's not fair.*

I hate having to talk like this. I wish I could see your face and hear your voice. I miss you so much.

> *I know, I miss you too.*

Really?

Of course really. I can't wait to get back to you.

:) x

Okay, I'll text you later once I've seen the undertaker, okay? Xxxxxxx

Love you xxxxxxxx

Occasionally, I wonder if one day Daniel will realise he's lost the career he could have had because he, not I, became the full-time parent; or worse, become belatedly successful and leave me for a starry-eyed groupie who'll follow him wherever he leads. But even after seventeen years together, Daniel still panics when we disagree. Even after seventeen years, he still misses me enough to text me before I wake. I'm so lucky to have him. He was right. I was trying to start a row. It's being in this place, surrounded by a million memories that don't include him. Maybe Lily is haunting me after all, trying to break up my marriage.

"I'm sorry for your loss," the undertaker says.

The undertaker wears a dark grey three-piece suit in an ugly old-fashioned cut, his face clean-shaven, his hair clipped short and neat. His outfit forms an uneasy disguise for the man beneath it, who is slim and muscly, younger than me, and rather good-looking. He can't possibly have chosen that suit himself. It must be a requirement of the job. What does he look like in private life? I try to picture him dressed casually for a night out, considering how that haircut would go with black skinny jeans and a hipster t-shirt. Perhaps he's forced to adopt the preppy look, button-down shirts and thick-rimmed glasses. If Daniel was here he'd be watching me for signs that I like the look of this young man, irrationally anxious in case I decide a quick fling with a pretty boy outweighs the profound comfort of a long marriage. He'd be the first to admit that he's prone to jealousy.

Since Daniel's not here, I can look all I want and no one will know. If Lily was here, she'd approve. She liked to encourage me in acts of mild transgression. Rule-breaking satisfied her. I don't like being here, sitting on Lily's sofa, thinking these thoughts while a near-stranger tells me with apparent sincerity that he's sorry for my loss. I wish I'd said we'd meet at his offices instead. I wish there was someone else I could palm this task off to. I wish I wasn't here.

"No need to be sorry." Beside me on the sofa, Marianne sits quietly, her hands in her lap, watching how it's done. "She was very old, she had a good run."

He smiles at Marianne. "And you're her great-granddaughter?"

Marianne nods cautiously.

"Wasn't she lucky to see her family continue into the next generation?"

Marianne hesitates and looks at me for guidance. He realises he's misjudged things somehow, and looks shyly down at his hands. He looks about as old as the graduate trainees we recruit every year.

"We weren't really in touch very much," I say, and then stop, because surely it shouldn't be me trying to make him feel comfortable? He's the professional here, he must be used to dealing with awkward situations. Including those where the person arranging the funeral resents every moment she has to spend here, and only wants to go back home to her real life. Daniel and the undertaker, and downstairs the rude and mysterious James Moon, three little boys tugging at my skirts. Meanwhile Lily, voiceless but demanding the most from me of all, lies silent and enigmatic, in the cool dark. I don't want to be here, I'd give anything not to be here. My rage must present as upset; Mr Corrigan nudges his box of tissues a little closer, and Marianne strokes my arm comfortingly.

"Sometimes it's difficult over long distances," he says.

And sometimes it's difficult when one of you's a monster. I didn't know I still had it in me to be this angry, but this place, this room, its faded glamour briefly reawakened by sunshine and the deep clean, has opened the wound again. I take Marianne's hand and hold it like a talisman. I have to behave for her. She doesn't need to see her mother rage and storm for events that were over before she was born.

"That's true," I say, and make myself smile. "But yes, I suppose she was lucky really."

"Indeed. So, um, I know we've talked by email but I wanted to go through it in person, so everything's how you want it." He catches himself in an eager smile, and I wonder if he's new to his trade. The surname on the crisp cream business card, Corrigan, matches the name of the business. How odd to grow up among the paraphernalia of the dead, to be raised by parents who put food on the table by laying other people's loved ones to rest. Of course, any upbringing can seem normal from the inside; and besides, it doesn't seem to have done him any harm.

He takes out a very neat black notebook and an old-fashioned fountain pen, working his way down a bullet-pointed list that's beautifully handwritten in blue ink. Lily, who never owned a typewriter and who could be quite appallingly rude about people whose handwriting failed to meet her high standards, would have grudgingly approved.

"We'll call for you here at ten o'clock on the morning of the service. We'll have two cars, one for Mrs Pascoe, and one for yourself and, and…" He glances at Marianne, sitting wide-eyed and enthralled beside me on the sofa, and I see the flush in the sensitive skin above the crisp white shirt collar, because he's forgotten her first name. "And Miss Webb." Marianne blinks at this formality, and glances at me. I give her a tiny wink. "Am I right that there won't be anyone else travelling with you?"

I think about James Moon, who knew Lily well enough to recognise her nightgown. A decent person would bury the hatchet with him and invite him to join us in the cortege. A less-than-decent person might do the same thing. *Heaping coals of fire on their head* is the phrase Lily used to use, which sounds much more poetic than passive aggression. I, however, am an entirely different kind of bad person. There will be no room in the limousine for James Moon.

His face when he walked in and saw us, as if we were the intruders and he was the one in danger. I thought he might die of fright when he saw me coming out of the kitchen. What was he doing? He talked about her rings, about me stealing them, and I can believe they're valuable enough to be worth stealing, but that doesn't feel right. Marianne pats my arm.

"What about Mr Moon from downstairs?" she asks.

"What about him?"

"He knew her. And he might find it hard to get to the church. He's quite old and he might not have a car."

I suppress a smile. James Moon is undeniably old, but he has the look of wiry endurance that comes with a lifetime of sea air, daily walks and frequent yomps up and down the beach. I can imagine him in his swimming trunks, strong muscles beneath slack skin, joining the elderly mad people who swim all the year round, immune to the icy waters.

"Why would we offer him a lift?"

"Because it's a nice thing to do."

"And does he seem like a nice person to you?" A bad question. Of course he seems like a nice person to her. "We don't know him well enough."

Mr Corrigan is carefully not watching, although I can see he wants to. He turns the page in his notebook, makes a mark that's meant to look like a word but that I can see is only a squiggle, then turns the page back again and makes a fat blue dot in the top corner.

"But he's a neighbour," says Marianne. "We ought to try and be friendly."

"He's not our neighbour. We don't live here, remember?"

"He was Lily's neighbour, though." I can see how strange

she still finds it to speak of Lily in the fractional hesitation before she says her name. "They were friends. Maybe she would have liked us to take her friend to her funeral so he could be part of it too?"

I will not lose my temper. I absolutely will not. I will not be ashamed that my daughter is behaving better than I am.

"It wouldn't be appropriate," I tell her instead, firm but kind, so she knows I'm not cross. I'm the chief mourner, so whatever I say goes. I'm not going to invite James Moon to share space with us on the way to Lily's funeral. If he can break into her house he can certainly get himself to the church. He can make his own way there, in his own car or by bus or taxi or perhaps via a lift from a friend, or else not get there at all, I don't care. If Lily felt that strongly about him being there, she should have told me. Although I'd probably have ignored her anyway.

"But—"

"Shush." I look over at Mr Corrigan to let him know that he can join us again, and see that he's given in to temptation and is openly gazing at us with the fascination so many people have when they see me talking to my daughter, and my daughter answering. When I catch his eye, he looks embarrassed.

"I didn't mean to stare," he says. "But it's so beautiful to watch. It's like a dance or something. I'm sorry, you must hear that such a lot." I leave a pause so he can reconsider what he's said. "Oh... I'm sorry... I mean... I didn't mean..."

"It's just me talking to my daughter," I say, then see the look of misery on his face and instantly feel mean. It's the millionth time I've heard that *it's-so-beautiful* line, but it's probably the first time he's said it. These days, people like me are an endangered species. "Forget it, it's fine."

"I really do apologise."

"Really, it's fine. We were talking about who's going in the car."

"We were. So, um, will there be anyone else joining you?"

"No," I say firmly. "There won't be anyone else."

Young Master Corrigan makes another small note. The top of the page is headed, *Mrs Lily Pascoe*. No mention of a funeral, simply Lily's name, as if she's still present and he's planning a party on her behalf. Which I suppose he is.

"And after the service, you'd like the mourners directed to the Memorial Hall for refreshments?" I nod. "Excellent. Just so you know, the caterers will come in and set up during the service. We've worked with them before, they're extremely discreet and professional. There won't be any disruption."

I wonder what sort of disruption he thinks I might worry about. What's the worst they could do? Subject us all to the sight of food being brought in? Would that be so terrible? We're all still alive. We have to eat and drink, carry on with the business of life until it's our turn to leave the party.

"About Mrs Pascoe's outfit. I wondered if you've chosen the clothes you'd like her to wear?"

Oh God, her clothes. I was supposed to go through her clothes. It was one of the jobs on my list, the list I made while trying to calculate exactly how few days of my life I could devote to the last fragments of Lily's existence. The list I talked Daniel through so he'd know how long I was going to be. The list I'm already falling behind with.

"Yes, I remembered," I lie. "I have something ready. Wait a minute and I'll get it."

I'm reluctant to leave the room but I make myself do it. I hope Marianne will be all right with Mr Corrigan. Sometimes she handles situations like this with aplomb. Sometimes she reverts to shy little-girl behaviours, hiding in her hair and refusing to answer questions.

Here I am in front of Lily's wardrobe. Should I choose something pretty, or something she wouldn't mind seeing go up in smoke? Would she rather see her best dress donated to charity, or burned? And how can I possibly know which of her clothes she loved the most?

I plunge desperately into the folds of fabric, hoping for

inspiration. Dresses and dresses and more dresses. I never once saw Lily in trousers, even though she was born in the time of Coco Chanel. Jeans she regarded as a form of tribal dress – fine for the people who belonged in them (including me), but ridiculous for someone of her class and generation. As I flail hopelessly among the clothes, my wedding ring catches on a frail white muslin bag hanging from the rail. I pull impatiently at it, tearing the fabric. Crumbs of ancient lavender rain down on me. They feel like tiny insects landing on my hair. I have to force myself not to flail at my head in a panic.

I pull a dress at random from a hanger, and take it to look at in the mirror. It's a silky delicate shirtwaister with long sleeves and mother-of-pearl buttons and a print of blue and purple pansies. The kind of dress worn by chatelaines of large country houses, on the days when they're not storming briskly round the garden in Hunter wellies and a Barbour jacket. It would be too small for me. Lily had that whippety thinness that came from living through a war and learning the hard way how to moderate her appetite. It would have looked beautiful with the golden white of her hair. But then, all of Lily's clothes looked beautiful, in their way.

Will this do? It'll have to. I won't waste my time on choosing an outfit for a corpse. I can feel tears gathering in my chest, ready to catch me unawares. I take a deep breath and return to the sitting room.

Marianne seems surprisingly at home in the company of Death's attendant. She's taken a huge heavy book from the bookcase and she's showing it to him, turning the pages slowly. He's left the winged armchair and joined her on the sofa, moving slowly and cautiously as if he's afraid of frightening her away. She's telling him something about the book, although what this could be I can't imagine, but he's looking at her. When she smiles at him, I see a ghost.

Lily could enchant anyone when she chose, especially

but not exclusively men. It was a seduction I watched her practise on many others, but that I never recognised when used on me. Like the lighting of a lamp, her charm would draw everyone around her, creeping closer to the warmth and the glow until finally they tumbled at her feet, dazzled and lost.

And what does the undertaker see when he looks at Marianne? Does he see the charming child she still occasionally resembles, or the subtly enchanting young woman she's about to become? When he turns towards me I'm relieved to see his face is innocent of furtive pleasure. Instead he looks as if he's been, quite literally, away with the fairies. I move closer, then feel my skin shiver and tingle with memory.

"Marianne was showing me some of your family photographs," he tells me, his smile sweet and foolish.

I could dispute the *your family* claim, but I'm too entranced by what Marianne's found to speak. It's not a book, it's a photograph album. The photograph album. The one Lily kept all her life. I'd forgotten all about it. How could that have even happened?

"Where did you find this?" I take the album from her hands.

"It was on the bookshelf. I found it while I was cleaning. Do you mind me looking? Is it private?"

Everything else in Lily's house has faded, but the leaves and flowers that frame the photographs are as fresh as when they were picked and pressed. Accompanying each picture, a few handwritten lines, the letters so sharp and crisp it hurts my heart. Some photographs are accompanied by odd little souvenirs: a button, a railway ticket, a fragment of shell.

Here I am aged six, wearing a red swimming costume with a white frill around the bottom. My feet are planted firmly in the sand and my right arm is outstretched, the palm facing out towards the sea. The wave breaks at my feet, seemingly in obedience to the fierce will written on my face.

The photograph is framed with a frond of red seaweed and a spray of ash leaves, dotted with a single whorl of periwinkle. Underneath, Lily has written a few words like an incantation:

My darling Jen, indomitable

Ash is for protection; I remember that. She gave me a frond of pressed ash in an envelope at the end of every summer, telling me to keep it at the bottom of my school bag. I don't know what the seaweed means, but its frail red feathers spread across the page like blood vessels. For a healthy heart, perhaps, like the hawthorn she used to secrete in my father's belongings, or perhaps just a memento. That was the first summer after we all knew I'd never hear again, and the first time my father brought me to stay by myself. I wonder what my mother did without me. I suspect it involved a lot of crying.

I turn back several pages and find a photograph of my parents' wedding. My father looks harried, my mother blissful. A tiny button covered in cream silk nestles in a corner. The blue flowers that twine around the photograph are easy enough to identify, but Lily has added a note anyway:

Convolvulus
A twining plant with trumpet-shaped flowers,
sometimes considered an invasive weed

Marianne and the undertaker are looking at me. I try to make my face neutral.

"It's all right," he says. "I wasn't trying to hurry you."

"Sorry." I snap the album shut and lay it down on the table.

"There's no rush. Take your time."

I don't like the compassion in his eyes. I told him Lily and I weren't close. Why is he looking like that? "It's all right, really. I'm done." The dress has slithered to my feet in a silky mound. It's cold and frail against my feet, like a shed skin. Trying not to shudder, I hand it to the undertaker, realising I should have brought a carrier bag; but he's prepared for this, taking a black canvas bag from an inside pocket and folding Lily's dress into a neat careful square. His attention to detail is commendable.

Such a pretty dress. How will they get her into it? She'll be cold and stiff, hard to move and manipulate. Will they lift her up like a doll? Probably they'll leave her lying there, cut the back open with shears so they can fit it onto her. Is she naked right now? Do the dead still wear shrouds? Is she wrapped tightly like a mummy, or merely covered in a sheet to keep the chill from scorching her flesh? How cool and gentle her hands were when she tucked me in beneath a single layer of crisp white linen, on the nights when the sun stayed up until nearly ten o'clock and every room was hot and airless.

"I know you've requested no flowers apart from your own," Mr Corrigan says, oblivious to the terrible images flitting through my brain, "but we sometimes find people don't realise and send them anyway. Quite often families send them to the hospital where their loved one died. We can sort that out for you, if you like?"

"They can go with the coffin to the crematorium, it's fine."

Another little blue-ink notation.

"And is there anything you'd like to send with Mrs Pascoe?" he asks. "We don't recommend jewellery for a cremation, but if there are any other personal items, photographs or favourite books, for example?"

Imagine sending her belongings with her to burn, as if they'll follow her to the afterlife. I smiled at Marianne's burning boat, but how Viking-like we are after all, we sensible twenty-first-century human beings. I think of her diaries, her photographs, the copy of *The Great Gatsby* that she left, part-finished, beside her bed. Her camera, which I can't find. The album I've been looking at, her oblique and pithy commentaries on those she loved or didn't love, like a faded book of spells. Would she want these things to be burned?

The cremation process reduces a whole human body to a few handfuls of fine grey ash. It's the most complete disposal I can imagine. All the memories, the truths and the lies, the pretences and the realities locked in her brain, burned away. The thought is both sad and comforting. If I could, there are a few black moments of memory I'd like to drop into the coffin alongside her.

Marianne touches my arm and I realise I'm staring blankly at the wall. Always painfully aware of what's acceptable, she's embarrassed on my behalf. She has no idea just how peculiar you're allowed to be in proximity to death and its associated rituals.

"No," I say. "Nothing else to go with the coffin."

Chapter Eight – Lily

My mother calls twelve an *awkward age*. A label used for everything from the speed I grow at, to whose decision it is about cochlear implants, to whether I am, or am not, allowed to watch *Drop the Dead Donkey*. I don't feel awkward. What I feel like is a cocoon about to split, my whole self folded tight and uncomfortable into a space that was once sufficient, but is no longer. I can't wait to crack open my shell and spread myself out to dry. I can't wait to see who I'm going to be. Does Lily sense this potential in me? Or does she still see the child she's loved so fiercely?

Adolescence has re-set my body clock. I read until late, fall asleep around midnight, have to be shaken awake each morning, and at weekends gorge myself on slumber, sometimes not getting up until noon. Night-time in Lily's house is a new territory. As I tiptoe down the corridor from the bathroom I imagine myself expanding like a telescope. Will I one day outgrow my visits to Lily with the same ease I've outgrown last summer's clothes? My summers with her, which once seemed as enduring as the seasons, are already drawing to an end. Five more, perhaps, and my childhood will be entirely behind me. With every year I grow taller, Lily grows one year closer to death. What will happen then? Where will I go when I need sanctuary?

The sight of Lily, seated at her desk in the window, brings me back to my senses. My eighteenth birthday is so far in the future it's like another world. This house, this room, my grandmother at her desk, the lamp all rosy and bright, is as real as it is unchanging. Her hair is in a knot at the nape of her neck and she's bending over some papers on her desk. The clock over the mantelpiece show it's nearly midnight. This makes me think of the phrase *the witching hour*, as does the sternness of Lily's profile. If this was my mother, or my father, I wouldn't dare stand watching like this. They still want me tidied away into storage by half past seven. But Lily surely won't mind.

As far as I can tell, I'm not doing anything to make noise, but somehow she knows I'm there anyway. She turns in her chair and for a moment, I see fear in her eyes and the leap of her hand as she presses her heart back into her chest. Then she smiles, takes off her glasses and beckons me forward.

"You look like a little ghost," she says. "You frightened me."

"Are you all right? Is your heart all right?"

"Good Lord, why are you worrying about my heart? My heart is fine. Do you need anything? A drink? Something to eat?"

What I want is to look at what she's doing. I can sense she's not quite willing to let me see, and with a spoiled child's contrariness I'm determined to find out. Trying not to be too obvious, I peer over her shoulder. I'm disconcerted to see myself looking back.

"What are you doing?"

"Oh, dull old-lady things. Would you like some cake?"

"No, thank you, but can I see?"

"It's really nothing interesting."

"Is that me? Is it a photo of me? When did you take it? I promise I'll be careful."

She's reluctant, but I'm her spoiled and beloved granddaughter and we both know I'm going to win. Graceful in surrender, she puts her arm around my waist and draws me into the pool of light.

This year at the beach, someone's moored a diving raft a hundred feet from the shore. I'm standing on the edge, looking down at the water. I'm ambivalent about the shapes my body makes these days, but somehow Lily's managed to capture me in the act of appearing – if not beautiful – then at least acceptable. The raft was crowded that afternoon, but clever framing makes me appear alone. As I look, my feet remember the sandpaper roughness. I feel the sun on my back, and shiver in anticipation of the cold waves. On the desk beside the photo is a heavy leather album, open at a pristine creamy page, and Lily has begun to lay out a spray of pressed flowers, white-petalled with yellow hearts and flat leaves that make me think of elephants' ears. Four tiny white corners show where the photograph will sit. Beneath the empty space are the words:

On the cusp

"I didn't know you did this," I say, aware that I must sound accusing. "How long have you been doing this?" I start to turn the pages to look back at the rest of the album, but Lily takes my hand and stops me.

"Don't do that. It's not dry."

"But are there more? Of me?"

"One for every summer," she says. "I'll show you another time, if you like."

The album is thick and heavy; there are many more than twelve pages. "And who are the rest of?"

"Nobody in particular. Just people," she adds as if this tells me anything more.

"What people? Family people?"

"Some of them. You know, Jen, it's nearly midnight. Maybe we should go to bed."

"What flower is this? Is it a daisy?"

"Its Latin name is *Sanguinaria*." She spells the word carefully, giving me time to follow what she's saying. The

98

name makes me think of *sanguine*, a word I've learned reading *Mansfield Park* at school. I wait for more – for Lily, plants always have a reason – but she seems oddly embarrassed.

"Sanguine? Like hope?" I ask, pleased to have the chance to show off. "Is it to do with hope?"

"Why," says Lily, laughing a little, "I suppose in a way it is." She glances at the clock. "Look at that. Here comes tomorrow. Would you like to sleep in while I go to church?"

"No, I'll come with you."

"Then I'll wake you at half past eight."

I glance one more time at the ordered clutter on her desk, at the album so like a spell book, at the space where my image will go.

"Lily," I say, fired with a sudden impulsive courage, "if you believe in all of... you know... all of this, why do you go to church?"

Her look is roguish. "So you don't believe that God made all creation? Plants and herbs and all?"

I'm not sure if I believe in the power of either gods or vegetation, but whichever side Lily's on, I don't want to hurt her feelings.

"It never hurts to be sure," she says, and I can't tell if she's mocking or serious. "And besides, the Lord's a busy man. A wise woman takes care of her own. Sweet dreams, my darling."

My sleep that night is restless and heavy. I dream I'm becoming a plant, drawing up moisture from the soil. It pools in my belly and spills out over my thighs. Waking a scant six hours later, I find for the first time in my life that the sheets bunched between my legs are stained and slimy with blood.

Chapter Nine – Saturday

Morning gorgeous wife xxxx

Hey there lovely husband xxxxx

So this is it! The big day.

Well, I suppose that's one way to put it.

By the way, I read last night that it's not compulsory to wear black to funerals any more.

What? What, what? Are you sure?

Yep, definitely sure. I read it on Emily Post.

As if that makes a difference. I've already done enough to earn the wrath of everyone who knew Lily. A friend of hers once talked for an hour about a woman from down the road who went to her son's wedding in a cream trouser suit, although Lily herself maintained an enigmatic silence.

Well I'll bear that in mind for the next funeral I go to.

You've still got time to get changed for this one :)

Come on, put on your best knickers and a party frock and celebrate a bit.

Celebrate?

Yes, celebrate! This is a good thing! Ding dong, the witch is dead? We're rich thanks to her, remember?

I take a deep breath and remind myself that Daniel and Lily never liked each other. I could tell him he doesn't have to see the black suit because he's not here, but that would only remind him how much he hates us being apart. I could lie and tell him I've got changed, but he might ask for a photograph.

Well I haven't packed any party frocks so I'll have to stick with the black suit. Sorry.

It's all right, I'll forgive you. As long as you wear your best knickers. And send me a picture later.

What's Marianne wearing?

Marianne is curled quietly into a corner of the sofa, earphones peeking out from beneath her curls. She's also in black, but because she's had to improvise, nothing quite matches and the overall effect is both romantic and incongruous, as if a very beautiful wandering Goth has accidentally crashed a funeral.

She looks lovely.

Is she all in black too?

Well yes, actually.

She could wear that red dress she had for Liz and Owen's wedding. Why don't you tell her to get changed?

A red dress at a funeral. I imagine the expression Lily's long-ago friend would be making. Apparently the noise that accompanies it is called a snort.

Well I'll ask her, but I'm sure she doesn't have it

It's her best dress, she'll have it

No, Daniel, she just calls it her best dress, to give her an excuse to not wear it ever again, after you bought it without checking and then went on and on and bloody on about how beautiful she looked so she felt like she didn't have a choice. What you're remembering is her not *wearing it. As in, I can't wear my red dress, Dad, it's my best and I'm saving it. Your daughter is far more clever, not to say far more tactful, than you realise*

Where on earth did all of that come from? I delete the words as fast as I can so he doesn't get suspicious.

Okay, I'll check but if she doesn't have it then we'll have to wait for the next funeral. Anyone in your family showing signs of dying?

Not yet, but you never know. Okay, got to get to rehearsal, hope it all goes okay. And don't flirt with the minister :) xx

I put my phone away and smooth the skirt of my single, precious and sinfully expensive Armani suit over my knees. It was the first year I got a bonus, and I was going to put half the money into paying our credit card bill, and the rest towards buying Daniel the new keyboard he needed. Then I was sent to London for a training course and a colleague dragged me for a dizzying visit to Oxford Street. Daniel said it was the most corporate thing he'd ever seen me wear. I never dared tell him how much it cost or where I got the money from.

"Do I look all right?" Marianne asks, taking out her earphones and tugging at the ribbed sleeves of her cardigan.

"You look beautiful," I tell her, because she does.

"I don't look as smart as you. I'm sorry, I did my best."

"You're young. You're not supposed to dress the same as your mother. Do *I* look all right?"

Marianne studies me carefully. "You look like you're going to a really posh wedding. Only without a hat."

Is this a good thing? And would black to a wedding have been more, or less, outrageous than the cream trouser suit? "Well, thank you. I think."

"Mum, are you supposed to wear a hat to a funeral?"

"According to your dad you don't even have to wear black, so I doubt it. He thought you might wear your red dress. You know, the one you had for Liz and Owen's wedding."

"No, I think I should definitely wear black, I'd rather be traditional. Anyway I don't think I brought it with me. Did I? Or did Dad… I mean, did it get packed anyway?"

"Don't worry, it's back at home."

"I do really love it," Marianne says. "I just don't think I should wear such a lovely dress to a funeral. It's for parties. Isn't it?"

"Of course it is." I feel mean for teasing her. Let her think she's successfully kept her secret.

"You could wear a hat if you wanted to, though, couldn't you?" Marianne asks. "It wouldn't be rude or anything?"

"Why do you keep mentioning hats?"

"Could I try something?"

"I don't know. What is it you want to try?"

"Wait a minute."

She disappears into Lily's bedroom. A minute later she re-appears carrying a cream leather hatbox with a brass clasp.

"Oh, I really don't think—"

"Please try it, Mum." Marianne already has the lid off. "Just to see how it looks. If you don't like it you can take it off again."

"It'll mess up my hair."

"I'll sort it out for you afterwards." I hesitate; she knows how much I like having my hair fiddled with. "Come on, Mum, free hairdressing! And all you have to do is try a hat on. It's the nicest one in the cupboard, I promise."

The hat sits in her hands like a neat little black cat, smooth and round and soft, inviting you to touch. The veil at the front makes me think of whiskers. I sit down so she can put it on me. She draws down the veil so it covers my eyes, frowning in concentration as she tucks strands of hair neatly away and settles the hat into place. Then she steps away so she can admire the effect.

"How does it look?"

"You need to see this," says Marianne, with a fervour that does nothing to warn me if I look nice or ridiculous.

"If it looks daft I don't want to see."

"Come and look," Marianne repeats, leading me to the mirror over the mantelpiece.

I sigh, then give in to the inevitable and look in the mirror. I see myself, looking out from beneath the veil of a hat that, despite my best efforts, somehow suits me, making me look mysterious and dramatic in a way that I never knew I could, and that I can't decide whether or not is appropriate for a funeral. But for a moment, before I focus properly and remember what my face looks like, I see Lily.

Wearing my hat, I stand in the window, behind the curtain, watching for the cortege. It shouldn't take two cars to transport three people three-quarters of a mile, especially when one of them is dead. But standard funeral protocol is that the dead person gets one car to themselves while close family follow in another, and going with the flow seemed easier than thinking of an alternative, so that's what we're doing. Sunlight flashes off windscreens as two polished limousines pull up on the stately gravel half-circle.

There's Colin Lightfoot again, doing a ninety-eight-point turn. I'm surprised they let him keep his licence. A non-driver herself, Lily still felt perfectly qualified to comment on the relative competency of other people. And now there she is in the back of the very largest car I've ever seen, travelling in state and splendour.

The door opens and Mr Corrigan climbs out, followed by the swirl of his frock coat. It suits him much better than the ugly old-fashioned suit he wore for our meeting. We're supposed to wait here until he's crossed the yielding gravel (accumulating dust on his immaculately polished shoes), climbed the shining stone staircase, trodden the hallway to Lily's front door; but suddenly I can't bear the thought of inviting him in. I'd rather go to meet him on the stairs, like a strangely over-eager date.

"Let's go," I say to Marianne. "Come on, let's go!" I repeat, as she wraps her earphones into a careful coil. She smiles tolerantly, so I flap my hands to shoo her along. "Go, go, go, go, go! Abandon ship! Women and children first!"

"But we are women and children."

"So move! Quick! Before we drown!"

As we leave, Marianne adds the final touch to her outfit; a black knitted beanie hat, worn on the back of her head so the end flops over like the peak of a little black hood.

"Does this look all right? I don't want to be scruffy."

Marianne's dark eyes look very big against the dual frame of her thick spirally curls and her soft black hat. She looks like one of the girls you see on stationery for moody teenagers; like a waif or a pixie. Lily would have adored her, in the fierce protective way she adored me.

"You look perfect," I say.

Mr Corrigan meets us on the stairs. He's carrying a top hat under his arm. When he sees me, his eyes widen a little. I have to resist the temptation to take his arm. He walks behind us down the stairs and across the hall, then takes three quick strides across the gravel to open the car door.

Lily always liked to encourage me into flirtations with boys, no matter how wildly unsuitable they were as long-term prospects. *Holidays are for having fun. You're young, you should enjoy yourself.* How very unlike my mother, who was alarmed by any sign of my taking an interest and did all she could to discourage it. Months of famine, and then a brief smorgasbord of sun-soaked and grandmother-sanctioned romances; no wonder I grew up so baffled by my own capacity for desire. If I hadn't married Daniel in a brief moment of sanity, who knows what might have become of me?

The door closes and Marianne and I sink into the impersonal air-conditioned comfort of the back seat. The driver wears a peaked cap and a sombre dark suit. In front of us, the hearse trembles like a horse waiting for the signal to depart. I'm expecting Mr Corrigan to join us but instead he puts on his top hat and walks in front of the cars, his head bowed, his hands behind his back, leading the procession towards the gateway.

In your face, James Moon, I think as we pass his flat. The view from his windows must be both chilling and magnificent.

"Do they always do that?" Marianne asks me.

In the mirror, the driver is discreetly watching us.

"I don't know," I confess.

"Well, I think it's..." Marianne considers. "Really elegant."

Elegant. Yes, that's exactly the word for it.

Lily, are you watching? Is this what you wanted?

The distinctive smell of the church – clean stone, hymn books, old wood – coils around my brain, whispering of long-vanished summer Sundays. There's a respectable sprinkling of people gathered in the lobby, mostly women and mostly elderly. Twenty or thirty pairs of eyes bore painfully into us, trying to work out who we are and then trying not to look like they're staring, realising none of them are sure if or how to introduce themselves. Marianne moves closer to me.

The minister takes the lead by shaking my hand, then Marianne's. This starts a slow chain reaction of formal greetings that draws in everyone in the lobby, as they filter past us and up the stairs to the chapel. Marianne and I stand at the base of the steps and nod and shake hands, nod and shake hands, trying to wrench our faces into some semblance of appropriateness. Who are all these people? Am I supposed to remember them from before? Not wanting to meet their gaze, I focus on their mouths, watching painted lips and wrinkled chins form the same words over and over: *So sorry for your loss. Sorry for your loss. I was so sorry to hear about your loss.* Their hands are extraordinary to touch, the skin warm and alive but the flesh pared down to bone and sinew, sometimes deformed with arthritis but still surprisingly strong. Most of them have worked out who I am now. I can tell by their poorly hidden disapproval of me, which softens into tenderness as they take Marianne's little paw within their own.

People lie best with their mouths, which is what makes life among other humans bearable. Imagine if what we said aloud was as honest and true as what we say with the rest of our bodies. *You're a cold-hearted bitch*, these women tell me as they take my hand, *and you broke Lily's heart. I hope you're happy now she's dead; I hope you don't choke on the money she left you. It's not your fault, little one*, they add as they move on to Marianne. *Your mother stole from you too, when she never let you get to know Lily.* Perhaps when they look at her they're imagining their own potential descendants, and wondering if they'll live long enough to meet them. Perhaps they're praying that the bonds they've built will be strong enough to hold. Or perhaps they're hungry for the touch of young flesh. Sometimes, even now, I still give in to the urge to steal a taste of my daughter; a sneaky little lick when I kiss her cheek, a pat of her leg, a nibble of her outstretched finger. The last remnants of the days when I was allowed to smother her in kisses. Marianne and Daniel, they're what's real, not this stone space that smells of face powder. Today is simply something I have to get through. I hold in my head the picture of Marianne as a newborn in Daniel's arms, a talisman against the dark.

The last of the parade has filed by. It's our turn. Lily, in her pale ash-coloured casket, will travel separately. As we climb the stairs, I realise I haven't seen James Moon. Perhaps he decided not to come after all. Or perhaps he decided to continue his policy of outrageous rudeness and simply walked past me without speaking.

Good for you, I think reluctantly. The world's more interesting when people speak and act how they secretly want to. In my experience, funerals give everyone a free pass to follow this principle to its most terrible conclusions.

The man who opens the door for me looks familiar. Within the nest of wrinkles, I see the face of Harry Rose, who used to greet me with a dry kiss on the cheek every Sunday morning of every summer, and who also (I now realise) used to discreetly flirt with Lily. He would hold her elbow as he guided her into the pew, and she would smile at him from underneath her hat before settling down for a good talk with me. Fascinated onlookers always assumed Lily was translating the sermon but in fact we were gossiping about the poorly chosen outfits and terrible husbands of the rest of the congregation.

He's a wicked man, Harry. Lily, settling herself into the pew beside me. A pause, a quick glance around, and then she turns towards me like a conspirator. *Do you know, he parked right in the middle of town the other Sunday morning, where there used to be car parking at the weekends. Only now it's pedestrianised, but he parked there anyway. Then the traffic warden came in during the service and asked him to move it or else they'd have to tow his car.* Her wicked smile as she told me this story; the mischievous gleam in her eye. She was always on the side of the law-breakers, never the traffic wardens. I don't want to remember how funny she was, how bewitching, how lovable. I can't afford to. This is an administrative duty. Once today is over I'll never come here again.

Thank God for Marianne, tugging gently on my sleeve to prompt me. Lily's pew is at the back and on the right, but I don't look into it. I don't want to see someone else in her place. I'd prefer to imagine it perpetually empty. Actually, now I stop to think about it, I'd prefer it to be torn up and burned. We walk down to the front of the church instead. The air throbs with the deep notes of the organ and when I put my hand on the back of the pew, I feel the wood buzzing beneath my fingers.

This feels wrong, all wrong. I want to be at the back, where I can see what's happening but no one can see me. Suddenly I see Lily, not tall and upright and elegant but hidden away in the ash-coloured box I picked from a webpage and ordered by email. She is riding on the shoulders of four solemn-suited men, all supplied by the undertaker, all strangers. I can smell the pollen from the heap of lilies. Lily pollen stains terribly and is poisonous to cats; if you have them in a flower arrangement, the advice is to cut out the stamens. Marianne is holding my hand. I clutch it tightly for a minute, then force myself to let go and give her a reassuring smile. I don't want to frighten her. Death is part of life. This is simply a task I have to get through.

The coffin is lowered onto a stand. The bearers melt discreetly away. Dwarfed by the lilies, two other floral offerings have made their unauthorised way into Lily's final public appearance. A cluster of long-stemmed red roses, swathed in gypsophila and tied with ribbon, scentless and soulless, the overpriced choice of clueless or guilt-stricken men. And beside them, a wilting tangle of green leaves and stems, like a bunch of stinging nettles.

The lily pollen tickles my nose and I rummage for a tissue, aware of the subtle rearrangement of faces and upper bodies as my actions are misinterpreted and judged. *Too late for tears now*, say the shoulders of the woman in the navy-blue coat. *Theatrical, like that hat of Lily's you've helped yourself to, although you didn't bother to make sure your daughter was dressed appropriately*, says the hand movement of the woman on the left, minutely adjusting her own black hat, sitting atop her sensible short-clipped grey hair like an upturned dog bowl.

I can't begin to follow the sermon, and singing has never been my strong point, so I float through the service in a determined haze. My spine prickles with memory. *That's where the choir sit; remember that summer when Lily's friend was in the choir and you saw her sing a solo on Easter Sunday; that's where that baby was being christened and it was sick over the minister's shoulder and down his back and he said it was a badge of honour and wore it all through the rest of the sermon and next week you could see the patch where he'd washed it out; that's the window where they had the Harvest of the Sea display and the cardboard mackerel fell off on everyone's heads.*

I distract myself by thinking about the flowers. Who sends red roses to a corpse? If I'd expected anything, I'd imagined mixed bouquets in shades of white, blue and yellow, inexpensive and unobjectionable. Red roses mean passion, sex, occasionally guilt. Do these things still happen to you when you're ninety-five? They draw my eye like a fluttering flag.

And what's the deal with the nettles? Are they from the same person? Taken together with the roses, do they form a message? *I love you, but you're wild and dangerous and painful to touch*? Lily would have enjoyed that. Or are the nettles from some other wronged soul? *You were an unwanted poisonous invader in the perfect garden of my marriage*, perhaps. *You stung me whenever I got near you. I hated you so much I sent weeds to your funeral.* Also possible.

You can't buy a bunch of nettles. They must have been picked by hand. I remember the bony strength of the hands I shook earlier, the warmth and the clumsiness, and the skin that was thin like wrinkled silk. The sender must have worn gloves. Marianne is bored but hiding it well. I can tell she wants to get her phone out, but she knows better than to actually do it. She sits up straighter in her pew and neatens the cuffs of her cardigan as if reminding herself of her duty.

From above his round white collar, Robert the minister gives me the nod that tells me the service is coming to an end. It's time for us to leave. Lily will ride solemn and stately to the crematorium, where she and the flowers will be burned to a fine grey ash that I'm supposed to scatter into the ocean where she once taught me to swim. Her will explained it all, simple and suitable; the gathering in the Memorial Hall downstairs afterwards, the catering supplied by a firm she knew from her hotel-owning days, a respectably lavish menu and a chance for everyone to relax into their natural selves after the strain of the service. I will go through the motions as correctly as I can – *trying to make up for all the years you never bothered with her*, says the lifted chin of the woman in grey in the pew to the right – to properly honour the Decencies, those terrifying well-dressed maiden aunts who stand between us and their wilder cousins, the Furies. I will keep this last goodbye dignified and quiet. I won't let anyone see how I really feel. I won't descend to Lily's level. I follow Marianne out of the pew and think how strange it is that Lily's funeral should be so much like the dark companion of a wedding: guests, formal clothing, an entrance and an exit, beautiful flowers and the knowledge that in the time we've spent together, a profound change of state has occurred.

I was going to simply lead the congregation out, but instead I find myself taking five quick steps to Lily's coffin. Amid a ripple of interested and disapproving faces and movements, I pinch off a leaf from what I thought was a bunch of stinging nettles but that I now see is something else, something with tender green serrated leaves and a minty, herby scent that's maddeningly familiar. I tuck the leaf into my sleeve. Marianne looks at me, unsure if this is some arcane funereal rite I forgot to mention and that she's supposed to follow me in. I shake my head and lead the way down the aisle as if nothing has happened.

Someone else is leaving ahead of me. Someone who's had the brass neck to take over the vacancy in Lily's pew, someone wearing a dark suit and a crisply ironed shirt, someone tall and upright with a shock of white hair. The man who knew what Lily's rings looked like, who shouted at my daughter for seeing him cry and then apologised with a glass of lemonade. He must have come early and hidden himself away in the chapel. There's no way I would have missed him if he'd waited in the lobby with everyone else. As I watch him disappear from the service, the identity of the leaf tucked into my sleeve suddenly comes to me. It's catnip.

"So what happens now?" Marianne frowns at the plates of dainty sandwiches with the crusts cut off, the canapés, the quivering slices of quiche Lorraine. "Are we supposed to eat all this? Have we got to stay?"

"Of course we've got to stay," I say, a little more sharply than I intended because today's gone on for too long already. I want to tell my fellow mourners exactly what I think of them and their judgement, then march straight out and leave them all to it. Instead I have to stay here and make some semblance of polite conversation with a gaggle of elderly people who have no interest in me beyond a vague malice for the way, as they see it, I heartlessly abandoned Lily. This isn't how Lily would have put it to them. Admitting that I'd walked away from her would have been too difficult for her pride to swallow. More likely she wouldn't have mentioned it at all, instead behaving as if I was a welcome and expected visitor who had simply been unavoidably detained for a few days or weeks, but who would be arriving very soon. The other mourners are assessing the food with greedy glances.

"It's all covered with cling film," says Marianne.

"We'd better take it off then."

"Do you think we should?"

"I'm paying for it, so I'll do as I wish."

"You're paying for it? You don't get it for free?"

When Marianne asks questions like this, I remember how young she is.

"Of course we have to pay for it. Why would anyone give it to me for free?"

"I just wondered. You know, because it was a funeral."

I don't laugh. I used to think funerals would bring out the best in other people too.

The other guests are staring at us, in that way they do stare. Wondering what I'm saying, and if I'm taking advantage of knowing no one else can understand us. They're all hungry but none of them like to be the first ones to descend on the food. I begin to offer round plates of sandwiches.

"A very beautiful service," says a woman in a severe grey dress and an elegant black coat. She is far younger and looks much richer than the others, and her perfume has the subtle lingering elegance that you only get with the most expensive scents. "It's all right, you're not supposed to know me. I'm Laura Crane. I was Mrs Pascoe's doctor."

"Nice to meet you," I say, then bite my lip. I'll never be here again, but I still wish I'd thought ahead about what to say to people. I glance down, and discover I especially like Doctor Crane's shoes. Black patent leather, with a thick high heel and a low-cut front.

"It was quite quick and painless," she tells me, the movements of her mouth very clean and precise. "She was

113

as sharp as a tack, very fit and healthy, right up until the end. Then one day I called round, and she wasn't. Into hospital within a day, a week on the ward, two weeks in a respite home and then gone in her sleep. Very efficient, exactly how she'd have wanted it. I hope I don't sound too blunt. People go all round the houses trying to work out how to ask, so now I just tell them straight."

"Thank you."

"Something else," Doctor Crane says. "She was adamant that when the time came, you weren't to be bothered until it was over. She made me write it into her medical notes. And she asked me to tell you that she loved you. That was how she ended every appointment. In fact, those were the last words she said to me before the ambulance came. *Remember you're not to bother my granddaughter with any of this and when I've gone, you tell her I love her.*"

"I'm so sorry."

"Don't be. It's no trouble." Doctor Crane reaches into her immaculate handbag and hands me a tissue. "I don't get involved in my patients' private business but you know how Lily was. And she meant it, you know. She didn't hold a grudge. She loved you very much."

Her words have unlocked a floodgate and now all the tears have no choice but to gush out. I squeeze my face up tight to try and keep myself together. Doctor Crane pats my arm.

"It's all right. You're allowed to cry. All quite normal. Best get it out of your system. Okay, I have to go before people start mobbing me for extra consultations."

A subtle queue is already beginning to form, little clumps and clusters of two and three, waiting in ambush to capture a few moments with the doctor. She picks her way unerringly through them with clean quick steps, turning her head to the left and to the right, smiling and nodding but never pausing long enough for a conversation to start. I stand uselessly by the buffet table, a clump of tissue clutched in my hand, and try to stop the tide of sorrow that's pouring out of me. I hope I'm not making a noise.

There's a warm hand on my back, rubbing gently as if I'm a small hurt child. It's Marianne, her face tight with anxiety but doing her best. I want to stop the tears but it takes me a few tries. I'm grateful for the veil of my hat, which will go some way to concealing the wreck of my make-up. At last I have the torrent back under control.

The other mourners are carefully not looking at me. An unexpected kindness, from a group of people who have no reason to be kind. Or perhaps they've turned away from my grief in the same way a hungry dieter looks away from the baker's window. Perhaps the scent of my tears will rouse them to vengeance, and if I get too close to them they'll turn on me and rip me to pieces with their harpy claws.

Chapter Ten – Lily

I'm fourteen years old and I'm lying on a towel on the sand, my seawater skin prickling and drying in the heat. I'm thinking drowsily about the boy, a year or perhaps two years older than me, who looked at me earlier as I bought ice cream. His two friends wrestled and kicked sand at each other, but he was watching me, transfixed as I licked a dribble of ice cream off my wrist. When our eyes met, my stomach turned over.

My mother has firm views on what I'm allowed to do with boys, which is essentially to share classroom space with them and absolutely nothing else. She says she doesn't trust them, but in fact she doesn't trust me, either to know how to behave or to keep myself safe; the same battle we've been having since I was six. The more female my body grows the crosser and more anxious she becomes. What would she say if she knew this boy had looked at me? What would she say if she knew I'd looked back?

I roll onto my front and squint through my sunglasses at the ancient canvas chair where Lily sits with her dress turned up two inches above her knees. Her wardrobe makes no concessions to the beach. When her strappy cream kitten-heeled shoes become too irksome she simply takes them off and packs them into her handbag, then unclips her filmy stockings and folds them away too, revealing feet ruthlessly crushed by decades of painful footwear. I'm always slightly frightened of Lily's feet, which seem like an awful warning of the price of elegance. It occurs to me that, in her way, despite her age, Lily is still beautiful.

"Did you ever want to get married again?" I ask her, then bite my lip in case this is rude. According to my mother, I've become very rude recently.

Lily looks at me, then at the ocean, then at the sky, and then back at me again. She is silent for so long that I wonder if she hasn't understood my question.

"I suppose I could have done," she says at last. "I did have offers. But it never quite seemed worth the effort."

"Is it hard work being married, then?" This is definitely a question my mother would class as rude, but Lily laughs.

"Well, you live with two people who are married, don't you? What do you think?"

Here's how my parents' marriage operates: my father goes to work, and my mother runs the house – *which is a full-time job, thank you, Jen, a very thankless and unpaid one but if I didn't do it, then who would? That's what I'd like to know.* I asked her once if she didn't ever want to get a job instead. Asking once was enough.

My father earns the money, my mother runs the house. That's the theory. But it's often hard to see exactly what my mother does. I come home to a house that seems no different than when I left it. The washing pile will be as tall as before and contain the same items, and we'll generally have run out of something vital, like bread or milk or teabags. And yet if either my father or I dare to ask about any of this, we're accused of ingratitude and thoughtlessness and thinking everything gets done by the fairies. For a long time I took it for granted that my mother was right and I was being ungrateful and thoughtless, not to say a traitor to the sisterhood by presuming it was my mother's job to do these things. Recently I've begun to think the real problem is that my mother is basically inefficient at everything.

My father solves this as well as he can by furtively

117

finishing the undone household tasks, taking care to complete them in the moments when my mother isn't looking. If he gets caught, he explains that it's only fair he does his share. Sometimes this explanation's accepted. Sometimes it ends in arguments and tears. Occasionally, when it occurs to me, I'll join in and help him for half an hour, but more often I watch in fascinated horror. I sometimes wonder how my father copes. I'll be out of there in a few years, but he's stuck for life. Lily looks as if she can see exactly what I'm thinking.

"They're very happy really," I say, and then, because I don't like lying to Lily, "but they argue about housework sometimes."

I want Lily to tell me this is normal, but she sighs and looks at the ocean.

"Did you and your husband argue?" I ask.

"Not very often. We didn't have long enough. We were married during the war, and we were only together when he came home on leave. Then of course, he was killed."

"And they sent you a telegram to tell you."

"They did." Lily's face is serene, as if she's discussing something that happened to someone else. "But I knew anyway."

"How did you know?"

"I dreamed about him. I dreamed we were at home together at night, and he was putting on his raincoat, ready to go out. And I said, *But it's raining*, and he said, *That's right. The biggest storm I'll ever see. Stay in and keep warm, Lily girl, and I'll see you again soon*. Then I woke up and I knew. You might find the same thing happens to you," she adds, as if this is the most normal thing in the world. "These things often run in families."

"What things? You mean, like second sight or something?"

"Oh, nothing that exciting. Just a sort of private line to each other."

I remember the time I fell off the bars in the gym at school and broke my arm. My mother had to be called, and then an ambulance. When I got home, my arm already itching beneath the cast, we found my father on the phone, apparently trying to reassure someone that everything was all right. "That was your grandmother," he told me. "She thought you'd been in an accident for some reason, God knows where she gets these ideas. Where have you both been, anyway?" Then he saw my cast, and swallowed hard and looked apprehensively at my mother, who didn't have any sort of second sight and had to be notified via a boring old phone call.

"So did you know when Margaret was going to die?"

This is all just ancient history to me, so I'm not prepared for the expression that scuds briefly across Lily's face, like the shadow of a cloud crossing the ocean. It makes me catch my breath and wonder if I've said something terrible. Then the moment passes and Lily is herself again.

"My poor darling little sister. She was never very strong. Yes, I knew it was coming, we both did, we'd known our whole lives. I was lucky to keep her for as long as I did." Perhaps she sees that I'm still worried, because she reaches down and touches the soft place under my chin with her long finger. "And before she died, we bought our hotel together and had a whole lovely spring and summer by ourselves, down here by the sea."

"So she was happy?" This surprises me. From the elegiac photographs I've seen, I've imagined Margaret as a sad lost soul, lacking Lily's essential power and gutsiness, pining away for her dead love. "Even though her husband was dead too?"

"Oh." Lily's mouth looks as if she can taste something sour but satisfying. "Well, my darling, I promise you Margaret mourned him quite as long as he deserved. But life has to go on. So we enjoyed our last few months. Jen, I think that young man's hoping to spend some time with you. If you go down to the water you might get talking."

It's the boy who was watching me earlier at the ice-cream booth. The way he looks at me makes me tingle.

"Can I? Don't you mind?"

"Why would I mind? It's natural to take an interest."

You need to concentrate on your schoolwork, my mother likes to tell me. *Yes, Jen, I know you get good grades, thank you, and do you know why that is? Because you're not distracted by running around after boys.* This boy is throwing stones into the sea. Each time he turns around to choose a new pebble, our eyes meet for a moment.

"I can't talk to him. What would I say?"

Lily's hand dips into her handbag.

"Take him this. Ask him how far he can throw it."

You're too young for all of this anyway. Why do you want to be going out with boys? You're only fourteen. You might think you're very grown up and ready to handle all that nonsense, but you're not.

In Lily's pleated palm lies a smooth white pebble shot through with a pink band of quartz. It's almost too pretty to throw away. Almost as pretty as the boy's brief, shy smile.

"Is it magic or something?" I'm not sure how I feel about walking down the beach with a magic pebble in my hand.

I don't care what all the other girls in the class are doing, Jen. Their parents might be perfectly happy with their daughters wasting their lives, but you're not going to. Do you understand me?

"Well, what do you think?" Lily asks. "Does it look magic to you?"

Besides, my mother continues, *you need to be more careful than most girls. Because, you know, you're vulnerable, Jen. No, don't close your eyes at me, thank you. You might not want to hear this but you need to listen anyway. They might try to take advantage of you being…*

The pebble fits snugly into the palm of my hand. As I fold my fingers around it, my mother falls blissfully silent.

"It has rose quartz in it," Lily says. "It'll help. You'll see."

I stand up and weigh the pebble in my hand. So easy after

all, to get past merely looking and giggling. All I have to do is take it to the boy and ask him to throw it.

"But what do I say to him next? What am I supposed to talk to him about?"

Instead of answering, Lily laughs and ruffles my hair, and returns to her book.

Chapter Eleven – Saturday

Now then gorgeous. How was this afternoon? Did anyone turn up?

> *Yes, actually. Quite a lot*

Blimey. I thought they'd all be dead by now

> *Well, apparently not. The church was pretty full. Most of the food got eaten*

Ah, that's it. They were only there for the sandwiches afterwards :)

> *That's a horrible thing to say*

Hey come on I'm only kidding

> *Well it's not funny all right? I just said goodbye to my grandmother and I don't feel like laughing about it*

What's the matter with you? You're the one who keeps saying it's only boring admin so we can have the money

I have no idea what the matter is, or why I'm berating my

husband for making the same jokes I've made myself, or why there are tears pooling in my eyes.

I'm sorry. You're right. Forgive me?

You know I do, I always do. I love you even when you're horrible

So what are you doing now?

I'm sitting at Lily's desk, watching the shadows gather in the corners of the sky. The wind has changed direction and a storm is blowing in. On the sofa, Marianne sits flushed and sleepy in her pyjamas, making herself small with a book in the hopes that I'll forget she's there and not send her off to bed. My open notebook lies discarded on the edge of the desk, its pristine pages a small reproach as I slowly turn over the heavy pages of Lily's photograph album.

Working out what the household contents are worth.

Christ. Really? Can't you make something up?

??? No of course I can't.

Course you can. Just pick a number, no one cares.

On the roof of the gardener's shed, two herring gulls hunker down in the slight shelter of an overhanging branch. As I watch, three more fly in to join them. I can smell the change in the air as it blows in through the half-open sash window and riffles the empty pages of my notebook. There are a million jobs I should be doing, but the funeral has drained me of all my will.

I can't lie to HMRC. It's got to be right or they'll query it and the whole thing will take twice as long. I do actually know what I'm doing you know.

I don't want you wasting time and driving yourself mad, that's all.

Yes I know, and you're lovely, but there's no point trying to make it easier, because there are no shortcuts. And I'm getting through it all as fast as I can, I swear

Let's talk about something else. Talk to me about your day. How's the music coming?

Slow. Not very productive. I keep thinking I can hear you and Marianne and then you're not here after all. I love you so much and you're not here. You seem so far away. And whenever we talk you're cross with me.

Don't say that, you know that's not true. I'm not cross with you.

Yes you are. Whenever I ask anything you bite my head off. I knew this would happen. It's being in that place. I think she's trying to come between us.

Oh come on. She's gone, remember?

And I'm sorry I've got to be here, I don't want to be. And I'm tired and I've got too much to do and that's the only reason I'm grumpy. I promise.

I can't stand being without you Jen. I need you back home

Then let me get on with it and I'll be home as soon as I can xxxxx

I turn quickly past the pictures of my childhood. I can't bear to be reminded of how close Lily and I once were. I go back in time instead, to the days when my father was still alive, then the days when he was small, and then before he was born. I linger over the small, dark-haired woman, framed with big green serrated leaves, like blackberry leaves but lighter and fresher. Lily's sister Margaret, who I never met. Margaret is leaning on a seafront railing and looking pensively out towards the ocean. I wonder what she's thinking. Beneath it, Lily has written:

This is where your life begins

Why does her life only begin in this picture, when she was so close to death? Did she know her remaining time was measured in months and weeks and days? One more page back is a photograph of Margaret's husband, Stanley, caught in the act of going out through the front door of a house. He's a shadow man, barely there, his face turned away from the camera and his left arm and leg already over the threshold, and the ominous atmosphere is enhanced by the words Lily has written underneath:

Stanley Walker
1907–1947
Wishing you the peace you deserve

I force myself to push the album away and turn to my notebook. The breeze that caresses my hair and tickles the back of my neck is like the caress of Lily's hands. Is she reading my text messages over my shoulder, enjoying the snags in my marriage? *Household Contents*, I write on the first page of my notebook, liking how smooth and definite the ink looks against the paper, the past confined and catalogued. *Furniture. Jewellery. Pictures. Other.* One page for each category.

I'll begin with what I can see. *Desk.* It's old, possibly valuable. Maybe I can find something out online. *Chair*, I write. When I was small, I believed the chair's ball-and-claw feet came to life when I wasn't watching. *Dining table.* How big does the table get when it's fully unwound? I'll have to try it out.

You could leave all of this until tomorrow, Lily says to me, *and take Marianne down to the beach and get some fresh air into her. She'll sleep better for it, and besides, there's a storm rising.*

We've been inside far too much today, it's true. But we've been too busy for anything else, and besides, this isn't a holiday.

It could be if you want. Just for a little while.

As if I can possibly complain to Daniel about how much I have to do, then walk away from it to play around on the beach.

Daniel wouldn't have to know. And he's not exactly working his fingers to the bone himself, is he? I can see Lily so clearly, her smile covering the sharpness of her tongue, the bite of her teeth. *You could stay another day or two. Say the paperwork took longer than you thought. What could he do about it?*

Before I can stop it, I'm picturing the beach the way it is before an evening storm, the sand grey and dusty in the twilight, and the waves shattering like glass. Maybe Daniel is right and Lily is haunting me. Marianne is holding her book but watching me over the top of it.

"Are you okay?" I ask.

"I'm fine. I like watching you, that's all."

Her expression is so sweet that I can't complain. Nonetheless her gaze prickles along my spine. I remember the fascination of watching adults going about tasks that had absolutely nothing to do with me. It was strange to realise they had an entire existence where I didn't feature, filled with people who knew them intimately, but who I'd never seen. I become oddly self-conscious, monitoring my movements as if I'm on stage, trying to look purposeful and decisive.

Rings, I write, as a subheading to the *Jewellery* page. *Diamond hoop. Square-cut sapphire. Pearl daisy. Emerald-cut aquamarine.* They would have been expensive to buy, but their resale value will be much lower. *Brooches.* Lily wasn't much of one for necklaces but she had many brooches, some of which may be worth something. *Gold bar with pearl and ruby. Emerald pin. Marcasite rose.* This is pointless. I can't possibly parse out all the complexities of setting, cut and stone size into a sensible estimate. I'll have to take them to a jeweller. The seagulls are pressed close against the roof of the gardener's shed and the sky is dark and heavy with rain. I lean on the sash window to force it closed, step back and find Marianne standing a few feet behind me.

"Am I disturbing you?" she asks. "I'm sorry."

"No, it's all right. Come and look if you want. It's not very interesting though."

She peers at my notebook. I take her arm and turn it towards my mouth so I can kiss the soft place inside her elbow. Marianne gives me a tolerant smile and takes her arm back.

"Diamond hoop," she reads. "Square-cut sapphire. Are these what you're going to buy with Lily's money?"

"No, it's her jewellery. I have to work out what they're all worth and tell the tax people."

"Oh, yes, the probate thing."

"How do you know about probate?"

"I was looking at the list you did for Dad." She strokes the edge of the album cautiously. "Did Lily do this?"

"Yes. She loved photography. She had a darkroom down in the cellar."

"That's Margaret, isn't it?"

"That's right. This must have been taken just before she died."

"If she'd had children," says Marianne thoughtfully, "they'd have been my aunt or uncle. And if *they'd* had children, they would have been my cousins. Is that right?"

"Close enough. But the doctors told her not to. Then she died anyway." Marianne's fingers are picking delicately at the leaf that grows out of the border and over the photograph. "Don't do that, you'll ruin it."

"Sorry." Marianne snatches her hand back guiltily. "*This is where your life begins*. What does that mean?"

"That it was a new beginning, I suppose. They'd only recently bought the hotel, her and Lily, I mean."

"Not their husbands?"

"No, they were both widowed by then."

"So your dad was alive? Is he in the pictures too? Where is he?"

I take the album from her and return it to its spot in the bookcase. "Come on now. It's bedtime."

"Can't I stay up a little bit longer? I can sleep in. I don't have to get up for school in the morning."

Sometimes I think Marianne believes Daniel and I are the ones haunted by terrible dreams – dreams in which our daughter screams in terror at things she sees in corners, or roams the house like a ghost and tries to get outside.

"No, it's bedtime."

"But—"

"I know, I know, it's a tough world. Bed."

"But can't I stay up and watch you a bit longer?"

"Bed."

"But what if—"

"No more questions. Clean your teeth."

I see her nestled into bed, her book in her hand, her face lit by the nightlight. The monitor that will tell me if she sleepwalks is in its place on Lily's desk. I can see the rising wind in the whip and toss of the trees and the shiver of the

128

curtains. I trudge grimly onwards through my list. *Books*, I add under the *Other* category. Are Lily's books valuable? Surely not. She was generous with books for me but rarely bought any for herself, preferring the company of the few old friends she'd loved for years. I run a finger along the shelf and find Jane Eyre still keeps company with Lucy Snowe, Jay Gatsby and Rebecca de Winter's poor un-named successor. My fingers, knowing what I want, skip past the books, find the photograph album and pull it out again.

Is it wrong to read the private thoughts of the dead? I turn over the pages anyway, telling myself it can't matter now. Here's the photograph of Margaret again, pensive and wistful, an attitude I find irritating even though I know she was ill. The leaf Marianne was picking at earlier has begun to dissolve. Tiny papery fragments of long-preserved greenery crumble beneath my fingers.

I blow hard on the page to get rid of them, and then breathe in sharply. In the newly revealed portion of the photograph, I can now clearly see that Margaret is pregnant.

Perhaps it's a mistake. Perhaps it's just the way her dress falls. I look again, more closely. There's no mistake. She's definitely pregnant, at least five months, maybe more. And Lily photographed it, put it in her album, and then hid it.

I don't care about who my grandfather was, I never met him and he's only a name on a page to me. But my grandmother – the woman who gave birth to my father, the woman who I have always known in my bones to be Lily – this matters. So what does this mean? What happened to Margaret's baby? Was it ever born? Is this why Margaret died? Is this who my father…

Stop it. Stop thinking about it. Stop, right now. I can't stop. My brain flicks coldly through the possibilities. Option one: my father was indeed Lily and Richard's child, born two or three years earlier than we always believed, a mistake so simple that even the official who registered his death failed to notice it. Surely not possible.

Option two: Margaret's baby died and, as lost babies so often were, was erased from the family record. Meanwhile, Lily became pregnant by some unknown man, and gave birth to a child of her own. This can't be right. The coincidence is too great.

Stop thinking. Stop it. Stop it now. I can't stop it. My head is out of my control.

Option three: my father was Margaret's child. The pregnancy killed her, as everyone always told her it would, and Lily – not my grandmother but my great-aunt – raised her sister's baby as her own. But this can't be right either. It was the nineteen forties, in a modern prosperous town. There would have been questions, records, enquiries; both the birth and the death would have been documented. Surely not even Lily could lie so successfully, pretending to a pregnancy that never took place, concealing the birth that killed her sister?

I look again at the photo, willing it to show me that I'm mistaken, and Margaret is not pregnant, but only wearing a badly cut dress. The beautiful swell of her belly remains stubbornly visible.

Lily, I think, pathetically. *Please help me. Make it all go away.*

I catch a breath of lavender on the breeze from the window. And then, like magic – or perhaps because I've reached the limit of the amount of shock I can deal with – the chatter in my brain stops and I'm in control again.

None of this is important, I remind myself. *They're dead, they're all dead, and you're the only person left who cares. Leave it alone. Stop thinking about it. Forget you ever saw anything.*

I take a deep breath. I close my eyes and turn over a fat handful of pages, then another, then another. When I open them again, I find a picture of myself, taken in the hallway. I'm standing in wellies and soaking-wet pyjamas, my cheeks rosy with cold, water dripping off my chin. Despite this, I am laughing.

A flare of green light on the monitor sends a shot of adrenaline through my body. I put the album down and scurry into Marianne's room. She's sitting up in bed, her hair around her face, her expression sleepy and unfocused.

"I was dreaming," she says, rubbing her eyes. "Dad was playing a red guitar on a boat that was being washed out to sea, and you were on the beach watching, and I could see you but I was still in bed here, only someone was opening the door. It's so loud outside. Is the roof going to blow off?"

I take a peek outside and see the storm has begun flinging handfuls of rain against the window. The pine trees are bent double. Marianne looks out at the weather in awe.

"Is it safe? Is the house safe?"

"Oh yes. They get a lot of storms like this. The whole bay fills with ships come in for shelter. The waves blow up like mountains and when the tide's high they come right up the beach and wash over the seafront. Sometimes—"

"Yes?" Marianne's eyes are huge and dark.

"Sometimes," I say slowly, "the whole beach moves. Come on. I'll show you."

"We're going out? Do I need to get dressed?"

"You can stay in your pyjamas, but put socks on, and a jumper, and then another jumper. Then a coat."

"Are we allowed?"

"Are we allowed?" I look at Lily in disbelief as she stands in my bedroom doorway with a torch, her head covered with an elegant black rain hat that slopes down her back, her body wrapped in a Burberry mac.

"I don't think the police will stop us."

"But is it safe?"

Her eyes are bright with wickedness.

"Let's find out."

"But, did Mum and Dad say I could go out at night?"

"Well, my darling," she says. "They never said you couldn't, did they?"

131

If Marianne reminds me that Daniel would forbid it, I'll admit she's right and let her go back to sleep. Instead, she looks at me for a minute, then scrabbles out from the covers and rummages wildly for her clothes. As we creep out like conspirators, for a minute I can see Lily's slender shape slipping down the staircase before us, leading the way.

The wind pushes hard against us as we walk. Beneath Lily's rain hat, Marianne's face is radiant with laughter. When we reach the seeming shelter of a lamp post, she stops to catch her breath.

"Are you all right?"

Her face is sallow and jaundiced in the dirty orange sodium glow. "Can people tell I'm wearing my pyjamas? Does it matter that they're getting wet?"

There are no other people on the streets. Everyone's hunkered down inside, waiting for the storm to pass.

"No, it doesn't matter. Come on, we're nearly there now."

Panting, we breach the crest of the tall hill. From here, it's a clear straight run down to the beach. Marianne stops, but not to rest. Vast walls of water pile up and fling themselves against the shingle. As we watch, a splatter of yellowy foam flies high into the air, floats a moment then drifts down to the pavement to mingle with the rain.

Marianne's hand clings tightly to mine. I loosen it so I can speak to her.

"Do you want to go down onto the beach?"

"Really?"

"It's all right, we don't have to. I just wanted you to see this. We can go back now if you want."

She looks at the waves a moment longer, then runs on ahead of me, into the dark.

Down on the beach, the wind's so strong I think it will blow us over. I must be careful now, make sure we don't stray too close to the waves' path. If they grab hold of us as they pour back down the beach, they'll surely drag us with them. From a distance the water looks like cloudy grey walls of glass, but when I shine the torch on them we see the coiled streaks and strands of weed, torn from underground beds only to be piled up on the beach to rot. We edge closer, mesmerised, then retreat again as the waves fling themselves at us, trying to catch us. After a few moments it becomes a game. We follow the water down as it retreats, getting as close as we dare, stumbling back as the next wave breaks.

It's a dangerous game and there's no room for error, but the beach is ours alone and we're both alive with the wild magic of the storm and we can't bear to stop. Marianne is bolder than I've ever seen her, edging closer to the water with every pass, resisting my attempts to hold her back. We're having too much fun to feel the cold, but I'll have to take her back soon. The band of pyjama fabric between the tops of her wellies and the bottom of her raincoat is soaked with spray.

As Marianne races to chase another wave away, I feel the vibration of my mobile phone in my pocket.

Hey gorgeous. Are you in bed yet? X

Marianne's getting too close to the water. I call her name, hoping the wind won't snatch it away before she can hear it, and wipe the rain from my screen so I can reply.

Not yet. Still up working. Won't be long. I'll text you when I'm going to sleep, same as always x

Is Marianne all right? Send me a photo of her so I can see her all asleep

She's as far from sleep as she's ever been. She's dancing with the ocean, Lily's rain hat flapping against her back, her curls blowing wildly.

I'll take one when I go to bed. I don't want to disturb her twice.

Can I have one of you as well?

Go on. Pull up your top and take a shot xxx

Oh, shit.

I tell you what. Wait till I've had a bath and I'll send you one x

Can't I have one now and one later? I'm VERY lonely

Shit shit shit. What can I say? What?

Hold that thought. Monitor's flashing. Give me ten minutes in case she's wandering

I put my phone away and turn back to impending horror. In the few moments I've been distracted, Marianne has got too close to the waves. Dancing among the seaweed, captivated by a gleaming pebble, she's failed to notice the wall of water bearing down on her.

I skim over the sand so fast it feels like flying. Marianne looks up and sees the wave about to crash over her head. She scrabbles backwards, falls over her own feet. The wave breaks; her head disappears. I feel myself scream for help, feel the word vibrating in my chest and throat like an incantation.

And then, like magic, like I've conjured it, a rain-slicked figure looms out of the dark and reaches a long arm into the water. A tense second and then Marianne's head appears, followed by her body, slick and skinny like a half-drowned cat. I'd thought we were alone on the beach, but it turns out there's someone else who, like Lily, like me, knows how much fun it is to dance in the rain at the edge of the angry ocean.

I'm there, my arms reaching for my daughter, clutching her tight against me, checking she's real. In the small fractions of attention I can spare, I take in the details of the stranger who saved her. Taller than me. A man. An older man. Old. In the moment of shared relief we look into each other's faces, and I see that Marianne's saviour is James Moon.

I was trying to say *thank you*, but it wasn't going well to start with, and all I can do is stare. I look deep into his eyes and he looks into mine, and in this brief fragment of vulnerability before he realises who I am, I see inside him and I know what he was doing in Lily's hallway that first morning.

Just like me, James knew Lily to the bone. He knew she had secrets. He was trying to help her keep them.

A deathbed promise? Or a self-imposed duty? And why did he know what I didn't? If I can hold his gaze a moment longer I'll have it from him. Then another wave crashes at our feet, long salt fingers reaching for our shoes, and he shakes his head and waves his arms and shouts something I can't quite get, but that is surely some bitter commentary on my shoddy parenting skills, and stomps off up the beach, as anxious as I am to avoid having to walk home together, even in the blessed chaos of the storm.

"Time to go," I tell Marianne, putting my arm around her shoulders and pulling her close.

Thankfully, she doesn't argue. She's already shivering, although she seems calm enough. I don't think she has any idea what almost happened, how close she came to being swept away. The sea still wants her – the waves break and break, trying to claw her back into their embrace, even as I peel off her coat and wrap her in mine. We set off for home. What am I going to tell Daniel? What was I thinking? No wonder he worries so much. No wonder he feels he has to check on me. I can't be trusted. I nearly lost our daughter. I am a terrible, terrible mother.

You're a wonderful mother, Lily says. *She'll remember*

tonight for ever. I shake my head to banish her and hit myself painfully in the eye with a strand of my own wet hair.

"This is real, isn't it?" Marianne asks as we stand shivering beneath a lamp post and pant for breath.

If only I could tell her it was simply a nightmare, so I can hide my incompetence for ever.

"Yes, of course it's real," I say instead. "Can't you tell?"

"It's just so lovely it seems like it must be something from a dream," Marianne says, and kisses me on the cheek with blue-tinged lips.

Chapter Twelve – Lily

I'm fifteen years old, and I'm in the back seat of my parents' car, on our way to Lily's house. Cars are apparently better than trains, but personally I can't see why. There's far less to look at, and the scenery that scrolls past the window mostly consists of other traffic. I can't get up to stretch my legs or buy a snack, and if I try to eat a snack before my parents think I should be hungry, I'm reminded that if I eat all the snacks now, there will be no snacks left for later. If I tuck my feet up I'm told off for putting my feet on the upholstery, and if I take off my shoes I'm told off for taking my shoes off.

I've been forbidden to read in case it makes me travel-sick. I could argue about this too, pointing out that reading on the train has never made me sick, but I don't feel like being told that I'm being rude and argumentative and while other people's parents might accept this kind of behaviour, they're certainly not having it from me. So I sit with my shoes on and my feet in the footwell, watching the road signs and trying to calculate the time until we arrive.

I can't see what my parents are saying, so I watch for clues. My mother's rigid posture and the shape of my father's shoulders tell me my mother is upset and my father feels guilty. My mother is easily upset. I do my best, but I still seem to make her that way. The car smells of greasy sandwiches and thermos coffee and bad tempers. After a while I'll get used to it.

We approach Lily's house from a different direction, and I have a sense of vertigo as the world whizzes into place. Never mind; we're here now. My mother takes a deep breath and loosens her shoulders, shaking her hair back.

Lily is waiting on the steps. In repose, her face looks rather stern, the wrinkles around her mouth carving deep lines of disapproval into her skin. But when we catch each other's eyes through the window, a huge smile spreads across her face to match the goofy expression that I know is on mine. I leap out of the car before my dad even has the engine off, and overcome with relief and happiness, fling my arms around her and hold on tight. This is worth every moment of the long drive.

Then I remember my parents, watching me bestow on Lily all the wild affection I never give to them. Guiltily, I drop my arms and move away.

My mother and Lily embrace carefully, their faces meeting, their upper bodies stiff. It's been years since they spent time together. My father struggles with the suitcases. I put on my rucksack so I have both hands free to help, but my mother waves me away. Then she lifts one herself, winces, puts her hand to her lower back, and glares at me and my father as if it's our fault. Lily, her face carefully neutral, picks up my case and carries it inside. She looks back at me, inviting me to hop along beside her as I always do, but my parents are still here, luggage and pillows and camp beds spread out around them, and I don't dare leave them behind in case my mother is angry.

"So how was the journey?" Lily asks, and passes my mother the potatoes. "Have more, Amanda dear, there are plenty."

"This is all I need, thank you. It was ghastly; so slow and exhausting. I thought we'd never get here, but never mind, we're here now."

"Still, at least you can have a little sleep in the car while Richard's driving," says Lily. "Richard, you look thinner. Have some more potatoes."

"He's actually been putting on weight this last year," says my mother. "But he's trying to lose it again, aren't you, Richard?"

Lily passes my mother the gravy. My mother pours a temperate puddle, then does the same for my father. My father takes the jug, adds a little more, ignoring my mother's expression, and passes it round to me. My mother cuts a very small slice off her chicken and puts it in her mouth as if it might bite her. I drown my food in a rich savoury lake. My mother frowns.

"I've told you before, Jen, don't pour out so much gravy. You'll spill it on this lovely tablecloth. Why don't you listen?"

"Don't worry her about the tablecloth," Lily says, smiling at me. "She's on her holidays."

"She's not allowed to ruin things because she's on her holidays. I won't have it."

"My tablecloth will wash," says Lily, still smiling at me.

My mother glances at my father.

"Be more careful, Jen," he says. "This is an old table, if the gravy gets through to the wood it'll damage the finish."

I haven't even spilled the gravy, I think incredulously, and slice off a long spear of chicken. Lily catches my eye and gives me a tiny wink.

I'm in Lily's house, but it feels like I'm somewhere new. The atmosphere's all wrong. The familiar smell of roast chicken mingles with the alien scents of my father's aftershave, my mother's face cream, the dustiness of the camp beds. My parents are impatient and snappy, and Lily is subtly annoying them, and it's all centred on me. Everyone is on their very worst behaviour. In the circumstances, the best thing I can do is to go to bed as soon as possible. I wonder how I'm going to explain to Lily, but when we meet briefly in the hallway and she takes my hand and kisses me on the forehead, I know she understands, and she's still on my side, and she still loves me best.

This should make me feel better, but it doesn't. Instead I'm resentful. Why are they all doing this to me? I go into my room and shut the door. Perhaps I'll lock myself in. That would show them.

In the garden, the shadows are gathering and a little cat is stalking a seagull that sits moodily in the centre of the lawn, eating bacon rind and glaring about for competitors. The cat is about half the size of the gull. The seagull must have decided the cat's not a serious threat. There's no way it can't have noticed it creeping over the grass. Apart from anything else, the cat is bright orange. It's the least subtle hunting attempt I've ever seen.

When I grow up, I decide, I'm going to get at least three cats. An orange one, a tabby one and a black one. And they'd better all get on all right. I'm not having cats that argue. There are too many arguments in the world.

In Lily's kitchen, my mother is apparently making dinner. This began in a conversation at breakfast ('No, Lily, I insist, I'll cook.') and has now sprawled over the entire day. Each distinct stage, from menu selection ('But what if they don't *have* sausages?') to shopping ('Maybe we should just get fish and chips if it's going to be this difficult.') to the return journey for missing items ('How was I supposed to know we don't have gravy granules?') to preparation ('I can't work this cooker, I'm not used to it.') has been a cacophony of tense shoulders and angry gestures and doors shut a little bit harder than necessary. None of this, it has to be said, is coming from Lily. To an outside observer, she'd seem serenely oblivious to the chaos unfolding in her kitchen. I can tell that she's enjoying the spectacle immensely.

Despite how badly she's behaving, I feel reluctantly sorry for my mother. To help her, I've been down to the shops on my own account and am now making a rice pudding. I don't especially like rice pudding, but it's easy and quick and I can make it in the small corner of the kitchen that's still unused. Fat dusty white rice grains swirl and drag at the spoon while my mother makes the batter for toad-in-the-hole. Every time she crashes her whisk into the bowl, I see a tremor on the surface of the rice pudding, as if a dinosaur's walking through the garden.

"Where's all that milk you bought?" My mother's face looms into my line of sight, flushed and anxious.

"I got two pints and it's all in the pudding."

"Why?"

"Why what?"

"Why did you only get... Oh, never *mind*, I'll manage somehow." Her whisk drips fat cream drops onto the worktop. I move my pudding bowl out of the way.

"But another time," she adds, "maybe you could be a bit more considerate and make sure there's enough milk for everyone."

This is so unfair that I can't begin to respond. I turn back to my basin, trying to decide if I'm upset enough to cry (because when did I become responsible for the household milk supply?), or if crying would make it a million times worse (because Lily will, inevitably, take my side, and my father will, inevitably, side with my mother, and even though we're technically in the right, Lily and I will, inevitably, lose, and then what will become of us all?).

When Lily and I bake together, the kitchen fills with a serene peace as thick and golden as butter and egg yolks, and we clean as we go, so the kitchen always remains welcoming. Today, every surface is dusted with flour and covered with discarded spoons. My mother's batter is lumpy. If she keeps whisking, the clumps will disappear. I bet she won't though. I drop dots of butter onto my pudding.

"This looks beautiful," says Lily, looking into my basin with pleasure. "A proper old-fashioned recipe. Did they teach you at school?"

"Yep."

"How lovely. Amanda, isn't it wonderful that Jen's learning to cook?"

141

"What?"

"I'm sorry, I'm interrupting you."

"No, it's fine, what were you saying?"

"It's so annoying when batter goes lumpy, isn't it? I was saying, isn't it wonderful that they're teaching Jen to cook? I'm glad they've started teaching proper cooking skills again."

And the worst thing is, there's nothing my mother can say about it. She vents her feelings on me instead, shuffling me along the counter because I am, apparently, taking up too much space. I escape to the pantry for nutmeg, and eat six glacé cherries with the door shut.

Back in the kitchen, a new crisis is brewing. After a frantic but mystifying few minutes, my mother manages to make me understand that my rice pudding will take two hours to cook, but she needs the oven for her dish after the first hour, and it's not all right for them to go in together because rice pudding needs a cool oven and toad-in-the-hole a hot one.

"We can manage," says Lily. "Put the rice pudding in right now, and we'll have dinner a little late."

"But then we won't be eating until nearly seven o'clock!" My mother is close to tears. "It's too hot for a stodgy pudding. We'll have ice cream or something instead."

I feel myself turn pale with anger.

"No, that's not fair," says Lily. "Jen's worked hard on this pudding, we all want to eat it. Don't we?"

So there, I think with satisfaction, and look at my mother. Lily stands beside me, poised and triumphant. My mother is flushed and unhappy, her hair hanging limply round her face, her eyes shiny, her lips drawn tight. I'm in the right, I'm winning, my mother has nowhere to go; so why do I feel so empty?

"We'll have a snack now," Lily continues. "We have plenty of fruit and cake. Then we'll go down to the beach while the rice pudding cooks. It's a shame to miss such a beautiful day. It'll do you and Richard both good. And Jen can have a swim, I know she'd like that, wouldn't you, darling? Then when we come back, you can put the toad-in-the-hole in the oven. That's all fine, isn't it?"

And it is fine, in every detail. Lily's plan has thought of everything. Including how it feels to my mother to have a mother-in-law who is so visibly, effortlessly better at managing her family.

We're walking back from the beach, tired and damp and sandy. Lily takes my hand, giving me the power to tackle the hill without pausing as strength flows through her skin and into mine. I look back to see how my parents are coping. My father, out of condition but still game, is laughing and red-faced. My mother lags behind, stopping often to catch her breath. This morning I would have called her expression *sulky*, but now I see more clearly.

As gently as I can, I remove my hand from Lily's. I stop on the pavement and wait for my mother. When she reaches me, I put my arm around her waist to give her a hug.

"Not now, Jen," she says, shaking me off. "I'm tired too, and I've got this bag to carry. And I've got to cook dinner when we get back. I said you'd be tired but you *would* go swimming, you've only got yourself to blame."

I let go of her waist and kiss her cheek gently. Then I take the bag – heavy with sun cream, spare shoes, unwanted cardigans, a purse stuffed with small change, extra pairs of sunglasses, all of it hers, none of it needed – add my own small burden of wet towel and swimsuit, and swing it over my shoulder.

"Don't put your wet things on top. You'll make everything damp."

Dizzy with understanding, I take the towel off the top and tuck it under my arm.

"Thank you," she says, in surprise, and then, "and when we get home you can help me cook, if you like."

It's the end of the most exhausting week of my life. Even our

143

departure feels wrong. Instead of the brisk walk down the hill, secretly blinking away tears and then the train and the familiar sadness of passing all the milestones I eagerly watched for on the way down, I have the awkward boredom of my father, my mother and Lily performing an elaborate departure dance. Careful embraces. A handover of sandwiches. A slightly spiky conversation concerning the provenance and ultimate destiny of said sandwiches. (My mother has already made her own, less appealing, sandwiches, and is trying to return the new ones on the grounds that we'll never eat them. Lily, of course, is having none of it.) The ritual of the missing coffee thermos. My mother's final return to the house to check nothing's been left behind, the squirmy feeling inside me as I imagine her going into my bedroom. I've never been happy to leave Lily's house before.

Bored of poking the gravel with my shoe, I look up and see Lily watching me. When she sees me looking, she tries to smile, but can't quite manage it.

There's a lump lodged in my throat as I hug her. She flinches and steadies herself when I squeeze a little too tight, because I'm still angry with her for the way she treated my mother – who, despite the way she behaves, is so much weaker and more vulnerable than Lily. She hugs me back with fingers that feel like bony twigs. Her mouth is against the top of my head and I feel the puffs of warmth as she murmurs something to me. The words she always says. *I'll always love you best.*

And I know she does. She's better at everything than my mother. A better cook, a better planner, more interested in me and my life, kinder, gentler, more accepting, less angry, more responsive. Unfortunately for Lily, what I've learned this holiday is that no matter what, my mother is my mother. Lily thinks my mother bullies both me and my father, but that's because she herself has always been strong. She doesn't know what it's like to be someone like her daughter-in-law, always struggling and always falling short. She needs protection and understanding, not to have her faults pointed out to her. I don't like seeing cruel behaviour, even when its purpose is to protect me.

I hold on. Hold on. Breathe deep. Let go.

Chapter Thirteen – Sunday

Are you awake yet?

Are you awake yet? Come on Jen, please don't do this to me again

Yes I'm here xxxx

Sorry. I only just woke up.

Busy night last night? :)

He has no idea what I really did last night. I distracted him with sex. My heart thumps with guilt.

It was. Paperwork. You know how it is.

You stayed up… afterwards… to do paperwork?

Had to make up for lost time. :)

This is a lie. I was so tired after the funeral and the beach that I could barely stay awake long enough to satisfy Daniel with blurry photographs and words of simulated passion. The sleep that followed was dark and dreamless, unbroken by memory.

Was Marianne all right for the rest of the night?

Not a peep out of her. Must have been a one-off.

Marianne slept without stirring, but I must have been sleepwalking again because I'm wearing one of Lily's rings. This time it's the hoop of diamonds that swings loose and heavy against the palm of my hand.

Right, I'd better get on. Loads to do today

What sort of things?

What do you mean, what sort of things?

I just wondered what you're doing all day.

Wow. Okay, well today I have to go to the solicitor and go through the paperwork so we can get probate, then go to the bank to find out why they're being awkward about me paying the undertaker's bill despite having the will and the death certificate. Then I need to chase up all the estate agents so I can get three valuations and take an average, pay the undertaker, cook, clean, talk to Marianne, find a jeweller to value the rings and maybe an antiques person to look at the furniture and then I think I might stop to breathe for a minute or two before getting on with my choice from the many exciting forms I have to complete so I can finally get this bloody estate wound up and come home. Does that cover it?

Did I write all of that? I stare at the screen of my phone in disbelief.

Don't be like that, I wasn't having a go. I miss you, that's all.

Yeah, I know. I miss you too. And I'll be back as soon as I can

You could send Marianne back home if she's getting in the way

No, she's fine, she's being a huge help actually

She said you hardly let her do anything and she wishes you'd give her more to do because you're working too hard :)

I'll get right on that. Child-Exploitation-R-Us

Okay, really got to go now. I'll talk to you later xxxxx

I love you xxxxxxx

Maybe I should send Marianne home. I don't want to, but that's me being selfish. I should ask her what she wants. Except she won't tell me what she wants. She'll tell me what she thinks she ought to want, or possibly what she thinks I want her to want. Working out Marianne's true wishes is always a ticklish business, or at least it is to me. Daniel never seems to find it a problem… I remember the red velvet dress with the Peter Pan collar that still hangs at the back of her wardrobe, and wonder if that's because Daniel's never realised how rare it is for Marianne to simply say what she's thinking.

It's almost ten o'clock, and Marianne is sitting at the desk with her legs tucked beneath her and looking out of the big bay window. Her hair, newly washed, hangs down her back in a tangle of spirally brown curls and when she turns to look at me, her skin glows golden. I catch my breath at how beautiful she is.

"Sorry I slept in," I say.

"I don't mind. You were tired." She smiles shyly. "I came to check on you. You looked sweet."

I've reached the age when my daughter comes to check on me as I sleep. I hide my embarrassment by going to the kitchen. I put bread in the toaster, then come back out. "Have you had some breakfast?"

"Yes."

"Promise?" The kitchen looks very clean.

"Yes! I had toast and jam and some orange juice."

I surreptitiously inspect the contents of the cupboards. One of the plates is slightly damp, one of the glasses distinctly smeary; but considering she's grown up in a house with a dishwasher, it's not a bad attempt. Daniel always tells me to stop worrying, not to nag, that I'll make her weird about food and she'll eat when she's hungry. My toast pops and I prop the slices against each other to cool. Sometimes Daniel makes my breakfast, but he's never yet understood that when I say I like my toast cold, I really mean it. I brew a pot of tea and take down an extra cup for Marianne. The table in the alcove has a sprig of buddleia propped in a dainty silver bud vase.

"Did you do that?" I ask, pointing at the buddleia.

"Someone was cutting it all off with a hedge-trimmer. It was on the ground so I thought it would be all right to take it."

"It looks lovely."

"If they complain you can say it was me, I don't mind. I don't want you to get into trouble for something I've done."

"You daft article. Who's going to tell you off for picking stuff up off the floor?"

"Well, I don't know how it works, do I?"

"Nobody's going to shout at you, all right? And if they even try, they'll have to deal with me."

"But they might shout at you too."

"Fortunately I won't have to listen."

"But—"

"But nothing," I say firmly, and pour her a cup of tea. She doesn't really enjoy tea but she likes sitting with me while I drink mine. At home, she sits quietly and pretends to sip from her orange-cat mug. Then when she thinks I'm not looking, she pours the tea into the Christmas cactus that is mine and Daniel's only successful attempt at owning a houseplant.

Lily's porcelain cups are yellow and green, rimmed with gold. As an incentive to finish our tea, when our cups are empty we'll find a painting of a rose on the bottom. The china looks delicate but it's withstood decades of heat and tannin, lemon and milk, hot water and scrubbing. To my surprise, Marianne seems to actually be drinking her tea. At some point between last night and now, the album has moved again. It's open on the table at a photograph of me. I feel as if I'm looking at a loaded gun.

"That's you at the beach." Marianne strokes the pages reverently. "I like your plaits. I wish my hair was straight like yours."

"Well, I wish my hair was curly like yours, so I suppose it just sucks to be us." She laughs in the half-reluctant way she has when I venture into teenage slang. "Maybe we should shave our heads and make wigs and swap."

"Mum! You can't say that, that's horrible."

"Is it? Fair enough. Let's put this away now. What do you want to do today while I'm busy?"

Marianne turns over another handful of pages. "There's you when you were a baby." She's found the picture of me holding my feet, as if it's a job I've been given that requires all my attention. "And that's… Who is that? Is it your dad?"

My father, a young man, laughing and holding a crab towards the camera. The crab hangs pathetically, legs dangling, claws splayed, resigned to its fate.

"That's right. Come on, let's put it away now, it's boring."

"No, it's not, it's beautiful. She was so clever! I wish I could take photographs like this. And make an album like this as well."

"You can, if you like. I don't know where Lily's camera's got to but when it turns up you can take some pictures. And I tell you what, why don't you go down into town this morning and choose yourself a photograph album?"

"Maybe later. Look, there's your dad when he was a baby."

"Seriously, it'll be fun. I'll give you some money. You can take all morning, if you like; there are loads of little shops to look round. You can go by yourself, if you like."

The look on her face reminds me of times in my childhood when my mother would get an idea for something she thought I ought to enjoy, then force me into doing it. Like a cat on a mouse, she would drag me away from my game or my book or my drawing, into organised craft activities with children I didn't like or know, trips to museums that didn't interest me, expensive days out I hadn't chosen. She would watch my face for clues, alert for any sign that I wasn't enjoying myself. If I failed to show enough enthusiasm she would become furious, then tearful, and declare me to be spoiled and ungrateful. It was such a relief to escape to Lily, who was perfectly happy to let me do whatever I wanted, from sitting at the dining room table balancing a pickle fork on a glass, to running breathlessly up and down the beach pouring seawater into a hole in the sand.

Marianne turns back through time. My father grows smaller and younger. We're perilously close to the photograph of Margaret. How can I distract her? I take the book away and turn forward instead, through my own childhood and into adolescence.

"Look at your clothes!" Marianne looks as if she can't quite believe what she's seeing. "Did you really wear things like that? Like, all the time, not for fancy dress?"

The photograph is framed with the delicate petals of sweet peas. I still have the purple-fringed scarf I tied around the brim of my black felt boater. That was the day a boy first told me he loved me.

"If you're going to laugh then let's keep going, shall we? Look, is that any better?"

"Why is your fringe sticking up like that? Is that on purpose?"

"Yes, it is, you cheeky mare. That must be the last one, that was the summer before I went to university." I shut the album, but Marianne opens it again.

"There's still some more. Look, it's all pictures of old people. Who are they? Oh! Is that... is that... Why is he here?"

We stare at the photograph in perplexed silence. From a border of sage leaves, James Moon looks back at us. Beneath it, Lily has written:

Why should a man die who has sage in his garden?

"Well, there you go," I say, and shut the album. "I suppose that shows you're never too old for it. Why don't you go outside for a bit? I'll come and get you when lunch is ready."

With Marianne safely distracted from the album, I sit down at the desk, but I can't settle. Yesterday has drained me of all my efficiency. With our one immovable deadline out of the way, I feel limp and lost. On the edge of my notes, I see Marianne's scribbled sum, a tiny reminder of a mystery, and shake my head before the thought can take hold again. I decided yesterday that it didn't matter, and I'm sticking to that. It's the photograph album, its dreamy images and necromantic words, getting into my head and convincing me there's something here I need to do or to discover. Lily and Margaret. One of them my grandmother, one my great-aunt. But which way round was it? Whose grandchild am I really?

I don't have time for this. My real life is waiting for me. I pick up my pen, lay it down again, pick it up again, lay it down again. Maybe I need a break. Maybe a few minutes will clear my head and restore me to my normal efficient self.

Maybe I should read, escape into another world for a while. I scan the bookshelf, but nothing appeals.

Tucked in among the untidy bundle of papers at the end of the shelf is a slim hard-backed notebook. When I take it out, the cover's stained dark with spilled vanilla and the pages inside are yellow. But the handwriting is as clear and neat as it ever was, counting out quantities and times and temperatures, the luscious alchemical secrets her friends used to enquire after, but were never allowed to share. Lily's recipe book.

Baking is a kind of magic, Lily tells me. *A very gentle kind. It's good for your soul. Like meditation.*

I think about Daniel, pining for me like a neglected dog. Every hour I spend away from the jobs I'm supposed to be doing is another hour before I can be back where I belong. I don't have time for this.

Baking helps you get your mind in order when you have something hard to think about.

But I don't want to think about it, I argue weakly. *That's the whole point.*

Then why not do it just because you enjoy it?

I leaf reverently through the pages. Which would I choose if I could? Quarter cake, Madeira cake, devil's food cake, angel cake, the same basic ingredients of flour, eggs, butter, sugar, mingled with flavours and fillings and endlessly combined into a million bewitching confections. Lily was renowned for her cakes. They took pride of place at church bazaars, each slice commanding a premium over its less-well-regarded companions.

You work so hard, my darling. Take some time for yourself.

A cake implies sociability, steadiness, permanence. It's a ridiculous thing to make in a house that's not your own and that you hope to leave in a couple of days.

It's never ridiculous to do something that makes you happy. Only an hour or so for yourself, that's all. What harm can it do?

I pause on Lily's recipe for Victoria sponge, rich with butter and golden with eggs. I never have the time to bake at home. When will I get the chance again? I can picture Lily nodding approvingly.

With every moment I spend in the kitchen, I sink deeper into memory. I remember the glint of the sugar as it poured into the scale pan, the luxurious weight of the butter, the gradual transformation from rich gold to richer cream. (*Always keep your butter in the pantry*, Lily reminds me as I work the mix with a wooden spoon, my arm aching with the effort. *It helps keep the sponge light*.) I remember the decadence of seeing Lily crack six eggs – a whole box! – into a basin, and the anxious thrill the first time she let me try this for myself. The slow peaceful steadiness of baking, each step in its own order, impossible to hurry, fills me with contentment. All the tension slides from my shoulders. I feel as if I'm walking in my sleep.

Don't let it curdle, Lily warns as I add the egg a tablespoonful at a time, stirring as fast as I can. *Fold in some flour if you need to. Add the vanilla after the flour. Then straight in the oven. Perfect. Now, while the cake cooks we can clean and tidy…*

The flour jar goes back into its spot on the pantry shelf. The sugar jar is nearly empty – I must remember to buy more. The little brown bottle of vanilla goes back into its home in the spice rack. I crunch the eggshells before I throw them away. *It stops a witch from using them to cast a spell*, Lily told me once, laughing at her own superstition. The water is so scalding hot that everything dries almost instantly. A quick wipe of the surfaces and the kitchen is clean again, scented with the treat growing golden behind the oven door.

Then I glance at the clock and see to my horror that it's nearly noon. I've wasted the whole morning.

Jen's exceptional ability to focus on the detail is an asset to the team. My boss Ken wrote that in my Performance Review a few months ago. What's happening to me? Maybe

I need fresh air; fresh air while the cake cooks, and then lunch. The blank screen of my laptop stares at me accusingly. I slam it shut so I won't have to look at it, and go to look for Marianne.

The trees have grown taller and the shrubs woodier, but the lawn is still soft and velvety, mowed in stripes by the gardener. The datura, poisonous and beautiful, still shades the bench where Lily's neighbours sometimes sat to enjoy the sunshine, and the tough little holly tree tucked away between two rhododendron bushes still drops thick brown leaves like caltrops. I stepped on one with bare feet once. I still remember how my whole body convulsed with the shock, a great rush of air pouring out between my lips, and when I looked around, Lily and her two friends were hurrying, white-faced, across the lawn. As I tried to explain, I accidentally stood on another holly leaf and did the same thing again, and the woman closest to me covered her ears and cowered. Lily said afterwards that she saw three birds fly off in a panic. I apologised, but she didn't seem angry. In fact, she looked rather proud. Today I have shoes on, but nonetheless I tread carefully. Marianne isn't here, but I hadn't expected her to be. She'll be in the quieter, more secret part of the garden, down by the wall where Lily grew herbs even though the gardener wanted carnations, a sunny spot where you can lose yourself for hours. I push between two tall camellia bushes, picking petals from my clothes as I go.

Marianne is kneeling by the wall, her nose close to the earth. The air smells sweet and minty, as if something has been freshly crushed. She's petting a little tabby cat with a white bib and socks that rolls and rolls in the sunshine, green eyes half-closed, belly fur stroked smooth by Marianne's gentle hand. The cat is lying in a patch of what looks like miniature green nettles but is, of course, catnip – which explains the tranced delight that surrounds it like a cloud.

"I found a cat," Marianne tells me, dazed and blissful. "I

found a little cat and she's such a darling. She even lets me stroke her underneath."

"I wouldn't, she might bite—"

Marianne's fingers trail through the cat's soft underbelly. The cat wraps velvet paws around her arm and purrs. Her teeth gleam as she rests them against Marianne's skin, so gently there's not even an indentation. Marianne looks as if she might be purring herself, a low repetitive vibration of sensual pleasure as the cat twines more firmly around her arm and writhes among the green leaves. I wonder if catnip has any proven effect on humans.

"Hello then, cat." I stretch out a finger and the cat sniffs briefly at it before relaxing back into her patch of catnip. I run my hand over her glossy coat. She's compact and muscly, a lean little moggy whose translucent claws glow pinkish-white as she kneads at the air.

"She likes me," Marianne says. "She likes you too." The half-crushed patch of catnip, sweetened by sunshine, is a little patch of feline heaven. I'm tempted to lie down in it myself.

"Is it a girl?"

"She looks like a girl," Marianne says. Her hands smooth longingly over the cat's side. "Do you think she has a home? She's not lost?"

"She's not lost. Look how friendly she is."

"She might just be pleased because she's found some people who like her."

"And she's nice and healthy."

"Maybe she's good at looking after herself."

A shadow falls across the patch of catnip. All three of us squint up through too-bright sunshine at the upright figure and frowning face of James Moon. I gather myself together, ready for battle. Marianne stops stroking the cat and moves closer to me. The cat herself carries on with her blissful rolling, purring so hard her little ribcage vibrates with it. James Moon bends into our space and his hands reach towards us and I flinch back, unsure what's going to happen. He scoops

156

up the cat and tucks it under his chin, where it wriggles for a minute and then nestles against his chest, absurdly tiny in his large hands.

"Might have known you'd be poking around down here," James says to me. "Can't you leave anything alone for one bloody minute?"

"We were only petting her," Marianne says, speaking and signing at the same time so I can follow what she's saying despite the sun that's right behind her head. "We're not trying to keep her. What's her name?" James Moon looks mutinous. "Please tell me. I promise I won't laugh."

"Doesn't have one. She's just called Cat."

Marianne's hand reaches up to the cat as it sits, quiet and resigned, under James's chin. "Hello, Cat. I like your name."

"It's a bloody stupid name," says James. "I didn't choose it. Like calling your child *Daughter*."

"So why didn't you change it?" Marianne asks, still hovering and dabbing at the cat. Long rabbity back feet dangle between James's fingers. Marianne touches the white toes in fascination.

"It's not your cat." I suddenly know this for a certainty. "It's—"

"Lily's. Course it bloody is. Been looking after it since she went into hospital. If you'd bothered to stay in touch with her you'd have known about it and made arrangements. As it was, you've got me to thank for not walking into a flat full of dead cat stink. Don't think you're getting it back either."

"If I wanted a cat I'd buy my own. I don't have to steal off my neighbours. Have it if you want. A present from me."

"Don't want the damn thing. Bloody nuisance it is, always wandering off, I don't know why she bothered." He strokes the top of the cat's head and she turns into his caress, arching her neck and closing her eyes. "Got it from a shelter. Previous owner up and died. Lame duck. Lily always liked lame ducks. Like you."

The unbelievable hurt this causes me strikes me

157

momentarily dumb. Through the red haze, I see James Moon look – am I imagining it? – briefly ashamed.

"She's so cute," says Marianne, continuing her investigation of the cat's paws.

"Catnip," says James. "Sends her off her rocker. Can't pick her up like this normally, she won't have it. Let Lily do it, of course. Thing was crazy about Lily. Sometimes I'd hear it meowing for her—" He stops talking so abruptly it's like having a door slammed in our faces, and turns away so we can't see his expression.

"The funeral notice said no flowers," I say very loudly to his retreating back, hoping the sob in my chest isn't leaking out. "And she never liked red roses either. She'd have laughed and thrown them in the bin. You didn't know her as well as you thought." His shoulders quiver as he slows his pace. "If the cat's such a nuisance I'll send it to the shelter. Then you'll have more time to spend breaking into people's houses and being rude to strangers, you miserable old man."

James Moon stops, hesitates, then turns around and looks me in the eye. I brace myself for the next verbal onslaught, but he simply stands there, swallowing hard, one hand still holding the cat that now appears to have gone to sleep against his chest. His mouth works and his face is crumpled. Despite my best efforts, a tear crawls down my cheek and I realise with a jab of shame that we've each reduced the other to tears.

Then Marianne, my gentle frightened Marianne, beckons James towards her, then reaches out and takes first my hand, and then his, so we stand on the grass in an awkward, reluctant trinity, or perhaps a quartet if we're counting the cat.

"I think you both loved her and that's why you're both sad," she says. "Maybe you should stop shouting and each say one thing you loved best about Lily."

If anyone else suggested this I'd laugh in their face. I keep my eye fixed on James, daring him to hurt Marianne's feelings so I can tear another strip of flesh from his poor hurt bones. The pause stretches and stretches.

"That what they teach at school these days?" James says at last.

"We learned about conflict resolution in PSD," says Marianne, looking modest. "It might feel weird at first but you should give it a go. It worked for me and Ellie and Grace when we had a big falling-out at the end of Year Six."

James shakes his head a little, but holds his tongue.

"Come on," says Marianne. "You just need to be brave."

James Moon shakes his hand free of Marianne's and holds it out to me instead.

"Time we called it a truce," he says. "Be civilised at least, shall we? Don't have to *like* each other, of course. God forbid."

I shake his hand, still a little reluctant. A small mean part of me has enjoyed the freedom to be as rude as possible, on all available occasions. Marianne nods approvingly.

"You look like her today," James says to Marianne, apparently surprising himself. His gnarled hand tugs gently at her curls. "Your hair's your own though. What you finding to do with yourself? Must get bored with your mother so busy?"

"She's fine," I say. We've agreed a truce. Why he is undermining me?

"I'm fine," Marianne agrees. "It's awesome here. The garden's great." She reaches up again for the cat, who's begun to come out of her catnip trance and glares warningly at Marianne from one slitty green eye. "And now I can play with the cat."

"Not supposed to be out here," says James. "Indoor cat all its life, apparently. That's why they let it go to someone with a flat. Not that she took any notice. Never took any notice of anyone she disagreed with. You'd have liked her."

I don't like the rapport that's developing here, while I stand around like a spare part and look from one to the other to follow the conversation. I break the moment by coughing loudly and then stepping between James and Marianne, resisting the temptation to sneak a stroke of the cat's plushy fur as I do so.

"We need to go," I tell Marianne.

"Are we going out somewhere? To the solicitors?"

"I've made a cake," I say, half proud, half confessional.

"You can make cakes?"

"Of course I can make cakes. I just don't often get time. We need to take it out the oven before it burns."

James frowns and watches our hands, as if concentrating hard for five seconds will somehow unlock the key to a whole new language.

"See you later," I offer, out loud.

"You could come too," Marianne suggests.

"Come where?" James looks bewildered.

"Come and have some cake with us." James's expression of horror must match mine. "You don't have to, but I thought you might enjoy it. Everyone likes cake."

"Marianne," I say warningly. She ignores me, swinging her hair across her face so she can pretend not to see me. "Marianne," I repeat, out loud this time.

"Don't worry," says James, with a look as dry as the Sahara. "Got too much to do to stop for cake. But thanks. That's a nice thing to say."

"Maybe I'll see you later then," says Marianne. She glances longingly at the cat once more. "Goodbye, Cat."

"How do you lot say that?" James asks abruptly, looking at me.

"Excuse me? My lot? I'm English, you know, the same as you are."

"Like this," says Marianne, showing him.

We walk briskly back across the lawn, Marianne struggling to keep pace with me.

"Why did you ask him in?" I demand as soon as we reach

160

the cool quiet of the hallway.

Her dark eyes are troubled. "Are you mad?"

"No."

"Yes, you are. I'm sorry."

It's very hard to lie with your hands.

"Maybe a little bit mad. But that's not fair, I know you're not trying to annoy me."

"But you are annoyed?"

"I wondered why you asked him in, that's all."

"He knew Lily."

"What?"

"He knew Lily," Marianne says, as if this is explanation enough.

I stop climbing the stairs so I can make sure I've understood this correctly.

"Why are you interested? You never even met her."

"Yes, I know. I'd like to know more about her. And I know you don't want to talk about her, and anyway you've got loads to do. So I thought if I got to know Mr Moon, he could tell me. And I've got to do it now because once we leave I won't ever see him again probably, and then he'll die and there'll be this whole bit of my family I'll never know about."

What can I say to this when everything I thought I knew seems doubtful? From behind the half-open door, the scent of Victoria sponge cake coils around us.

"Isn't the cat sweet?"

"It's all right," I say, refusing to let myself dwell on the treacherous softness of her paws wrapping around my arm, her wet little nose nuzzling against my thumb. In the kitchen, the cake is golden and perfect. I put it on the wire rack to cool, then take out the bread for sandwiches. What if James and Marianne become friends? What might he tell her? What then? Marianne helps me with the margarine.

"I tell you what," I say after a minute. "Tomorrow, let's go to the beach."

"Seriously?"

"Of course seriously." If I keep Marianne out of James's way for a day or two, perhaps she'll lose interest. Or perhaps he'll think better of it and stop encouraging her. "What do you think?" Or perhaps he'll die. *That would work too*, I think, surprised by my own malice.

"But what about the list?"

"It'll be fine. I'll work twice as hard the next day."

"But won't Dad be mad? I don't like it when he's mad with you."

"Dad's too far away to find out," I say, which is a terrible answer, but the only one I can summon. "We've earned a day off and we're going out. That's the end of it."

Of course, Marianne's right. If Daniel finds out I've frittered away a whole precious day at the beach, he'll be upset. Nonetheless, I'd thought Marianne was still too young to notice tensions between adults, or to resist the promise of a day spent on swimming and sunshine. Instead, she looks sad and anxious, until she sees me watching her and flashes me a bright smile that's almost real enough to be convincing.

Chapter Fourteen – Lily

"And I hear you're a musician," Lily says, passing Daniel a slice of cake.

"I want you to meet Lily," I say, as we lie, resplendent and sweaty, in his room in a shared off-campus house. I have my own room in my own shared house, but I'm in it as little as possible. My housemates joke that if Daniel decided to murder me, they wouldn't notice for weeks.

"Who's Lily again?"

"My grandmother. My dad's mum."

"Oh yes, I remember, down in the South West. Do we have to?"

"Yes we do."

He kisses my shoulder.

"I'd rather stay here in bed."

Daniel takes the plate, rewarding Lily with the smile that melts my heart and loosens my joints. Her answering smile is smaller and more guarded than I'd really like.

"So, how did you and Jen meet?" she asks, correct and sweet.

Oh God, I think. *She doesn't like him.*

The Students' Union, sweaty and crowded, a roomful of uncertain young adults trying to prove themselves. Everyone's stricken by the irrational terror that if they don't meet people right now, tonight, this instant, they'll be alone in their rooms for ever. I say *they* as if I'm immune to this, but seeing it in others doesn't stop you feeling it yourself.

Nonetheless I'm determined to take my time and be choosy. Unlike everyone else, I don't have the excuse of being distracted by the noise. My attention snags on a tall boy, fair-haired and green-eyed, long-lashed and pretty in the way musicians often are. He's at the centre of a group who look vaguely alike, as if they're all siblings. I can tell from the casual way he takes the drink offered by the girl on his left that he's used to adulation.

Why are the good-looking ones always such tossers? I wonder.

"So when I saw this gorgeous girl looking at me, I was stoked. I mean, you know, really pleased. And then she just smiled and looked away again." Daniel is quick to sense other people's moods. I can feel his anxiety, aware that he's missing the mark. "So obviously that made me want to talk to her even more."

"Naturally." Lily nods. "I wonder, why did you look away, Jen?"

I accept a drink from a boy who I'm sure told me his name at some point, and who keeps touching my forearm in a well-meant attempt at non-threatening contact. He's decided the way to impress me is to painstakingly list the names and academic histories of everyone he's met so far. I nod and smile as he works his way round the bar ('That's Josh, he's on my corridor and he's doing PPE, he applied to Cambridge but didn't quite get the grades and this was his second choice, that's Liz and she's doing Sociology, she nearly chose Durham instead but she thought the campus here looked better.') and try out various labels to see if they'll attach themselves to my companion. *Hi, I'm Dave and I'm doing English Lit. Hi, I'm Andrew and I'm doing English Language with French*. Is that a real course or did I make it up? I'm sure English came into it somewhere. *Hi, I'm Steve and I'm doing English with Linguistics*. The fair-haired musician and his coterie have vanished into the crowd.

Daniel leaves the room to use the bathroom. Lily waits for me to speak.

I look at her, and she looks at me, but for the first time I can remember, I have no idea what to say.

Dave-or-Andrew-or-Steve is at the bar when Daniel finds me, materialising by my elbow like a magic trick. He looks shy, uncertain. I have to remind myself that good-looking people don't need to worry about first impressions, that this is simply an act he's learned works.

"I know this'll make me sound like a twat but you look really nice and I wondered if I could talk to you," he says, and despite my resistance I can't help finding his expression appealing.

"Daniel's a musician," I say at last, hoping this will gain Lily's approval. She already knows this from my letters, but perhaps now we're together, I can explain Daniel so he'll make sense to her in the same way he does to me.

"That's very interesting. What sort of music does he play?"

"I'm going to write a whole new kind of music," Daniel tells me when we've known each other for a week. "It'll be based on vibration and sensation – playing with sound waves to create an experience. They'll be songs you'll hear with your whole body."

"What will that sound like? To everyone who can hear, I mean?"

"That won't matter. It'll be just for you."

"Just for me? Not very commercial."

"I don't care about money. It's the music that matters." He kisses my naked shoulder. "And you."

At this point everyone else asks the obvious question. Some people come straight out with it; others dance delicately around the edges; but they all want to know what a musician is doing with a girl like me. The implication is generally that I'm the lucky one.

In Lily's hand is a smooth green pebble, striated with rings like a tree. She turns the pebble over in her hand and watches me with eyes as bright as a bird's.

"Lie here," Daniel says. He's sweating with the effort it's taken to move the furniture, roll back the carpet, rearrange his kit on the bare floorboards. "Next to the amp."

I stretch myself out, unsure what shape to make. Do I curl up like a newborn, or cross my hands like a corpse?

"Can I have a pillow?"

"No, it'll absorb the vibrations. Close your eyes."

The unshaded light shows me the blood vessels in my eyelids. I feel exposed and ridiculous. I breathe deeply and try to concentrate. There's a faint vibration beginning beneath me.

The rhythm is insistent, growing in complexity. I lay my palms flat so I can feel more intensely. I open my eyes and see Daniel watching me and smiling.

"This is amazing," I tell him, unsure if he'll be able to hear. He smiles victoriously. The door opens and Daniel's housemate Nick glances in.

"Bloody hell," he grumbles when he sees what we're doing. "Can't you two just stay in bed all day and have sex like you normally do?"

Still holding the pebble, Lily raises her cup to her lips, watching me over the top of it.

"And does he make a good living?"

"I'll make our fortune," Daniel tells me. The sunlight is thick and honey-coloured as it pours in at the window and pools onto the floor, lending loveliness to everything it touches, even the dust, even the discarded plates, even Daniel's socks. "And we'll build our own house. Nothing like this one. A beautiful clean white house with a massive studio. Out in the country so no one can bother us."

"How will I get to work?"

"You won't need to work by then. I'll take care of you."

I don't want a huge white house in the country. What I want is for time to stand still so I can keep what I have right now. I want to live for ever in this golden autumn, in the arms of the man I love, watching his face as he spins his dreams into our future.

Lily puts down her cup, reaches out and takes my hand for a minute, then lets it go again.

"I can see how much you like him," she says. "So tell me, does he make you happy?"

Christmas separates us for the first time in ten weeks. We sob shamelessly on the station platform, oblivious to the spectacle we're making, and write to each other every day, counting hours and minutes until we can be together again. The long erotic fantasies he sends me make my skin flush. On Christmas Day, frantic because there's no post, he calls my parents and asks them to tell me he's thinking of me. On Boxing Day there's no phone call, but I dream he's being dragged naked through snow by two angry giants in matching hats and scarves. The day after Boxing Day, I fling myself onto the first train and race down the platform to meet him.

Three minutes after we arrive at his parents' house, he tumbles me onto his bed, tearing frantically at my clothes. I'm not really ready but he crams himself inside me anyway.

I'll be sore and tender afterwards. It doesn't matter. I don't care. We're back together. I bite his shoulder, matching his ferocity with my own.

"I'm so sorry," he says as we gasp for breath afterwards. "I know that was too quick. I just missed you so much. You can't ever be away from me that long again. I can't compose without you. It feels like I'm missing my soul. And I'm sorry I couldn't call yesterday. I was thinking about you, I swear. But my—"

"—parents made you go out with them," I say. "For a long walk. You were freezing but they made you do it anyway."

"How do you do that?" I shrug. "You always know things before I tell you. You've got second sight."

"No, I haven't."

"Yes, you have. I wish I had it too. I want to be able to watch you when you're not with me."

He kisses me again, his lips rough and insistent, almost too rough. I've never felt so needed, so longed for, so loved.

"Have some more cake." Lily's silver cake slice makes a neat sharp division in the buttery sponge. As Daniel passes his plate, a fat crumb falls onto his knee and he brushes it absent-mindedly to the floor. Lily doesn't pause, doesn't flinch, doesn't miss a beat.

"Do you think you two might get married at some point?" My dad, vague and gentle as he always is when our conversations turn personal, seeking only a quiet life, with a moderate and conventional happiness for those he loves. I wonder if my mother has told him to ask.

"I don't know. We might one day."

"Not that it matters these days, of course."

"Well, we might do, okay?"

"And you're keeping up with your work? Course you are, you always have. Only, you know, make sure you enjoy yourself as well." His smile is crooked. "Do all the terrible things we wouldn't let you do while you were living at home."

"That's not really me," I say.

"I know." My dad pats my shoulder, his hand damp and soapy from the washing-up. "You're having a good time though, aren't you? Not studying too hard? Making the most of it?"

Daniel and I, lying in bed in the stolen quiet of a Saturday night, briefly rich from Daniel's weekend of busking, eating strips of rare steak with our fingers, bloody juices dripping onto the sheets.

"And what are your plans after graduation?"

"Jen's got a place on a grad training scheme so that's sorted out where we're living. It's a bit further north than I'd have liked but the train connections are good, so I can commute to London for meetings and stuff."

"Commute to London? Goodness, that'll be expensive, won't it?" Lily blinks benignly at him, the perfect facsimile of a sweet old lady. And all the while her bright sharp gaze, skewering him like a lab rat ready for dissection. "Or perhaps there are, I don't know, grants or something? I'm afraid I'm out of touch."

"We'll be fine," says Daniel, reaching easily for my hand. "We'll live on Jen's salary while I get started, then when I'm making decent money she'll leave her job and I'll look after her."

"I see." Lily's eyes twinkle with what looks like merriment, as long as you don't look too closely. "Well, things have certainly changed since my day!"

"It'll be perfect," Daniel tells me as we stand shivering in the snow, throwing bread to the ducks. Later we'll go into town to choose luscious uncomfortable underwear to dress me up in. I want him to save what was left from the steak dinner for his share of the electricity bill, but he insists that's what his overdraft's for and this is bonus money, to be spent on frivolities. It's only since I've known him that I've understood what *spending money like water* really means, or how much fun it can be.

"But what if I fail my exams and they fire me?"

"Of course you won't fail, you're brilliant."

I want to ask *But what if it doesn't work out for you?* Instead I break off more bread and throw it to my favourite duck, a foolish orangey creature with a tufted back and a startling ring around his eyes, like white eyeliner. My trust, my confidence, mean everything to Daniel. And I do believe in him. I do.

Can he tell she doesn't like him? Why doesn't she like him? Even my mother understands that we come as a pair now, that our lives are utterly intertwined and there is no having one without the other. If even she can accept this, why can't Lily?

"It was so lovely to meet you, dear." Lily kisses Daniel goodbye, then rests her hand against his cheek for a minute. Her nails gleam in the sunlight. For a minute I think she might scratch him.

"She hates me," Daniel says.

The cider is cold and delicious and the scent of cooking meat is tantalising. Perhaps if I bury my nose in my glass and let the bubbles burst on my tongue, I can pretend not to notice what Daniel's saying. A hand reaches across the table and takes my glass away.

"I know you're listening, Jen. She hates me."

"She's just difficult," I hedge. "She's not good with new people. She'll love you when she gets to know you."

"No, she won't. She thinks I'm not good enough and I'll sponge off you for the rest of our lives and I'll never amount to anything and you should get rid of me right now."

"Don't be ridiculous." I'm amazed how well Daniel has read Lily's mind. "Hey, you're not upset, are you?"

"Suppose I took you to meet someone who really mattered to me."

"Like who?" I don't mean to say this out loud, but I'm upset and defensive too. I want Daniel to tell me it doesn't matter if he and Lily get along or not. Instead he's giving me those frightened puppy-dog eyes, begging for validation. "You don't care what anyone in your family thinks."

"That's not fair. I do care about them, but I care about you more. You're the most important person in my life."

"And *you're* the most important person in *my* life."

"You mean that?"

"Of course I do."

"And if she made you choose—"

"That's ridiculous, how could she possibly make me choose?"

"But if she did?"

"I'd choose you."

He strokes my fingers then, his huge green eyes fixed on mine, and lifts my hand to his lips. I see the woman on the next table sigh with envy. He looks at me for a minute longer, then pulls me to my feet.

"Come on. We're going back to the B&B."

"What? Now?"

"Right now."

"But we've ordered food."

He fumbles money from his pocket to the table.

"But I'm hungry."

"Oh, so am I."

"But what's the hurry—"

His kiss is so deep and sudden I can hardly breathe. For a minute I think I'll die of embarrassment at being kissed so needily in public – we're in our twenties now, we're getting too old to behave like this. Then his fingers tickle the back of

171

my neck and all I can think is *yesyesyes*. We run back to the B&B hand in hand.

"And you don't think she's right?" he asks me afterwards. "You believe in me?"

"You know I do. You'll be a superstar. You're going to set the whole world on fire."

He falls asleep with his face in my hair. I consider moving him so I can go for chips from the takeaway down the road, but I don't want to wake him. So instead I admire the planes of his face, so innocent and boyish when he sleeps. To everyone around us, I'm the one batting above my average. His need of me is baffling, but irresistible.

There's something pressing against the base of my spine. Trying not to disturb Daniel, I wriggle one hand beneath me and find Lily's green pebble. It's malachite, found occasionally in the deep mines whose wealth once built Lily's house, and said to be good for dreams. Lily has sent me home with a dream in my pocket. I'm not sure I want to know what she's given me, but its fat shape fits so comfortingly into my hand.

I fall asleep and find I'm at the bottom of the hill that leads to Lily's house. I've promised her a visit, she's waiting for me, but Daniel is kneeling on the pavement, his face buried against my legs. He clings to me like a child and begs me not to leave him. As I watch him weep, the knowledge suddenly comes to me that Lily has made me a promise that I can live with her for ever, but only on condition that I kill Daniel. When I wake up, my face is wet with tears.

Chapter Fifteen – Monday

So what's happening? How's the list going? Are you still coming home tomorrow?

You still there?

I know you're still there, I can see those little dots appearing and disappearing. What's the matter?

I take a deep breath.

> *It's taking longer than I thought it would.*

Oh.

> *There's so much to do and everyone keeps losing the pieces of paper they're supposed to have and no one but me cares about getting it done. It's a nightmare, it's absolutely doing my head in. I'm so tired each night I can't tell you. xxxxx*

Do my words sound authentic? They ought to; I've borrowed the script from my mother. I feel guilty, but not guilty enough to stop lying.

> *I know. I'm sorry.*

I need you back. I can't work without you, the house is a mess, I need you here to support me.

How much longer are we talking anyway?

    Till the end of this week I think

The end of the week? Jesus what are you doing? Can't you bring some of it home with you?

    I know, I know

And what about work? Are they going to let you have this long?

I have no idea. I honestly have no idea. I only know I can't come home yet.

    It'll be okay. They'll understand

Unlike your grumpy miserable husband you mean

    I didn't mean that and you know I didn't. Look I know how hard it is for you. I'd rather be anywhere than here.

Is that true?

    ??? Of course it's true

I feel like you're drifting away from me. The only times we ever argued were when you went to see her. She never liked me and now you're back in her house surrounded by her stuff and I hate it.

    Daniel please, I love you. I swear I don't want to stay

here a minute longer, I'm doing literally nothing but bloody forms and emails. I'll come home the second I'm done xxx

And then we'll be rich, remember?

Okay, now you're the one with the little dots.

It's nothing

Come on. Tell me

Well, you know the other night when you dream-stalked me and I had a red guitar?

Yeeessss…

Well, I've kind of still got it.

I knew it. I bloody knew it.

It has the most amazing tone. I could play it for hours. Actually I did play it for hours

He said he'd hold it for me for a couple of days. It's a bargain, he could get five grand for it easily on eBay but he offered it to me for three and a half

I couldn't say no, Jen. It's the most beautiful thing you ever saw

So I bought it

I PayPalled him the money last night

Oh God. Oh God oh God oh God oh God, fucking fucking

fuck. This and the payment to the T-shirt guy and the first part of the undertaker's bill; we'll go over our card limit now for sure. I'll have to try and increase it. Can I do that online?

Never mind. We've managed before. We'll manage this time too. And when Lily's flat is sold…

You know, it's a bloody good thing I love you

So you're not mad?

This is my penance for taking our daughter out to dance in the storm and nearly losing her, and for pretending I've been working hard when in fact I've been bone idle.

No I'm not mad.

You really mean it?

I really mean it

Oh my God you're amazing. THANK YOU

AS LONG AS I don't have to fall over the damn thing all the time because you leave it lying around

Don't worry, this baby won't be lying around anywhere, I swear

And as long as you don't get mad with me for needing longer here

It's a deal. Only till the end of the week, right?

About that yes. Maybe a day or two longer. But that's all. And then we'll be home

I love you xxxxxxx

I know xx

The secret negotiations of a long marriage.

"Are we taking lunch to the beach?" Marianne's like a mouse getting ready for winter, all bulky burdens and anxious scurrying. It wouldn't surprise me to find she's stashed something inside her cheeks. "What shoes should I wear?"

"Whatever shoes you want. And we can take lunch or get something there, whatever you want. There's a café, or there used to be."

"What sort of food will they have?" Marianne is sensitive about food, a deep anxiety that goes far beyond *picky*, combining childish dislikes with odd taboos picked up at random from government leaflets, Food Science lessons and conversations with Daniel. At present she's not eating potatoes in any form, but has a passion for porridge with jam stirred through it, and the kind of part-baked bread that comes entombed in thick plastic, and which you sprinkle with water and finish off in the oven.

"I don't know, the usual stuff."

"What's the usual stuff?" She looks genuinely baffled. "And what should I wear?"

Just when I think I've finally managed to herd her to the door, she vanishes again. I run her to earth in the bathroom, scrabbling through her small assortment of make-up.

"What are you doing? You don't want mascara, it'll run in the water."

"I want to look nice."

"Why do you… You do look nice, you look lovely."

"But it's a special occasion," says Marianne.

How many times in my childhood did I run up and down the streets that lead to the beach? Hundreds. And now my daughter stands in front of Lily's bathroom mirror, making herself beautiful for a special occasion. I take the mascara from her and reach instead for the scarlet lipstick that she loves.

"Put this on," I tell her. "And get a move on or I'm going without you."

At the top of the steep hill that flows down to the seafront, we stop to catch our breath and to gaze at the sea, bright and choppy and glinting. When I feel Marianne beside me draw the air deep into her lungs and see her shoulders relax and her face break into a huge goofy smile, I feel again the stab of guilt that I kept this treasure from her for so long.

"It looks so different," she says. "Are you sure it's the same beach?" I laugh and she looks at me shyly. "Did Lily bring you? Even though she was an old lady?"

"All the time. Twice a day, sometimes. We'd go home for lunch and come back again. And sometimes in the evening, to watch the seagulls going to bed."

"I didn't know old people did stuff like that."

I think about my mother, alone and grumbling in her frowsty existence; of Daniel's father, who has opinions about whisky and thinks of himself as a dog-lover even though he's never owned one; of Daniel's mother, who is ruthlessly organised with a terrifying garden. What a contrast with Lily, mysterious and magical, capable of conjuring wonders. "Some of them do and some of them don't. I think you got the sort of grandparents who don't. Sorry."

"Don't be sorry. I wouldn't be me without them, would I? They're sort of like the foundations. And you and Dad are the house. And I'm standing on the roof like a seagull."

I'm used to thinking of Marianne as the bottom of an inverted pyramid, in danger of being crushed by the weight of the generations above.

"It would have been nice to meet her though," says Marianne, almost to herself, and it's only because her hands are moving along with her lips that I know she's talking to me at all.

We spread out our towels and settle ourselves under the sea wall. Marianne looks longingly towards the water.

"It'll be cold," I tell her.

"I don't mind."

"Go on then." She'll never get past her knees, but if it makes her happy to try I don't mind.

"Aren't you coming with me?"

"Maybe in a bit." It's been years since I've been in the ocean and I'm not sure I still have the mental toughness to go through with it.

"But am I allowed by myself?"

"Course you are. Off you go."

"I want you to come swimming with me. Please, Mum."

I'm startled. It's very unlike Marianne to ask directly for anything.

"Please," she repeats. "I want you to come swimming with me."

"How about you swim and I'll paddle?"

"Okay. But you've got to watch me, you can't go back."

"It's a deal."

Do I take off my jeans or roll them up? Roll them up, I think, even though I'll end up wading too deep and getting them soaked. Marianne sheds her clothes and abandons them in an uncharacteristic heap, hopping over the pebbles in her sensible black racer-back one-piece, chosen for school swimming lessons because it was exactly the same as those worn by the identikit smooth-haired orange-tinged girls who Marianne isn't quite friends with, but who aren't enemies either. The water's so cold my feet hurt, and Marianne contracts into herself with the shock, but then to my astonishment she pushes on anyway, with a determination I can't begin to muster.

Watch them going in, Lily tells me. *Look how they all do it. You can learn a lot about a person from how they go into the sea.*

Three young men race down the sand, splashing and

flapping, sending up heavy globs of water. They're acting as if they'll swim to America, but I already know they won't make it in past their waists. The older woman with the tousled salt-and-pepper hair and the deceptively youthful figure is an experienced swimmer; I can tell by the way she wades through the water, unhurried but unhesitating, and launches straight into a smooth clean breaststroke. A little boy beside me is lost in his own world, racing to meet each wave and then running back up the beach as it reaches his toes, halting at the tideline and stretching out one arm as if he's casting a spell. I wonder what magic he's conjuring and whether his ritual will work. Marianne is up to her waist now, her arms wrapped tight around her ribcage.

Keep watching, Lily says. *She'll get there. Just like you.*

Marianne's shivering and I wonder if she'll give up after all, but she takes a deep breath and stands up straight. Then in one quick movement she brings her hands into a point and dives into an oncoming wave, neat and precise, emerging on the other side all slick and wet and gasping with shock.

"Good work!" I call out and wave. I see several people glance at me, then away again. Despite my best efforts, I'm self-conscious about my speaking voice and dislike being stared at, but suddenly I don't care. Marianne's looking at me, so I repeat it: *Good work*. So what if people stare? This is me.

Marianne waves back, then begins to swim the width of the beach. I'm astonished at how competent she is. As a toddler in the swimming pool she was timid and unwilling, clinging tenaciously to my hip when small, becoming whiny and reluctant as she grew. I remember Daniel peeling her arms from around my neck, ignoring her panicky protests and carrying her into the deep end of the pool, forcing her away from his chest so the water could lift and support her little body. *I know what I'm doing*, he always said when I tried to intervene, and I always gave in because after all, he spent the most time with her. But once she grew old enough for swimming lessons at school, I took care to find other things we could do at the weekend.

Now I watch Marianne plunge and laugh in the salty water, and I'm ashamed at how simple the answer is. This is what we should have done. We should have brought her to the ocean.

There's someone else walking into the water now; a tall man with white hair, well-built despite his age. His stride is long and determined, his back strong, and he enters the sea with a no-frills, no-nonsense approach that Lily would have approved of.

If he and I were fifty years younger. Lily chuckles. *But we're not. Ah well.*

And then, of course, I realise that the man – who else could it possibly be? – is James Moon.

Maybe he feels me looking at him, because he turns round and scowls, then swims off towards the horizon in a steady crawl. His progress is slow but relentless, taking him on a beeline towards the spot where Marianne, floating blissfully on her back with her hair spread out like seaweed, is propelling herself with enthusiastic strokes of her hands and feet. Does he have to swim exactly in the spot my daughter's already in? I brace myself for conflict, ready to leap to Marianne's defence if he dares say anything to her, but he stops before they collide. When he swims on, Marianne's following behind him, further out to sea. What's he doing? What's he saying to her? They stop and tread water, and Marianne's face creases with laughter and James Moon gives her an approving nod then swims off again, still heading away from the beach, his arms cycling round and round.

The sun's warm on my back, but my feet ache with cold. As soon as I can catch Marianne's eye, I beckon her in. She pretends not to understand, but I beckon again and she reluctantly swims into shore. She's glowing and golden in the sunshine and her eyes are bright. Before getting out she ducks her whole head under and emerges as slick as a seal.

"You'll freeze," I tell her, and wrap a towel around her shoulders. "Come and get dressed."

"Can't I stay in my costume?"

"No, you can't, you'll freeze."

"But I'll dry in the sun. Won't I? I want to go in again later."

I'm suddenly paralysed by the memory of Lily, shaking her head indulgently as I plead to be allowed to dry off in the sunshine. *Do you promise not to get pneumonia?* she asked, and I, not really clear what pneumonia even was but secure in my invincibility, replied, *Of course I won't get pneumonia! It's warm, look, the sun's shining!* and Lily's reply, *Well, then we'd better buy you an ice cream and make sure your insides are cold too.*

"I saw Mr Moon in the water," says Marianne, cunningly changing the subject.

"I know, I saw him too."

"He told me about the warm current. Did you know about the warm current? You swim out a bit further and it's there. Nobody knows why, though."

"Why do you keep talking to him?"

"He's nice."

"No, he isn't. He shouts at us every time he sees us."

"He doesn't mean it, though. He's a bit grumpy but he's all right really."

"How can you like someone who broke into our home?"

"But it's not our home, is it?" Marianne looks at me in honest astonishment. "Are we keeping it, then?"

"Let's go and buy an ice cream."

"But are we?"

"No!"

"We could though, couldn't we?" Marianne takes my hand.

"Chilly little paws, missus. Put a fleece round your shoulders at least."

"But we could keep it?"

182

"Of course we can't keep it, you know that. We're going to sell it and build a house for all of us back home. Come on. Ice cream."

As we sit in the shelter of the wall and lick the last drips of ice cream off our hands, James Moon comes to claim the neat pile of belongings that have been left a few feet from ours, because of course, out of all the people at the beach this afternoon, they had to belong to him. All I wanted was a single, simple day at the beach with my daughter. Whatever I do, wherever I go, this man will haunt me, just as I'm haunting him. Someone has bound us together with a strand of red silk and now we'll never get away from each other. *Lily*, I think, *did you do this? Why?*

James's expression suggests he's as sick of our endless meetings as I am. He reaches into his bag for a sort of all-in-one towelling tent. After a minute of frenzied movement, his head emerges from the top.

"After all, it's a free country," he says crossly in my general direction, as if I've told him to go away. "Beach belongs to everyone. Used this spot for years."

I smile sweetly and put on my sunglasses.

"You came back in before you froze, then," he says to Marianne. The towel-tent quivers as he peels off his trunks beneath it.

"It wasn't too bad in the warm current," Marianne says.

"Not all it's cracked up to be." James reaches into his bag. I catch an unwelcome glimpse of a pair of giant white old-man briefs. "Don't go thinking it's actually warm. It's only the contrast." Another brief swish of clothing vanishing beneath the tent. "Shouldn't be going in on your own really. Don't know what your mother was thinking."

"Her mother's thinking it's nothing to do with you," I say loudly. "Do you know how incredibly rude it is to assume I can't understand you just because you're not talking to me?"

"Can't I say anything to you without taking offence?"

"It doesn't look good, does it? Are you going to be here all day?"

"None of your business." He emerges from the towel-tent, dressed in neat chinos and a short-sleeved cheesecloth shirt; an old man's notion of casual wear.

"Suppose she won't let me buy you an ice cream either," says James to Marianne, looking gloomy.

"That's right." I settle my sunglasses more comfortably on my nose.

"I've already had one," Marianne says regretfully. "But thank you."

"How about your mother? She eat ice cream? Or is it too much like fun for her to bother herself with?"

"Jesus Christ." I sit up and take off my sunglasses. "Buy us both a bloody ice cream if it'll shut you up. And if it makes Marianne sick I'm cleaning her up with your towel. What?"

"Nothing. You look like your grandmother."

"I bloody don't. I'm nothing like her."

"Not trying to insult you, you know. You always this prickly? Might as well give the cat a compliment."

"Can I help you carry the ice creams?" Marianne bounds to her feet.

"So one of you has manners. Suppose it skipped a generation." He holds out a hand to Marianne, and to my astonishment, she takes it. "Come on, then."

With my sunglasses on I can look wherever I want and no one can know. I stare at James and Marianne, hand in hand on their way to the ice-cream booth. To everyone else on the beach they must look like a loving grandfather and his cherished grandchild. He stops and picks up a shell for her, bending and straightening with difficulty.

It's disturbingly easy to eat two ice creams in quick succession. Rivulets of white trickle down the cone and into the creases of my hands. When I lick them off, I taste the salt crusting my skin. The silence should be awkward, but somewhat annoyingly, James Moon is rather restful to be with. Marianne sits between us, glancing from one to the other as she eats her ice cream with quick dainty licks. Her attitude suggests she's trying to persuade two angry, hissing cats to become friends, and has just begun to make progress. She finishes her cone and sits quietly between us, playing with a little shell she's found by her feet.

"Go on with you," James barks suddenly, and flaps his hand at her. "Let me talk to your mother. Go and have a swim or something. Wash your hands while you're at it." Marianne looks at him doubtfully, then at me. "For God's sake. Promise I'll behave. Can't speak for her, of course."

"Will you be all right by yourself if I go for a swim?" Marianne asks me. I swallow a smile.

"I'll be fine. Off you go."

"Wish you wouldn't keep doing that," James grumbles as Marianne runs down the beach.

"Talk to my daughter?"

James sniffs. "Wouldn't exactly call it talking."

"That's because you're an ignorant old man who doesn't know any better. But never mind, you can't help it."

"Suppose you think I should apologise for coming into Lily's place the other day."

"Breaking into my place, you mean."

"Didn't realise you were there, you see. Didn't think you'd bother coming, to be honest. Thought you might sort it out from a distance and sell up quick. Bit of a shock to find you there. You look just like her."

"I look like my ninety-five-year-old dead grandmother? Thanks so much."

"I'm trying to apologise to you, you stupid woman."

"I don't want your apology."

"You ate my bloody ice cream."

"That's because I'm a brat."

"I said I was sorry about that!"

"No, you didn't. You bought me an ice cream and said I looked like someone sixty years older than me."

"Well, I'm sorry."

"You sound it."

"You can't—" he stops himself.

"Hey, it's all right, don't hold back. Feel free to treat me exactly as rudely as you would anyone else."

He shakes his head and turns away to watch the sea. Marianne is diving for pebbles. When she pounces into the water, I'm reminded of Lily's little cat. James tugs at my arm to make me pay attention.

"Have the cat back if you want it," he says, and I wonder if he's seeing Marianne in the same way I am. "You're right. Damn thing's yours anyway."

"I don't want the cat, thank you, I'd never get it back on the train in one piece."

"Bloody nuisance it is. Wanders round looking for her. Think it misses her. Didn't know cats could. And it meows in the night and tries to get under the blankets. Suppose you'll be selling the flat."

His abrupt change of direction startles me into honesty. "I suppose I'll have to."

His glance is disturbingly shrewd. "You sure? No second thoughts?"

"What business is it of yours anyway?" I ask angrily, because I don't like that he can read me so well.

"You'll have to clear out all her clutter first."

"I know how to sell a house, thank you."

"Kept all sorts, Lily did," he says. "Women always do. Hoarders, the lot of you. Especially photographs. She loved that one you sent her. Of..." He jerks his head towards the water.

"I never sent her—"

"Course you did. Know you loved her really. She loved you too. Both of you. Kept it in her handbag."

"You used to go through her handbag?"

"Give over, you stupid woman. Trying to tell you something. I cleared out my wife's stuff after she died. Spent weeks over it. She'd kept all sorts. Letters. Old papers. Photos of people I'd never met."

He's trying to make it seem like casual advice, but the tension in his neck and shoulders tells me the truth. This is a warning. James Moon is warning me. It's suddenly very hard to breathe. I stare at his mouth so I don't have to look at his eyes, and wish I didn't have to keep listening.

"Want my advice?"

"See if you can guess."

"Well, you're getting it anyway. Don't go through everything. No point. Only upset you. Lily lived a long time and now she's gone. Anything you find you don't understand, don't waste time worrying. Chuck the lot and get on with your life." He blinks crossly and wipes at cheek. "Bloody sand gets everywhere – meant a lot to her, you know."

"What did? Are you going senile or something?"

"The little one. Just knowing she was in the world. Her great-granddaughter. Makes a difference when you're old. Of course you want to see them, make sure they're all right and they'll know you. But even when you can't, it's nice to know they're out there somewhere."

I swallow down the lump in my throat. "Why the hell are you telling me all this? Are you trying to make me feel guilty?"

"Think what you want. If you feel guilty it's your own damn fault. I'm only telling you what I think you ought to know." He stands up stiffly, pressing down on his thighs as if he needs to push his feet into the sand for balance, and collects up his damp swimming things. "Tell her she can come and see the cat any time she wants to."

"Tell her yourself."

"You never give an inch, do you?"

"Not to you I don't." He's giving me that look again. "If you tell me again I look like Lily I swear I'll come round in the night and burn your flat down."

187

"Won't do much for the value of your place."

"I've got insurance. Go away and stop bothering me. Do some gardening or something."

"Lily was the gardener. Thought you'd know that."

"I do know that! I was exploiting a lazy stereotype to cover up the fact that you actually made me feel better, you horrible old man."

"Not my problem how you feel. I'm just giving you some advice."

"Did she really keep that photo with her?"

"You heard me the first time," he says, and stumps crossly away up the beach.

Chapter Sixteen – Lily

The beginning of my twenty-third summer finds me restless with desire. What I crave is not sex but escape, to clamber on board the first train that will carry me and flee south to Lily. I look out of the air-conditioned office at the dusty sunny afternoon and think, *I should be by the sea.* I lie awake in the dark with Daniel asleep next to me and think, *It's too hot to share a bed with anyone.* I tell myself my longing for freedom is nothing more than the rhythms of my childhood that still refuse to leave me. I tell myself that I love Daniel as much as I ever did. I tell myself that I don't want to wake and find him gone.

Despite my best efforts, I've begun to feel detached from Daniel. The flow of energy has changed. I'm no longer nurturing him, worrying about him, making sure he remembers to eat and has bus fare. I've become utterly uninterested in his talk of the people he's met, the contacts he's made, the song he's almost ready to record. I step outside the warm cocoon of our love, where my existence is so entwined with his that I barely have time for anyone else, and think, *I wonder what Lily's doing now? I wonder if I could visit?* I begin to notice the existence of other men.

Daniel senses this. Close as we've been from the day we met, how could he not? He tries to win me back with words, telling me a hundred times a day how much he loves me. He makes dinner, or at least he begins to make dinner, until

I become infuriated by his endless questions about where everything is and how long it should be cooked for, and take over. He recreates the rituals of our university days, rolling back the carpet and inviting me to lie on the bare floorboards to experience the music he's composing. I take pleasure in refusing, telling him the neighbours will complain. He asks me what he can do to make me happy. I lie and tell him everything's fine. I feel both pleased and guilty at his confusion.

Why do I feel like this? I consider all the things I love about Daniel, all the reasons I fell for him in the first place. He's as passionate and full of dreams as ever. He's as fiercely committed to his music. He's still spontaneous, impulsive, hedonistic, prone to sudden wild improvisations of weekends away in borrowed tents and cottages or impromptu reunions with old friends or extravagant feasts eaten nude, in bed, on lazy afternoons. He still worships me for all the ways I'm unlike him. He's still astounded by my ability to get the bills paid and the shopping done regularly. He still considers my domestic skills an advanced form of witchcraft. He still needs me as much as ever.

We've built our lives around the premise that we belong together for ever. We've whispered promises to each other in the heady darkness of the dozen beds we've shared. He's put his trust in me, utterly and without reservation, believing that what I said to him (*I'll be earning enough for both of us while you get started, it'll happen more quickly if you can concentrate on music full-time, no of course I don't mind, I love you.*) would stay forever true. If I left him, he'd be destitute. The thought of tearing myself out of his life makes my heart hurt.

Something extraordinary is going to happen. I can feel it, the way you can feel thunder. The summer turns sticky and oppressive. At work, we scurry inside like mice, desperate for the air conditioning. When Daniel rolls towards me and lays a loving hand on my stomach, I want to shrug him off and tell him *no, I'm not in the mood*, but his need for reassurance is so obvious that I find myself submitting anyway. It doesn't hurt, after all; it's just a nuisance that stops after a while. Afterwards I wonder how he can possibly not notice how not-present I am, how I simply allow him to satisfy himself inside my limp body. When I sleep, I dream of train journeys and of the walk up the hill to Lily's house. Sometimes there's a child beside me, which makes me wonder if in my dream, I have become Lily.

It comes to a head one night when Daniel, in yet another attempt to reconcile the distance between us, has done the food shopping. To be specific, he's taken twenty-five pounds from my purse and – ignoring the list of essentials I keep pinned to the fridge – spent it all on red wine and fillet steak. The scent of the rich red flesh makes me want to claw his face. Perhaps I might devour him afterwards. When we've eaten, he presses me against the wall and sticks his tongue in my mouth. The sex is quick and frantic and leaves me unsatisfied.

Pleased with his success, Daniel tries to persuade me to join him for an early night, but I tell him I have to do some work. He accepts this and leaves me to sit on the sofa and brood. How much longer can we live like this? There's a heavy pressure lodged in my chest that starts off bearable but grows as each day goes on, only receding when I sleep. But I'm too tense to sleep.

I go into the bedroom and wake Daniel with a smack on the shoulder and a hand down the front of his pyjama bottoms. As soon as he's hard I climb on top of him, ignoring his bewilderment, slapping his hands away from my breasts, refusing to kiss him. He glances towards the bedside table where we keep the condoms and I know what he's telling me, but I refuse to stop, riding him relentlessly until the weight in my chest comes undone and my mind is blank and, in the aftermath of savage selfish pleasure, I can fall asleep, rolled into a tight ball, pushing him away when he tries to fit himself around the unwelcoming curve of my coiled spine.

The next day I come home from work, deliberately very late to minimise the time I have to spend with him, and tell him I'm taking a week off to visit Lily.

"Really? When are you going?"

"Tomorrow. First thing." Is there even a train? I don't care, I'll get there at half past six and camp out at the station if I have to. This must be how the geese feel when the southern sunshine starts calling. Is this it? Am I leaving him? "I've booked a taxi, you can have the car while I'm gone."

"Okay. Um. Do you need me to ring her and let her know? Shall I ring her now?"

"Don't. It's late. She might be asleep."

"Okay, I'll call her in the morning then."

"No need. She'll know."

Daniel's hand rests awkwardly on my shoulder. It feels clumsy and heavy, but he doesn't dare put it round my waist. He isn't sure any more how to touch me.

"I'll come too," he says.

"No! No."

"It's all right, I can make the time. We've got a gig but I can call someone in to cover. The only thing is I was going to drive the van so it'll have to be someone with a licence. Only I'm the only one named on the insurance so... God, sorry, what am I talking about? I'll come with you."

"No, don't. You'd hate it."

"No, I'd like to. Jen, I feel like we haven't been – I mean, we need to – I think we need some time away. We need to relax. Get a break. I'll start calling round, get the van thing sorted."

"Daniel." I speak very slowly and clearly. "I don't want you to come with me. I want to go by myself. I'm going to pack now."

The train station at six thirty in the morning is surprisingly busy. Grey-faced commuters grab five minutes of half-sleep with their heads propped backwards against the waiting room wall. A couple with brimful rucksacks, orange jackets and bobble hats kiss discreetly in a corner over paper cups of herbal tea. The special scent of dust and diesel, hot coffee and sleepy travellers, tickles my nostrils and flips my stomach over. I'm six years old again, standing beside my father, who is an omnipotent giant and whose vast hand engulfs mine. He shows me the line I have to stand behind in case a passing train sucks me under its wheels. When I climb aboard, I glance into the drop to the track below and hold my breath in concentration. It would be a terrible thing if anything of mine – my foot or my shoe or my teddy, or even a sweet wrapper – were to fall into the gap and be lost.

Did Daniel ring Lily after all? I forgot to ask. She'll know I'm coming anyway. She's been calling me home all summer. Am I leaving Daniel? Is this what leaving feels like? He wanted to wave me off but I refused, afraid that he'd talk me out of going. Or am I making too much fuss? It's only a week away after all. The tears have arrived at last, and I stand behind the line on the platform and feel them pour down my face.

After a minute a hand touches my hand and – without making eye contact – a woman my mother's age puts a packet of tissues into my fingers, pats my wrist gently, then withdraws. I mop at my face until the train arrives, and climb on board with the packet clutched tightly in my hand. When my weeping stops as suddenly as it began, I still have three tissues left. Another thing I remember well about train stations; the extraordinary kindness of strangers. I lean my head against the window and surrender to the journey.

After the first change, I sleep until the guard shakes me awake and warns me my station's coming up and I need to change trains again. The platform is full of students in shabby black clothes, their hair dyed pink and blue and scarlet.

They're only a few years younger than me but I feel shy and conspicuous. Daniel would look at home among them, but not me.

Onto the final train, and I have to force myself to stay awake. The carriage is warm and soporific, and the rhythmic rocking is comforting. When I reluctantly leave my little nest, the hill that leads to Lily's house seems to have grown very tall.

She's waiting for me on the doorstep, a tall gaunt figure with her thick white hair pinned into its immaculate chignon. She looks as if the sun is shining through her, and I feel ashamed of running to her like this, as if I'm still a child and she's still young enough to bear my burdens for me, my unconquerable grandmother, the matriarch who is always strong and right.

"How was the train?" she asks, completely unsurprised by my unannounced arrival, and takes my case from me as if I'm still a six-year-old girl. "I've made chicken for dinner."

Beneath Lily's roof I find a blissful temporary shelter. I savour every minute of the time I spend with her, wrapped tight in the clinging embrace of nostalgia. Lily is so much easier to live with than Daniel. She resolutely resists all my attempts to contribute, treating me like the honoured, indulged guest I have always been, or perhaps like an invalid in need of extra nurturing. Little gifts – a box of chocolates, a bouquet of moonpenny daisies, a slim book of short stories that unfold in my mind for days, a bright lipstick, a green cotton dress that looks like nothing until I put it on – magically appear in my room. My favourite foods are stealthily posted into the oven before I can even think about lunch or dinner, and after our traditional tussle over the washing-up (the one battle she allows me to win) I'm eerily free of responsibility. I'm aware that the phone rings often and that letters arrive for me with every morning's post, but I can't hear the phone calls and choose not to read the letters. Instead I wander

194

dreamily around the garden and along the beach, drowning in memories. When the soft dusk descends, Lily – a roguish gleam in her eye – presses her house keys into my hand and shoos me out to enjoy myself. I go out to make her happy, but I quickly discover that it's fun to be out in the dark in a town where nobody knows you. Neither of us ever mentions Daniel.

It's only as my blissful timeless week closes that I briefly glimpse another reason why she may want to send me out every evening. I'm a little drunk with my shoes in my hand, and my stockinged feet slip on the steps as I tiptoe up.

I open Lily's door to the sense that someone else has been here. The kitchen is immaculate and the sofa cushions plump and undented, but there's an unfamiliar scent of soap in the air, a warmth greater than a single body would produce. Who was it? It's late, so late it's early, and Lily's friends never call round in the evenings anyway. They like to get home before dusk and close the curtains, put the chain on the door and seal themselves away from the gathering night. These days even Lily herself rarely ventures out after dark. She isn't in the sitting room. She isn't in the kitchen. She isn't in the bathroom. I creep down the corridor towards her bedroom. Her light's on.

Lily sits on the end of her bed, fully dressed but with her hair around her shoulders in a soft white cloud. Her back is straight and strong and her hands are folded in her lap. Her face is crumpled into an ugly howl. When she sees me, she holds out a hand to me.

"What? What? Please tell me."

She shakes her head. I sit beside her, feeling the tension vibrate through her. Then she puts her arms around me and begins to shake. I'm aware again of that clean, soapy scent. Someone else has been comforting her in my absence. Perhaps the sofa is unruffled because they were here in the bedroom.

"What is it?" I repeat.

She releases me, takes a deep breath and wipes the tears from her face. She takes my hands and holds them, then lets them go. This is it. The final breaking of the storm I've sensed for weeks. Perhaps Daniel's called her and told her he's left me. Perhaps this was what was written in all those unopened letters. No, I would have known this as soon as I touched the envelopes; they were heavy with longing, not rejection. And besides, Lily wouldn't weep for my loss of Daniel.

"It was his heart," she says at last. "His heart. It gave out. Just like—"

This is how I learn that, while I was out, Daniel called Lily's house and broke the news he'd received from my mother, that my father was found dead that afternoon.

Chapter Seventeen – Tuesday

Paging Daniel Webb. This is your early morning wake-up call xxxxx

What? What time is it? Is everything all right?

Everything's fine. It's early. Thought I'd make a start on things. Get things ready for the estate agent. Find out how rich we're going to be.

So how's the new material coming?

Not bad.

That means very bad. Come on, what's the matter?

Nothing's the matter.

Course there's something the matter, I can tell.

How do you ALWAYS manage to do that? Even from a distance? What did you dream?

That Daniel was shouting at a man who refused to look at him. In my dream, Daniel grew increasingly frustrated, grabbed him by the shoulders and shook him, then finally punched him in the face so hard that he broke his nose, but my dreams often contain an element of exaggeration.

Repeat after me: There Is No Such Thing As Second Sight. I just know you really well that's all :)

Now never mind about me. Tell me what's happening.

Creative differences.

This is what finished everything the last three times. The Average Gentlemen are now a cover band, renowned on the wedding and party circuit. Truth Before Fiction have dissolved into nothingness and gone back to their day jobs. The Rabid Horseflies took a plane to Los Angeles, changed their name, found a new frontman and signed a contract, after which Daniel refused to discuss them any further.

They want to play it so safe all the time. It does my head in. Why bother if you're not going to take a risk?

I'm seriously wondering if we've really got a future to be honest

Oh come on. You can't decide that because of one little row

It's not one little row it's one huge difference of opinion

I mean, if they don't love it the first time they're not going to love it the second or the third are they?

They might. Give them a chance, let them hear it a few times. Great art isn't meant to be easy. Right?

Yeah well, I expect better of them

I don't mind if the audience don't get it but your bandmates are supposed to have your back, not tear you down

All the best bands have massive rows. You're a genius and sometimes genius takes time to sink in. Call them again today and ask if you can talk about it, see what they say

I wish you were here Jen. You make everything all right when you're here

Please come home. Please. Just drop it all and come home. I need you so much. I'm lost without you

Oh God I'm so sorry. I wish I could but I can't

I feel like you've been away for ever. I don't think I can stand it much longer. I'm begging you. Get on the train and come back to me

You know I can't. It'll be worth it when we bank the cheque

You're so far away. It's like you've left me

Please don't say that, you know it's not true. Only a few more days I swear xxxxx

The high street is hot and full of fumes. Marianne and I dodge lost tourists and delivery vans to shelter in the air-conditioned offices of a series of estate agents, who seem harassed and disinclined to deal with us. Everyone speaks quickly and with frequent interruptions, and after a few minutes I lose my concentration and Marianne has to interpret for me. She always swears she doesn't mind, but I very much mind having to ask her. The tension makes me snippy and irritable, and when I see the effect this has on Marianne as she diligently struggles to translate *probate valuation* and *vacant possession*, I find it even harder. Eventually we manage to arrange for three someones from three separate agencies to come round that evening to inspect and put a price tag on my inheritance.

"What happens now?" Marianne asks. She looks tired and anxious.

"Let's go home."

"Back to Dad? We're finished?"

"Sorry, no, I didn't mean home, I meant back to Lily's."

"Not to the jewellers?"

Bundled roughly together and tied up in a handkerchief, Lily's rings make a heavy weight in the corner of my handbag.

"It'll keep."

"And the antiques person? Weren't we going to do that too?"

I remind myself that Marianne isn't arguing, she's only asking.

"One more day. We've done enough for now. Let's go home and cook something nice for lunch." Fat tears gather in the corners of Marianne's eyes. "What? What's the matter?"

"I don't want Dad to be mad," she says. "He wants you to hurry up and come home, he's really missing you and I don't want you to be in trouble for wasting time."

"For God's sake! Your dad is not going to be cross. We need to go home and clean anyway so it looks nice for the estate agent people. Now stop it, all right? Give me a smile." She forces the corners of her mouth upwards. "That's better. Let's roast a chicken, how about that? You love roast chicken."

"A whole chicken just for us? And it's not even Sunday?"

"The whole damn thing."

I can see she's still worried, but I don't have time to deal with Marianne's anxieties. I think through in my head how much longer we'll be here. Today we'll get the estate agent's valuation. Tomorrow I'll go to the jewellers, the day after the antiques man. That takes us to Thursday. Travelling on a Friday will kill us on the rail fare, especially as we haven't booked. I'll have to find out what the saving might be for advance booking. If it's a big enough number I could get a whole extra week out of it. Although I don't want to hang around another week, do I? Daniel needs me. We'll go home on Saturday whatever it costs us.

This decision made, I can march into the tiny supermarket and select a bag of potatoes, an assortment of vegetables, a bag of flour, a loaf of bread, eggs, milk, three different kinds of sugar and an outsized chicken with a clear conscience. Of course I've forgotten to bring shopping bags with me, so I pay fifteen pence for three flimsy carriers and pray they'll see us home. It's not looking promising; even as we hurry past the brief bewitching glimpse of the harbour, the handles are already beginning to stretch, cutting deep red grooves into my palms.

"Let me take them." Marianne, hovering like a hawk, makes a grab when I put the bags down for a minute.

"No, they're too heavy." I try to fend her off.

"It's okay, I'm not little any more. I can manage."

"No really, I'm fine – no, come on, give that back." Marianne dives beneath my arm and snatches up the heaviest bag that contains mostly potatoes. I have no idea why I wanted so many. Even if Daniel was with us, we'd never get through them all in one meal. "Marianne, put that down."

"Nope." She turns away so I can't see her face and sets off up the street at a walk so fast it's almost a run. I swear to myself, then pick up the other two bags and follow her.

By the time we reach the driveway, all the handles have given up and we're cradling the bags in our arms. When I put my burden down to scrabble in my handbag for my keys, three onions leap out and bound joyfully away down the steps. When I get back, to my surprised relief, the door's opening.

"Might have known it'd be you." James Moon shakes his head disapprovingly. "Suppose you left your keys."

"You make less sense every time I see you. Do you hang around that door all day waiting to open it? If you're not careful they'll put you in a home. And leave that shopping alone, it's not for you."

"Give over, you stupid woman. You been eating this bag? All in shreds. Disgraceful, charging five pence for it." He stumps off up the stairs, carrying my bag of vegetables cradled in his arms. He's surprisingly quick for his age.

"Can't let you in here, you stole my key. Don't know how you're going to manage. Door's like Fort Knox. Have to call a locksmith."

"Unlike you I'm not senile, so I have my key in my handbag, thank you. You just didn't give me enough time to find it."

He blinks. "Why'd you ring the doorbell then?"

"I rang it," says Marianne. "I thought it would be all right."

"Course it's all right." On a less military-looking face, I'd say his expression was indulgent. "Don't mind letting you in. Look at you. Strong wind would blow you away. Mother should be ashamed of herself, letting you carry this bag."

"Oh, you're right, I ruthlessly exploit her for my own personal gain," I say, and unlock the door. "We should have a contest, see which one they lock up first."

He passes the carrier over the threshold. "Suppose you're not going to say thank you for carrying this, are you?"

"I suppose if I ask you for a late lunch you'll turn me down, won't you? Do you like roast chicken?"

"Not my favourite. Prefer a nice rare piece of beef."

"Well, tough, because we're having chicken. It's Marianne's favourite. Come back in two hours."

"Might be busy, you know."

"Course you're not busy. Now go away and let me cook." I give him a little push so he steps back over the threshold, then shut the door in his face. I try to ignore the small smile that tugs at Marianne's lips.

When James Moon comes back, the flat is luxurious with the scent of roast chicken. Marianne has rummaged in a drawer and found Lily's damask tablecloth, a little musty but still white and beautiful. She also found a canteen containing Lily's heavy silver cutlery, but I put my foot down and said we were eating with the everyday stuff from the kitchen drawers. I've seen Lily clean silver, and I don't want my food laced with traces of appalling chemical cleaner. As a compromise, I've sent her into the garden to pick a few sprigs of geranium to replace the buddleia in Lily's silver bud vase. I'm in the kitchen when I see Marianne getting up to answer the door. I peek at the chicken, which is browning beautifully, turn the roast potatoes so they will brown evenly, poke the tender stems of broccoli with a fork, then wipe my hands and switch on the kettle. For once, I'm ready and waiting for him.

James has changed his shirt, and I'm pretty certain he's had a shave. He's carrying a bottle of white wine sweating with cold, holding it by the neck as if he might need to bash me over the head with it.

"Don't know if you drink at lunchtime," he says, by way of greeting.

"Depends how badly you behave. How about you? Do you drink at lunchtime?"

"Don't drink at all."

"Too old?"

"Learned better. Help yourself though, don't mind me."

The wine is Australian Chardonnay, the choice of a true teetotaller. I would have guessed he was a whiskey-lover. I decide I need my wits about me and stash the bottle in the fridge for later. James hovers in the kitchen doorway.

"What? I can't talk to you and cook, if you want something just say."

"Thought women were born multitaskers."

"Let me explain. Do you notice how you're standing over there? And how everything I'm cooking is over here? And I can't look at you and at what I'm doing at the same time? Do you see how that works? Go and talk to Marianne, she seems to like you for some reason. You've only got ten minutes to fill anyway."

I wonder if Lily tolerated him in the kitchen while she worked, or if she banished him to the sofa. Perhaps she gave him a job to do, laying the table or chopping vegetables. I should have thought of this, and saved up the task of putting out the cutlery. As it is, Marianne will have to look after him. I risk a quick peek into the sitting room. There's no sign of either of them. At least they're not sitting on the sofa in awkward silence. The chicken sits perfectly crisp and delicious in its Pyrex dish, slowly reabsorbing the juices that have trickled out. In a minute I'll pour the rest into the gravy. The roast potatoes are golden and crumbly, the broccoli tender. I've made a plate of little cakes to follow, miniature sponges filled with jam and cream.

Back in the other room, James and Marianne look conspiratorial at the dining table. I carry through the dishes, blinking away the steam. The chicken's so tender it falls off the bones. Marianne looks from James to me, and from me to James. James gives her the tiniest wink when he thinks I'm not looking. I say nothing, but pass the broccoli. After a minute, Marianne takes a tiny sliver of chicken from the edge of her plate and drops it to the floor. It seems we have an extra visitor.

The chicken disappears at satisfying speed. Both Marianne and James are on their best behaviour; there's no gravy spilled, no water glasses upset, no broccoli surreptitiously smuggled back into the dish. To my astonishment Marianne eats a potato, then two, then a third, and drops scraps of meat

204

down to the stowaway guest lurking by our feet. As I reach for the gravy jug, I feel something lithe and muscly press against my ankle. Then a tiny prickly paw dabs speculatively at my calf.

"Do you always bring your cat out to lunch with you?" I ask sweetly. James is caught off guard, but recovers quickly, taking the time to finish his mouthful before he answers.

"Don't take the cat anywhere. Does what it likes. Not my fault if you don't keep your windows shut." I see Marianne very visibly realising that she doesn't have to say anything to contradict him. "Put it out again if you don't like it."

"It's begging for chicken."

"Come here, Cat." He peels a long sliver of meat from the leg and holds it down beneath the table. "No point asking her for anything. Heart of stone."

"Behave yourself or you won't get a cake."

"See? Heart of stone." He holds down another chunk of meat. The cat takes it delicately from his fingers and retreats beneath the table. Marianne catches her breath.

"Oh! Will she eat out of your hand? Will she do that with me?"

"Eat out of Jack the Ripper's hand if he had chicken. Most food-minded cat I've ever known. Just hold it out, she'll take it."

"No, don't just hold it out, get a plate. I don't want chicken fat all over my carpet."

"Thought you weren't keeping it."

"I'm not. We're not. The estate agent's coming later. I don't want everything filthy."

"So you'll want the washing-up done? Bet you only asked me so you wouldn't have to." I start collecting the plates but he slaps my hands away. "Give over, woman. My job, not yours. Sit down and have a rest."

"We haven't had the cakes yet."

"Cakes aren't going anywhere. Have them in a bit when the pots are cleared."

"You need someone to dry."

"Little one can help."

"No, she can't."

"Of course I can," Marianne says.

"Come on, then." James gives her hair a friendly tug.

Bereft of anything productive to do, I sit down on the sofa. The cat jumps up next to me and curls up with her spine against my leg. When I stroke her side I feel the vibration of her purr. I'm replete with food. My eyes begin to close. I force them open again. I never sleep during the day. I don't have time.

It's the air, Lily tells me. It's very strong. Good for you. Margaret and I were the same when we first moved here. It's all right, have a nap if you want, you'll feel better for it.

The cat unrolls and stretches, then re-rolls around my hand so my fingers are buried in the warm fur of her belly. I feel as if I'm wearing a single, too-small, very warm glove. A single, too-small, very warm, vibrating glove with tickly whiskers. The most non-glove-like glove in the world. My eyes fall closed again. I force them back open.

Shhh, Lily says. It's all right.

"I can't go to sleep," I protest. "I've got too much to do."

It will all wait. There isn't as much to do as you think there is, you know.

"Lily, I need to ask you something. Was Margaret my real grandmother?" Lily smiles, but doesn't answer. "Are you my great-aunt?"

You're my darling girl, and you always have been.

"But is that why I always called you Lily and not Gran? What happened to the baby Margaret was having? Was that my dad? And who was my grandfather?"

Would it matter so much either way? Whatever happened was all over long ago. You're thinking about the past when what matters is the present. You've got a hard decision to make, my darling.

"I don't know what you mean."

You will soon. You're too tired to see it yet, that's all. Sleep on it, and you'll see it all makes sense in the end. She glances over her shoulder and grimaces. *Oh dear. You're going to be interrupted. Again. I never liked him, you know.*

Lily turns away and disappears, and in the space where she was standing, I see Daniel. He's looking straight at me. I can't read his expression. He's naked.

The shock jerks me awake. The cat, woken by my sudden movement, stands up and stretches sleepily, her back arching up into an impossible tight curve, then stretching out low and long. My phone buzzes in the pocket of my dress. I hold my thumb over the button, open the message, then turn it over and glance around hastily. Daniel has sent me a photograph.

I miss you my gorgeous sexy wife. This is how you make me feel

> *I miss you too, but PLEASE don't send things like that in the day! What if Marianne saw it?*

That's why you have a lock on your phone :) Come on, send me one back

> *I can't right now. I've got company*

What? No you haven't. You don't know anyone down there

> *I didn't mean company company, I've just got someone round*

If I crane my neck I can see into the kitchen. Marianne is laughing at something James has said. Her skin glows in the slow afternoon sunlight. They look like an advert for Werther's Original sweets.

The estate agent. I've got the estate agent here. He's looking round all the rooms, I can hardly clear off and leave him to it

What's he like? Is he good-looking?

Oh yeah. He's fat and middle-aged with a bald spot. Utterly lush

He'd better be. What's his name? I want to cyberstalk him. Make sure he's a fit person for my wife to be around

This is why you should never lie to your husband. It gets out of control so quickly.

I've forgotten, I've got three of them coming and I can't remember which one this is

He's good-looking isn't he

No he is NOT, come on Daniel, don't be ridiculous, please

Look I'll check his business card in a bit okay? I've got to go and talk to him, give me half an hour and I'll let you know

Anyway never mind all this how did it go with The Talk? Are you all speaking again?

Yeah we are actually

Mac rang this morning and apologised. Said he'd needed time to get used to it but now he liked it

See? I told you. You're a genius

Okay got to go talk later xxxxx

"Are you all right, Mum?" Suddenly, I'm surrounded by people. Marianne next to me, James Moon in front of me.

"Of course I am, why wouldn't I be?"

"You look stressed. Are you and Dad fighting?"

"Why on earth would you think... No, of course we're not fighting." I wish I could stop myself blushing.

"We did all the washing-up and put everything away and then Mr Moon cleaned the kitchen."

"You're wonderful," I tell her, smiling. Then I look reluctantly at James. "And I suppose you're not the very worst guest I've ever had."

"Not the worst cook either. Ought to ask you back, hadn't I?" He pats Marianne on the shoulder. "Show this one how manners work. No chance she'll learn it from you. How about Sunday?"

"I think we're leaving on Saturday," I say, surprised by how regretful this makes me feel. Marianne's face falls. "What? Don't you want to go home?"

"Yes, I do, it's just..."

"Just what? Dad's missing us, you know. He'll have some new stuff to play us when we get back."

"I know. I miss him too. Saturday's great. And new music as well! Brilliant. That's really cool."

I don't like the way James is watching us both. I think I've finished having him in the flat now. I pick up the cat, warm and sleepy, and hold it out to him.

"That my cue to go?" He stows her carefully away against his chest.

"Not quite as senile as you look, are you? Marianne, get him a cake."

"See you before you go, will I?"

"If you look."

Marianne hands him a napkin-wrapped cake, to juggle awkwardly along with his cat.

"I'll come and say goodbye," she promises. I suspect she's talking to the cat, but James Moon looks pleased.

"Make sure you get a good price," he tells me.

"Why do you care?"

"Might want to sell up myself one day. Don't want you under-pricing everything."

"I'll give that all the consideration it deserves."

"See you soon, then," he says. Before I can stop him, he puts out one arm, cake and cat and all, and gives Marianne a quick rough hug, then does the same to me. His cheek – bristly despite the extra shave – scrapes against my cheek and I feel his jaw work as he swallows. Then he's gone.

Marianne and I endure a parade of men in suits, one two three in quick succession, like the people who come out of clocks and weather houses. Their conclusions are both reassuringly similar and dizzyingly extravagant. I had no idea. I honestly had no idea. It's more money than I'd let myself consider. There'll be some inheritance tax, but the cash in the bank will cover that. All things considered, it's been a day of excess all round.

I should close it by filling in the figures on the form the solicitor gave me, but instead I rummage in the hallway cupboard and find the old Scrabble set. Marianne loves board games but Daniel can't bear them, so playing together across the mahogany table feels like a subversive treat. I offer Marianne double points to make up for the age difference, but she refuses, and then goes on to surprise me by giving me a thorough thrashing. She's no better than I am at using up difficult letters, but she has an uncanny talent for extending additional words onto a double- or triple-score square.

"Right," I say, sweeping the tiles away. "You won so you can choose supper. Anything you want."

"I don't know. What can we have?"

"I don't know. Soup, sandwiches, cheese on toast." She's not looking inspired. "Pizza. Takeaway."

"Takeaway? Really? Can we afford it?"

I remember the astonishing price named by the three wise men from the estate agencies. "I think we can run to it. I tell you what – let's get chip-shop fish, no chips, just fish, and eat them on the seafront."

Half an hour later we're sitting in one of the shelters lining the seafront walk, licking salty fat and ketchup from our fingers as the battered fish uncoils clean fragrant steam into the air. The scent takes me instantly back to the days when Lily sat here beside me, smiling at my pleasure in the free wooden fork that always seemed so mysteriously special to me. Lily herself brought a fork from home, wrapped in a napkin and tucked in her coat pocket. I tell Marianne about this and she laughs and chokes over her mouthful of batter.

"And I used to keep my forks," I confess. "I had a stash of them in a special box in my knicker drawer. They were too special to be used. I thought one day they'd be worth a lot of money for some reason."

"What happened to them?"

"I can't remember. I must have thrown them away. I kept them for years, though. I think I still had them when I went to university."

"This has been such a nice day," says Marianne.

"Has it?"

"Yes. We went into town and I got you all to myself, and I got to play with the cat and feed it bits of chicken, and we had someone nice come for lunch, and we played Scrabble, and now we're having supper by the sea."

I think about my own version of today, littered with undone tasks and smarmy sales people and small lies to my overanxious husband, and feel ashamed.

"Maybe we can come back here for a holiday. That might be nice."

Marianne looks at me shyly. "Or maybe you and me could

come by ourselves. I don't think Dad would like it much. He likes camping and festivals and things."

"But where would your dad be if he wasn't with us?"

"He could do the things he likes to do. I wouldn't want leave him on his own for ages or anything, he'd get lonely and wonder if we'd left him for ever," she adds, seeing my face. "But I think he'd be all right without us for a few days."

She makes Daniel sound so much like a dog in a boarding kennel that I find it hard to keep a straight face, so I tell her it's time to go home. We tidy our papers into the bin, ignoring the meaningful glares of the seagulls, and go home. Sleepy with sea air and food, Marianne barely protests when I send her to get ready for bed as soon as we walk in.

I pass the time while Marianne is in the bathroom by sitting by the window and gazing out at the view. A few months from now, perhaps no more than a few weeks, and this will no longer be Lily's house. When I close the door and carry my suitcase down the stairs, it will be for the last time. I will take no souvenirs, store no possessions to remind me of the past. Daniel and I will use the money to buy ourselves the kind of airy modern space we've always craved, and Lily will become a fading memory, only resurrected when a friend marvels at the luxury we've bought ourselves and we casually answer, "Oh yes, Jen had a rich old relative who died and left us the money..." We'll have the money and time for friends. Between my work and Daniel's, between raising Marianne and keeping our household together, the concept of socialising with others has fallen by the wayside. All of this should thrill me. So why do I feel so empty?

Perhaps it's the draught from the sitting room window. I go to close it, and find the cat has somehow found her way back in and is lurking behind the curtain to watch the birds.

"You're a nuisance," I tell her. "Yes. Nuisance." The cat stretches her neck and puts her nose delicately against my hand. "Never mind giving me kisses. You don't belong here."

Marianne appears and reaches for the cat in delight. I look at her severely. "You didn't let it in, did you?" I'm not serious, but she looks guilty. "You did let it in? Really? How?"

"She was meowing at the bathroom window. I think that must be how she used to get in and out. Can't she stay for a bit? She's so sweet." The cat rounds her head beneath Marianne's caressing hand and blinks smugly.

"Mr Moon might want his cat back."

"If we leave the window open she can go home when she wants to."

I should take her back downstairs, but instead I carry her into Marianne's room and drop her on the bed. She glares, then settles, right in the centre so she's taking up as much room as possible. Marianne crawls into bed, fitting herself awkwardly around the cat's tiny form. Her hand, brown and smooth, caresses her soft fur.

I kiss Marianne goodnight, tickle the cat behind her ears, then return to the living room. I thought I didn't want any mementos of Lily's house, but now the moment to leave is nearly here I can't bear to simply walk away.

There's so little room in our suitcases; whatever I choose will have to be small. The photograph album is too heavy and bulky, but I could take the photographs out. They'd be small and light, easy to tuck safely into our belongings. Will this be possible? I don't want to tear them. I'll practice on the one of James Moon. He's been unexpectedly enjoyable company, but I don't mind destroying his picture.

As I lift the photo delicately from its mounts, I find a rectangle of card hidden behind it, covered in tiny notations in different inks, a log kept over a period of several months:

I hereby certify this is a true and accurate record of what I have heard from the flat beneath my own owned by Mr James Moon and Mrs Ramona Moon, recorded from 11 June to _____. I confirm that I have also heard and observed similar incidents over a number of years. I am willing to testify to this in court. – Mrs Lilian Jane Pascoe

11 June – raised voices, something breaking

12 June – met in hall. Carrying chair, broken

28 June – Shouting (no words heard). Sobs

14 July – 'no, please, stop'

15 July – met in garden. Bruises on face and arm

16 July – more breaking things – 'please stop, I'm sorry' GETTING WORSE?

31 July – Nothing heard but met in garden. Bruises and cut next to right eye

11 August – Very loud shouting. Called police. Apparently both refused to open door. Police claim they can do nothing

12 August – Heard voices. Single awful scream. Later we met in garden. Saw burn on arm, curved triangle with dot marks – I believe from the iron

19 August – Very loud shouting. Called police. Refused access again.

20 August – Something crashing below, ornaments shaking. 'Please don't, please don't, no.' First time it has happened in the afternoon

24 August – Called police. No access. What more can they do? What use is this log if no one listens? No one escapes this without help. I have to act because no one else will.

Tomorrow I will bake a cake, I think.

I take a deep breath, hold it, let it out. Breathe in, then out, in and then out, counting to seven on the in-breaths, eleven on the out. I hide the card carefully between the pages of my notebook. I close the album and put it back on the shelf. I sit carefully back down on the sofa.

No wonder James warned me not to go prying into all Lily's secrets; no wonder he told me to throw everything away. I continue to sit, still and quiet, not moving, simply breathing. I don't want to disturb Marianne. I can't imagine how I could ever explain to her that James Moon, the man who showed her the warm current and bought her an ice cream, who sat at our table and ate our food, who brought his cat with him to make Marianne smile, once used to hit his wife so hard that Lily could hear her cries for mercy.

Chapter Eighteen - Lily

I sit in the bathroom of our flat, watching the wall. Sunshine filters in through the window, illuminating the cheery yellow paint. Perhaps it will help with the condensation, which accumulates whenever we use the shower. We're supposed to open the window to let the steam out, but the sharp crisp air pouring onto freshly washed skin is too much to bear. The nausea is still there, but I feel no panic, only a serene and infinite stillness. I've added one more huge decision to my existing store of huge decisions, but I don't feel weighed down. What I feel is a mysterious freedom. My father is dead. I am pregnant. I am filled to the brim with the powers of life and death, of flux and stasis. I could do anything. Anything. Anything. Or I could do nothing at all.

The train journey is bewildering for both me and Lily, but we cling to each other like shipwrecked sailors and make it through somehow. By the time our taxi finally arrives at my parents' house – now only my mother's – Lily's face is grey with exhaustion. My mother falls onto my neck as soon as she gets the door open, throwing me off balance, and by extension Lily, whose hand rests in the crook of my arm. My other grandmother, Esther, holds her arms out to Lily, which Lily accepts with rigid grace. As far as I know, they haven't seen each other since my parents' wedding.

Naturally my mother hasn't got my old bedroom ready for

Lily. I have to remind myself not to be cross about this. She's lost her husband; she's allowed to be however she wants. I run a bath for Lily, turn on the radiator, move the suitcases and toaster boxes off the bed, rummage in drawers and on top of wardrobes and in the airing cupboard, assembling enough bedding so Lily has somewhere to sleep. Meanwhile, my mother hovers in the background and fails to make anyone a cup of tea. I do this too, once I've laid out Lily's nightdress and wrap. I'd imagined she'd go straight to bed, but instead she comes downstairs, elegant and fragile in her green silk wrap and black velvet slippers, and joins me in the kitchen. When I turn around and find her standing there watching me, the sight is so incongruous I have to put the mugs down before I spill them.

In the sitting room, my mother's crying again. Esther tries helplessly to comfort her. I put mugs of tea into their hands, move papers off chairs so Lily and I have somewhere to sit, find my notebook and pen and wait.

"I'm so glad you're back," my mother says at last. "It's been awful trying to get everything done." The tissue she's clutching rips in two. "I had to talk to the coroner. Did you know that because of how he died, very suddenly and without seeing his doctor, they have to—"

From the corner of my eye, I see Lily's hand twitch in protest, a gesture of weakness that she covers by leaning forward and placing her mug carefully on the table. Esther strokes my mother's back. I don't want to think about my father's empty shell, peeled and hollowed on the cold table. "I know, it's all right, you told me. So what did they say?"

"It's appalling. We shouldn't have to deal with all of this."

"Yes, but Mum, they have to check. I mean, supposing one of us had—" I force myself to shut up. There's no possible point trying to explain. "Have they… I mean, are they done?" She nods. "Okay. So have we got the death certificate?"

My mother looks confused. "I think so. They gave me a lot of papers and said something about me going to see the registrar. I couldn't follow it all, Jen, it was so bewildering and I didn't have anyone to help me."

I see a brown envelope that looks promising. I'll have to go through everything in the morning.

"It's okay, we'll sort it out later. Have you rung the funeral director?"

Lily reaches for her mug of tea. She takes a careful sip, then replaces it and folds her hands in her lap.

"Well, I started to think about it, and then I didn't know which one to choose. I mean, how am I supposed to know which one's best? How am I supposed to decide? It's all so unfair, I never asked for this. I'm too young to have to cope with it."

"How about I pick one and you call them in the morning?"

She looks hopeful. "Could you call them?"

I stare at her in disbelief. She looks confused, then guilty. "Oh yes. I forgot."

How can anyone possibly forget that their own daughter is deaf?

I don't have time to be hurt. "Did Dad ever say what sort of funeral he wanted?" One of us has to hold everything together.

"No, he didn't." She looks at me reproachfully. "I do know he wouldn't have wanted me to be worried. I don't know if he had any money put away to pay for it. You can guarantee it'll be expensive. It's a disgrace, how expensive everything is. There should be a law."

"And did he have a will?"

"He made one years ago, when you were born. But I don't know if it's still any good. It was a long time ago, it might not be valid any more."

"Of course it's still… never mind. Where's it lodged?"

My mum looks mutinous. "I don't know what that means."

"Mum." I force myself to stay calm. "Who's got it?"

"I don't know. I don't know where half his papers are."

Lily leans slightly forward, reaches behind her and pulls

218

out a squashed, crumpled cushion, marked with bleach where a stain has been viciously attacked with the wrong sort of cleaner. She lays the cushion flat on her lap, plumping it so the stuffing is evenly distributed, neatening the tangled tassles, stroking the velvety pile into the right direction. The cushion, worn and battered as it is, transforms under her touch, a treasured heirloom rather than a scrumpled back support. As I watch her do this, I remember that this cushion is one of a pair, a long-ago Christmas present from Lily. When they arrived, the cushions were rich and splendid, and quite out of place. I have no idea what's happened to the other one.

"We don't need to worry about his other papers right now, just the will. Can you remember who drafted it?"

"We made them at the same time. They were mirror wills, I remember that. We made mirror wills."

"And who drew them up for you?"

"It was someone in the high street, I think…"

I force myself to keep sitting in my chair and taking deep breaths. I don't think I have the patience for this tonight.

"You're home." Daniel stumbles over the threshold to greet me, warm with sleep. "Oh, thank God, thank God. I've missed you so much. Come here." He hugs me tight, and leads me to the sofa. "Jen, how did you know?"

"How did I know what?"

"That your dad was going to… you know." There's something in his expression I can't quite read. "I knew there was something wrong. When you went away I thought you were leaving me. But you were only getting ready."

He's relieved. My father is dead and Daniel is relieved. I should explain to him that what he thinks of as prophetic dreams and magical insights are simply coincidences, but he hasn't listened the other million times, so why should he pay attention now?

"So how are they all?" he asks.

"My mum's losing the plot. She can't remember where anything is or what she's supposed to be doing. God only knows where my dad's will is."

"Leave her to it. It's not your problem."

"Of course it's my problem. She's got no idea, she's hopeless."

"Well, she'll have to pull herself together. Let her sort it out. God, you're gorgeous. I missed you so much. Come to bed, it's late." He shambles off to the bedroom, a simple unencumbered animal waiting for his mate.

Daniel has no idea what I've left behind me in my mother's living room. Which is worse? My mother's soggy spinelessness and apathetic refusal to take charge? Esther's barely concealed relief that her child, at least, has been spared? Or Lily's cold strong fury? Her capable hands, stroking the cushion as if it was a familiar crouching on her knee. It was a mistake to leave her there. If Lily decides to attack, my mother will be helpless against her.

How am I going to get us all through the next few days?

"Have you thought about music?" The undertaker looks from one face to another, unsure where to direct the question. My mother, the chief mourner but far from the chief decision-maker. Esther, handing tissues. Lily, tall and silent, unforgiving. Me with my notebook, making suggestions that become decisions that become my responsibility. We are, as my father used to say, a terrible houseful of women.

"Music?" My mother looks at me, then away again, then back at me.

"Mum, come on." I'm nauseous with exhaustion and too many cups of tea. "How on earth would I know?"

"Daniel. He'll know." My mother calls him in. She talks too fast for me to follow, but I understand anyway. She's passed everything she possibly can onto me, from the shape and fitments of my father's casket to the time the cars will arrive to take us to the church. Now she's passing on the choosing of the music to Daniel. Daniel looks at her with perplexity, as if he can't understand what she's asking or why. Then he shrugs, nods and disappears again.

Lily is watching me, her eyes bright and eloquent. She seems constantly on the verge of saying something, but whenever we're alone, she fails to speak. Instead she offers small gestures of practical affection – making bowls of soup and insisting I eat them, plying me with tea and ginger biscuits, whipping a comb from her sleeve to tidy the tangles of my hair away from my face. There's something on her mind, but she won't tell me what, and I don't have the time to ask.

Once, my mother comes into the room and catches Lily handing me a plate of freshly prepared cheese on toast. The toast is crisp and golden, the cheese gently bubbling with a thin scrape of tomato puree beneath. I've felt sick for days and have begun to suspect the reason, but the plate looks delicious. My mother looks at Lily with baffled fury.

"You need to take care of yourself," Lily tells me, carefully not looking at my mother.

In my mother's hallway, Lily stands straight and composed, her rose-painted lips pressed tightly together. I wonder why she's waiting here like this – the cars won't arrive for another half an hour – but when I go into the sitting room, I see my mother on the sofa, and I understand. Esther sits beside her, trying helplessly to comfort her. My mother holds her arms out and draws me into a damp embrace. I close my eyes and cradle my mother for a minute, then let go. She looks at me in surprise.

"Lily's on her own," I tell her.

"She could come in here if she wanted to. She's happier out there in the hall. You know what she's like. Stay here with me, Jen. I need you with me today."

Being indispensable is far uglier and more painful than I ever imagined.

Besides the long black limousine my father rides in, there are two more cars, swollen and sleek like well-fed cats. Each car will take three people only. Esther, or course, will ride with my mother. I have to make a choice.

Esther goes first. My mother follows, then turns and looks at me. Lily's hand remains on my arm. Behind Lily, Daniel holds the handbags and waits to be told what to do.

"Which car are you getting in?" he asks.

I feel like I've been fighting this battle my whole life. I am so tired.

"I don't know."

"Come on, Jen. Pick a car."

My mother's mouth trembles. My ears sing and my stomach's sour and unhappy, a gift from the little stranger nestled below. Does it have arms and legs yet? Can it move? I'm already convinced my baby will be a boy. There are too many women in my family. We need someone to even up the balance. I don't know what to do, about any of it.

Then, as she so often has, Lily saves me. She slips her hand from my arm and pats my shoulder.

"Go with your mother. I'll ride with Daniel. Don't worry." And as I look at her in weary disbelief that this awful contest could be resolved so easily and ask her with quick small gestures if she's sure, she adds, "I'll always love you best, remember?"

I climb into the spot beside my mother, who is trying to work the central seatbelt. I keep my eyes down so I don't have to see what she's saying, and rummage between the seats. Despite age and arthritis, Lily never has trouble with seatbelts. *I'll always love you best*. It's the first time I've heard this statement for what it really is: a declaration of war.

The church is unfamiliar and forbidding and almost everyone in it is a stranger. Are they neighbours? Friends? Did my father know them from work? Did he have a hobby I don't know about? Was he secretly a member of a swinger's club?

How little I know about my father's life. My mother's eyes are fixed fearfully on the doorway where shortly, my father will make his last entrance. Lily is beside me again, tense and trembling. On her other side, looking bored, is Daniel. When the coffin comes in, my mother collapses back into the pew and covers her face. I feel Lily take in a sharp gasp of breath and her hand fumbles for mine.

The undertaker asked if I wanted an interpreter for the service, but I have no desire to hear whatever bland nonsense my father's boss has cobbled together to share with the rest of the mourners. I look up the hymns and follow the words. Beside me Lily holds her head high and sings, not even glancing at the book. 'How Great Thou Art'. 'Nearer, My God, To Thee'. The floor thrums with the notes from the organ. The vicar speaks; the man in the dark blue suit who I only know as Mr Landsborough speaks; the vicar speaks again. Everyone closes their eyes and bows their heads to pray.

I put my hand across my roiling stomach to quiet it and gaze around at the congregation. My mother's hair has its first strands of grey. Esther's hair is all iron now, a thick helmet that looks strong enough to ward off anything. Do I want to join them in the tribe of motherhood? Can the rewards possibly be worth the pain? Shall I wait and see which of their traits my child inherits? Or shall I visit the doctor, take the pills and watch him dissolve and disappear?

Lily isn't praying either. She catches my eye, gives me a knowing secret smile and squeezes my hand. She has something she wants to say to me. I watch her fingers. *Life goes on.*

The grave is as simple and terrible as these things always are; a steep-sided claustrophobic space, the sides sliced smooth by the blade of the mechanical digger. My mother stumbles against me, clutching my arm hard enough to bruise. Esther glances guiltily towards Lily and I know what she's thinking. *Thank God it was her child and not mine. Not my daughter. Not my daughter. Never my daughter.* Lily's face is very white and her eyes are fixed on the coffin, but her step remains steady and firm, one foot and then the other, carrying her through space towards the place where she'll bid her son farewell. Daniel glances into the hole, winces, and turns away.

The vicar's vestments are white and clean. I've read the words in advance so I know what's being said. I wish my dad was here, standing next to my mum and possibly engaged in one of the many minor squalls that made up the fabric of their marriage. What would they bicker about? My father's choice of shoes. His driving on the way here. His failure to listen to her directions, thus making them late. Occasionally he'd retaliate by saying they were late because she took so long getting ready. Yes, that would have been a good argument. I wonder what their last words were to each other.

The coffin is lowered by four solemn-faced men in suits. The sturdy nylon straps are ugly and industrial against the polished wood. They step back, hands folded in front of them. My whole body shudders and I force myself to stand straight and true. Dying is part of living. One day I too will end my days in either earth or fire, but until then, it's my time, and while my time lasts I will live in the best way I can, making my own choices and accepting the consequences.

It's time to leave. Time to go to the pub-restaurant I chose, eat the buffet foods I selected from the mid-range menu, shake the hands of those who came to say goodbye, all while trying to hold my mother together, before taking her home and putting her to bed with a sleeping pill. *I can't sleep*, she tells me over and over, *I wake up in the night and stare at the ceiling and weep*. Then at four o'clock every afternoon she will declare, *It's no use, I can't fight it any longer. I've got to get some rest*. And she will swallow her pill with a mouthful of milk, leave the glass on her bedside table to turn sour and lumpy, and fall into a drugged stupor that will take her through to the hours when I've left and Esther and Lily are both softly asleep in the spare bedrooms.

I'd hoped the horror of my father's death might bring out the best in my mother. Instead she's taking her widowhood as permission to behave in the most childish, helpless way she can possibly manage, transferring all my father's responsibilities onto my shoulders and adding the wearing complexities of death into the bargain.

"Come on," I say to her, and take her arm. To my surprise, she resists. I tug again, trying to get her moving. She shakes her head and says something I can't catch.

"I didn't get that."

"I can't bear it," she repeats. "I can't, Jen. I can't go to that restaurant and eat food and talk to people, and be polite, and let them tell me all about how much they liked him and how sorry they are. I can't do it." She looks almost proud of herself, as if she's achieved something morally worthwhile. "Can you go for me, Jen? You can go. Just you and Lily and my mum, everyone will understand. I'll go home and have a rest. You can explain."

"Mum."

"Thank you, darling." She smiles tremulously.

"Mum, please, I – okay, yes. No problem. I'll go. How are you going to get home? We need both cars."

"I don't know. I'm so used to your father doing the driving. Oh, Jen, how am I going to do without him?"

"It's all right, it's all right, we'll sort something out." I look around for help but most of the guests have already left. Daniel is studying the names on the headstones. Esther is speaking to the undertaker. Does my mother have a mobile phone? And what are the chances of persuading her to make a call?

"Come with me, we'll find the vicar and—"

And then Lily's there, her face transformed with passion, her fingers sharp and witchy, her hair flying around her face as her chignon comes undone with the force of her rage, and all the words she's been holding back explode from her mouth like poisonous toads.

"Don't you dare." She slaps my mother hard across the face, then grabs her by the shoulders and shakes her. "Don't you dare put everything on Jen. You're a vampire, do you know that? You sucked all the life out of my son, all those years and years of running round after you, as if you were a child. He's in his grave because of you. You killed him. You drove him to his death."

My mother has a cut where Lily's diamond ring has caught the tender skin at the corner of her eye. A thin little line of blood runs down her cheek. She puts her hand up to her cheek.

"I've been watching you," Lily continues. She's signing as well as speaking now, but she doesn't need to. I'm getting every word. "You sit there in that house, day after day, letting Jen run around after you, doing your shopping, cooking your dinner, tidying your mess." She jabs a sharp finger into my mother's chest. My mother staggers backwards. "Making her organise her own father's funeral. What kind of mother are you? You never loved her properly, not since the day you found out she wouldn't ever hear again. You'd have got rid of her before she was born if you'd known that was coming, wouldn't you? You always resented her — "

"That's not true!" My mother's hands, helpless and grasping, stretch out towards me. "Jen, that's not true. I've never, ever, ever wished that. I love you. You're my darling girl. I don't know what I'd do without you, I couldn't manage without you, I need you so much. Jen, I promise that's not true."

"Of course it's true!" Lily's face is vengeful and triumphant. "*I don't know what I'd do without you.* You think that's love? Love is giving, not taking. You've never loved anyone in your entire useless life." She spins on her heel, driving the sharp little point deep into the grass. "Listen to me, Jen. She's going to ask you to come and live with her.

226

Only for a little while, she'll say. Only while she gets settled. Only while she learns to cope. And every day she'll tell you how much she loves you, how wonderful you are, what an amazing daughter you are, how she doesn't know what she'd do without you. *He* won't hang around." She points contemptuously in Daniel's direction. "Not that he's any sort of loss, you'd be better off without him. But there won't be another one. She won't let you. She won't let you have anyone. Not even your baby. You'll never have your child in your mother's house, Jen. You won't have the strength. She'll take everything from you, and she'll live a long time, vampires like her always do, and when she finally goes—"

"Stop it! Stop it! Stop it!" My mother's hands, feeble little fists, beat uselessly against Lily's arm. Lily looks at her in surprise. "You don't know anything about it, you horrible old witch. Jen loves me. Not you. Me. Of course she'll take care of me, she's my daughter, she won't mind. Will you, darling? Just for a little while. I looked after you while you were little, all those appointments and learning to sign and finding a special school and everything, it took everything I had but I did it, because I love you. And now you'll do the same for me. Won't you?"

"It's all right," Lily says. "I'll take care of you. Both of you."

I feel so weightless I might float off into the sky.

Then Daniel takes my hand.

"Did Lily say you're having a baby?"

"Yes," I whisper.

"And… are you?"

"Yes."

"Seriously?"

"Yes."

"You're pregnant?"

"Yes."

"Oh my God!" He's laughing. "Oh my God, that's so cool."

"It's not cool, it's a nightmare. We'll have to find a bigger flat. And I'll only get six months' maternity leave. And we'll never afford childcare."

"That's okay. You go back to work and I'll be a stay-at-home dad."

"What about your music?"

"It'll be fine, I'll fit it around the baby. I gig in the evenings anyway and you'll be at home then. We'll manage. And when it's older it can come too, and hang out backstage. Is it a girl or a boy? Do you know yet? Have you had one of those scans?"

"It's a boy," I say. "There are enough women in this family. Mum, I'll see you tomorrow. But I'm not coming to live with you."

As we leave the cemetery, I look back just once. My mother looks confused but triumphant, and I know she's relieved I didn't choose Lily. Lily's face streams with tears, but she's watching me every step of the way. As I go, she raises her hand in farewell. She's saying something to me, and even though I'm too far away to see it, I know what she's telling me. *I'll always love you best.* The words she always says when we part. And today, we're parting for the last time.

Chapter Nineteen – Wednesday

Morning favourite husband. Just so you know I'm thinking about you when you wake up xxxxxx

Blimey, you're up early. xxxxxxx

Says you. What's got you up at this hour?

Can't sleep properly without you. Feels like you've been away for about a million years

So how will you manage when you're off on a mega-tour of the world?

You'll come with me of course :)

How about you? Why are you up so early?

I've been awake most of the night. More accurately, I've been half awake most of the night, that uneasy hyper-vigilant state where even though I'm nominally at rest (lying down, eyes closed, body immobile), I'm alert for the smallest sign of danger. There is an ogre living downstairs, and he could creep into our home at any time.

Thought I'd get an early start. If I get a wriggle on we

might be on our way home on Saturday

Oh my God that's such good news. Can't wait to see you. I'll buy steak so we can celebrate

Hang on don't buy anything yet, I only said might. Depends if I can get the house clearer sorted.

I thought you'd booked that ages ago

Did I say this? I might well have.

I found one but he suddenly couldn't do it for three weeks. New one looks good though. Just need to sort that out, pick the estate agent, last bits of paperwork with the bank and we're there

You keep saying that but you're still not here. Can't you hand everything over to the estate agent and let them do it?

Of course I can't

I bet you could, there must be a way. People die all the time and their relatives don't end up living in other places for days on end sorting everything out. You're super-efficient, surely you ought to have it all sorted out by now. Stop messing about and come back home to me :)

That's a horrible thing to say. You can't put a smiley face on the end of it and pretend it's a joke. I don't actually want to be stuck here you know

I'm starting to think you do

You know that's not true

No I don't. Not when you're not here. Come home to me soon Jen. I miss you and I miss Marianne and I want you back here where you belong. Promise me you'll get on the train on Saturday no matter what happens

I can't promise, you know I can't

But I'll do my best

Please. Or I'll have to come and get you :)

I put my phone back under my pillow and lie down. The sharp point of a feather scratches my cheek. I fumble for it, pull it out then turn onto my side.

James Moon is charming, I'll give him that. He'd begun to slip under my defences, begun to convince me that beneath the crusty-old-man performance there was a worthwhile human being. But I of all people should know that *charming* isn't the same as *a good person*. My notebook's on the nightstand. I open it up and look again at Lily's true and accurate record. When did this happen? Was this during my lifetime? Marianne said James remembered me as a child, but he and Lily weren't friends then because his wife was still alive. *Please stop, I'm sorry. Burn mark on arm – I believe from the iron.* Did he beat her while I slept obliviously above him?

Maybe she got away before she died. *Tomorrow I will bake a cake, I think.* Maybe that's what Lily did; she helped James's wife escape. Battered women are notorious for standing by their terrible husbands, but Lily could talk anyone into anything. She would have gained admittance with a cake, and from that built a friendship, weaving her slow subtle magic, filling James Moon's wife with the strength and power she needed to finally break free. Maybe Mrs Moon's death is a fiction, and she's living somewhere else, gloriously free.

Or perhaps James simply beat her to death one night, then passed off her injuries as a fall down the stairs.

It must take effort and strength to kill another human being, but James would be strong enough. I think about how small the cat looked when he held it, how easily he lifted my bag of potatoes, how effortlessly his arms cut through the water as he swam with Marianne. So strong still, even though he's old. But then if he did that, how could Lily and he have become…?

My bed's too hot and I can't get comfortable. I close my eyes and try to sleep, but I can't make it happen. Thank God I took the key back from him on that first day. But perhaps it wasn't the only one he had. Perhaps he had a copy. Perhaps he's been back in here while Marianne and I have been out. Did I remember to lock the door and put the chain on last night? I must have remembered. I always remember. Except that first morning when I didn't. Maybe I did that again. I'd better check, just in case.

I crawl out from the tangle of sheets and blankets. Marianne's bedroom door is shut, so I can't peek in. I could open the door, but if I wake her, she'll feel compelled to get up too, and then we'll both be awake at a stupidly early hour. Besides, I'm clutching Lily's true and accurate record in one hand, and I don't want Marianne to see it and ask questions.

The chain's on the door, as I knew it would be. Still holding the true and accurate record, I take the chain off to make sure. Then I turn the heavy key in the lock. I'd remembered that too. Now it's time for me to put everything back the way it was, but it seems I'm not going to do that. I open the door and glide into the corridor.

The tabby cat that used to be Lily's is pacing up and down the hallway. When she sees me, her tail goes up and her little mouth opens to expose the ridged pink mouth and needly teeth. I reach down to pet her. She wipes her cheek against my finger, lets me stroke her once from head to tail, then

232

dances off down the stairs, her tail still sticking straight up like a signal. *Come with me.*

I'm wearing one of Lily's rings again. This time my sleeping self has chosen the inky square-cut sapphire framed with diamonds. The soft cotton of Lily's nightgown is cool and comforting against my skin. I wonder if the cat understands that Lily and I are two different people, or if she thinks Lily has somehow come back to her and is following her downstairs to join her in her new home.

At James Moon's front door, she pauses to stretch luxuriously on the doormat. Her toes splay out as she digs her claws deep into the rough fibres so she can properly unkink her spine. Then she looks expectantly at the door. She wants me to get it open, but I don't have to do what the cat wants. I could go back upstairs and no one would know I'd been here. The cat presses against my calf, letting me feel the vital warm vibration of her impatient purr. There's a lovely old brass doorknocker shaped like a lion with a ring in its mouth. It must weigh a lot. I slide my fingers around the thick brass ring and lift it experimentally, and then drop it again as the cat stretches imploringly up my leg and puts out her claws.

Well, that's done it. I could pick up my skirts and run for it, but I don't feel like running. I feel like waiting on the doorstep and picking up the cat with my free hand. She opens her mouth again when my hands go around her middle, but then resigns herself. Not all cats tolerate being picked up, but this one's more willing than most. Her pretty white bib is soft against my forearm and she stretches up her muzzle to give me a soft whiskery kiss on the underneath of my chin. Then she looks expectantly at the door. I take a deep breath and kiss the top of the cat's head for courage. James Moon opens his front door.

I see my resemblance to Lily reflected in his face, a combination of terror and delight that shakes my heart a little and makes me wonder if perhaps I'm wrong. Then he realises it's only me, the annoying woman from upstairs, and he rolls his eyes.

"What do you want? It's too early." He holds his arms out. "And I'll have my cat back as well, thank you."

"How can it be too early when you're dressed?" I demand, not surrendering the cat.

"I'm dressed. You're not. What's the matter with you? Coming out in your nightclothes like that. No sense of decency. Come back here, you little beast," he adds, addressing the cat with an outstretched finger. The cat touches her nose to him politely. Then she gives a neat little wriggle and jumps out of my arms, her body flowing in a smooth elegant curve. James bends stiffly so he can give in to her impetuous demands that he pet her. His gaze falls on the true and accurate record. His hand stops halfway down the cat's stripy back. After a minute he straightens up and looks at me wearily and I know from the resigned expression in his eyes that there's no mistake. He recognises what he's done.

His lips move as he mutters something, to me or to himself, I can't tell and I don't feel like asking. I look back at him and wait to see what happens next.

"Are you going to answer me, then?"

"I didn't hear what you said. Speak more clearly."

"I said, what did you expect? Told you not to go through all her things. Couldn't let it alone though, could you? Not surprising. You've been through everything else of hers. Couldn't even keep your hands off her clothes. It's your own stupid fault if you find out things you wish you hadn't." He goes back inside, but the front door remains open. I wonder whether it's wise or even safe to follow him, but then the cat pops back out for a minute and gives me such an incredulous stare that I find myself following it down the narrow entrance hall. James Moon is very tall and upright and his body blocks all the light.

In the sitting room, he points towards one of the chairs. I sit down in it, wondering if this is where Lily sat in her time.

His face has that expression again, the one that tells me he's both thrilled and haunted by my resemblance to the woman he loved. I grit my teeth and remind myself that love, like money, never made anyone a better person.

"Suppose you want to hear all about it," he says. "Haven't got the sense to let sleeping dogs lie. Well, just you remember, she's dead now, all right? She's dead and gone and there's nothing to be done. Want some tea or something? I don't have coffee. Never liked it."

"How dare you?"

"Not have coffee?" He looked genuinely confused.

"You make me sick. How dare you be so smug about it? *I can hear them through the floor.* That's what she said. How long did it go on for? How often?"

He shakes his head wearily. "Wasn't anyone's fault. It was the drink, you see. Terrible thing when it gets hold of you. If it wasn't for the drink we'd have got on well enough. Got worse when the boys grew up and we moved here. Thought we might be better with a smaller place. Less to worry about. Now you know why I don't—" He sees me looking at him, and his face turns an ugly shade of brick red. "Don't know why I'm explaining. Not your business, is it? It was a long time ago."

"So?"

"So you don't know what it was like. Different time."

"Oh, right. A time when it was okay for a man to beat his wife." The blankly innocent look on his face infuriates me. "Did she know you were sneaking upstairs to see Lily? Were you lovers while she was still alive? Did you kill her so you could be with Lily all the time?"

"Good God, I didn't... She wasn't well, all right? She died in hospital. Doctor came and everything."

"Shut up. I don't want to hear another word from you. I can't believe I let you talk to Marianne. Don't you dare come near her again, you hear me?"

That makes him flinch. What a strange and tender monster he is, this man my grandmother loved.

"And I'll tell you something else," I say. "Before we go, do you know what I'm going to do? I'm going to call the estate agent and tell them I want to rent out Lily's flat to students. I'm going to convert her bedroom to two smaller rooms, and put in a new bathroom with a decent shower, and then I'll find the dirtiest, skankiest, druggiest, noisiest students in the whole damn town. I'll give them a killer deal on the rent. I'll tell them they can have as many parties as they like. I'll fill the fridge with beer as a welcome present. I'll buy a bag of weed and leave it in the kitchen. I'll leave all her china for them to smash."

"No. Don't. Not for me, but for her. She'd have—"

"I know. She'd hate it. That's why I'm going to do it. I'll show both of you. I'll buy them a firepit. I'll tell them they can have barbecues in the garden. I'll tell them I'll give them a discount on their rent if they'll redecorate. I'll tell them they can stay for the summer without paying. And I'll keep doing that every year until the whole place is ruined and you've either moved out or died from all the disruption. I think that ought to make up for it, don't you? About time you had to listen to something unbearable through the floorboards." James flinches. I refuse to let myself feel bad. From his table of photographs, Lily's face beams up at me. Lily's face, and someone else's. "And where the hell did you get that?"

"What are you talking about now?"

"That baby picture of Marianne. Did you steal it from Lily? Why did you want it?"

"But... but that's... yes. You're right. I stole it. Souvenir. Stupid thing to do. Don't know what I was thinking. Let me keep it. Something to remember them both by. Please." His hand reaches out for the photograph. I move it out of reach. "I admit it. Admit everything. Now give it back and get out. Put it down. Please, Jen, I'm begging you to put that photograph down and stop rummaging and go away!"

I think he keeps talking, but I don't have time to listen any more. The baby in the photograph looks exactly like

Marianne, but she's wearing an outfit I never put her in: a little blue knitted cardigan and a matching blue bonnet. The photo has a yellowish cast that tells me it's old, and when I look more closely I can see the white border at the edge of the print. The baby in the picture is a boy, not a girl, and the table is covered with photographs of him as he grows. There he is as a chubby toddler, fat stumpy legs and cheerful smile, the resemblance to Marianne shrinking now but still visible in the shape of his chin and the curl of his hair. A sturdy boy sitting in a deep hole on the beach, his skin the golden olive that Marianne turns in the summer. A lanky teenager, shy and surly, offering as little of himself to the camera as possible. I nearly recognise him now, although I don't want to. For thirteen years I've lived with a comforting uncertainty, and I don't want the mystery put to rest.

And there he is, looking like a boy to me now although at the time we'd have said we were adults. Dark hair, dark eyes, dark skin. Spanish-looking, the way so many of the Cornish are. James's hand is slamming down the photograph as he did once before, only this time it's too late, I've seen what he didn't want me to see. He knew before I did. He tried to hide it from me. Why? I've threatened him with everything I have, I've told him exactly how I'm going to ruin his life, but his expression as he looks into my eyes is one of guilty tenderness.

"How did you—"

"Suspected as soon as I saw her. Looks exactly like him at that age. Well, like a girl version of him. Bit of you in there too, obviously."

I can't think of a thing to say.

"Thought I was going mad. Imagining things. Never even met you, as far as I knew. Then I remembered. That summer. Summer your father… you know. You were both down for a visit. Lily wanted to introduce you. Told her not to interfere. She said sometimes you had to. Thought I'd talked her out of it. Then I caught her stealing his hairbrush."

"He said he was staying with his granddad. That was you? You're Marianne's—"

He touches my cheek with a thick, clumsy finger. "He's out in New Zealand. Got married to a local girl. Got a baby on the way. He'll never find out. Not from me, anyway. Forget you ever saw anything. Don't cry. Not worth it. All a long time ago now. Her dad's her dad. Not just about genes."

"Don't talk to me. Don't look at me. Just... leave me alone."

He puts a hand on my shoulder to try and make me stay, but I shrug him off. Then I scurry out through the hallway, falling over the cat as I go, and race back up the stairs to the sanctuary of Lily's house, where Marianne still sleeps peacefully, not suspecting that the man who lives downstairs now has the key to the secret that could shatter our lives.

Chapter Twenty – Lily

I'm here at Lily's house, and in the slow lazy rhythm of late mornings and steep hills and clean sunshine, it's slowly dawning on me that I may have left my boyfriend. I keep this thought at the back of my brain and examine it in small glimpses, wondering when I might be ready to bring it into the light and look right into its ugly face.

If and when I finally find the courage to admit this, everything about my life – present and future – will have to change. So I put it off, hour by hour and day by day, and for a lot of the time I can pretend there's nothing wrong at all. I'm free, in the haven of my childhood. Lily presses me to go out into the fresh air. I visit the sea and find it's the same as it always is. My dreams are fragmented and meaningless.

My time here feels limitless, but in fact I have only a week. When I wake each morning, my sense of well-being dissolves into the knowledge that I have one day fewer to hide from choosing. In the fresh green morning sunlight I can withstand the letters from Daniel appearing on the doormat, but by mid-afternoon my strength is failing and I have to hide in my room and pretend to nap. When I cry, I muffle my face in my pillow. I don't want anyone with me as I grieve, not even Lily. I can't yet bear to admit that she was right.

Then I fall asleep, and dream I'm standing at my parents' kitchen sink, watching my father walk down the garden path in the rain; and it's afternoon, and then evening, and it feels like a new day.

"You should go out," Lily says, over dinner. "It's a beautiful night. Don't waste it."

The scent of evening is its own invitation, whispering through the open window and drawing me outside. I've slept all afternoon and now I'm filled with a restless disoriented energy. I shake my head, feeling guilty, but Lily's smile is as beguiling as ever, tempting me into the kind of mild wickedness she loves. I'm in my new green dress and halfway down the street before I can stop myself.

The whole world seems happily tipsy on sea air and cider. I normally dislike drinking alone with strangers, but tonight I plunge gladly into the warm press of bodies at the bar, waving my ten pound note to catch the barman's eye and finally receiving my reward of a brimming pint of pale bubbling gold. I carry it to the mantelpiece over the open fire, lit even though the pub's already unbearably hot. Around me, people cup their hands around their ears and mouth, *Sorry? What? Come again? Didn't get that?* at each other, which makes me feel I'm among friends.

At the other side of the fireplace, there's someone watching me. He catches my eye because he looks so entirely unlike Daniel. When I put my hand in the pocket of my dress, I find a polished rosy pebble.

"We're moving on. Want to come?" He has a nice face, a Cornish face, tanned and freckled, his whole self all tangled and unkempt as if he climbed out of the sea two hours ago. He's bought me a pint, laughing and pushing my arm away when I tried to return the favour. He's told me his name, which I forgot instantly, and now I'm hoping I can pick it up from someone else, or that that I'll make it through the evening without needing to know it at all. He likes me, in that easy holiday way I remember from before Daniel. We touch each other a lot as we talk, gentle friendly touches on

240

the arms, the hands, the shoulders. The night's still young.

'On' is a minibus crammed with, apparently, half the pub, shuddering with music that vibrates against my skull. The driver has sunglasses on even though it's dark, and steers us into the unknown with cool professionalism. I turn over the pebble in my pocket and think of ferrymen, of skeletons with dark robes and scythes, of that inevitable one-way journey we'll all make some day. Of what Daniel might do if I tell him I'm leaving. I think of the phrase, *you're a long time dead*. I have no idea where we're going.

The bus rocks and rolls around the tight country lanes and I wonder if we'll finish in a wall or a ditch, but suddenly we're in a field of mud where a large tent pulses with light. The ground throbs and my hand is in his. He offers me a pill. ('Nothing heavy, I promise. Good gear. We can split it, if you like.') I shake my head. He swallows the pill himself, and doesn't press me.

Inside the tent, reality dissolves into flashing lights and writhing bodies. The air presses against me in waves of sound. There's a bar, though most of its trade is in bottled water, and a thin man with giant earphones who has us all on a string. I hadn't known nights like this still existed and I'm charmed. We dance, laugh, point wildly in lieu of conversation. When we kiss, it feels like the logical outcome of everything that's gone before. He offers me a second pill, which I also refuse, and which he swallows with a single gulp of water. How will we get home? Or will we simply dance all night, then sleep where we drop?

As I'm wondering this, he takes my hand and leads me outside. It's normally me who calls time on the fun, dragging Daniel reluctantly away with the reminder that I, at least, have to be up for work in the morning, pushing his head off my shoulder as I drive us home, coaxing him up to our flat and our bathroom and our bed. It's strange to be with someone who's happy to take charge.

Outside it's very cold. In the dried mud beneath the

floodlights, he wraps me in his jacket and, perhaps forgetting that I passed on both the pills, insists on my drinking deeply from a bottle of water.

"I can't hear a thing," he says, laughing and pointing to his ears. "Deaf as a post now. Probably done some permanent damage."

An improvised taxi service is scooping up tired revellers. Young men who, in different circumstances, might have been at the rave with the rest of us, yawn and rub their eyes behind the wheels of battered but cherished first cars. We climb into the back seat of a Vauxhall Corsa and my companion passes a fistful of money to the boy in the baseball cap. He spins the wheels getting out of the mud, but once we're on the tarmac he seems competent enough. I close my eyes and accept the gentle kisses brushing across my face and neck. His skin feels cool and damp. When I lick my lips I taste sweat.

The car halts by the sea; we stumble down the beach. The tide's well down and the moon's painted a wide yellow path across the water. It's light enough to see each other, but dark enough to pretend we have privacy.

"Sorry I can't take you back to my place," he says, as his hands slide beneath my dress. "I'm staying with my granddad."

"And I'm at my grandmother's. Sorry."

"And I'm moving abroad soon."

"I—" I manage to swallow the potentially complicated truth that *I'm living with my boyfriend but I think I might have left him*. "Where are you going?"

"New Zealand."

"Good choice." I tug at his belt buckle and find the skin beneath his clothes, astounded by my own brazenness, without even the excuse of alcohol. "When do you leave?"

"Two days."

"So I'm your last hurrah?" I find I'm relieved. Whatever happens now, none of it will be quite real. "I'll make the most of you, then."

He looks at me seriously. "You're sure that's all right?"

"I'm sure."

It's more than all right. It's delicious and perfect and raw. I think it must be the shock of freedom that makes me so eager, as if someone's peeled off the thin film of reluctance that's smothered me for years. Or maybe it's the late hour, or the sea air. Maybe I've been fantastically lucky and the man I chose at random in the pub is a secret Casanova. I don't care. I think briefly of Daniel, but I don't feel even faintly guilty. The sand isn't as soft or as comfortable as it looks, but we're too far gone to mind.

His jacket and T-shirt are beneath my head and his jeans are around his ankles. My knickers have disappeared into the shingle. He gently resists my attempts to draw him closer to me. He's saying something to me but I can't make it out.

"I can't hear you," I tell him.

He turns me gently around so we can see each other in the moonlight.

"I said, is this all right to do?" he asks me.

"Is what all right?"

"I don't, you know, have anything with me."

"Doesn't matter," I lie. "I'm on the pill."

"That's fine then," he says with a smile, and these are the last words we say to each other as we lose ourselves and all our inhibitions, and the little speck that will one day become Marianne begins its slow journey to creation.

Afterwards, I doze briefly against his chest, then wake up feeling damp and chilly. While he sleeps I can study him as much as I want to. I wriggle back into my dress, steal his discarded jacket and wrap it around myself, then sit for a few minutes and consider him. He's shorter than Daniel, narrower across the shoulders, his skin browner, his eyelashes longer, his body hair denser. Do I like him more or less than Daniel? Irrelevant, since he's going to New Zealand.

He looks like a local boy. The kind of boy Lily has always

secretly hoped I'll marry one day. Perhaps she conjured him for me, out of a tangle of hair, a drop of seawater and a mandrake root. A boy for one night of wild joy and measureless freedom, who will dissolve into nothingness when the tide turns.

I could wait for him to wake, but I think it would spoil the moment to kiss a slow goodbye and then watch him leave me, stolen away by the land of the long white cloud. I'll leave him instead, and he'll be left wondering if he dreamed me. I'd like to keep his jacket, but I leave it beside him, with Lily's pebble tucked in one pocket.

None of this counts for anything, or has any connection to our lives together or our lives apart. It's simply something that happened. Whatever happens to us next, Daniel doesn't need to know about it.

I run back home barefoot, shoes in hand, too elated to feel the chill against my feet. When I get back to Lily's house, the storm will finally break and show me, not the end of me and Daniel, but the end of my father. But for now, in my last few moments of ignorance, I'm wildly happy.

Afterwards this all seems like something I made up, or perhaps dreamed many years ago. When Daniel looks at his arm next to Marianne's in the bath and exclaims over how dark she is compared to him, I laugh along with him, carefree and conscienceless, and marvel out loud at the mysteries that hide in our DNA, waiting for the right combination to spring the lock. When I look at Marianne, her spirally hair, her olive skin, her lean shape, the darkness of her eyes, I refuse to understand or to remember. Even on the day when, dreamy with oxytocin, I take a picture of Marianne and slide it into an envelope, add Lily's address, and drop it in the postbox, I refuse to let myself see what I'm really looking at.

For someone so dependent on her sense of sight, I'm remarkably good at not seeing.

Chapter Twenty-One – Wednesday

Being awake, alone, indoors, rapidly becomes unbearable. I pace from one room to another, checking the clock every thirty seconds. When Marianne finally appears, yawning, in her doorway, I chivvy her out of her pyjamas, into her clothes, then hover over her as she eats breakfast. She looks confused, but accepts my explanation that we have errands to run. Closing the front door behind us is a deep relief.

"So where are we going?" Marianne asks, trying to keep up with me.

"Estate agent."

"Not the house clearer?"

"I... no." Will I be able to rent Lily's house with what's in it now? Of course I can't; some of it at least will have to go. But what can I leave, and what must I throw away? My new plan is still half-formed and ill-considered. "Not today, anyway."

"Not today? But I thought we were going home on Saturday? Will we have time if we don't do it today?"

Maybe the rent will be enough to pay for our new house. Maybe I can mortgage Lily's house and use the rent to pay that mortgage, then spend what we borrow on our own home. That's an absurd and inefficient way to do it, but revenge is expensive. "We'll have time. Or we'll have to stay a few days extra after all."

"Or we could ask Mr Moon if he'd mind—"

"No."

"Just to let them in, not to be in charge or anything—"

"No." I'm sharper than I meant to be. She looks at me in bewilderment, trying to work out what she's done wrong. "Look, forget it. You don't have to worry about it, I'll sort it."

"Mum, we're going past the estate agent. Or was it the other one you wanted?"

I don't know which one. I'll have to start the whole process again, work out who will be the best choice for renting rather than selling. There'll be alterations to pay for, decorators to find, furniture to buy. And we don't have the money – only what Lily had in the bank, but we need that to pay the inheritance tax. This is all impossible, or at least it's impossible to sort out in the ninety-six hours I've allowed myself before I have to be on the train. Daniel won't tolerate me staying any longer, he's made that clear. Damn Lily and damn James and damn everything about this week. Why couldn't Lily leave her money to the local cat sanctuary?

Because I promised I'd always love you best, of course. What else would I do but leave it to you?

"Mum? Are we going in this one?"

"No, not this one."

I need more time to think. We had a plan, a plan to sell Lily's home and use the money to secure our future, but now I have a different plan. Except my plan is ridiculous, driven by nothing more rational than a desire for revenge on an old man who beat his wife, a woman I never met.

I could go to the police. But what would I say? *The old man who lives downstairs from my dead grandmother used to hit his wife, who is now apparently dead. My evidence is a list of dates and incidents from God knows when, with no names on, written by a woman who's also dead. I want you to do something about it even though you couldn't do anything then.* They'd laugh in my face. I need more time to work out what to do. Daniel. What am I going to tell Daniel?

"Are you all right, Mum?"

"Yes, I'm fine."

"You look worried. Can I help? I can translate if you're tired."

"No, it's fine, I'll manage. But thank you."

"So which estate agent are we going to?"

"We… oh, hang on." My phone's vibrating. "It's your dad. Let me see what he wants."

How's it going lovely wife? Nearly ready to come home?

I'm doing my best, I can't promise but I'm doing my best

So what have you been doing all morning?

Uncovering old secrets. Rattling the bones of the family skeletons. Wishing I'd never set eyes on James Moon.

Never mind me, tell me about you. What's new for you Mr Music Man?

Well since you ask, I have got some really cool news

Go on then

WE GOT A GIG AT THIS NEW FESTIVAL NEXT SPRING

Hey that's fantastic! Well done! Tell me about it!

Dorset, Easter weekend. Not costing us a bean, we get free tickets for the day and our lunch and dinner thrown in

Except there'll be the van hire and the insurance and the petrol down there and the petrol back and the beer and the tickets for the days they're not playing but that they'll want to be at anyway and he'll want Marianne and me to go with him.

That's really awesome! So proud!

Marianne's watching a dog down on the quay. The dog is losing its mind because it can see a seagull eating scraps from a discarded chip wrapper. With every morsel the seagull gulps down, the dog becomes more and more agitated, straining against its lead until it's barely anchored to the ground. Its owner, oblivious, is talking to her friend. She turns to look at me.

"Is Dad all right?"

"Of course he is, why wouldn't he be?"

"Is he angry?"

"No, he isn't angry, why would he be angry?"

Maybe now is a good time to tell him my new idea, while he's happy and excited about the festival. My phone vibrates again.

They sent me some details and it's going to be amazing. They're planning three stages, one for electronic, one for Indie and one for more mainstream stuff. We'll be on the Indie stage.

It's a chance to make some good contacts, get our names known.

AND Six Music might be there for some of it. I know I'm going on but really excited about this one, could be The Breakthrough!

Yep, it really could! Sounds like a really brilliant gig. Well done for getting asked

And I know it's not paid exactly, but it won't cost anything and it really is great exposure

Yes I know, it's brilliant! So proud

The only thing is you and Marianne won't be going for free

Of course we won't be. We never are. Marianne, lured by the dog and the seagull, has wandered onto the quayside and is now studying the blackboards.

"What have you found?" I ask.

"Boat trips. I don't want to go on one or anything, I'm only looking."

It's okay, we'll find the money somehow

??? We're rich now aren't we? Or we will be by next summer anyway :)

Yes but that's to build our house remember?

Oh come on, it won't cost that much. Festivals are dead cheap, everyone knows that

Not the way Daniel does festivals.

Well look we'll find the money whatever happens, okay?

Got to go. Estate agent visit looming xxxxx

xxxxxxx

I put my phone away, but I don't go back to the high street. Instead I stare at the board, still thinking about Daniel and the booking for the new festival. What must it be like to be him? Where does he find the dedication to keep on and on and on, relentlessly focused on his passion, never doubting the worth of what he does, no matter how many times his almost-breakthroughs come to nothing? How does he withstand the knowledge that he's barely made a penny from his music? Sometimes I forget that I'm proud of him.

The blackboard is filled with timetables. The regular ferry across the harbour. A pleasure cruise that takes you inland up the river. Fishing trips. Each one the promise of escape. I want so much to escape. If I could, I'd board a boat to South America right now, me and Marianne, and run away from everything, the paperwork and the secrets and the unmet obligations. We could start new lives in another land where nobody knows us.

"Let's do it," I say to Marianne.

"Let's do what? A boat trip? Really? But we have to—"

"No, we don't. Come on. One more day of fun."

"But Dad—"

"Dad won't mind." She's tempted, I can tell. "When will we be here again? It's now or never. Which trip do you fancy?"

She looks wildly around.

"Which one can we go on right now?"

"There's a ferry in ten minutes."

"But how long does it take? When do we have to be back?"

I'm giddy with the illusion of freedom. "Doesn't matter. We don't have to be anywhere. We can do whatever we want and stay out as late as we like."

"What about the house-clearing people? And the antiques man?"

"It'll keep." It won't keep. If we do this now there's no way we can go back on Saturday. But I don't care.

"Seriously?"

"Seriously."

Marianne thinks for a minute. I wonder what's going on

in her head, what mysterious calculation she's undertaking to decide if she can allow herself to give in. Then she puts her hand into mine and kisses my cheek. The baby softness is all gone now from her fingers. They're muscly and capable, the palm almost as big as mine. It can't be long now until the last time she'll take my hand for comfort. This could even be the last time.

The ferry is the only practical way to get between the towns that stare at each other across the harbour and it's filled, locals making room for the well-off tourists with their Mini-Bodened children. I sit beside Marianne in the prow, and think about the subtle signals that tell me who lives here and who's on holiday. The newness and the brightness of the waterproof coats. The endless performance of putting on and taking off layers. The elaborate choosing of where to sit, while the locals simply grab a corner, dogs and shopping bags lodged between their feet. Tourists and residents. I never belonged in either category. Instead I was a *visitor*, which doesn't sound too different from *tourist* but in fact made all the difference in the world.

"What are you staring at?" Marianne asks.

"Just the people."

"Which people? Those really loud ones in the corner with the bright yellow matching macs and the stupid dog that keeps trying to jump overboard?" I touch her hands warningly. "It's all right, Mum. They can't understand us."

"You never know."

"Your yellow macs look so stupid even your dog is trying to escape," Marianne says very slowly and deliberately. The father, oblivious, pulls his daughter's thick blonde plait and she jerks it away from him. "See?"

"It's still not very nice. Oh, all right then, yes, I was looking at them. I was thinking—"

"What?"

That Lily would have laughed at them too, and called

251

them Hooray Henrys or Weekend Sailors. She'd have said they'd end up drowned by the end of the season. She'd have hated their dog, too. She couldn't bear dogs that climbed all around people and jumped up with scratchy muddy paws. "They look like they'd be annoying to listen to."

"They are," says Marianne. "The big sister's mad because the little sister got a new outfit for her Bratz doll and the boy keeps standing on the dog and making it yelp. It's quite funny really. What do you think they're called?"

I glance discreetly over at the family and consider.

"The older daughter's called Incontinentia."

I don't think this is all that funny, but Marianne's face crumples with laughter. "Incontinentia? Is that even a name?"

"Course it's a real name, it's in a film. She was named after her great-great aunt who was the King's second cousin by marriage."

"Which king?"

"Any king. Don't interrupt. And you can't laugh either, you need to listen." Marianne straightens her face and looks at me expectantly. "And the second daughter, she's called Dalmatia, because when her mother was pregnant she had a pet Dalmatian that she was very, very fond of and when it died she had its pelt made into a little teeny small spotty baby outfit for her newborn baby, and the head was made into a baby hat. And the son's called—"

"Horsefly," says Marianne.

"Horsefly?"

"Yes, Horsefly. Because he's annoying and whiny and they don't like him but somehow they can't get rid of him."

I'm laughing too now. The father glances over at us, then away again, and I feel mean for laughing simply because they look rich and have matching yellow macs. Then he taps his son on the shoulder, pointing us out as an Interesting Spectacle, and suddenly I'm not sorry after all.

"The father," I say, "is called Bumface." Marianne is helpless with mirth, leaning against me for support. "Of course he tells everyone he's called Boom-Far-Say, but everyone knows really that it's Bumface. And his wife's called Stinkerbell."

"What about the dog?" Marianne manages between gulps of laughter.

"Oh, the dog's called Rover. A moment of clarity." Marianne collapses into my lap and lies there, twitching and gasping. "And… my work is done."

I try to remember when I last saw Marianne laugh with this kind of abandon. The older daughter's holding her sister's Bratz doll over the side. She's getting away with it because the mother's showing her little son the man in the wheelhouse, and the father's lost in his phone.

"You made me snort like a pig," Marianne says at last. "What's a moment of clarity?"

"When you suddenly realise how daft you've been and make a good decision for once."

"Did you come on this ferry when you were little?"

"Yes," I say, caught by surprise, and then lay my hands back down in my lap.

"And what's at the other side?" She looks at me anxiously, worried that she's ruined the moment. "I only want to know."

Blackberries. You walk out to the point and pick blackberries, bags and bags of them, and you bring them home and boil them up and strain them and make jelly. I can't tell her about this, it hurts too much. James Moon is a predator and I never want to see him again, but he's right about one thing. The past is a creature best left alone. Like the poor little dog who's crept away from the boy's oblivious feet and found damp, chilly sanctuary beneath a lifebuoy.

"A fishing town," I say. "Quite pretty."

"I like the colours of those macs," Marianne says. "Just not the people inside them. Do you think you could own a bright yellow mac and *not* be annoying? Your phone's going."

"Is it?" I'd thought the trembling against my leg was the vibration of the engine. "Thanks. Oh, it's your dad again."

Marianne sits up and takes herself discreetly off to the stern of the boat to watch the churning water. I straighten out my coat, take a deep breath and take out my phone.

I forgot to tell you, Jaz says Mel's coming to the festival and bringing the boys

That sounds nice

They're hiring a luxury yurt. I know it sounds a bit wanky but it looks great, you get your own toilet and a hot tub and real beds and a fridge for your beer

Glamping in action

If we get in quick we could book one too. Fifteen hundred for four days, what do you think?

I sigh and count to five, slowly.

You still there?????

It's just quite a lot of money for four days in a field

Oh come on, it's not four days in a field, it's four days in a yurt! It'll be fun. You need to learn to relax a bit, we're rich now

But we won't be for long at this rate, and if I rent Lily's place instead of selling it we won't be rich at all. Do I even dare to carry out the threat I made to James this morning? Daniel's instincts are razor-sharp. All it would take is one letter, one photograph, for him to see the truth. Would James do that to me? Of course he would. If I pushed him enough, he would.

Well we'll see, okay? Let me look at some figures and see what I can work out. Tell me about the festival. How long's your set? What time?

Not sure yet. We'll see. I'll text Jaz and Mel now, okay? Let them know we'll be camping out with them

Can we PLEASE hang on until tonight so I can check we've got the money?

Not a chance, the yurts'll sell out if we're not quick. Stop worrying so much!

Okay I've got to go out so I'll talk to you later okay? Give M a massive sloppy kiss from her dad xxxxxxxxxxxxxxxxxxx

I join Marianne at the stern of the boat and stare down into the churning indigo, the white froth around the propeller. A cloud is crossing the sun and there's a chill coming off the water.

"Was that Dad?" Marianne asks. "What did he want?"

"He was just checking in. Oh, and Storm Interference have been booked for a festival next year, isn't that cool?"

"Are we going to see him play?"

"Course we are."

"Camping?"

I make myself smile.

"Yep. Maybe a posh yurt. How does that sound?"

"Did you tell Dad what we're doing right now? The boat trip, I mean?"

I hesitate.

"I was thinking," she says. "Maybe we shouldn't tell Dad about going on the ferry. I don't mean lie to him or anything," she says, seeing the expression on my face. "I only mean maybe not mention it."

"Let's see how it goes," I say ambiguously.

"Well, I won't tell him anyway," says Marianne, and bends to stroke the little dog, which has crept out from beneath the lifebuoy and come to lean against her legs.

Hi gorgeous. Yurt all booked. They wanted a 20% deposit so I put it on the card.

Are you all right?

Okay I guess you're with the estate agent. Hope it's the bald fat ugly one, I don't want him stealing you away :) And hope you're getting a good price! Love you xxx

Marianne and I stand on a pebbly beach and throw stones into the water. A swan glides around the shallows, elegant and disapproving. Its wings make the perfect shape to hold flowers. I can picture it perfectly. Forget-me-nots and freesias, armloads of gypsophila, a scattering of long-stemmed roses bowed over by their own weight. I say this to Marianne, and she looks at the swan, then takes out her phone and snaps a picture, before kneeling to pick up a tiny yellow periwinkle. I prop myself against a hunk of rock and lose myself in the sight of my daughter, unselfconscious and forgetful, pottering quietly among the shingle.

"Be careful," I say automatically, even though the water's only a few inches deep. Across the harbour, the ferry powers through the water, making its way back to us. We should leave now, before I say or do something I'll regret.

The blackberries are ripe. Lily's face, smiling at me over the breakfast plates. *Shall we go and pick some? Or do you want to go to the beach instead?* As if there was ever any doubt about the answer. Jelly-making was like witchcraft to me. Each summer I would return with six jars of bramble jelly in my suitcase, which somehow always had more room in it when packed by Lily, despite the extras. While my mother fretted about whether we might have accidentally picked something poisonous, every morning until far into the autumn I would savour the sharp-sweet taste of brambles on my toast. Before I know what I'm doing I'm beside Marianne at the tideline, urging her to put her shoes back on.

"Where are we going?" She's confused but willing, hopping along beside me as she struggles to cram her foot back into her shoe.

"To the supermarket to buy carrier bags. And then you'll see."

"What about the ferry? Won't it go without us?"

"It runs twice an hour until late. We've got time."

"But what are we doing?"

"You'll see in a few minutes. What?"

"I like it when you're like this," Marianne says.

The blackberry bushes rear up like giants, blocking out the sea. The sun is baking hot on our heads and the scent of the ripening berries is lushly seductive, rich with sugar, its subtle smokiness conjuring the bonfires of the coming autumn. Armed with our clutch of plastic bags for life, we begin our harvest.

Blackberry-picking is addictive. The more you look, the more you see. First you pick off the easiest ones, and think, *right, that's this bit cleared out*. Then as you press forward into the yielding vines – prickly and resistant, but willing to let you in as long as you take it slowly – you find more and more berries within your reach. You want to go on and on and on, reaching for the highest, heaviest fruits, regretting each one that tumbles from your fingers. Marianne has never picked blackberries before but she takes to it instantly.

Working in a dreamy trance, oblivious to scratches, I pluck berry after berry and think that must be how it was for the prince who came for Briar Rose, facing the wall of tangled roses. Perhaps the heart of these bramble bushes holds their own sleeping princess. Suddenly the bushes shake and tremble, and when I look around I see Marianne tearing herself recklessly from the tangle, followed by a phalanx of wasps.

"They're chasing me," she says. "I think one of them stung me. Come away quick, they're chasing you too."

We make an undignified retreat across the grass. The wasps chase us for a few yards, then turn and disappear, their work apparently done. Marianne's finger is swelling, but she manages a heroic watery smile.

"I'm sorry." I cradle her hand remorsefully.

"No, it's fine, I don't mind." She wipes her nose absent-mindedly on the back of her hand. "They were just telling me those were their blackberries."

"You poor thing. We can walk back down and find a chemist, get some cream or something. What are you doing?"

"I saw the nest," she says. "It looked like a lampshade. How can insects build something like that? Come and look. They won't mind as long as we don't get too close."

I'm not sure I trust Marianne's assessment of the wasps' good nature, but I follow her back to the bushes and wait nervously, ready to drag her away if necessary, as she gently moves aside the heavy woody briars. And there it is, impossibly suspended from a heavy branch; an elegant creamy pendant, a city of busy workers, ruled not by a sleeping princess but a queen.

"It's beautiful," Marianne says. "I thought it would be ugly but it's lovely. How can something that lives in bins and stings people make something like that?"

"I don't know, but it's a good question. What are you doing?"

"Picking more blackberries. We don't have to go home yet, do we?"

"But doesn't your finger hurt?"

"I'm fine," says Marianne. "Let's get more."

We work our way along the rambling curve of the point, hardly feeling the weight of our bags. It's only when I reach a spot where the cliff has fallen and the bushes have not yet grown in to fill the newly exposed earth that I see the harbour and remember we have a ferry to catch.

"I think it's time to stop," I say out loud, tugging on Marianne's shirt. She emerges slowly and reluctantly, stopping to gather a last handful to drop into her brimming bag. She's a mess, her face and fingers stained purple, her arms and legs scratched and streaked with juice. From the expression on her face, I look even worse.

"We have to get the ferry," I tell her.

She looks longingly at the blackberries.

"Let's get a few more."

"No, no more. Look, we're already got pounds and pounds."

"Have we?" Marianne blinks. "So what do we do with them now?"

"We boil them, then strain them, then boil up the juice with sugar, and then we'll have bramble jelly."

"How much will it make? A whole jar?"

"Oh, loads more than that." I take the bags from her hands and weigh them. "Say about fifteen, twenty jars maybe?"

"Twenty jars? How long will that take?"

"We'll strain them overnight and make the jelly tomorrow morning."

"But how will we get it back home?"

"We'll take a few jars in our suitcase."

"But what about the rest?"

"I… oh."

Marianne's looking at me with an expression I can't quite read. Is she sad because all our hard work will be wasted?

"Maybe the people who buy Lily's house might like it," she says, and takes one of the bags from me to carry.

"Maybe they will," I say.

The blackberries drop thick juice from the corners of the bags. From a distance it must look as if we've killed and

259

butchered something. Marianne raises one of the bags above her head and lets it drip into her mouth, grimacing because it's not as sweet she expected, and across the road a man stops to watch her in shock. She looks like a wild warrior child, savouring the sweetness of her first kill. My chest aches with love.

You should see yourself, Lily says to me as we wait for the ferry. With clever, gentle fingers she teases a fragment of bramble from my hair.

Why? What do I look like?

You look beautiful, she says, with such gravity and firmness that when I shut myself in her bathroom and stare in bewilderment at the suntanned, purple-streaked, wild-eyed girl waiting for me in the mirror, for a second, I almost believe her.

"What?" Marianne asks me, licking juice from her lips and smiling. She has a blackberry seed trapped between her two front teeth. Perhaps this is her Happiest Day, the one I should preserve for ever and use to make a charm that will secure her a hundred happy days to come. I wish I'd found Lily's camera.

"You look beautiful," I tell her, and mean it.

Hand in hand, we run back to the end of the quay, where the ferryman is tying the boat up with a thick rope that trails acid-green weed from its lower reaches. On the way back, Marianne leans against my shoulder and unexpectedly falls asleep for a few minutes. Her eyelashes are so long they cast shadows on her cheeks. I think for a minute what it would be like if it was Daniel here and me back at home, a lost soul haunting a temporarily discarded shell. And we've spent the afternoon picking blackberries.

When we get off the ferry, I buy a postcard and a stamp from the souvenir shop and, holding my hand away from the pristine white surface to avoid smearing it with blackberry juice, scribble a message to Daniel. Perhaps we'll beat it home. Or perhaps not.

Darling husband,
We love you and we miss you and we can't wait to
come home to you
Jen xxx

I pass the pen to Marianne and she draws a fat arrow, then adds her own boisterous message:

This is true Dad! We want to be back with you! Lots of
love Marianne
xxxxxxxxxxxxxxxx

We drop it in the postbox on the way back to Lily's house. I have to stop myself from calling it 'home'.

From the bottom shelf of the pantry I take out the marmalade pan, huge and heavy like a cauldron. As Marianne soaks in the bath, the smoky scent of gently stewing blackberries fills the kitchen. It's a melancholy smell, because it reminds me of the end of the holidays and the train that waits at the bottom of the hill to take me back to reality. Sometimes, watching the rich black juice dripping from the jelly bag, I would feel weighed down by sadness, knowing the summer was nearly over. I'm a grown woman now, I have my own home to go to, and this time the journey will be filled with the excitement of knowing our future's finally beginning. The sadness is only because I'm tired and my head is full of memories. Or perhaps they're because I feel guilty, about taking a whole precious day to run away and pick blackberries, preserving fruit for a future that will never come because we'll be elsewhere.

Daniel is always telling me I need to relax and let the little things go. I stand in the kitchen and think about the row we almost had, about whether it's okay for Daniel to take jobs that only pay him in burgers and tickets to see other musicians, and whether we can afford a yurt rather than our usual second-hand family-sized tent. I think about the deceptions Marianne and I have practiced on him recently, deceptions meant to save his feelings. I wonder if lying to your husband about everything you've said and felt and done for nearly a week is one of the little things, or the big things.

Chapter Twenty-Two – Lily

I'm sixteen years old and it's raining, so I'm hiding out in the pantry. I've stolen half a packet of biscuits, several slices of ham, the long-haired cat (now rather old and battered) from down the road, a pair of nail scissors I found in the bathroom cabinet and Lily's hairbrush. Now I'm dividing my time between eating the biscuits and brushing the cat, which fell on the ham as if it hadn't been fed in months and is now reluctantly submitting to a good grooming. Its response to the hairbrush flip-flops between bliss and loathing, and I have to keep a close eye on it to make sure it doesn't scratch me in one of its periodic transitions to fury.

"You'll feel so much better when you're all finished," I tell the cat, as it grabs at the hairbrush and gnaws wildly on the handle. "No, that's my hairbrush. Give it back now. Thank you. No, no biting… no biting… that's it. Good cat. Good cat. Now keep still while I cut this lump out. That's it. Good, good cat." As its tangled coat grows smooth, the cat grows calmer, until it slowly collapses onto my feet, its paws padding at the air, claws sliding in and out, eyes half-closed.

The pantry door opens and Lily glances in. I swallow my mouthful of biscuit, hide the hairbrush behind the potatoes, sweep clots of fur behind me and wonder if I'm going to be in trouble, but the look on her face tells me she's just amused.

"I thought you'd be in here," she says. "Why do you like

it so much? I see that poor old cat's still on the go. Did it follow you?"

"I tried to shoo it away but it didn't work." What actually happened was that I ran down the road in the rain, scooped the cat from beneath its usual shrub and held it under my coat, where it obligingly stayed, warm and purring against me as I smuggled it inside.

Lily looks at the cat severely. "Have you been brushing it? It looks cleaner."

"They don't look after it properly," I say. "It was all knotty. Long-haired cats need brushing every day, they can't look after themselves. And it feels thin as well."

"So you cleaned it up?"

"Someone's got to. If I lived here, I'd steal it."

"You know, Jen, it's against the law to steal people's pets."

"Well, then it's a stupid law. Stupid laws should be broken."

"Wouldn't you worry about getting into trouble?"

I shrug. "I'd make sure I didn't get caught."

Lily laughs. "That's my girl. Can you pass me that little vase from the bottom shelf? No, not that one, the thin one. Thank you, my darling."

The cat, put out by Lily's arrival, trots out of the pantry. In the kitchen, Lily fills the vase with pansies. The water in the vase quivers slightly, and when I put my hand on the table I feel a tremor in the wood. *It's an old house*, Lily told me once. *Its bones creak. Don't worry, it's only a lorry passing outside*. The petals of the pansies tremble with raindrops. On the table beside the pansies, Lily's gardening gloves cradle a handful of spiny-looking things like conker shells.

"Don't touch those," Lily warns. "That wretched datura is growing thorn apples again. I don't want the birds eating the seeds."

"Would birds eat them if they're poisonous?"

"Of course they would. Have you ever seen a bird skull? They have barely any brain at all. There, that'll do nicely."

I follow Lily into the living room and watch her put the vase in front of the photograph of Margaret.

"It's her birthday," she explains, as naturally as if Margaret will be dropping by for afternoon tea and cake. The cat creeps under Lily's feet, begging to be noticed, and she bends down and ruffles up the fur along its cheek.

"What was she like?" I'm not all that interested, I'd rather be playing with the cat, but I sense Lily would like to say more.

"She was very sweet," Lily says. "And she always loved animals, especially cats, like you. I took this on her wedding day."

Margaret's soft dark hair and small face are framed with a white veil. She looks cripplingly shy.

"She was so sad when he died," Lily continues. "They weren't well suited I thought it might be a relief, but—" her fingers gently rearrange the pansies. "So I insisted she needed a new start, somewhere by the sea, where she could be happy again. We had to borrow to buy the hotel, and she was afraid it would fail. I bullied her into it really. And then we only had one summer before she died. I sometimes wonder—"

This startles me. I've never seen Lily be anything other than sure of herself.

"But she was happy? Once you'd moved, I mean?"

"Oh yes. She loved the sea. She walked down to look at it every single morning, even in the season. She'd get up extra early to see what it was doing before we had to start the breakfasts."

"So you were right, then, weren't you?"

"Was I? I don't know."

"Of course you were. She spent her last few months happy. It was the right thing."

"Do you think so? It must have been the right thing, mustn't it? If a person's heart is weak, it wouldn't make things worse to move somewhere new, would it?"

"I don't know," I say, because I don't know, and then,

"I mean, of course it wouldn't. It's like a..." I'm going to say *a bomb going off*, but manage to stop myself. "Like a clock running down, isn't it? They don't stop sooner because they're in a different room. In fact, maybe it even made her live longer because she was happier."

"Maybe it did." Lily looks heartened.

"Sometimes," I say, bolstered with all the confidence of a successful cat-kidnap and the invincibility of sixteen years of life, "you have to be a bit bossy and firm with people. Otherwise everyone talks about how awful things are but nobody gets round to sorting it out. You can't sit around and watch everyone be miserable when you know you could fix it for them. Somebody's got to be in charge."

Lily is looking at me with a curious intensity.

"My lovely granddaughter. When did you get to be so wise?"

I feel embarrassed, so I pretend I haven't seen her and instead bend down to stroke the cat, which has stretched itself out long and contented beneath the sideboard. As long as I'm here, I decide, I'll collect the cat every morning and bring it up here to brush it. Maybe its owners will be shamed into doing a better job of taking care of it.

Chapter Twenty-Three – Thursday

A second night of not-sleep. After three hours of staring blankly at the ceiling, I give up and crawl out of bed, throw on some clothes and, my heart hammering with guilt, creep downstairs and run down the road to the all-night supermarket. Leaving Marianne alone while she sleeps is another thing Daniel wouldn't like me doing, another item on my list of things I must remember not to mention. Halfway back up the hill, carrying what feels like my own body weight in sugar, I'm suddenly convinced Marianne has left her bed and stumbled, confused and frantic, down the stairs. But when I fling myself in through the front door, the hall is as peaceful as when I left it. Lily's front door is still closed. Marianne is fast asleep, cocooned in her sheet, the blankets crumpled in a heavy heap around her feet. From the warm space behind her knees, the tabby cat regards me with a suspicious gaze.

Radiant with exhaustion, I shut myself in the kitchen and ladle thick jugfuls of red-black juice with Lily's pint jug. I weigh out the sugar, a pound to a pint, and stir over a low heat until it dissolves. I turn the oven on low and fill it with Lily's store of jars, hoarded as carefully as if there's still a war on. My favourites were the ones that once held Roses Lime marmalade, because of their intricate shape. I turn up the gas, put two saucers in the fridge to cool, and skim off the foamy lilac scum that rises to the surface. I don't even know why I'm doing this, it's a ridiculous thing to do. What could anyone do with all this jelly?

That's what you said about the cake, says Lily. *And the cake got eaten, didn't it?*

But this is different, I tell her. I must look insane. Thank God there's no one here to see. *This is enough to last all year.*

That's the point, my darling. To make enough to last until next year. Remember to stir it. You don't want it to burn.

I turn back to the stove and stir around and around, tracing out crosses and shamrocks and figures of eight, enjoying the viscous weight that drags at my spoon. I take a saucer from the fridge, drop a teaspoon of liquid onto it and wait a moment for it to cool. When I push it with the spoon, it wrinkles. Encouraged, I dab at it with my finger, then shudder and wipe it off again. It looks like a clot of half-set blood.

How could you let James near you? I ask. *Was it…because you were… lonely? Was it my fault because I never came to see you after…?* Lily looks at me gravely. *Please. Tell me. I can't sleep until you tell me.*

You can't sleep, my darling, but that's not why. None of that matters now. You need to stop thinking about the past and concentrate on the future.

You keep saying that but I still don't know what you mean.

Don't worry. You will. That jelly's ready for pouring now. Her hand against my cheek is like a blessing. *And when it's done, you'll sleep.*

"You let the cat in last night," I say to Marianne as she stands in the kitchen doorway, and she looks at me with a sleepy, guilty smile. "It's all right. She can visit. As long as you don't feed her." Marianne yawns and mumbles something at the same time, stretching as she does so. "Speak English, girl."

"Would it count as feeding her if I gave her little bits of ham out of the fridge?"

"Why? Have you been giving her little bits of ham out of the fridge?"

"Maybe just once or twice. She looked so hopeful." Marianne strokes the cat's long back, not looking even faintly sorry. The kitchen still smells of boiled fruit and sugar. Twenty-one jars of slowly cooling bramble jelly are lined up on the worktop, as pretty as well-cut jewels. The fruits of insomnia.

My lack of sleep manifests as ravening hunger. I take eggs and bacon from the fridge and begin cooking an enormous breakfast. At some point today, Marianne is going to suggest that we take some of the jelly down to James Moon. What will I say when she asks? *Lily*, I think again, gnawing at the thought like a bone, *how could you?*

The smell of toast mingles with the sprinkles of hot fat from the frying bacon. Marianne looks into the pan with pleasure and rummages in the cutlery drawer for knives and forks. I'm already looking forward to the crisp salt of the bacon combined with the smooth oiliness of perfectly fried eggs.

The trick is to cook them slowly, Lily tells me over a long-ago breakfast in the alcove. I've just told her how different her fried eggs are to my mother's: undersides brown flecked with black, and raw-looking jelly on the top. *And you have to make sure the frying pan is really clean*, Lily adds, her face dreamy and innocent. My mother's pan was crusted with what she claimed was the non-stick coating. I slide two eggs onto Marianne's plate.

"Will you be busy today, Mum?"

"Why? Do you have a plan?"

"I was thinking I might go down to the beach. I'll go by myself, you don't need to come. And I can text you when I get there and when I'm coming back so you know I'm all right. And you could always ask Mr Moon to keep an eye on me. He swims every day so he's bound to be there."

"You really like him, don't you?"

"He's nice."

"He's the rudest man I've ever met."

"Yes, but he doesn't mean any of it. He's nice underneath it."

Can she possibly know, in some deep way, what he is to her? I think of how she is with Daniel's parents, patient and polite, as if being nice to them is a piece of homework she's been set. Adoring her, Daniel's parents try to bridge the distance between them with presents, days out, sleepovers. The last time Marianne saw them was for two nights in half-term. They took her to the cinema, then for dinner, and to a local zoo for an animal-encounter experience the next day. When they brought her home late on Thursday, she kept her bright delighted smile plastered to her face until the front door shut behind them. Then she leaned against me and I felt the deep breath go right through her body. "Gran and Grandpa are lovely," she said, "but, oh, Mum, it's *so* nice to be home again."

And now she sits opposite me at Lily's breakfast table, eating bacon and plotting how to spend time with an old man she met a week ago.

"Marianne. We need to talk about this."

"I'll be fine, I really will. I won't go in the sea if it's rough. And I'll wear my watch and I'll only stay in for the time you say I can. So if you say I've got to come out after ten minutes, I will, even if I'm not cold. It's waterproof and everything, I checked in the bath last night."

"It's not the water, sweetpea, it's… Mr Moon. I need to tell you something about him, and I'm trusting you to be sensible about it."

Her eyes are very dark and anxious as she watches me to see what I'm going to say.

"You see, I found something in Lily's things," I say slowly.

"I know he was Lily's… boyfriend? Is it still a boyfriend when you're old? It's all right, Mum, I think it's sweet."

"It's not that, chicken. It's… Look, you know he used to be married?"

"Oh. So he was cheating on his wife? With Lily?"

"Actually, it was worse than that. He – well, there's no easy way to say this, really – he used to hit his wife. Quite often. And very hard. Lily used to hear the screaming through the floor."

The room has turned very cold. I feel as if I've crushed something small and precious.

"But he's nice," Marianne falters.

"He might seem nice, but that's what Lily heard. She kept a sort of diary of it, she even called the police a few times. And… and I went to see him yesterday and I'm afraid he admitted it. I'm so sorry."

"But," Marianne says, "maybe it was a mistake? Sometimes people make mistakes, don't they? And they can be forgiven. And maybe his wife made him angry. Maybe she upset him and he couldn't help himself."

"Don't say that, Marianne. No one ever deserves to be hit by someone they love. Not ever, not for any reason. Do you understand me?"

"I'm sorry, Mum, I didn't mean to make you cross, I just—"

"It's all right, I'm not angry, I just want you to understand. This is really important. Are you listening? It's never all right. There's never an excuse."

"But—"

"No. No buts. That is never, ever okay. It doesn't matter what they say afterwards or how sorry they are. It's not okay."

"But, Mum—"

"But nothing. That's what he did. And that's why I don't want you spending any more time with him. Do you understand?"

"But he's nice," Marianne says again. "It might have been a mistake. And anyway, he doesn't have a wife any more. She died."

"We're not discussing this. Eat your bacon."

Marianne spears a large slice of crisp bacon as a tear rolls down her cheek.

Damn it, Lily, I think to myself. *What were you thinking?*

I invite Marianne to come into town with me, and then as an alternative I tell her she can go to the beach by herself, as long as she promises not to go swimming or to talk to Mr Moon. But she prefers to stay at home, reading quietly in her room and hoping for a visit from the cat. Her face is pale and reproachful. To my surprise, I'm as upset as she is. I'd begun to feel a reluctant tenderness towards James Moon, who loved Lily so much more successfully than I did. But no longer. There's no place in this world for a man who hits his wife.

I'm tired, and it takes me a while to make sense of the conversation with the estate agents. Eventually we all manage to understand that I'm still considering my options with regards to Mrs Pascoe's property and that yes, they do indeed have a lettings division, and they would be very willing to meet with me to talk further. Yes, I have a phone number, but they can't call me on it. Texts only. Why is that? I give the boy my best patient look, watch him turn crimson, then feel mean for teasing him.

Is there any way I could be wrong about James? Could there be a justification for what he did? I'm surprised by how badly I want to have made a mistake. We'd begun to build a friendship of sorts. An awkward spikey argumentative friendship, held together mostly by Marianne's earnest desire to steal his cat, but nonetheless, there was a connection there.

Some people are so charming they don't have to bother with being nice, Lily tells me. *Do you know anyone like that, my darling?*

I can't trust her any more. I always thought she was a good person, on the side of the victim not the bully. And now I find out her man friend was a wife beater, and yet she loved him anyway, welcoming him into her house and her life and maybe even into her bed.

But you don't understand, Lily says.

I turn away. I don't want to listen.

When I get back, the cat's asleep on the sofa with her paws over her eyes. Marianne sits beside her, idly stroking the tight curve of her head. I should put her out again, but I don't want to upset Marianne any more than I already have. She has dark shadows under her eyes and her gaze is troubled. Desperate for something to do, I go to the linen cupboard, then to Marianne's room to strip the sheets off the bed. Halfway through the job, I stop and stare down at the floor.

How did he do it? What precise form did his violence take? Did he chase her around the house and trap her? Did she cower, sobbing, in the corner of the room? Or was it more sudden and surprising than that? What excuse did he make? And when she died, was she angry for the waste of her life, or simply glad to escape?

Marianne appears by my side. I wave her away, but she's determined to help, lifting the mattress with all the force of her slim little frame, her ribcage heaving, so I can fold the sheet beneath it.

"It's all right," I say as soon as my hands are free. "I can manage."

"I need to learn, Mum. Let me help. Are these the right sheets? I thought bottom ones had sort of elastic in them."

"Most of them do, but Lily was old-fashioned. These sheets are probably older than I am. That's why they're so thick and heavy."

"And is that why there aren't any duvets? Just blankets?"

"We can buy a duvet if you want one," I say, remembering even as I speak that we'll be leaving in two days.

"It's all right. I like the blankets." She picks up the top sheet. "Wow. This is heavy. What do we do next?"

"Spread it out. No, the other way. It's longer than it is wide, you see? Pull it all the way to the top."

"But then I can't get in when I go to bed."

"You fold it over the blanket so it's not scratchy."

"Oh, I see. So, Mum, if you get into a fight at school with your friend and you hit them, is that the same as when two people who love each other hit each other?"

"No."

"Why not?"

"Because… well." The difference is so obvious, I can't explain it. "Okay, so, when you're at school you're still learning how to be a civilised person, so you get a pass on some things. But when you're a grown-up you know better. And you shouldn't hit someone you love. Not ever."

"Not even if they're really annoying you?"

"Are you really annoying sometimes?"

"Yes."

"How about me? Am I ever really annoying?"

"No, you're not."

"Course I am. And do I ever hit you? Do you ever hit me?"

"No!"

"Well, then."

I'm braced for more questions, but the next thing she asks me is whether she could make a roast chicken for dinner, 'all by myself, but with you watching in case I make any mistakes'. I agree instantly. It's extravagant and wasteful and means we'll have to go shopping again, but if eating roast chicken for the second time in three days will make Marianne happy, we'll do it.

The cat coils around our legs, twining and twining and opening her mouth in that pleading way that I secretly find adorable. Marianne, fussing over the last scrap of peel on a knobbly potato, stops what she's doing to look at the cat critically.

"This cat has the whiniest meow you ever heard," she says, picking her up. The cat gnaws ecstatically at her chin, tiny white claws flexing against the tender skin of Marianne's neck. "I still like her though."

"She's not biting, is she?"

"No, it's a lovey bite, not a bitey bite. Anyway, I wouldn't mind if she did bite, I'd still love her."

"Well, you should mind. You can't let her hurt you." Why do all our conversations today lead back to love and violence? "Maybe you should… no, never mind."

"What?"

I keep forgetting James Moon is no longer someone we can visit. It's hard to think of him as the slouching beast he really is.

"Don't worry about it. Put that cat down and we'll finish the potatoes."

"What happens if we don't finish the chicken tonight? Can I give it to the cat?"

"No, you can't. We can have it in sandwiches tomorrow."

I can tell from Marianne's expression that she's plotting a secret feast for the cat as soon as my back's turned. She's only known this little creature for a few days and already she's pouring all her soul into winning its ungrateful feline heart. I should have bought her a cat years ago. I'm a mean mother and a bad parent. I tap her on the shoulder to make her look at me.

"It's all right. You can give the cat some too. Just make sure there aren't any bones in it."

"Will Mr Moon be angry?"

"I hope so," I say before I can stop myself. "I'd like to make him as angry as I possibly can."

"But aren't you scared?"

"Why would I be scared?"

"Because he used to… you know."

Oh, yes. Why can't I get it into my head?

I move Marianne's curls away from her cheek so I can

kiss her, and she offers me a brief half-smile before returning to her potato, looking as if she's trying to kill it rather than simply peel its skin off. I look at the curve of her cheek, the shape of her chin, and most of all at the spirals of thick dark hair that fall around her face like the hair of a storybook princess, and feel a chill.

I could put students into Lily's flat, and take a long-overdue sisterly revenge on a violent man on behalf of a wronged woman. And in return, James has a secret that could destroy me. He promised me this morning he'd never say a word, but why would I trust his promises? Mutually assured destruction is as good a place as any to start bargaining.

The roast chicken is perfect, at least as good as the one I made for the three of us (four of us, counting the cat) two days ago. Marianne shreds her meat into strands and studies them critically, scraping off the gravy so she can see more clearly.

"Is it supposed to do this?"

"Do what?"

"Go into all little bits like this."

"Of course it is. It's delicious. Can't you taste how good it is?"

"But is it supposed to look like this? Or did I cook it wrong?"

"Even if you did it wouldn't matter – since it's the first one you've ever cooked – but as it happens, it's perfect."

"You helped, though," says Marianne. "You told me when to put it in and what time to take it out and when to put the potatoes on. I don't think I could remember by myself."

"Why would you need to?"

Marianne looks uneasy, as if I've caught her trying on my clothes. "Well, one day I won't live with you any more."

"But that's years away. You've got years to learn how to cook."

"But there's everything else," Marianne says, putting down her fork, so comical in her despair that I have to bite hard on my lip. "How to make the bed and how to clean the kitchen and how to make breakfast and how to pay the bills. *And* all my schoolwork as well. I don't know how you do it all."

"Well, for one thing I don't have to do your schoolwork as well."

"But you go to work."

"And I've got your dad to help."

"No, you haven't. He doesn't help at all."

"Marianne, that's rude."

"No, it's not. It's true. You do the housework."

"I do *my share* of the housework, when I get home. Your dad does his share while you're at school. You might not see it, but that doesn't mean it doesn't happen."

"But he—"

"That's enough." Marianne looks as if she might keep going, but I shake my head and point at her plate. "Eat your dinner. No? Okay, so how about pudding? Would you like chocolate pudding in a mug?"

"I don't want you to have to make anything for this dinner." Marianne's mouth quivers.

"You cooked the nicest dinner I've had for ages, and I'm not just saying that, I really mean it. And if I'm in the kitchen making pudding, then I can't possibly be in here seeing you feeding the cat, can I? How does it keep getting back in, anyway?"

"So I'm allowed to feed it?"

"No, but if I can't see you it doesn't count. Don't leave bits on the floor or we'll have mice."

"She could catch them."

"Or we could not have them in the first place. Anyway, we won't be here much longer. I know I keep saying it but we really are nearly finished now. And we can go back home to Dad."

"That's nice," says Marianne, without conviction.

"And maybe when we get back," I say slowly, "we can think about getting a cat of our own. *Maybe*," I add hastily, knowing how little Daniel wants the increased responsibility and loss of freedom that comes with a pet, "and we need to talk to Dad first, and I'm not promising. But we'll maybe look into it. Okay?"

"Or maybe we could keep this one," Marianne says, her face turned slightly away from me so she's almost talking to herself. "I like this one. She's got a black spot on her back sock."

It's late when I finally escape from Marianne. She's normally happy to be tidied away into her own space, quietly reading or drawing until she's ready to put out the light, but tonight she's uncharacteristically clingy, drawing me back again and again. Am I sure Mr Moon used to hit his wife? Is it really okay to not forgive him? But it wasn't us he hurt so shouldn't we be nice? Is hitting his wife as bad as murdering someone? But he didn't kill her? Or did he? Would I tell her if I thought he had killed her? How did I know he didn't? Question after difficult, unanswerable question, all with a generous helping of anxious brown eyes and pale cheeks. Eventually, at the end of my patience, I tell her sharply that it's time to stop, I'm not discussing this any longer, and turn away so I don't have to see her cry.

I take myself off to the sitting room where I find that the cat has, yet again, crept onto the sofa and curled up among the cushions, even though I put her out on the landing and sternly instructed her to go home. I prowl around and eventually discover that the top window in the bathroom is open, although how she managed to swarm up and through the gap is beyond me. I shut the window tightly, then go back to the sitting room, scoop her up around her muscly middle and hold her firmly against my chest.

"I'm taking the cat back," I say to Marianne, through the crack in her door. She nods quietly, turning her face away so

I won't see she's still crying. I'll have to apologise later, but first I have to go and talk, again, to James Moon.

Outside the flat, the cat stops wriggling and rests her chin on my arm so she can see where we're going. Perhaps she's hoping I'll take her downstairs and open the front door for her, but it's not going to happen. Tonight she has a job to do. She's my thin excuse for paying a visit to James.

He opens the door before I even knock, which annoys me.

"Heard the cat," he says in explanation. "Got a meow on her like a sobbing baby, that one. Goes right through you. Can't ignore it. Well, I suppose you can. No offence meant."

"Please stop talking." I hand him the cat, who scrabbles up over his shoulder and disappears inside. "I'm not trying to steal her, she keeps—"

"Coming in. I know. Gets in through the bathroom window. Seen her do it. I suppose you want to come in."

"That's putting it a bit strongly."

"Wish you'd stop acting like I'm the enemy."

"Well, I wish… I wish…" To my horror, there's a hitch in my throat. This isn't what I meant. I want to be tall and righteous, clutching what I know about him as my shield against what he knows about me. I want to be made of steel, of cold iron, or maybe piercing glass. I want to be cold and pure, ready to strike a bargain with the devil. And now my nose is full of snot and my face is getting red and James Moon waves a huge handkerchief that looks like a sign of surrender but is actually a victory flag. I snatch it from him and follow him inside.

"Here." In the sitting room James gestures towards one chair and begins to lower himself into another that stands in front of the lamp. "Sit there and we can talk."

"That doesn't work for me. Give me your chair and you have that one."

"What's the matter with you now?"

"If you sit with your back to the light I won't be able to hear what you're saying."

"You sure you're not making this up? Playing on it to annoy me?"

"I've got better things to do than make up problems I don't have to annoy you." My brain knows what he is but my heart won't feel it. We were sort-of friends, and now we're not, and I can't get used to it. I take the seat by the lamp, wondering if my face is as inscrutable to him as his would have been to me.

"Meant what I said," he says, before I can speak. "Won't say a word. You're not the first to pull that trick. Won't be the last either. Probably a couple more cuckoos in her class who don't know it. None of my business. Doubt your husband would listen anyway. No one your age has time for anyone my age." He shrugs. "There. Said my piece. Now you can say yours."

"Stop being so bloody nice. It won't work. I still know what you did."

"What are you talking about, what did I? Oh, that."

"I suppose you think *that's* none of *my* business," I say. "But for the record, you make me sick. I can't believe I ever spent time with you. I can't believe I let my daughter come into your home."

He stares at me defiantly. He doesn't look ashamed. Instead he looks as if he's enduring my rudeness for some private but noble reason of his own. Why is he letting me speak to him like this? He's been far nicer to me than I've been to him. How could this gentle, forbearing man have attacked his wife so savagely that Lily could hear it through the floor? Tears gather in my throat again. I hope he can't see. Did he ever hit Lily? Surely she wouldn't have allowed it. But what if he did? What if she spent her last years in terror? James stands up and reaches over me. He takes his handkerchief from where I've stuffed it down the side of the chair, careful to keep a respectful distance, and puts it back into my hand.

"Wash it before you give it back," he tells me. "Don't

want your snot all over my clothes. Disgusting."

"You blow your nose and keep it in your pocket all day, and you think I'm disgusting?"

"Better for the environment."

"Tissues are biodegradable."

"Mucky old process to make them though. Ever seen the mess that comes out of a paper mill? Come on, woman, say what you came here to say. Got better things to do than watch you sob into your hanky."

"You mean, your hanky."

"Stop being pernickety."

"How could you do it? Tell me."

"Thought you wanted to talk about those students you're going to put into Lily's flat to drive me mad. Want me to beg you not to?"

"Of course I'm not going to let the bloody flat to bloody students, you stupid old man. I only want to know why you did it. I thought you were a nice person."

"Course you didn't think I was a nice person!" He's trying to look angry, but instead he looks hunted. I suddenly have the scent of blood in my nostrils. "Stop trying to butter me up. Glad to hear about the students. Now go home and leave me in peace."

"No, I won't. Tell me. Tell me." I stand up and now he's the one cringing as if he thinks I might attack him. I loom over him, trying to be as imposing as I possibly can. "Tell me! I don't even care about you, I want to know about Lily! Did you hit her too?"

"What? No!"

"So what did you do? What did you do to make her like you? She hated bullies, all her life she hated them. So why would she like you?" I clench my hands into fists. "Tell me!"

He sits up straight and yells something into my face, but his face is so distorted with emotion that I can't make sense of it. Then he shuts his eyes and turns his face away. He looks pale and exhausted.

"I didn't get that."

"Don't be stupid."

"I'm not being stupid. Tell me again."

"I said," he repeats, looking right into my face and moving his lips slowly and with great care, "you got it the wrong way round. That clear enough for you?"

"What do you mean, I got it the wrong way round?"

"It was the drink," he says, and swallows hard and rubs fiercely at the end of his nose with the back of his hand. "The drink. Not her. She wasn't happy. Drink made her feel better. Then it made her angry. Couldn't let her do it in public, shouting and threatening to... the boys would have died of shame. Seemed easier to stay with her. Let her take it out on me. She was always sorry afterwards."

I feel the click in my head as I finally understand what should have been obvious all along.

"So why didn't you tell anyone?"

He glares at me.

"Why doesn't anyone tell anyone? No one's business but ours. Besides, it was never serious. Could get worse falling down the stairs."

"But why did you let me believe—"

"Because I was ashamed!" He's yelling at me now, his face red and angry. "I was bloody well embarrassed, all right? What kind of a man gets hit by a woman? Should have been able to stop her."

"So why couldn't you?"

"Well, I'd have flattened her, wouldn't I," he says, as if this is obvious. "Only a little thing. Not even your height. Couldn't hurt her."

"But you let her hurt you."

"I could take it. She couldn't. She was unhappy. Couldn't fix it for her, so the least I could do was... all right? Got your pound of flesh now?"

"But," I say slowly, "why did you tell me not to go through Lily's things? Why did it matter if I found out?"

"Not discussing it," he says, and waves an imperious hand. "Take the cat with you, if you like. She likes your daughter better than me anyway."

"You mean, your granddaughter."

A tiny smile crosses his face.

"Little monkey she is. Glad I've met her. But I'm not her grandfather, not really. Just some old fool who lives downstairs and shares a few chromosomes."

The cat's waiting by the door, but I refuse to be moved by her luminous green eyes or the softness of her fur as she comes back presses against my leg. I get up, shoo her back inside the room and close the door on her pink little meow of outrage, pressing my hand against the latch so I can feel the click as it closes.

It's a relief to be here in the cool of the stairwell. I take the climb slowly, relishing the familiar shapes of the steps. The fifth from the bottom has an inclusion that's remained hard and rough over the long years of use – not enough to hurt, just enough to feel different and interesting when I scrunch my toes around it. The third step from the top slopes down and back, threatening to tip you backwards into space. The coil of the bannister as I reach the landing is as fat and satisfying as ever. All these things are home to me.

The flat smells comfortingly of chicken. I need to pick the meat off the bones and put it in the fridge. But first I have to talk to Marianne, who hovers like a wraith in the doorway of her room, her too-short pyjama bottoms clinging around her calves and her cloudy hair tumbled about her face.

"Mum," she says. "I need you to listen."

"What's the matter? You should be asleep, it's getting late—"

"Mum! Shut up!"

The sharp imperious gesture is so unexpected that I'm shocked into silence.

"You need to listen, okay? And you can't talk until I've finished. That's the rule. All right?"

"What?"

"Are you going to keep the rule?"

"Marianne—"

"Shush! Are you going to keep the rule?"

I nod.

"Okay. So, Mum." Her hands very careful and deliberate. "You need to leave Dad."

I begin to speak, but she shakes her head and pushes my hands back down.

"No. You promised you'd listen. You need to leave him. You stay here. You'll be safe here. I'll go home on my own. I'll keep an eye on him, we'll be all right. I'll come and see you every other weekend. And all the holidays." Her hands tremble. It's costing her everything she has to say these words. I try to take her into my arms but she won't have it. "No, stop, you promised! I'll be fine, I promise, he won't hurt me, he never has, it's only you he does it to. You said yourself you shouldn't hit someone you love, not ever. So you have to stay here. And then he can't do it any more." She takes a deep breath. "All right, that's it, I've finished talking now."

"Marianne, my darling. What are you talking about? Your dad has never, ever—"

"Yes, he does! I know he does! Stop lying! You try and hide it from me but I know he does, okay? I'm not a little kid any more. I know you don't fall down stairs and walk into cupboards."

"I – that's really what – you sleepwalk, you see things, you know that."

"It's not okay for him to hit you," Marianne repeats, and although she's trembling, I can feel the inexorable strength in her. "Maybe Lily knew and that's why she left you this place. So you'd have somewhere to go. I think she wanted you to come home."

Chapter Twenty-Four - Daniel

The first time it happens is when Marianne is about eighteen months old. I've spent the day in London in a succession of tedious Head Office meetings, which are somehow going to enhance my skillset and allow me to progress in my career. (Somehow.) I could have stayed overnight, they were willing to pay for it, but I've chosen to come home. I've scurried across London and bullied my way into crowded Tube cars and shouldered fellow passengers out of the way to make the earlier train, which gets me home just in time to put Marianne to bed. Her little face as she sees me come through the door is the one golden moment in the day.

I kiss Daniel's face, which is smudged with tiredness. I peel Marianne's grimy T-shirt off over her head, and watch her stump around the bathroom on chubby legs, bending over to inspect the toilet brush, various scraps of tissue and the discarded plastic shell that once held a contact lens. I wash my hands before I put her in her bath, watching her splash busily about, pouring water from cup to cup. Bath. Teeth. Pyjamas. Story. Kisses. Nightlight. More kisses. A drink of water. Still more kisses. A stealthy descent down the stairs, to where the adults live. Daniel is slumped on the sofa with his eyes closed.

"What do you want for dinner?" I ask, meaning, *Have you bothered to make any dinner, or have you left it to me, as usual?* The things I say to Daniel increasingly come with a dissatisfied subtext. *How many nappies have we got left? Are there any potatoes? Does Marianne's bag need packing for playgroup?*

"I haven't really thought about it," he replies, giving me a smile that's meant to make up for this. Normally it's enough to calm me down. Normally I smile back and sort it out. Normally I'm not this angry. I stamp into the kitchen, opening and shutting cupboard doors, trying to assemble the bare makings of a meal for two. Frozen sausages. An elderly onion. Tinned tomatoes, tinned kidney beans. Sausage casserole it is. Herbs. Garlic. Do we have enough bread? Of course we bloody don't.

"We need more bread," I shout to Daniel, without bothering to go into the sitting room. He hates it when I do this because if he wants to reply, he has to get up to come and talk to me. I'm aware that I'm being rude. I don't care. He slouches resentfully in the doorway.

"Why do we need bread?"

Because you didn't go to the shop and buy any.

"Because we don't have enough."

Daniel rummages in the bread bin.

"We've got four slices."

"And that's not enough." I turn away and get on with chopping the onion. Daniel touches me on the arm to get my attention.

"We don't need more than two slices each. Do we? What are we having? Sausage casserole? Two slices is plenty."

I lay the knife down and sweep the onion into the casserole dish.

"Marianne might like toast in the morning."

"She'll be fine with cereal."

"Okay, then I want toast in the morning."

"Can't you have cereal instead?"

It's too much.

"Why should I have to have bloody cereal? I don't want bloody cereal, okay? I want toast! That's all I want!" I want

Daniel to be frightened by my rage, but instead he looks baffled.

"How can you have such a strong opinion about breakfast?"

"All right. All right. I don't just want toast. I want toast, and I want someone else to worry about whether we've got enough bread, and I want dinner cooked for me for once, instead of having to come in from work and do everything, every night, all the bloody time. I mean, what do you actually contribute? You don't cook, you don't clean, you don't do the washing—"

He looks like a hurt puppy now, and this should be enough to make me stop, but tonight I have no pity left in me. I want to hurt him. I want to make him feel useless and a burden. I want to make him sorry.

He holds up his hands as if I'm physically attacking him. "Jen, that's not fair! I do contribute! I look after our daughter."

"Yes, and she's eighteen months old! She goes to playgroup every day, morning and afternoon, five days a week – even though she's the youngest there by a bloody mile, you couldn't wait to get her out of the house so you could have your mates round and mess around in that music room, full of equipment that *I* paid for, incidentally – and of course you don't have to do anything else, you've walked three minutes up the road with a pushchair so that gets you off the hook for the whole bloody day, you can leave me to sort out everything else—"

I can see I'm getting to him, but it's not until the blow smashes into my face, slamming my head back against the corner of the cupboard door and turning the edges of my vision black, that I realise how successful I've been. We stand in dazed silence, staring at each other. Then Daniel looks towards the kitchen door. Marianne stands in the doorway with her best teddy bear under her arm and two fingers jammed in her mouth.

"Are you all right, Mummy?" Her pudgy hands move

along with her perfect little mouth, making sure we both know what she's saying. It's the first time I've seen her do this. It's the longest sentence I've ever heard her say. Daniel stares at me beseechingly. I have never seen him look so loving, or so remorseful.

"We're fine, baby," I tell her. My head swims as I scoop her up, but I can't stop to think about that. I have to be strong. "Come on. Back to bed."

Marianne touches her fingertips to the tender orbit of flesh along my cheekbone.

"I know, baby. Mummy bashed her head on the cupboard. Don't worry, Daddy will look after me. But we have to get you back to bed first. No, it's too late for another story, but you can have one more cuddle, and then you have to go to sleep, all right? You've got playgroup in the morning. Night night now, baby. No, really, night night. Sleep now." Her eyelashes are already casting shadows against her cheeks. "That's right. See you in the morning."

I have to hold on to the bannister to make it down the stairs. I can feel the beat of my pulse thudding in the lump on the back of my head, in the ache along my cheekbone. I should go and look at it, see how bad the damage is, but I don't want to. I'd rather not know. I'll wait for the morning, when everything will seem better. Right now we have to talk. Daniel hit me. Did he mean to? Yes, of course he did. But no, that can't be right. I was yelling at him. What did I think was going to happen? I even wanted him to, maybe. Maybe I was deliberately that awful so he'd hit me and then I could…

Daniel isn't in the sitting room. He isn't in the kitchen either. Not in the hall. Not in the music room. Where has he gone?

He's in the bedroom, throwing clothes wildly around in a flailing attempt to pack a suitcase.

"What are you doing?" I grab his arm to make him stop, then flinch back when he tries to stroke my face.

"You see?" His eyes are wild and panicky, as wild and panicky as I feel inside. "You don't even want me to touch you. I can't touch you. I can't touch you ever again."

"It's not that. It hurts a bit, that's all."

"I don't blame you. I don't deserve to touch you. I don't deserve to stay here in this house with you and Marianne. I don't deserve either of you. I'm so sorry. I'll go."

"What? Where are you going?"

"I don't know, somewhere, I'll find a hotel or sleep on a mate's floor or something. Or I'll go to my mum and dad's."

"But what are you going to tell them?"

"That you asked me to leave. I'll say you asked me to leave because I... oh God, I don't even want to say what I did. I can't even say it. So on top of everything else, I'm a coward. How am I going to tell my mum and dad? What are they going to think of me? I'll have to tell them why you threw me out. I've ruined everything."

"No, you haven't. You haven't got to tell them anything. It's all right. We can get past this."

I can feel the words coming out of my mouth, so I must mean them. I must genuinely believe we can get past this. This must be me speaking. It will feel real soon.

"But I—" Daniel presses his hand over his mouth so I can't understand what he's saying. His eyes are huge and terrified. I take his hand away from his face, and this time he lets me touch him.

"It was my fault." I stroke his hand gently, seeing him relax and begin to believe. Such power I have over him; the power to make things right or wrong, the power to keep our family together or destroy it. "I was being a bitch. I shouldn't have said any of those things."

"Yes, you should. You're right. I don't do enough round the house. I'm a useless husband."

"You're not. You're a wonderful husband."

"No, I'm not, I'm useless. I don't know how to cook, I don't know how to clean. I don't bring in any money. I haven't written anything new for months. I don't get to enough rehearsals, I don't know how much longer the rest of them are even going to put up with it. They need someone who can commit properly."

"Because you're looking after our daughter. It's a hard job, the hardest job in the world."

Where has all my anger gone? Half an hour ago I was desperate for him to acknowledge all these things that seemed so true. Now he's saying everything I've nursed in the darkness of my heart, and all I want is to kill the words stone dead. I upset him so much that he hit me. I nearly destroyed everything we have.

"You'd both be better off without me."

"Of course we wouldn't! I love you. We both love you. You know that."

He takes my hand and rubs it against his cheek. His tears are warm on my fingers.

"You and Marianne," he says, "you're all I've got. All I've got. The only thing in my life I've ever done right. If you left me, what would I even be? I don't know what I'd do. That's why I was so upset when you said I—"

"Don't. Please. I'm so ashamed. I shouldn't have said any of that."

And it's true. I do feel ashamed. It's hot and burning in my chest. How could I have been so awful to my husband that he had to hit me to make me stop talking?

"You're only saying what's true." His nose is running and he wipes it with his sleeve. "Do you think I don't notice when you come home and start cleaning and tidying and cooking dinner and stuff? It makes me so ashamed. And then I feel so useless and then I can't write or play properly, and I start wondering what you're even doing with a loser like me. I mean, would you even still be with me if it wasn't for Marianne?"

"Don't even ask that. You know that's not true."

Except it just might be. It's one of the thoughts I haven't

dared let myself think, because there *is* Marianne, small and innocent, sleeping quietly in her bedroom lit by the soft pink of her glow-lamp. She is what matters. I can't let her family be destroyed. What if there was no Marianne? Imagining a different life is imagining her gone, which is unbearable, so I don't let myself think it.

"Look what I did to you." He touches my face and the back of my head with his fingertips. I try not to react but I can't help it; when he touches the duck-egg beneath my hair the world turns black around the edges and I clutch his T-shirt.

"And I haven't even looked after you. I let you take Marianne back to bed by yourself. I should have sat you down and got you a cold compress. I'm a waste of space. I'm useless and I hit my wife. Why am I even still alive? I should be dead."

He collapses at my feet, his head against my knees like a tired child. My anger has slunk away like a kicked dog. All I feel is tenderness. I kneel down too, stroking his face and arms to show I mean him no harm. He looks at me and winces.

"You look so pale. Should I take you to hospital?"

Maybe he should. I feel dizzy and light-headed, as if I'm not quite in my body at all. But then we'd have to wake Marianne again, or – worse – call Daniel's parents and ask them to babysit while he takes me. Would they see through our subterfuge that I fell and hit my head? Would they find this convincing? The thought of them realising what happened between Daniel and I is shameful. Tonight is our own dark and terrible secret, a holy mystery that, paradoxically, will bring us closer together.

"I'll be all right. You'll see. I'm made tough."

"You're amazing. You're so amazing. I don't deserve you. And I swear this will never, ever happen again. Oh, Jen, I thought I'd lost you. I should have known better. I should have known you'd never leave me and Marianne—"

And he's right. I really won't leave him and Marianne. I've learned something about myself tonight. I am strong and powerful, far more than I ever imagined. I nearly broke Daniel. I took a gentle, kind, loving, slightly feckless man and turned him for a brief minute into someone else. If I chose to, I could do it again. I've found the key that unlocks another, darker Daniel, and if I make him come out again, it could destroy us all. I sit on the floor of our bedroom and promise myself that I will never, ever, ever repeat the words I said tonight. It's too frightening. Meanwhile, Daniel leaves the room and returns with an overfilled bowl of too-hot water and a scrumpled wad of tissue that he uses to dab painfully at the back of my head, spilling water on the carpet as he does so. I see him looking at me to see if I'll say anything about the mess, his face anxious and vulnerable. I'm ashamed of how deeply I've hurt him. He hit me, but he was only fighting back.

He dabs the back of my head, and I tell myself that as long as there's no blood there, I don't need to go to hospital. I hold my breath as he dips the tissue back into the water. It instantly dissolves into a mass of floating shreds, but there's no blood. I must be all right after all. Only a bad bump. Nothing to worry about. Daniel takes my hands between his.

"I love you," he tells me. "I love you more than anything else in this world except Marianne. You've given me everything in my whole life that's worthwhile and I swear I'll never, ever… and I know you're right and I'm not good enough for you… I was so scared you were going to leave me that I… I couldn't help it…" I stroke his face gently. "Oh, Jen. Are you sure you forgive me?"

I blink, and that must be enough for him, because suddenly he's all over me, sweeping me up and carrying me to the bed, pulling at my clothes in a frenzy.

We haven't had sex like this ever, not even when we first met. The strange thing is that despite the headache and the soreness in my cheek, I'm as eager for it as he. Everything he does makes me hungry for more. I take his hand and press it hard between my legs, and when he finally touches me the way I want, I bite him because it feels so good. His face is contorted with need and from the way he presses his fingers over my mouth, I know I must be making noise. Afterwards, we lie in each other's arms and I feel the movement of his chest where his blood still pounds.

It's not his fault. I made him do it. Of course women who have been hit always say this, but the truth is that it really wasn't his fault; I really did make him do it. My head is a perfectly divided vessel with two chambers. One holds the knowledge that you should always, always leave a violent partner because they will inevitably do it again; the other, my unshakeable understanding that, alone of all the women in the universe, I really did bring it on myself. I've always thought not leaving was weak. Now I understand it takes a special kind of strength. The strength to take responsibility for my part in a terrible incident, to ensure Daniel's mistake never happens again. I am the singular exception to an otherwise perfect rule. Context is everything.

I dream I'm walking up the winding hill towards Lily's house. I'm the age that I am now, but my hand is still tucked into hers, and when we cross the road, she makes me change sides so that she can continue to shield me from the traffic. It's only when we reach the driveway that I realise Marianne is with us too, toddling along on stumpy legs that tremble with the exhaustion of the climb. I swing her onto my hip and we stand together in a little cluster, three generations of women drenched in the evening sunlight that slants between the trees and warms our faces.

"You can stay here with me for ever," Lily tells me.

"But where's Daniel?"

"You left him behind," Lily says, calm and smiling. "I told you he wasn't good enough for you, remember? So you saw to it that he'd never hurt you again."

And as she speaks these words I remember something terrible. When Marianne and I left that morning, I closed the door of our bedroom on Daniel's cold corpse as it hung and twirled from the light fitting.

I wake with my heart and my head pounding, wondering if I've screamed aloud or simply in my head. Daniel sleeps peacefully beside me. I'm ravenously hungry – we both skipped dinner – so I creep downstairs to find something to eat. The kitchen is a mess. The whole house is a mess. But I can fix it.

Moving stealthily and carefully, I unload the dishwasher, and refill it with dirty pans and crockery. I throw away the chopped onion from the casserole and hide the sausages in the fridge. I empty out the washing machine, transfer the clothes into the tumble dryer, creep into the bathroom and gather up another load. A quick wipe around the surfaces, a few minutes straightening the lounge, and my house feels an entirely different place. Later, when Marianne and Daniel wake, I'll make us all pancakes.

I crave toast, crisp and crunchy and laden with lime marmalade, but when I take the bread out, I see it's spotted with mould. I open a box of cereal instead, shivering in the cold kitchen as the milk chills me from my stomach outwards. I try to forget that last night in my sleep, I killed Daniel so I could leave him.

This is the first time I have this dream. It will not be the last.

Chapter Twenty-Five – Friday

When I wake, Marianne is up before me, pottering around the kitchen in her ludicrous pyjamas, making pancakes in that meticulous way she has. Every step is checked at least three times against the recipe on her phone. The egg whites are whisked into smooth foamy peaks, the tops scrutinised to see if they stand up (acceptable) or flop over a little (more whisking required). Each spill and spatter is instantly wiped with the damp cloth that remains within arms' reach at all times. The smile she gives me looks natural and relaxed, as long as you don't look too closely.

"I thought I'd make you a nice surprise breakfast," she tells me. "You sit down and I'll make you a cup of tea. You deserve a rest."

In any normal household I would revel in this unexpected gesture of thoughtfulness, but this is what Daniel and I always do the morning after we've—

—*the morning after he's hit you*, says Lily. *It's all right, you can tell me. I knew it the first time I saw him. I tried to warn you, but I don't blame you for not listening. No one ever wants to believe it.*

It's become almost routine, in its own hideous way. Or perhaps not a routine, since I never know exactly what will trigger it off. Maybe a ritual. Yes, that seems right. Blood and sex, feasting and mystery, power and terror; an ecstasy of self-abasement. In the very worst times (which are also the very best times, for the passion that comes after) I wonder if I deliberately provoke these episodes, because the time after is when we're closest. The moments when his hands, remorseful, caress my back, my face, my breasts. His vulnerability, as he pours out all his sorrow and need. I bring it on myself; I know that he hates being reminded of the imbalances between us, but I remind him anyway. This is what all women in my position say: *It's my fault, I wind him up, he can't help it.* But that doesn't make all of us wrong. Some of us have to be telling the truth.

And now my daughter, my beautiful only child, is in the kitchen making pancakes and wiping the surfaces clean, because this is what she's seen her parents do whenever they're confronted with the violence that lurks at the dark heart of their marriage. Cook something nice, clean the kitchen, act as if everything's all right. Shove the beast back in its cage.

"Do you have a lot of jobs today?" Marianne asks me, her face very bright and cheerful.

"A few." I'm cautious and careful, treading carefully around the subject we're not ever going to discuss. "Sorry."

"No, that's okay, I don't mind."

"You know what? Let's go to the beach again."

"No, Mum, I didn't mean that."

"No, I know you didn't. But I think we should."

"But you've got stuff to do. You've got to get everything sorted out here."

"We can afford a day off to go to the beach."

"Dad will be angry."

"No, he won't."

"Yes he will. He texted me last night to ask me what we'd been doing."

"What did you say? No, never mind, it doesn't matter. These pancakes are delicious."

"Yes, it does matter. I told him you were working really hard, Mum. Because I don't want him to be mad with you."

The pancakes are light and fluffy and the golden syrup pours clear and delicious from Lily's dainty cream jug. I force myself to smile and swallow. "Don't be silly. He won't be cross."

"Yes, he will. I know what he does, Mum. You don't have to hide it from me and pretend."

"Look, you might think you sometimes saw—"

"I know what I saw. I know I sleepwalk sometimes and see things, but I can tell the difference." She's hesitant but clear. "Please, Mum. Listen to me. You can leave him. And I'll go home and look after him. I don't mind."

"We're not talking about this any more. Eat your pancake."

"Think about it."

"Here, have the rest of this syrup."

"I'm fine, I've finished."

"Then I'll make you another."

I suspect Marianne's telling me she doesn't want another pancake, but I turn towards the stove so I don't have to see and ladle out a perfect pale circlet of batter. Little bubbles rise and pop on the thick surface. The edge begins to crisp, and I flip it onto its back so it can cook through. When I drop the pancake onto Marianne's plate, I give her the brightest smile I can muster, to show I'm not angry. She eats the pancake dutifully, her dark eyes never leaving my face.

If I keep moving I don't have to think. I clean the kitchen, scour the bathroom to a polished shine, then whirl towels and swimming costumes into a bag so we can go to the beach. Marianne tries to protest, but she's only twelve and the lure of sunshine and seawater, topped with the promise of an ice cream after lunch, combine into something she can't possibly resist. I march proudly down the stairs with the bag on my shoulder. My phone vibrates, warning me Daniel is trying to reach me, but I ignore it. I don't need to jump to Daniel's command. I can ignore him and afterwards claim a flat battery or a dropped signal, and nothing bad will happen. I'm a strong woman and I'm taking my daughter to the beach, because I'm not afraid of my husband.

The hallway is cool and empty. Marianne glances towards James's door, but it's closed. There's no sign of the cat. Perhaps she's finally got the message and accepted her new home. The gravel shifts and yields beneath my firmly planted feet.

"Let's run," I say to Marianne, at the top of the hill.

"But what about the road?"

"We'll stop at the bottom."

She starts to say something else, but I take her hand firmly in mine and run down the narrow pavement. We dodge bin bags and car mirrors, leap wildly around a man wearing an anorak and carrying two shopping bags, skitter to a halt at the bottom to check for cars and then career on again, upwards this time, gasping and uncoordinated, arms flailing, hopelessly out of time with each other. We stop for breath at the crossing and Marianne tries to ask me why, but then the green man beckons us over and we're off again, tearing down the broad slope toward the beach and the ocean, until Marianne suddenly tugs hard on my arm and stops, pressing her hand against the spot beneath her ribcage.

"I've got a stitch," she says. Her face is crumpled with pain. "Sorry, Mum. You go on. I'll catch you up."

"No, it's all right. I'll wait for you."

"Honestly, I don't mind. I've got to learn to be more independent."

"Don't be daft. You're only twelve."

"Exactly. I won't always live with you."

"What on earth are you talking about?"

She looks at me steadily and I feel a chill. She is terribly persistent, this daughter of mine. She takes her time to think about things, but once she's made up her mind, persuading her to change it back is difficult. I can't think of a time when I've ever managed it.

"I think you should leave him. I don't want him to hurt you any more."

"But you could live with me?" This isn't what I meant to say. We can't discuss this as if it's a thing that might actually happen.

"No, that's not fair on Daddy. We can't both leave him."

"But… do you want to live in a different house to me?" I ask. This is unforgiveable. And besides, she won't choose me. Given a choice between two options, Marianne will always select the less desirable one. *Is this what I've taught her to do?*

"I want him not to hurt you any more," she repeats, and walks away from me, towards the beach.

Panic, shame, terror; these are hard emotions to sustain. If you'd told me a week ago that I'd be openly talking to my daughter about all that I thought I'd hidden so successfully, I would have pictured the end of everything; torn hair, torn garments, smashed possessions, myself lying shuddering, dying by inches so I wouldn't have to face any further discussion. And yet here we are, sitting peacefully against the sunny wall, sifting through the sand for tiny shells, negotiating over ice creams and when we can have them. Only intermittently does the horror come over me, like a wave of scalding water, like a curtain whisked back to show the seething blackness behind.

It's my fault. I provoke him. If any other woman said it, I'd tell her she was deluding herself. But, unlike all these other imaginary women conjured into my head by magazines and newspapers, I really do provoke him. I'm hard to live with. I complain when he makes a mess. Although I've never said it out loud, I don't believe in him or his music. I have no faith that it will ever come to more than what he achieves now, which is essentially a time-consuming hobby that occasionally brings in a few hundred pounds.

I've lied to him for the last twelve years, passing off another man's child as his own.

Does it matter that Marianne is, strictly speaking, not

his daughter? He wasn't there when she was conceived but he's been there for every moment after. He held her when she was less than a minute old, stroking her sticky head in wonder. Whatever else is wrong with our marriage, we've both loved Marianne. Sometimes it feels as if she's the only thing holding us together. Maybe that's because she is the only thing holding us together.

She's in the water now, splashing around and laughing. The curtain has fallen and we're a happy family again, a happy family of two, playing in the sunshine on the beach where all my best memories were made. Marianne, I can see now, is made to live by the sea. Her olive skin is designed not for the cool pale comfort of city living, but for the sharp bite of the Cornish wind and sunshine. Her hair wasn't made to be straightened and styled and smoothed to a glossy shine. It's at its best soaked with salt water and left to dry in spirally unbrushed tangles. She's terrible at team sports and uncoordinated on a tennis court, but in the water, her jerky anxious movements become lithe and graceful. This is the life we could have had, if I'd made a different choice that day in the churchyard. This is what Lily was offering.

You can still have that life, Lily tells me, kneeling down beside me on the warm sand. *It's not too late.*

I could have taken Lily's hand instead of Daniel's and left my job and come back here to live. While Marianne was tiny, we would have lived with Lily, and when I found work and a place for us to be independent, Lily would have helped me. Her tall upright figure, crowned with white hair, would have greeted Marianne's rosy face as she came out of school on the days I was working late. There would have been family trips to the beach at the weekend, and in the long summers, I would have enrolled Marianne at the surf school. She would have grown up knowing this place deep in her bones.

A terrible houseful of women, Lily laughs. *But that's all right. Sometimes life is better without men.*

Would there have been any men? What about the boy who got me pregnant? I can't think of him as Marianne's father, any more than I can think of James as her grandfather. All I can remember now is that he was gentle and sweet and not very curious, on a night when gentle and sweet and not-very-curious were exactly what I craved. Would we have had a future together? Surely not. He had his own plans, none of which involved making a life with a stranger whose only connection with him was a single evening of fruitful pleasure.

He wouldn't have had to know, Lily says, serene and powerful. *It's easy to keep that kind of secret if you want to. Women have done it since the dawn of time.*

His grandfather lives downstairs. How was he not going to find out?

He moved to New Zealand that summer. That's why he was visiting. He came to say goodbye.

James knew as soon as he saw her.

James would have kept quiet. He's good at keeping secrets.

I look up from my handful of shells and see Marianne making her way up the beach, laborious and shivering, her feet wincing away from the pebbles.

"Let's get you dry." I wrap a towel around her trembling shoulders.

"Who were you talking to?"

"No one. Myself."

"I never saw you do that before," Marianne says, not challenging me exactly, but clearly worried. No one likes to see their parents doing something new. "Is it because you're thinking about—"

"Shush."

"But Mum—"

"No, I mean it. Shush. We're having a nice day. Let's not spoil it." Except by saying the words, *Let's not spoil it*, I've managed to remind her of what I want her to forget. "Do you want to go and get us some ice creams?"

"Will you come with me?"

"There's only two of us. Can't you manage?" Too late, I see that this is the wrong thing to say. What's the matter with me today? I can usually read Marianne's moods as if they're my own. "Actually, no, I'll come with you."

"You don't have to, I can carry them."

"I know you can, but it's easier if I help. They melt so fast, it'll drip all over you."

"But I need to be independent!"

"No, you don't, not yet."

"But Mum, I have to learn. I can't rely on you to look after me all the time."

"Please stop going on with all that rubbish about being on your own. And stop worrying about me."

"I've got to worry about you. You don't worry about yourself. Someone has to."

She's right, says Lily. *You don't worry about yourself. I think it's time you started.*

"Look." I stroke Marianne's cheek with the ball of my thumb. "You need to stop fretting."

"But what are you going to do?"

"I don't know, but we'll work something out."

I can see from the look on Marianne's face that she has no faith there can be any plan better than hers. She's already shutting down, withdrawing, saying goodbye. She's preparing for a future without me in it. When she takes my hand on the way up to the ice-cream stand, she clutches it tight. The quivering of her fingers is not solely from the cold water.

The ice creams are no fun but we gulp them down anyway, forcing ourselves to finish them even though we're both pushing them past the knots in our throats. It's a feeling I've grown familiar with over many years of putting a brave face on for Daniel. How many other times has my daughter been my silent companion, gallantly playing her part to keep up the loving fiction that Daniel is a good man, a successful husband, a successful father? Afterwards I send her down to

302

the rock pools with a bucket, telling her to try and find me a crab. The rocks have been picked bare by a century's worth of beachcombers; she'll be gone for a while.

I need to evaluate my options. Evaluating options is what I do, it's the way I make my living. I assess the possibilities, I assign each one its costs and benefits, and I recommend what will be, on balance, the most rewarding course of action. Sometimes I'm listened to, sometimes I'm not; sometimes I point out a risk that never materialises, sometimes the solution I propose proves unworkable; but on balance, my answers are generally good ones. I don't have my spreadsheets, I don't even have a pencil and the back of an envelope, so I arrange shells in patterns to help me think.

Option one. I could leave Daniel, taking Marianne with me, but stay close to him. With the money from selling Lily's home, we'd be able to finance two separate dwellings. Of course, running costs would be a problem, and Daniel would have to get a job; which he would hate, and which would prove difficult, since he's spent the last fifteen years dossing around the house pretending to be a professional musician. But with care, we could manage.

Benefits: I'd no longer have to live with Daniel, but I'd be close to my daughter, seeing her regularly.

Risks: Daniel would not go quietly. He's told me over and over that Marianne and I are the only things that matter to him, that without us to love and cherish, his life would have no meaning. In my heart I know that Daniel's plans for his music career will never achieve anything, that he has talent but not genius, good looks but not stage presence, technical skills but no fire in the belly. But what I know is unimportant. Daniel would not forgive me leaving. Daniel would be heartbroken. Daniel would be ashamed of his failure. Daniel would want to make me understand how much I'd hurt him.

Daniel would kill you, says Lily, shaking her head. *Tell the truth, Jen.*

I know. Daniel would kill me.

But you don't believe that.

No, you're right, I don't. Murderers don't sob on the floor and clutch your knees and beg for forgiveness. He's wearing and he's suffocating but he's not frightening.

That's because you're frightened of the wrong things.

You know what? I don't want to talk about this any more.

Option two. I leave Daniel, send Marianne home on her own and stay here.

Benefits: no more Daniel. No more getting up in the middle of the night to complete the chores he can't stand to see me doing, but seems incapable of doing himself. No more Saturday night duty sex, which means drinking white wine until my head swims, then climbing into bed and gritting my teeth and pretending to enjoy his lips searching for mine, his tongue licking at the roof of my mouth, his fingers fumbling for my nipples, his flesh pressed inside me. No more tender places marking the times when I've failed to successfully maintain the fiction that I'm content with him, that his contribution is adequate and even generous, that he is a successful musician and a wonderful father and a beloved husband. No more tightening in the belly as I turn my key in the door. Instead, the vast peaceful comfort of a home empty of resentment.

Risks: Marianne. Even if I could bear to leave her behind – which I can't, because I'm at least as greedy for my daughter as he is – if I decide not to live with him, I can't let her do it either. I sweep the cluster of shells away with my hand.

Of course you can't leave her with him. My darling, he really has beaten you into submission, hasn't he? But don't worry. Keep thinking. You'll find the solution.

So, on to option three. Marianne and I stay here. We'll walk away, the two of us, leaving everything behind. Daniel can have the house, take over the tenancy. The furniture, the music room, the contents of the kitchen cupboards. He can have our savings. He can keep the car. I'll mortgage Lily's flat to pay him his share of what I've just inherited. Once I find a new job, I'll pay him a monthly allowance if that's what it takes.

Benefits: oh, everything, everything. Our own little home, the perfect size and location, in a place that, for me, is crammed with happy memories. A place where Daniel has barely been. The beach for Marianne; a new start in a new school. The cat can live with us too if she wants, that's probably why Lily bought her in the first place…

Well, of course it is, says Lily. *I'm surprised it took you so long to realise. Something for Marianne, to make up for leaving everything else behind.*

Risks: as if Daniel would ever let that happen. He'd come down in the night and burn the place to the ground first.

Yes, says Lily. *He would.*

Which leaves only option four. I keep on doing what I've done for years. I do everything Daniel wants. I put Lily's home on the market. It will sell quickly, of course – a dream purchase for any well-heeled yachting type or newly retired business owner. We bank the cash, in the full knowledge that we'll never build our own house because Daniel will fritter it away in dribbles and chunks, paying for producers, studio time, session musicians, trips to Los Angeles, always convinced the next bend in the road will bring the lucky break he craves.

And what about you? What will you do with the rest of your life?

I'll go back home. I'll try harder. I'll accept that I've made my choice and if I want to keep my daughter, this is what it will cost me. I'll work on my career. I'll find satisfaction in knowing I've done my best.

Benefits: Marianne.

Risks: Marianne.

All the options are impossible. There's nothing I can do.

There's always something you can do. Lily is willing me to understand something. *Don't give up.*

So what am I supposed to do? I beg. *You had a plan for everything. You must have had a plan for this part too. How do I get him out of our lives?*

I've already given you the answer, Lily says, and stands up to leave. *You'll find it if you look hard enough.*

I feel her feathery kiss on my forehead, and then she walks away from me and towards the water, the sunshine shining through her, pausing briefly to run her fingers over Marianne's rough hair as she toils back through the sand, her bucket held carefully in two hands as if she's carrying something precious.

"Look," Marianne says as soon as she gets close enough. "Look what I found."

Resting in the bottom of the bucket, a tangle of pinky-green tentacles clings to a rock, swirling and drifting with the movement of the water.

"I found this in a pool," she tells me. "But I don't know what it is. Is it a plant?"

"It's a snakelocks. A type of anemone."

"It's so beautiful."

I put my hand in the bucket and rest the tip of my finger in the tangle of the anemone's tendrils, feeling the tingle as it clutches and stings at my skin.

"It's very beautiful," I say. When I take my hand out again, there is the slightest red flush where the anemone's venom has touched me.

"Is it poisonous?"

"Only to tiny sea creatures. It tingles, that's all. You can try it, if you like."

Marianne puts her finger doubtfully down towards the anemone.

"It's all tickly. How did you know it was all right to do this?"

"Lily showed me," I say, and take a deep breath. "She would have showed you too if I'd ever let you meet her. I'm so, so sorry."

"That's all right," says Marianne automatically, still busy with the anemone, and then, "sorry for what?"

What am I sorry for? For everything. For making such a mess of our lives. For thinking all this time that I was doing the best I could, when it's becoming increasingly clear that I've made the worst possible choices at every opportunity. What am I sorry for? It's too big a question. I kiss her instead, and tell her how clever she is to find the snakelocks.

"I know you said a crab, but I thought this was more interesting."

"You're right. It's much more interesting."

"There was someone else with a crab, but I think it might have been the only one."

"They're not as easy to find as they used to be."

"Have I hurt it bringing it in the bucket? I put some seawater in it and it's got its own rock."

"It'll be fine. Sea creatures have to be tough. We should probably take it back, though." Marianne looks at the distance back down to the rocks, then nods stoically. "Unless you want me to take it for you?"

"No, it's all right, I'll come with you."

"I don't mind going if you're tired."

"No, I don't mind. It's a different sort of tired down here, isn't it?"

"What do you mean?"

"Oh, you know. It's the sort of tired that makes you sleepy. Not the sort that keeps you awake. Are we going home after this?"

The corner of the curtain twitches again. How many nights has my daughter lain awake, listening to what I'd always thought was secret? When it happens, do we make a noise that she can hear? I have no way of knowing.

"Yes, if you like. And we can get takeaway pizzas for tea and eat them out of the boxes."

"And can we make chocolate pudding in a mug for pudding?"

Fat and grease and salt and carbohydrate, followed by fat and sugar and chocolate and more sugar. "Oh, why not? Let's go for it."

Our feet sink into the loose shale. Marianne's anxious to find the place the snakelocks originally came from, but I persuade her that it will be perfectly happy in any sunny pool that's covered at high tide. After some thought, we choose a deep gully and drop the rock carefully in, watching it sink down and down and down towards the bottom. The rock twirls and sways as it falls and I wonder if it will turn over in the current and crush the little snakelocks, but no, it rights itself and comes to rest on the pebbles.

"And now it's got a new home," says Marianne in satisfaction, and empties the bucket of water in for good measure.

On the walk back home, Marianne's slow and sleepy. She leans against me as she walks, in a way that is confiding but also hard to manage, and it takes us a long time. When we get home, I tell her to jump in the bath and wash the salt out of her hair, while I walk down the hill into town to buy pizza. She tries to convince me to let her come with me, but I can tell her heart's not in it. When I glance at our open bathroom window from the driveway, I see the small flick of a stripy tail as the cat leaps inside.

We eat our pizzas straight from the box. Marianne keeps one eye on me as she eats, and quietly drops oily strings of cheese for the cat that hovers, all pink mouth and melting eyes, whenever she thinks I'm not looking. Cleaning up is ridiculously easy. Next, chocolate pudding. Merely standing in the cool comfort of the pantry is a pleasure, among the ingredients arranged in neat orderly rows, every jar filled, every space occupied.

Do you remember? Lily asks me.

You know I do.

You spent hours in here. Especially when it rained. If I

couldn't find you I knew this is where you'd be.

Did you mind?

Of course not. I used to make sure I had everything I needed out on the counter the night before so I wouldn't disturb you.

I never knew that.

I never wanted you to know that, says Lily. *That would have spoiled it for you. I told you, didn't I? I always loved you best. And I still do. That's why I'm saving you.*

We're having a peaceful evening, Marianne and I. I turn away from Lily so I don't have to look at her, and spoon out flour, sugar, cocoa, oil. An egg. Chocolate drops. Vanilla essence. Stir well and into the microwave for three minutes. In the short time I've been gone, Marianne has curled up on the sofa and fallen asleep with the cat tucked into the crook of her arm. As children do when they sleep, she's regressed to her baby self, her cheeks soft and flushed, her lips slightly parted. I kiss the top of her head, stroke the cat's outstretched stripy paw, and go to the kitchen to turn off the microwave.

The sun's beginning to sink behind the trees. I light the lamp in the bay window and admire the paradox of the two light sources together. It reminds me of the print that hung on the wall of the room Daniel and I shared in those first blissful weeks at university. *The Dominion of Light*. Those weeks were happy ones, good ones. Surely we can get back to where we were then? How did it all go so wrong?

In the corner beside the lamp, Lily raises her hands to speak, but I turn away. I don't want to talk any more. I don't want to hear her opinions on Daniel and me.

Why is it always her talking to me? Why does she get to judge me and my marriage, while her own past remains a closed book? She's dead and I'm still alive. I should be the one defining her, summing her up, tidying her existence away and moving on to the next thing. That's what I'm here to do. I reach for the photograph album and carry it to the sofa.

I'll drown out Lily's judgement on me by forming my own judgements of Lily.

Here is Margaret again, the woman who might or might not be my real grandmother, swelling with life even though her own death was so close. My finger runs over the curve of her belly. Is this my father? Or some poor lost baby who didn't even live to be named?

Beneath Margaret's skirt, my fingers find a long flat ridge like a fold. I trace its path, follow it along the whole length of the photograph and up the side. There's something hidden behind this picture too.

Stop it, I tell myself fiercely. *Stop thinking. Stop looking.* Lily is dead. Margaret is dead. My father is dead. All of this is ancient history. I'll close the album and pretend I never found anything. Except I can't. I can't. I can't make myself stop. My fingers delicately prise out whatever Lily has concealed beneath the portrait of her pregnant sister. What will I find? My father's real birth certificate? A signed confession?

It's another photograph, badly composed and clearly taken in haste. The world it captures is tilted within its frame. Margaret sits hunched on an unmade bed, one blurry arm held in front of her as if trying to ward off a blow. There is dried blood at the corner of her mouth. One eye is swollen shut. Her face and neck are stained with bruises.

I have to clutch the arms of the sofa to keep myself from floating away into space. The photograph flutters from my fingers. My heart beats against the wall of my chest, trying to escape. Who did that to Margaret? Why would Lily record it? What does it mean? What should I do?

Beside me on the sofa, Marianne sleeps on, undisturbed. The cat rolls onto her side and stretches her back legs blissfully. I was afraid I might have made a noise, but it appears not. I take a deep breath, pick up the photograph and force myself to look again.

Margaret's face, bruised and terrified, her arm going up to shield herself from the pitiless gaze of the camera. Had

Lily done this to her? No, that's not it. Margaret is afraid of the camera, not the person holding it. She's begging Lily not to take the picture. The injuries you want to hide are the ones that come from someone you love. And Lily, ignoring her sister's pleas, took a photograph as evidence, just as she kept her meticulous, furious record of what was happening to James. She refused to let it stay hidden. But would anyone have taken any action?

Of course they wouldn't. Lily is with me again. No matter what I do I can't get away from her; she won't be denied when she has something to say. *It's hard enough now, but you can't imagine what it was like then. No one wanted to hear what Stanley was doing to my sister. So I had to deal with it myself. Margaret thought she was trapped, but she got away.*

My accountant's brain begins to tick, assessing, evaluating, looking for the thread that holds everything together. At some time after this photograph was taken, Margaret's husband died and she and Lily moved here to open their hotel, two young widows making the best of a tough situation. *This is where your life begins.* I think about James Moon, who allowed his wife to take out her rage on him. I think about how ruthless Lily was, how cruel she could be on behalf of those she loved. No, that's ridiculous. Lily was a lot of things but there's no way she was a…

Lily looks at Marianne, and smiles.

How well did I know Lily? Who was she really? My father's mother, or my father's aunt? The wise beloved matriarch of my childhood, or the banshee at my father's funeral?

She was a woman with her own opinions, confident and secure in what she believed. A woman with the charm and cleverness to carry off a deception so successfully that I may never know for sure whose child my father was. A woman who could scream insults at her daughter-in-law over a freshly filled grave. A woman who tried to help her downstairs neighbour escape from the hell of a violent marriage. A woman who knew plants and their uses, so well I used to think she was a witch. A woman who believed in taking action. I turn the pages over.

And there he is again, on the page before his pregnant wife. Margaret's husband Stanley, a black shape passing through a front door, caught in the act of vanishing. And beneath it, Lily's inscription:

Stanley Walker
1907–1946
Wishing you the peace you deserve

Innocent enough, a simple and elegant memorial to her sister's husband. Except that the picture is framed with foxgloves, which even I know can be deadly for the heart.

I turn more pages, over and over, passing through my father's childhood and my own, onto the handful of photographs that come after. A page before the picture of James Moon, I find an old woman sitting on a bench in the garden. She looks tiny and wispy, as if a strong wind might blow her away.

Ramona Moon
Lost in Paradise

Ramona sits beneath the strong impetuous tumble of a huge tropical shrub, long orange flowers dangling like trumpets above her head. Lily has echoed this in her choice of blooms for the border. The datura blossoms have lost some of their vibrancy in being pressed, but there's no mistaking that distinctive tubular shape. Datura is a poisonous hallucinogen. Lily never let me even touch its flowers. Foxgloves and datura. For Lily, flowers always had meaning.

Did James know? Is this the secret he was keeping for her? Was he trying to protect me from this final discovery?

Beside me on the sofa, Marianne stirs. I pat her gently

on the shoulder until she breaks through the surface of her slumber and sits up, bleary and blinking. The cat jumps to the floor and begins washing her face. I help Marianne to her feet and steer her to the bathroom, putting toothpaste on her brush for her as if she's still four years old. I can tell from the way her feet stumble against the tiles that she's not properly awake. In the morning she'll have no memory of how she got into bed, and when I tell her she cleaned her teeth and climbed beneath the covers basically in her sleep, she'll look at me as if I might be the one who dreamed it.

You were the same, Lily says. *You used to sleepwalk sometimes. I'd find you in the hallway or in the pantry, sitting and staring at the shelves. I used to worry you were going to eat things and make yourself sick.*

I remembered the conversations in the morning, but not the wandering itself. *Do you remember getting up in the night?* Lily would ask me, her face amused and mystified. *No*, I'd say, and then she would describe to me what I'd done – the rooms I'd wandered into, the words I'd said – none of it even faintly familiar. It wasn't until the first time I found Marianne, eyes unfocused and face soft, standing mutely at the bottom of the stairs, that I realised how strange my sleepwalking must have seemed. Back in the sitting room, the cat sits up like a meerkat and begs to be stroked.

I'm trying hard not to get fond of her, but she's a dear little thing. Marianne, of course, has already given her heart entirely away. I run my hand down her arched back and up the long, striped length of the tail. Is the cat a witness to a murder as well? Or was she merely Lily's familiar?

Perhaps there's one more way to be sure.

I go to the pantry, climb the steps and peer onto the very highest shelf. A bottle of sherry. A bottle of rum. A bottle of brandy. At the back of the shelf, the keys to the cellar. Lily always kept the key high and hidden, claiming she was afraid I might go down by myself and fall on the steps.

Shutting the door in the cat's face, I run down the stairs and go to the entrance built into the stairwell that leads down to the house's roots. Four separate households share these cellars, but only Lily ever came down here.

At the very back of the long damp strip-lit chasm is the door to Lily's darkroom. The padlock is rusted slightly shut, as if even now Lily doesn't want me to get in here, but I jiggle the key and tug at the lock until finally it gives way. I shut the door and turn on the red lamp and look around to see what there is.

Lily's worktable is as neat as it always was. Here, at last, is her camera, and the neat row of chemicals lined up at the back, against the wall. Above my head, the line of pegs for hanging. The developing trays laid out side by side. One is covered with a sheet of greaseproof paper.

I lift the sheet and there they are, the dried prickly cases like conker casings, and within the tight-packed seeds that looks like apple pips. Thorn apples.

I touch one cautiously with my fingertip, and watch the seeds dislodge from their casing, pouring exuberantly out onto the paper. So small and innocent-looking. I wonder what the lethal dose is. Can datura be absorbed through the skin? I must be sure to wash my hands carefully before I eat anything.

"Lily," I say out loud, and wonder what my voice might sound like in the cool confinement of the darkroom. "Lily, what did you do?"

Chapter Twenty-Six – Jen

My unconscious is trying to warn me of something in a way I haven't felt since I was pregnant with Marianne. All week I've been dreaming of storms and journeys, of strange rooms and lost cats and railway-station partings. For the last three mornings I've woken to find myself standing by the front door with my keys in my hand. My bones hum with the awareness that something's about to change. What will it be? The answer lurks in the dark, but I can't yet bring it into my consciousness.

I try to hide all of this from Daniel, but he knows me too well. *What's going on?* he demands, and when I answer, *I don't know, it's just bad dreams, why does it have to mean anything?* he accuses me of hiding things from him. He texts me dozens of times a day, growing frantic if I don't answer immediately. Twice he turns up at the office, allegedly to take me out for a nice lunch, but in fact to make sure I'm not meeting someone else in the only scrap of potential free time he's unable to account for.

I'm desperately sorry for the pain I'm causing him, but I can't seem to stop it. No matter how warm and loving I try to make our partings and greetings, no matter how diligently I respond to his text messages, no matter how much simulated passion I offer, he insists I'm withdrawing, growing distant. I deny all of it, and redouble my efforts. Marianne wakes me multiple times each night, screaming inconsolably in her sleep. My boss takes me to one side and asks me if everything's all right. When I tell him I'm fine, he looks at me very seriously and says that I don't need to tell him what's going on but he's on my side and he's got my back and if I need some time, I should take it.

It comes to a head in the way these things always do for us: an argument that spirals into the inevitable violent confrontation. It's my fault for provoking him. He's bought a second-hand amp from a mate in the pub. I know how sensitive he is about money. His self-esteem is worth far more to me than forty-five pounds. But I can't seem to stop myself. Maybe I even crave it, as a release from the tension that we're living in. Afterwards he holds me and sobs against my neck, and I stroke his head and tell him it's all right, we will be all right, we'll find a way through, it's only the pressure of being short of cash, but soon everything will come right and then we'll never have to worry again.

"But what if we never do?" he asks. "This isn't where we're supposed to be. We're supposed to be rich by now. I was going to make our fortune."

"You still will. There's all the time in the world."

"But what if I don't?"

I don't have an answer for that, so instead I comfort him in the way we both know always works. In the wild tenderness that we only find in the aftermath of our periodic storms, we fall asleep in each other's arms, sated and at peace. I wake the next morning to find Daniel has me by both shoulders and is shaking me so hard my teeth rattle against each other.

"Wake up, wake up, wake up!" His face is like a marionette's, set in a single terrifying grimace. "Wake up! Wake up! Stop it! Wake up!"

"All right, I'm awake, I'm awake, stop it, please. I'm awake." He lets me go and takes a deep breath. "Shush, you'll wake Marianne. What's the matter?"

"You were crying in your sleep. On and on and on."

I touch my face. My cheeks are wet.

"What were you dreaming? Were you dreaming about leaving me? Is that why you were crying? Who is it?"

"Of course not! I'd never leave you, you know that."

"What else would make you cry like that?"

"It was just a dream!"

"Your dreams are never just dreams, you've got second sight, you know you have. If you leave me I'll kill myself, I can't manage without you. Were you dreaming about me being dead?"

"No, of course I wasn't! I... wait—"

"What? What?" He grips my arm. "Talk to me!"

It was a dream about death. That sounds familiar. In fact, all of this is familiar. When have I felt like this before? I remember all of it from some other time; the dreams, the discord, like a storm about to break. I remember death and new life; leaving and returning; the heartbreak of a terrible choice. I remember my dream from last night.

I was in my bed at Lily's house, half awake in the comforting glow of my bedside lamp. When Lily came in, she was wearing her raincoat and her slick black rain hat. She looked old and tired, but also serene.

Well, my darling, she said, *this is it.*

Are you going out? To the beach? Is it raining?

Oh yes. The biggest storm you've ever seen.

Can I come with you to watch?

Not this time. Now, I've left everything as tidy as I can, but I'm afraid there are some things I had to leave for you to do. But don't worry. You're my clever granddaughter and you'll know what to do when the time comes. She bends and kisses my cheek. *Get some sleep. You'll have a long journey ahead of you.*

"The phone's ringing," I say to Daniel. "You need to answer it."

"How do you know the phone's...? It doesn't matter, ignore it, the machine can pick it up, we need to talk."

"No. You need to answer it, right now. It's important."

Daniel's face is white and frightened. "Don't worry. It's going to be all right."

"Who… who is it? What do they want?"

"I don't know who it is," I tell him, "but they're calling to tell me that Lily has died."

Chapter Twenty-Seven – Friday

It's evening, and Marianne and I are walking up the hill from the station. She's holding my hand even though these days she employs all sorts of gentle strategies to avoid this, which tells me that she's as tired as I am. Her lips are smudged with the scarlet lipstick she loves, and there's a large ladder in the back of her tights. The street is bathed in the thick light that haunts my dreams, the slow summer evening sunshine of the Cornish coastline, honey-coloured and drowsy-sweet.

"Only a bit further," I tell her, squeezing her hand. She smiles at me and pushes her hair off her face, and I'm struck again by how little she resembles Daniel. For all the years of her life I've watched for signs of him, his mother, his father, searching, wondering, always looking, never finding. Now I know why. Tonight I see myself and Lily, traces of both of us in the shape of her eyebrows, her chin, her eyes. "Nearly there, I promise."

"Will Lily be waiting for us?"

"She's been waiting for us since before you were born."

"But isn't she dead?"

"That doesn't matter. She still knows we're coming."

"But what about Dad?"

And with that, I feel horror creeping up on me, and I know we have to run, towards sanctuary, towards the safe place, because Daniel is coming for us. He's coming for us and when he catches us, he'll kill us both. If we can just get to Lily's house, we'll be able to shut the door and keep him out. If we can just get to Lily's house, everything will be fine. But the hill is steep and our legs have turned to jelly and we can't run fast enough, and I realise this is a dream, I'm dreaming again, and no matter how hard I try, I'll never get away from this dream, just as I'll never get away from Daniel, because he'll follow me everywhere, anywhere, to the ends of the earth, until I die, until we're both dead, until it's over.

I wake up on the sofa with a crick in my neck and Lily's camera on the floor. Perhaps it was the camera falling that woke me, the vibration in the floorboards as it landed, the leap of the cat as she jumped away in protest. I can feel the warmth where she was snuggled against me, the chill now she's gone. I've only been asleep for a few minutes; the bar of late sunshine slanting across the sofa has hardly moved. I pick up the camera tenderly.

Tomorrow I will bake a cake, I think. Lily, my grandmother, loving and ruthless. Once she was on your side, she was on your side for ever. Did James know what she was going to do? No, Lily was too clever for that. She would have made many other cakes first, small gifts from one woman to another, a token between neighbours, establishing a habit so that when the time came, James would be able to look the doctor in the eye and say, *No, nothing different. Nothing different at all.* Did anyone ever suspect? Of course not. Why would they? Ramona was an alcoholic, and the symptoms of datura poisoning resemble those of alcohol withdrawal. No one would have questioned what they were seeing. How did James feel, watching his wife struggle and die in her hospital bed? I can't begin to imagine.

Of course you can imagine, Lily says. *You can imagine very well. How would you feel if it was Daniel?*

But it never will be Daniel, or at least not until we're both old, too old to bother with anything more than *what shall we have for dinner* and *do you want to watch this now or later?* Daniel's vice is not drink but delusion, and delusion kills only those around you.

Imagine anyway, Lily says. *Imagine that he's dying. Imagine he's in front of you right now, dying, or maybe even dead. Imagine he's gone out of your life for ever. Imagine you're free. Now, what would you do to make that happen?*

Well, what can I do to make that happen? I ask. I see my hands moving in the reflection in the mirror over the mantelpiece and feel ridiculous, then frightened. What am I contemplating?

It was easier for Lily because her victim was old, old and ill with the kind of illness no one wants to look at too closely. Her death would have been described as a merciful release. Daniel's young and strong, healthy and good-looking, presenting the perfect picture of a devoted father and a loving husband. Strong young men with health and good looks aren't expected to get sick and die. People take notice. Questions are asked. Especially when their spouse has recently inherited a property hundreds of miles away and promptly decamped to live in it, along with their only child. I could hardly look more suspicious if I tried.

So what wouldn't look suspicious?

I don't know. I don't know!

Then you need to think. Keep trying, my darling. You're clever enough to solve this.

I scoop the cat up and tuck her against my chest, feeling the vibration as she purrs. If I'm going to be a witch, I might as well have a familiar. We go into Lily's bedroom and sit down at the dressing table. The cat wriggles free and sits at the end of the table, tall and elegant, blinking slowly at me as I slide Lily's rings onto my fingers, one by one. I open Lily's powder compact, hold it to my nose and am instantly engulfed by her presence, encoded deep in the scent of her face powder. Her little bottle of violet scent sits at the back

321

against the mirror. I dab a spot behind each ear, and follow it with the pearl-drop earrings.

Next, my hair. Lily's hair grips live in an old-fashioned pot that I think may have originally been made to hold hatpins. I twist my hair into a pile on the top of my head and jab it ruthlessly into position with pin after pin after pin, feeling a breeze against my neck like a caress, or maybe a kiss, or maybe the touch of Lily's ghostly fingers as she hovers behind me, watching.

Now I look like Lily, like Lily in a way I never saw her, as a powerful younger woman, sure and certain in her own mind, doing what it took to defend her sister from a violent husband, creating a new life for them both with a handful of wildflowers and the strength of her own will. Was my father Lily's child, or Margaret's? I'll never know now.

It doesn't matter, Lily tells me. *Concentrate on what you're doing.*

What am I doing? I'm not sure myself. An act of necromancy. I'm trying to conjure the beloved dead, to help me escape the living. I'm transforming myself into the likeness of the woman who tried, in her own way, to save me. The woman who is still trying to save me now. I open the drawer and pull out one of her nightgowns. Another minute and my clothes are in a puddle around my feet and the nightgown falls around me in soft lavender-scented folds.

What do I have of Daniel's? The basic principle of magic is that you have to have something of the other person's essence. Marianne, the child he thinks is his, sleeps soundly down the hallway, but she's a cuckoo child, and whatever I can steal from her person will do me no good at all. We had sex the night before I left, but that was over a week ago and I've bathed many times since. I brought nothing of his with me when I came here.

Something vibrates against my foot. My mobile phone. It's Daniel. Of course it's Daniel. I've been ignoring his messages all evening.

Where are you Jen? Come on, this isn't fair. You're late. Xxxxx

His words. I have his words.

Jen, for God's sake, I hate it when you do this. You know how much it worries me. We swore you'd stay in contact the whole time so I know you're both okay. You promised. Remember? Now where the hell are you? Xxxx

My heart is like a drum in my chest and my hands shake. My pulse throbs through my temples. I used to think this was a sign of our enduring mutual passion. Now I recognise that what I really feel is cold terror. I'm terrified even though he's hundreds of miles away. I'm terrified of what he's going to do when I tell him.

I don't want to feel like this any more. I want the feeling of peace I had when I woke up here that first morning. I want to go to work, to come home, to cook, to clean, to care for my daughter, without the impossible pressure of also trying to hide what I do, terrified I'll injure Daniel's self-esteem by reminding him of his own weakness and failure. I want to know he'll never hurt me again.

I want this to be the last time I ever speak to him.

I'm here

THANK GOD

WHERE THE ACTUAL FUCK HAVE YOU BEEN

I know. I haven't been checking my phone

What's the matter with you? How could you possibly forget?

I didn't forget, Daniel, I

No. Not yet. Take it slowly. Lily was careful. I need to be careful too. Delete. Start again.

I'm sorry. I've been busy

What were you doing?

Oh, this and that. How about you? What are you up to?

What do you think I've been doing? Worrying. Sending you messages that don't get answered. Drinking beer. Trying to keep calm

How many beers? Have you had dinner?

No I haven't had bloody dinner, I've been too worried. And I don't know how many beers. Don't get all sanctimonious with me

He's been drinking. He's been drinking. He's been drinking. How can I use this? How?

Daniel, we need to talk

I agree. You need to come home Jen. This is getting ridiculous. It's well over a week now. Get the bloody place cleared and on the market and come home. And we can start making plans for the money

I think it's best if I don't come home actually

I try to picture his face as he reads these words. Will he believe them straight away? Will he be bewildered? Or will he jump straight to rage? If I was there, I know exactly what he'd do. But I'm not there. I feel as if I am but I'm not. I don't need to cringe. I force myself to breathe deeply, to move normally and stand up tall.

Don't be stupid. I can't move down to the back of beyond, you know that. We're on the verge of breaking through. The festival gig's the start of big things. I've waited for years for this, I put everything on hold for Marianne and now it's time to concentrate on my career

And anyway, you can't exactly commute to the office from there, can you?

How typical of Daniel, the dreamer, the impractical one, putting his own fantasy of fame ahead of the job that actually pays for everything.

I mean, if we were a bit more established, maybe we could have kept it on as a holiday place or something, but there's no way it's going to fit into our lives now, is it? We talked about this, remember? I think the air down there's softening your brain

I know. I know all that. I wasn't expecting you to move down here. It would never work

I know you weren't. You always understand. That's why I love you so much. Even when you scare the shit out of me by dropping off the radar :)

What I meant was, I'm staying here and you're staying there

Sorry, what are you talking about?

Deep breath. This is the moment. You've looked through the keyhole. Now walk through the door. Do it. Do it now.

I'm leaving you

You what? Is this some sort of joke? Because it's not very funny

No, it's not a joke. It's the truth. I'm leaving you

This is the deceptive peace that comes when you stand in the eye of the storm. I fill the pause that stretches out by stroking the cat under her chin and admiring the way the light catches the diamonds in Lily's ring.

That doesn't make any sense. What the hell do you mean?

Please, Daniel, I need you to understand. I'm telling you our marriage is over. That's what I'm talking about. It's not working and I'm leaving you

Fuck off, you are not leaving me Jen. You are absolutely not. I need you. You know that. There is no way in hell that you're leaving me, do you hear? I'm not having it

It's not up to you, Daniel. It's up to me. You can't make me stay married to you

Look I know sometimes I'm not easy to live with. You're an angel for putting up with me. I need you so much and you've been so amazing. You can't give up on us now. You absolutely can't

I can and I am. It's too much. I can't live with you any more

We're not calling it quits. We're going to counselling

   No, we're not

Yes we are. I'll go by myself as well. I think there are special courses to help when you have anger management issues. I've been thinking about doing one anyway. I know I get angry but I don't want to be like that, you know that. You know how much I hate myself when I get angry with you. You promised me you'd help me

Angry. Anger management. The way we both step around the real problem, the ugly naked truth of what he does to me. I don't want to say the word even now. Only Marianne has ever dared to truly name what happens between Daniel and me when he loses his temper. Is it possible there is such a thing as a course that could make him stop?

And Jen, I'm sorry. I'm sorry. I'm sorry. How many times do I have to say it before you believe me? You're all that matters to me, you and Marianne. If you leave me, you'll be killing me. I can't make it without you, I'll kill myself if I have to live without you

If I was there with him he'd force me to listen. He would push me into a chair and make me look at him, putting one hand over my mouth, holding my wrists with the other, to stop me from speaking to him even in the language he's never bothered to learn properly.

   I'm sorry to hurt you. I am. But this isn't working. We both know it

So what, you're making me homeless? Where am I supposed to go?

You can keep the house. We're living here

And how am I supposed to pay the bloody bills?
You're being so selfish, I can't believe how selfish
you're being. This isn't you talking. You're having
a mental breakdown. That's what's happening. I'm
going to call the doctor and tell him you've gone
mad

In fairness to Daniel, this does feel like madness. My head
is so light I think it might float off my shoulders. My feet
feel as if they're a thousand miles away. I'm expanding like
Alice, growing up and up, away from the ground and into the
ceiling. Is this freedom? Am I free yet?

No, Lily says. *Not yet. He's angry, but he's not angry*
enough. You need to goad him into action.

What action?

You'll see, Lily says.

And what about Marianne? Have you even thought
about Marianne? Come on Jen, if you won't stay for
me you can at least stay for our daughter. She deserves
to have her parents together

Marianne's fingernails, unbitten; Marianne's anxieties and
worries, fading; Marianne's inability to express herself,
dissolving; the look of fear on Marianne's face, smoothing
out. This is for Marianne. To keep the monster away from
my daughter I have to become a bigger monster, breaking
Daniel's heart in order to set us all free.

Of course I've thought about Marianne. She's staying
here with me. One less thing for you to worry about

She bloody is not. She needs to come home. She belongs
with me. I raised her while you went to work, that

*means I'll get custody. You're not taking my daughter
away from me*

If I was there instead of here, he would already be raging
through the house, shouting, throwing things. Storming into
Marianne's room. Putting on the light. Waking her up, her
little face soft and protesting at first, then dissolving into
terror. His face, so huge and terrifying, pressed tight next to
hers. 'Who do you want to live with, Marianne? Me or Mum?
Mum's making you choose, she says she doesn't want to live
with us any more. But you won't leave me, will you? You'll
stay here with me while your mean mum moves away. We
don't need her, do we? She can pay for us both to live here
and go away and be all by herself. We'll be fine.' I won't be
able to follow the words because he'll be turned away from
me, but I'll see their impact in her face. This is how it would
happen if I was there instead of here. This is why I've never
dared to speak before.

Instead, we're both here. And he's there. But he has the car.

Yes, says Lily, and strokes my face. *He has the car. Be
brave. Keep going.*

*It's not custody any more, it's residency. And she's old
enough to choose for herself. And she wants to stay
with me, not you*

*You talked to her? You talked to our daughter about
this? You absolute bitch. How could you? I'll kill you
when I see you, I swear*

I force myself to breathe in, then breathe out. Breathe in.
Breathe out. Wait.

*Oh shit. Jen. You know I didn't mean that. I'm sorry. I
didn't mean it. I wouldn't hurt you. I'd never hurt you.
You know that*

You do hurt me. You hurt me all the time. But not any more

I know. Not any more. I don't want to do it any more. I want to stop. You've got to help me. It's an illness, there's something wrong with my head. I need you to help me get better. I can't do it without you. You know that

My backbone feels weak and dissolving. I've accepted this so many times over the years. Accepting it one more time feels so easy, so right. *Help me, Lily. Make me strong.*

No. That's not going to happen. I'm not helping you. I'm leaving you. It's over.

You don't get to choose. Why do you get to choose? This isn't fair. You promised me for better, for worse, remember? You can't walk away from that. I get a say too

Our wedding day. The sunlit room in the office that was once a beautiful Georgian house, municipal carpet on the floor, Daniel in his only suit with a clean T-shirt underneath it, me in a silvery dress I'd bought from Monsoon a few hours before. Two of Daniel's friends, who for the purposes of the day were also designated as my friends, as witnesses. Marianne slumbering within the slowly burgeoning curve of my stomach. The registrar smiling and congratulating us. The single glass of Prosecco I allowed myself in the restaurant. At the time, a good day. In retrospect, a frightening one. Why did I let myself marry a man who laughingly refused to invite any of my family or friends to witness it, a man chosen in the teeth of Lily's warning? Why did I stay for all the months and years afterwards? Why did I go back to work while he stayed at home? Why, why, why, why, why? Was every choice I made wrong, from the day I took Daniel's hand instead of Lily's and ran away from my father's graveside? Are the choices I'm making now any better?

> *You've had your say. You've spent our entire marriage having your say. Now I'm having mine. You have to listen to me for once. This is over. All right? Do you understand? This is over and there's nothing you can do about it*

I'm afraid even though I know he can't hurt me. I can feel myself cringing. I don't want to be doing this. I'm afraid of what's going to happen.

> *Yes there is. I'm not accepting it. You're not allowed to dump me without even seeing me and talking about it. We have to talk first. We're not ending it. We're going to counselling at least. Come home right now and I'll call a counsellor in the morning. You owe me that much*

I've kept him in clothes, food, accommodation and transport for over a decade. He's had the use of my house, my bank account, my car and my body. I don't owe him anything more.

> *I'm emailing work tomorrow to tell them I'm resigning with immediate effect. You can send up the car documents to me and I'll transfer ownership to you, you drive it more than I do anyway. I'll email the letting agent and tell them we need to transfer the tenancy into your name only. And you'll need to get a job as well, I'll pay you what I can but it won't be enough to live on*

> *And how am I supposed to get Storm Interference going around a job stacking bloody shelves in Tesco?*

You're being spiteful now. You're punishing me for being a stay-at-home parent. This isn't fair

Maybe it isn't fair. Maybe I am being spiteful. I don't feel spiteful. I feel as if I'm going to die. My heart's pounding out of my chest. If I take a single step I'll fly into the sky. I feel as if the datura I touched earlier has seeped into my skin. Is this magic? Or is it just madness?

I don't want to talk about this any more. I'm tired and I want to go to bed

You're tired? YOU'RE TIRED? You stupid little bitch, you've done nothing but laze around and have fun without me since you got there. You could have got that flat on the market in four days if you'd put your mind to it. Have you met someone else? You've met someone else, I know you have. No one ever leaves a happy marriage unless there's someone else. Who is he?

He's someone I met thirteen summers ago, and haven't seen since. I didn't keep him around either.

Of course I haven't met someone else. It's over, that's all. Now I'm going to bed and I suggest you do the same

You can actually sleep after what you've done?

Goodnight, Daniel

What do you think you're doing? You don't get to say when this conversation is over. I need to talk to you some more

*Come on Jen, don't ignore me. That's bloody childish.
We're not throwing away fifteen years because you
want to act like a kid*

Answer me

I know you're reading these, I can see on my phone

Right, that's it. I'm coming down to see you

Oh God. Oh God. Is this how it ends?

> *No, please don't come down. You don't need to come
> down*

*Don't tell me what to do. I'll fight for this marriage
even if you won't. The roads are quiet. I'll be there in
about six hours*

> *You can't. Please don't. Let's be civilised, try and sort
> this out like adults.*

*Like adults?! Adults talk face-to-face. They don't hide
behind their phones*

> *Please, Daniel. Don't come down now*

Too late. I'm getting in the car now. I'm on my way

> *Then put your phone away at least*

*Stop trying to control me Jen. I'm not going to be pushed
around. You think you're in charge of everything but
you're not*

> *Daniel, please please don't come down. I'm sorry. I*

*didn't mean it. I'm not leaving you. I'll come home on
the next train, I'll*

No, says Lily, shaking her head. *That's not the real you
talking, Jen. Stay strong. I promise it will be all right.*

*All right, then. We'll talk when you get here. Drive
carefully*

I think I might actually die of the terror I feel. Daniel is
coming. He's in the car, right now. His hair will be falling
over his eyes in that flopsy, adorable way that catches the
attention of all the young clueless girls who always seem to
hang around studios, licking their lips at him like dreamy
predators. "You don't need to worry," he always tells me,
stroking the back of my neck or squeezing my arm. "I'm not
interested in them. Why would I be? I've got you." Was that
the truth? Has anything he ever told me been true?

Of course he was telling the truth, says Lily. *Why would
he want them? Would they pay for everything and do all the
housework and fund his daydreams, and provide him with
sex on tap and let him knock them around whenever things
didn't go his way?*

I don't want to listen to her any more. I don't want to do
anything any more. I want this all to stop. I have no more
strength.

You poor girl. Lily's hands on my hair as she removes
the hairpins and brushes out the tangles are very gentle, very
comforting. *You're worn out. It's all right. It's nearly over.
Sleep. Sleep now. Climb into bed and sleep now.*

But he's coming to—

*I promise you, my darling, after tonight Daniel will never
ever hurt you again. You've done everything you need to.
When you wake up, you'll see.*

I can hardly keep my eyes open. It's an effort to drag my
feet across the floor. The bedcovers are heavy and unyielding.

Sleep now, Lily commands me, and I fall down, down, down a tight spiral of exhaustion and land, as always, at the bottom of the hill, with Marianne's hand tucked securely into mine.

"We keep doing this," Marianne says as we reach the top of the hill.

"I know. But this is the last time."

"How do you know it's the last time?"

"Because this time it's different," Lily says, holding out her hand to Marianne. Marianne hesitates, then takes it, drawn by Lily's compelling charm just as I always was. I'm struck once more by how much they would have liked, as well as loved, each other. So many years I lost to Daniel.

And as I think his name, as if I've conjured him, he's there at the bottom of the hill, smiling and terrible, crawling slowly up towards us, teeth bared, ready to tear us all into pieces.

"You can change this," Lily tells me. "You're in charge now. You have all the power you need. Now it's time to use it."

"How? How can I change it?"

"You already have. You told him you were leaving him, remember? And now you're free."

"But he's coming. He's coming. He's coming to kill us both. I know he is. That's why I never dared say anything before."

"But he isn't coming," Lily tells me. "You killed him. Don't you remember?"

And then I see that Daniel isn't there at all, he was never there; it's only the way the light falls across the pavement, casting strange shadows. Daniel is somewhere else, somewhere crowded with traffic and lit by the orange-white flare of sodium, somewhere with sirens and blankets and strobing blue lights, and a rainbow leak of petrol spilled across black tarmac, trickling into the central reservation and pooling around the cat's-eyes. When Marianne was small, she loved to watch as they flashed by beneath the brief gaze of the headlights. Her favourites were the red and green ones that marked a junction, but when the lights of the police car catch the reflectors, I see that these are amber.

"It was for the best," Lily says. "Wake up now. Wake up, my darling. It's morning. A new day."

There's a seagull on the windowsill, peering in at me with an eye as yellow as poison. The floor is littered with everything I assembled last night: the hairpins, the nightgown, the perfume, my phone, Lily's powder compact. The sight makes me cringe with embarrassment. What if Marianne sees? I scrabble everything hastily up, putting Lily's things back in their places. There's something different. What is it? I glance at my phone and realise there's no message from Daniel.

It's nearly nine o'clock. He should have been here hours ago. Is he hiding in the sitting room? Surely he couldn't have got in without waking Marianne. I creep down the hallway anyway, irrationally terrified that he'll be waiting on the sofa, but the only person in the room is the cat, stretched out in a patch of sunshine. When I look out of the window, there's no car on the driveway.

And there never will be, says Lily. *Goodbye, my darling. I'll see you again one day.*

Where are you going?

I feel a kiss on my cheek, and the stir of the air as if someone has left the room. When I turn to look, I see Marianne standing in the doorway, tousled and sleepy-looking. I hold out my hand and she comes to stand beside me, bending down to stroke the cat as she twines around our ankles, pleading for attention or perhaps for food.

"Mummy," she says. "Is everything all right? Look, there's a car coming." She touches my arm to make sure I'm listening. Her fingers are very cold. "Is that a police car?"

I look round for Lily to advise me, but she's no longer there, and I understand that she will never be there again;

perhaps she never was, perhaps I simply conjured her to give me the strength and will to do what needed to be done. I have killed Daniel, just as Lily killed James's wife and Margaret's husband, and as surely as Lily escaped justice, so I will too. No one looking at our final text conversation will see anything other than a terrified wife trying to escape a violent husband.

"Is Daddy all right?" Marianne's eyes are very large and dark. "I dreamed he was in a car crash."

What do I say? Part of me wants to tell her the truth. *I think you're right*, I could say. *You have Lily Pascoe's blood in your veins, and whatever gifts she had, you'll have too. Sometimes you'll dream, and what you dream will turn out to be true.* But I don't know if that's right. I've never known if the things Lily seemed to see without being told, my apparently prophetic dreams, are a true supernatural power, or simply the knowledge that comes with knowing those you love to the bone.

He was never your father, I could say. *He was just some man I passed you off on for a time, because I was young and stupid and I thought I'd never manage by myself, and besides, he told me he loved me and I thought that meant I must love him in return, and then it was too late.* But no, that would be cruel. He loved her, in his way, and she loved him too. And besides, who's to say what makes someone a father? A grandmother? In the end, after all, in spite of everything, perhaps he was her father.

I killed him, I could say. *He's dead because of me.* I did what I had to, to free us both. But I don't think that would be any easier to hear. It's my job to keep the family secrets now, and if I can possibly manage it, they'll die with me.

So I pick up the cat and put her in Marianne's arms, and then I put my arms around them both and hold them close and secure against my chest, watching as the two men in uniform climb out from behind the wheel of the car and walk slowly, reluctantly, over the gravel to Lily's front door, heavy and solemn with the weight of the news they bear.

Acknowledgements

I'd like to say a special thank you to Professor Bencie Woll at University College London, for helping me understand how to accurately render into English the experience of speaking and hearing Sign. All mistakes are entirely my own.

Thank you, as always, to my wonderful editor Lauren Parsons, and to everyone else on the Legend team, for your support and your wise advice, and for everything you do.

Thank you to my parents, for a lifetime of support and inspiration, and for making the entirely wise decision to move back home to Cornwall.

Thank you to my brother Ian, for the conversation that sparked *Lily's House*. The story turned out kind of dark, but the image you described was beautiful.

A special thank you to my wonderful children, Becky and Ben, for being so kind, understanding and supportive, for giving me hugs whenever I need them, for lending me your thinking putty (and buying me my own), and for not minding when scheduling circumstances beyond my control required me to attend Parents' Evening in my book-launch party dress. You're the most wonderful supporters any writer could wish for.

Thank you most of all to my husband, Tony, for being my rock, my foundation, my best friend and my constant supporter. You make it all possible.

Finally, thank you to Audrey Fyson, Dorothy Hulley,

Mildred May and Anne Smallwood – the four beloved matriarchs of a magical childhood. I remember you every day, and every day you make me smile. If any part of us continues after death, I hope we'll meet again.

We hope you enjoyed *Lily's House*, the third novel from Cassandra Parkin and the latest addition to the author's growing list of beautiful stories.

Cassandra's debut, *The Summer We All Ran Away* was shortlisted for the Amazon Rising Star Award and described by international best-selling novelist, Katherine Webb, as 'fresh and original'. Following this fantastic read was *The Beach Hut*, described as 'beautiful' by Jen Campbell.

The Winter's Child is Cassandra's forthcoming novel, and tells the story of Susannah Harper when her son Joel goes missing without a trace. While trying to rebuild her life, a fortune-teller makes an eerie prediction and tells her that Joel will finally return. As her carefully constructed life begins to unravel, Susannah is drawn into a world of psychics and charlatans, half-truths and hauntings, forcing her to confront the buried truths of her family's past.

If you can't wait to read more, here's a sample of *The Summer We All Ran Away*, available online and from all good bookshops:

chapter one (now)

This Thursday, in the middle of August, had been the most terrible, apocalyptic day of Davey's nineteen years on earth. Getting drunk seemed the only possible response.

Slouched hopelessly on the grey-white steps of Trafalgar Square, his rucksack between his knees, he forced the vodka down his throat. Was it supposed to taste like this? Or were his mother and stepfather storing oven-cleaner in the drinks cabinet for secret reasons of their own? He imagined it burning through his stomach and intestines, fizzing gently, creating thick yellow fumes. Stubbornly, he took another swill, and wondered if he might go blind.

Of course, if he did, then maybe he wouldn't have to -

"Alright there, mate?" said a companionable voice.

Davey squinted up through dust and sunshine to the policeman who stood, sweating amiably, by the steps.

"Bit early to be drinking, isn't it? Not even lunchtime yet."

Years of public school training smoothed over his terror.

"Er yes, sir. Sorry, sir." His words slightly blurred by alcohol. The policeman nodded wisely.

"Good." His gaze took in the clean hands, the good jeans, the bottle of Stoli. The rucksack. The dark hair capping the young, weary face. The bloom of fresh bruises, one on the jawline, one high on the cheekbone. The crust of blood at the hairline. "You've been in the wars."

Davey flushed. The policeman sat down beside him.

"Need any help? Got trouble with them at home?"

Davey wondered what incarnation of *them* the policeman was picturing. An alcoholic mother. An unemployed father with a drug habit. A violent girlfriend.

"I'm f-fine," he said. His stammer peeking out from beneath its stone. Would the policeman read anything into it? "But, erm th-thanks."

The policeman looked thoughtfully at the rucksack.

"Running away's bloody hard, you know. You might think it solves everything, but it mostly makes it worse."

"I'm n-n-n-not erm - " Davey suddenly discovered he was a terrible liar, even to strangers. "How - "

The policeman gave him a penetrating stare.

"Look, you're not causing any aggro, so I'll leave you alone if you want. But you'd do better to sort it. If you're getting hit, we'll help, but you have to ask. Alright?"

Horrified, Davey stood up. The ground rocked treacherously beneath his feet.

"Where are you going?" The policeman had hold of his elbow, his grip firm and impersonal.

"Train station," said Davey, indistinctly.

"Yeah? Where you headed?"

Over the policeman's shoulder, a paper bag danced in the breeze. West Cornwall Pasty Company.

"Cornwall," said Davey, after a slight pause. "I'm g-ggoing to visit my Aunt."

"Your Aunt in Cornwall? What's her name?"

"Dorothy," said Davey, desperate. "My Aunt Dorothy. I'm g-g-going to stay with her for a bit. G-g-get my head together. You know?"

"You've got money for the ticket?"

Just let me go.

"Yes, yes, plenty." Davey showed his wallet. "See?"

"You sure there isn't anything you want to tell me? 'Cos they'll do it again, you know. They always do."

"Not if I'm n-n-not there," said Davey, and grabbed his rucksack.

"Alright, son," said the policeman, resigned. "Off you go. Good luck."

A blink, and he was on the tube. How had he got here? He remembered a barrier, a platform, a ticket machine, a handful of change, but couldn't string them together into a coherent narrative. But he was going to Cornwall. Guided by a paper bag. Well, why not? He had to go somewhere. His contempt for himself had his stepfather's voice. *Only cowards run away, real men stick around and sort it out*. He drowned it with vodka, and felt a giant wave of collective disapproval break over his head.

Above his head, the adverts were moving. A girl on a poster winked at him. She was pretty and confident, and had saved up to one hundred and fifty pounds on her car insurance because she was a lady driver. Davey's stepfather had tried to force him into driving lessons, but so far he'd managed to resist. Two panels down, a man dressed as Nelson had also saved money on his car insurance. Was that because he was an Admiral? The parrot's gaze was knowing and sly.

The lines of the tube map made him feel sick. Lying on the floor was a newspaper, open to the showbiz pages. An iconic British actress had walked off a film set because her husband was sleeping with the actress playing her daughter; a battered California starlet had wrecked her car and checked into rehab. Their faces stared accusingly up at him, as if these events were his fault. Regurgitated vodka crept up his throat. Was he going to be sick? He picked up the newspaper in anticipation. The woman next to him edged away.

Another blink, and he stood at the foot of an escalator. The platform swayed beneath his feet. If he was on a ship, would the ground feel stable? Was this why sailors drank? The handrail's speed was treacherously slower than the escalator and he had to keep letting go and grabbing on again, convinced each time that he would fall backwards into the chaos below. Staggering off the top step, he fell into a man in a suit.

"Jesus Christ, just *fuck off*, will you?" he snarled. Davey clung to the man's shoulder, trying to re-orient himself. "Let go of me or I'll fucking deck you." His expensive aftershave was like a scented cloud. "Are you drunk? Police, police, I've got a lunatic here, police!" A privileged voice, used to be being obeyed.

"No, I'm sorry, I'm *sorry* - " Davey let go and stumbled away. The crowd parted, then refused to re-form around him, leaving him for the policemen to find. He began to run, realised how stupid this was, forced himself to stop again. High-vis jackets over black uniforms appeared at the bottom of the escalator. The crowd rustled with excitement.

"I haven't got fucking time for this," said the man in the suit, and gave Davey a spiteful shove. "Piss off, you disgusting little shit." He straightened his jacket and marched away.

As if his departure proved that Davey was not, after all, a lunatic or a terrorist, everyone returned to their business. The police arrived, looked around, saw nothing, swore, began to ask questions. A woman with henna-red hair pointed them in the direction of the man who had called them.

Reprieved, Davey crept along the wall of the tunnel. His forehead was dewy with sweat. Was it against the law to throw up at a tube station? He began following a woman with a large suitcase, hoping she would lead him to the railway.

They crossed a huge white concourse, Davey's stomach clenching, the woman's sensible low heels clicking. Would more vodka settle his nausea? The phrase *hair of the dog* floated across his mind, but the thought of hairy dogs – stinking and drooling and wet – made him gag. The woman with the suitcase was climbing some steps now. Where was she going?

Clinging to the rail for support, he broke through the surface to open air.

Another blink, the smell of diesel, everyone with suitcases, whistles shrieking like birds. Was this the train station? A giant board filled with letters and numbers. Just when he'd got a fix on them, the display refreshed and he had to start all over again. Fast food smells coiled around his nostrils. Gulping desperately, he found the Gents, scrabbling in his pocket for change to get through the turnstile.

The steel toilet bowl looked dirtier than ceramic, even though it was probably more hygienic. The vodka tasted even worse coming back up than it had done going down.

By the basins, he took another deep swig from the bottle to cleanse his palate, aware of the basic stupidity of the action, but reluctant to disobey the stern signs over the taps: NOT DRINKING WATER.

"Where are you travelling to?"

A ticket-selling woman behind a glass screen, her voice coming to him via an intercom. There was a slight delay between the movements of her mouth and the arrival of the words.

Buy ticket. Get on train. Run.

"Cornwall," said Davey.

"Which station?"

"W-w-w - " His stammer loving the vodka. Was this why he'd never really liked to drink? "Which ones are there?"

"Information centre's over there," she said wearily. "Come back when you've chosen."

Davey found a touch-screen kiosk, but you could only operate it if you already knew where you wanted to go. Behind him, a woman sighed and said loudly, "You can't work it because you're *drunk* - " and Davey, ashamed, slunk away to a row of chairs. The carpet's pattern looked like germs swarming. He wondered if he was going to be sick again.

After a few minutes, the man next to him left. On his chair was a tourist leaflet.

A spreading ripple of movement and rearrangement, everyone sitting up, paying attention. Davey opened his eyes. Strangers opposite him; stranger beside him. Wide glass windows. The sensation of speed. He was on a train. Which train? A huge ogre squeezing his way towards him.

"Tickets, please." The guard was enormously tall and fat, barely able to fit between the seats. Why had he chosen a job he was so obviously not designed for? Or had he been thin when he got it, then gradually grown into his present size?

"Ticket," repeated the ogre, holding out his hand. Davey groped desperately back through the blankness of sleep. Did he have a ticket? Could he have got on the train without one? He remembered the ticket office, he remembered queueing, he remembered not knowing where he wanted to go. He found his wallet; there was a lot less money in it than he remembered. The other passengers watched with interest.

Panicking now, Davey began to rummage through his rucksack. On the very top was a bottle of Glenfiddich whiskey, half-empty. Had he drunk that? He remembered vodka, not whiskey. Then something flickered in his brain, just a couple of neurons mindlessly firing up, and he reached into his jacket pocket and found a rectangle of cardboard.

Together, they inspected it dubiously.

"Railcard," said the guard at last.

Davey rummaged some more, found a holder with a laminated card. He held it out and waited miserably for the guard to pronounce his fate. The guard looked at it for a long time.

"So you're old enough to be drinking," he said. "I was going to confiscate that bottle, son. If you give me any trouble, I'll have you put off the train."

"Okay," Davey agreed meekly.

The guard was looking at the bruises.

"Change at Truro."

The carriage contained nothing but staring eyes. Davey slumped down into his jacket. Outside, the world unspooled like a roll of film.

"Where are you headed?"

The woman next to him was speaking. Davey, head reeling from the inch of Glenfiddich he'd gulped down in the toilet, tried to focus on his ticket. Where *was* he going? Was this still the train with the fat guard? Alcohol had turned his memory into a swamp; no clues on the surface, hideous monsters lurking below.

You've made a complete mess of your life.

It's for your own good.

I'm trying to help you.

He shivered, and stared downwards. The letters on his ticket flickered and danced and refused to turn into words.

"Can I see?" She took his ticket from him. "You need to change at the next station."

"Thank you."

"No problem."

He studied her in shy glimpses. She reminded him of Giles' mother. Small and soft, fair wispy hair. The train was slowing.

"Okay," she said briskly. "This is me. And you. Up you get." She chivvied him out of his seat, handed him his ticket, saw him off the train.

"Thanks," he mumbled again, not daring to meet her eyes. He was terrified of needing help or asking for anything. Since he was three years old, *getting in the way* had been the unforgiveable crime.

"I've got a son your age," she said vaguely, and he stared at her in astonishment.

"Are you Giles' mum?" he called out as she disappeared across the platform; but she was already gone.

A sudden jerking stop, a sign right outside the window.

Another platform to negotiate. His rucksack caught in the

closing doors. The stillness of the ground was too much, and he was painfully, shamefully sick in a bin. He could hear the sound of judgement being passed, and blood singing in his ears. As he straightened up, he heard seagulls.

He stood in a steep street, a finger of tarmac leading straight down to the quayside. There were no barriers. How good would it feel to ride a skateboard down, down, down and off into the oily water? Did he have a skateboard?

He rummaged hopefully in the rucksack, but was distracted by the Glenfiddich. His mouth tasted like a drained pond. As he unscrewed the cap, he suddenly remembered the terror of stealing it, less than twelve hours ago.

On the other side of the harbour, a rose-coloured house stood by itself. In a high window, a tiny light hung like a red star.

A worm of memory wriggled at the back of his sodden brain.

"Steady there," said a man, helping Davey aboard the boat.

Dazed and mystified, whiskey swimming in his blood, Davey sat down on an iron park bench screwed tight to the wooden deck.

Where was he going now? On the quay was a shelter with walls of cool, cream-coloured concrete. He would have liked to rest his hot cheek against the wall and close his eyes, but instead he was on a rickety ferry that smelled of diesel fumes and sweaty humanity, going - somewhere. No-one else shared his bench. Did he now look so wild and unkempt that nobody dared sit next to him?

He realised he was starving, and looked in his rucksack again. Why on earth had he ignored the contents of the fridge and cupboards, but packed six pairs of black socks, a battered photograph album, a stolen newspaper and *Alice in Wonderland*? How could that have seemed like a good idea?

You're a total fuck-up from start to finish.

I don't know why I even bother any more.

The seagulls sounded like crying children. He was crying too, no tears, just a contortion of his face and a keening sound that escaped in gulps and bursts. The sea-spray had the approximate taste of tears but with more complex afternotes, like a good wine.

The boat sat alarmingly low in the water. Was it safe? Were there people who checked these things? The man in the wheelhouse smoked a cigarette and stared across the water. His expression reminded Davey of long-distance lorry-drivers at service stations; a professional surrounded by amateurs, inhabiting a different world.

The bump and scrape of wood against stone, ropes thrown and tied up. The same man who had helped him onto the boat now helped him off again. Davey marvelled at the unself-conscious way he touched Davey's hand and elbow. At school, physical contact was governed by unbreakable rules. Shoulders and upper arms were alright, as long as you slapped hard. Legs were for kicking. Heads were for capturing in a headlock and thumping. Penises, bizarrely, were acceptable, in certain situations. Hands and forearms were too close to holding hands, therefore a shortcut to social death. He tried to remember the last time he'd been touched gently by someone who wasn't his mother, and remembered a nurse bandaging his arm one night in casualty. "How did this happen?" she'd asked him, and when he'd stammered out something about a broken glass, she'd smiled cynically and shaken her head. He still had a jagged, silvery line to remind him.

He was exhausted, but something in him was forcing him on. He climbed a steep, narrow street – barely wide enough for a single car – and opened the whiskey bottle, now nearly empty. A woman walking her dog glanced at him in disgust. He tried to apologise, but his mouth was too dry. The double yellow lines were like those on the floor of the hospital, guiding bewildered patients around the labyrinth.

I've got to get up high.

Come visit us at
www.legendpress.co.uk

Follow us
@legend_press